A NOVEL

CHRONICLES OF
NICKY SPADE

BOOK 2: IT'S IN THE GENES

A NOVEL

CHRONICLES OF NICKY SPADE

BOOK 2: IT'S IN THE GENES

JANICE WILLIAMS
AND TRACEY SCHUMANN

Primix Publishing
11620 Wilshire Blvd
Suite 900, West Wilshire Center, Los Angeles, CA, 90025
www.primixpublishing.com
Phone: 1-800-538-5788

Published by Primix Publishing   04/01/2022

ISBN: 978-1-957676-10-4(sc)
ISBN: 978-1-957676-11-1(e)

Library of Congress Control Number: 2022905214

CONTENTS

PROLOGUE

How do you say goodbye to a rock icon? Someone who epitomized the world of rock and roll. Someone whose influence would be felt for generations. Someone who had inspired others to follow his path to the pinnacle of fame and fortune. Someone who most importantly had left behind his DNA pulsing through the veins of his only son, Cameron. Today, November 17th, 1987, the world would lay to rest a rock god, Nicky Spade.

As the hearse entered the long narrow drive into Memorial Gardens in Middleton, Michigan, a fine mist of rain began falling. Somehow it seemed surreal yet appropriate. The world was reeling with overwhelming feelings of grief and sadness. A native son was finally home and being laid to rest. News anchors and fans would be held at bay outside the massive wrought iron gates. Today there would be no televised coverage. Bruce insisted the funeral be private, to allow only the immediate family and members of Black Tie Affair to say their goodbyes.

Slowly the convoy of cars came to a stop. It would only be a short walk toward the immense array of flowers surrounding the open grave. Emerging from the limo, Cameron now became Jenna's strength. As her legs buckled from beneath her petite frame, Cameron held tightly to her arm. Opening a large black umbrella, he covered her from the rain.

Following behind the pallbearers that carried the love of her life, Jenna's mind became flooded with memories of her short time with Nicky. It would be all that remained except Cameron. Flashes of their night at the cabin on the lake brought tears to her eyes. Fate had dealt her some hard blows. However, she felt blessed to have their son standing beside her. Cameron embodied Nicky. He carried within him the genes of a rock star. She vowed to herself that he would not make the same mistakes.

Sitting next to the open grave, it seemed almost unbelievable that Nicky had been taken from her once again. It had only been six years since the night Nicky had walked back into her life. A short time to try and make up for all those lost years. Nicky's health had been spiraling out of control, but he had managed to hang on just long enough to witness the torch passed to his only son.

It was evident that Cameron was on the same path to fame. His childhood dreams were rock solid under the loving guidance of Bruce. However, there would be one difference.

As Jenna wiped tears from her eyes, she promised herself that Cameron would not be taken from her as Nicky. She wouldn't watch Cameron's career catapult him into a world of hard drugs and alcohol. It had cost her too much.

CHAPTER ONE

Déjà vu

Following the graveside service, the convoy of limos exited through the large wrought iron gates of Memorial Gardens. As was typical of Bruce, they were now on their way to the best restaurant in town. It just so happened to be Rosettas. It was the place where many years previous, Bruce had met with Nicky's parents to go over the numerous legal documents necessary to take their young son out of Middleton. So it seemed only fitting to Bruce that everyone celebrate Nicky's life and success in the music industry where it had begun.

Walking in, Bruce escorted Jenna to her seat. Looking around, she seemed comforted to know that neither Mr. nor Mrs. Spade would be present today. Nicky's parents had been tragically killed in a car accident almost a year ago. The unexpected news of their passing had dramatically affected him. For the first time in his life, he had felt guilty for pursuing his dreams. Dreams which had taken him far away from his home town and his parents. The impact of losing his parents had thrown him deeper into depression and addiction. The demons of depression, alcohol, and drugs had finally claimed their victim. Even though Jenna loved him more than what seemed humanely possible, it wasn't enough to keep him alive. Nicky had finally lost his battle to addiction. Looking over at Cameron, she smiled. Jenna knew that whatever it took or whatever she might have to do, it would be the one aspect of Nicky's career that she would not see passed from father to son.

After everyone was seated, Bruce offered the first toast to his beloved friend. His voice began to crack, and tears flooded his eyes as he lifted his trembling glass.

"Nicky, I loved you like a son. I felt like a proud father managing your career. When I first discovered you here in Middleton, my world was never the same. As lead vocalist, you took Black Tie Affair to staggering heights. Your fans adored you. You epitomized the words rock icon. Unfortunately, black Tie Affair and the world have lost a legend. You've been taken from us all too soon. Rest in peace. You will be sorely missed by those of us sitting here today. Here's to you, my son."

Jerry stood to give Bruce a much-needed hug. Then, looking over at Jenna and Cameron, seated next to Annie, Joey and Tony, he lifted his glass.

"Here's to Nicky. I always knew he was destined for greatness. Thank God I got to share in his long career, but more than that, he was family. Nicky, I love you. Thank you for all the unforgettable moments we shared."

Glancing over at his mom, Joyce, he noticed she was wiping tears from her eyes. Muffled sounds of crying inundated the room as piping hot plates of lasagna were brought out. Jenna was desperately trying to hold her emotions inside for Cameron. She needed to be strong. There would be time for tears, plenty of them, but this wasn't the place. There would be many sleepless nights in her future, spent with her head laying softly on a pillow dampened from a myriad of tears. Jenna knew there would never be a replacement for Nicky. However, she found comfort knowing that just as the morning she had woke early at the cabin to watch him breathe, his heart had always belonged to her.

It was time for the boys of Black Tie Affair to stand and offer one last toast to their friend. As David stood, he asked that Jeff stand beside him.

"Most of you know that our band, Black Tie Affair, lost two of our band members, Randy and Alex, many years ago in a horrific tragedy. If they were alive today, they would stand here with Jeff and me to recount the many memorable times we all shared with Nicky. Nicky first went onstage with us at a concert in Dublin," David smiled, glancing at Bruce. David continued. *"Most of you probably don't know the reason I left the band during that time. But let's just say Bruce made the right decision and leave it at that. Nicky came on stage that night as my replacement, and the fans fell in love with him. After losing Randy and Alex, Bruce again made the right decision to make a long story short. He brought Nicky upfront as the lead singer of our band and invited me back on board as well. Once again, the fans fell madly in love with Nicky. Who wouldn't,"* he winked, staring at Jenna. *"And the rest is history, as they say. Here's to you, my friend. I'll always miss you."*

With trembling hands, Jeff wiped his eyes.

"Nicky, I'm sure going to miss our long talks. So here's to you, man."

The whole room was a mixture of sadness and an unexplained peace. Those sitting here had been affected and influenced in some way by the life of Nicky Spade. After Jeff's toast, Todd walked over to hug Jenna and offer his condolences.

"Jenna, I'm so sorry. He loved you. He always loved you," he softly whispered in her ear.

Taking tissue from her purse, she looked up as she wiped the tears from her eyes.

"I know," she answered, trying to smile. "Thanks, Todd."

Afterward, he walked over to where Mike, John, and Pete were seated at the end of the long table, "Guys, please stand with me to offer our toast."

"Well, I guess it's time for the boys and me to stand and offer a toast to our friend," Todd announced, lifting his glass of Champagne.

"There was something about that kid," Todd smiled. *"I'll never forget that night in London walking out of the elevator and meeting Nicky for the first time. Bruce and Nicky had just flown in from the states. What made such an impression on the boys and me was that this kid had just entered a new country, a new time zone, a whole new world sort of speaking*

and still managed to go pub hopping in London with us later that night. We introduced him to the finest beer and ale London had to offer," Todd continued. "And you know what, he managed to hang with us even though I'm sure he was sleep-deprived. The boys and I liked him from the very start. He worked hard as a roadie, never failing to complete any task he was asked to do. If ever a kid deserved to make it, it was Nicky. The boys and I will always feel proud that we knew and loved him as a friend before the world ever knew his name. Here's to you, my friend."

"Guess I can speak for everyone standing here," Mike smiled, desperately trying to keep his composure.

"Nicky, we are definitely going to miss you. I'll never forget you. So here's to you."

"Cameron, if you ever need a couple of old roadies, Bruce knows where to find us. We're all so proud of you. We know Nicky will be watching your career and smiling from above," Pete added.

One by one, people walked over to Jenna and Cameron, offering their condolences. Jenna knew that Nicky had many friends here this evening. She knew her heartache for him was shared by those who had come to pay their last respects.

Reaching over to take Jenna's arm, Bruce whispered in her ear.

"Sweetheart, are you ready to go back to the hotel? The car is out front if you and Cameron would like to leave now?"

"Yes, Bruce, that is so nice of you," Jenna tried to smile. "I'll ask Cameron to come with us."

She needed to make her escape. She needed the solitude of her hotel room. A quiet place where she could just be alone with her thoughts. At times like this, the kind words of those around her would never be enough. Nothing could ever fill the void of living without him. Oh, how she ached for just one more hour, one more day with him. Just another moment to be held in his arms, to smell his cologne, to see his silly smile. She was silently dying inside. She only hoped those around her couldn't see how bad she needed and missed him. Why had fate brought him back into her life, only to rip him away after such a short time? For a brief second, she wished she had somehow died with him. However, seeing Cameron walking toward her, she knew why. She had her answer. It was Cameron.

"Mom, please have Bruce take you back to the hotel. I'm going to stay for just a while longer. I've got some things I want to discuss with David. Would you mind?" Cameron mentioned.

"Okay, stay and talk with David. I'll be at the hotel."

After giving her a quick kiss on her moist cheeks, Cameron walked over toward the end of the room, where he saw David talking with Todd and the boys.

Entering the limo, Bruce stepped in behind Jenna.

"So Cameron decided not to ride back to the hotel with us?" Bruce inquired.

"No. I think he wanted to remain behind with the boys for a while," she answered, wiping her eyes.

"Well, I hope he remembers that we'll be leaving for Vancouver early tomorrow morning?"

"Oh, I'm sure there won't be any problems," Jenna insisted, resting her head against the seat.

Seeing her so distraught, Bruce reached over to take her hand.

"Jenna, things are going to be all right. I promised your mom before she passed that I would always make sure you were okay. When I came back onboard to manage Cameron's career, I promised not only her but also Nicky that I would always be there for you both. I can't tell you the worries I had for him. I watched him slowly deteriorate, even before you came back into his life. Jenna, Nicky loved you. I honestly believe the years he spent without you, along with his eventual drug use, caused his untimely death. I will tell you for sure that Cameron will never be on that same path. Sometimes, I felt like I had abandoned Nicky. When things began spinning out of control with his drug use, I couldn't stand by and watch his demise, so I chose to leave."

"Oh Bruce, it's not your fault for leaving. Nicky was a grown man. He knew what he was doing. No one could have saved him, not even me," Jenna whispered, taking a Kleenex from her purse to wipe her eyes.

It wasn't long before the limo entered the drive of the Carlton Hotel. Bruce saw Jenna to her room. Then he headed immediately down to the lounge. He needed a stiff drink. The thoughts of how Nicky had spiraled downward so quickly after reuniting with Jenna made him no longer wish to remain sober. He was now managing the fast-rising career of Cameron. Again, he promised himself that Cameron would never fall prey to drugs as his father did. Bruce knew all too well the trappings that can sometimes come with being a rock icon and the high price that Nicky had paid.

Finally, alone in her room, Jenna threw herself onto the huge bed. Not even bothering to remove her clothes, she felt hopelessly lost.

Nicky, how could you leave me? How could you? I can't do this. I just can't.

She cried rivers of tears for what seemed like an eternity until she fell asleep from pure exhaustion.

Not waking until the following day, it seemed somehow miraculous that she had even managed to drift off. Maybe somehow, someone was watching over her. Walking over to the television, she turned it on without thought. Catching the early morning news, it was detailed coverage concerning Nicky's untimely death. It caught her by surprise. Quickly changing the news channel, she didn't want to hear details about Nicky's remarkable career. Jenna didn't care that the world had lost Nicky Spade. She had lost her husband, the one whom her whole world revolved around. How was she ever going to be able to live without him?

Hearing a knock at the door, she walked over to answer it.

"Good morning, Mom," Cameron said, hugging her. "Mom, you look as if you slept in your clothes last night," he mentioned giving her a quizzical glance.

"Oh, I guess you would be right," Jenna replied, looking down at her wrinkled Versace original. "Suppose, I must have been pretty tired. I can't remember the last time I slept in my clothes."

"Mom, get changed. We're supposed to meet Bruce downstairs

in the lobby for breakfast before leaving. I think Aunt Joyce, Annie, Joey, and Tony will be joining us before we leave for Vancouver," Cameron insisted. Hurriedly, opening the drapes, the room was immersed in the warm morning sunlight.

"That will be nice. I wanted to see them before we left. I don't know when I will be back, and Vancouver is a long way from Middleton," Jenna replied as she shuffled through a rack of clothes. Finally finding the perfect outfit for the morning, she disappeared into the bathroom to change.

"Okay, guess I'm ready. Have you called for someone to take our suitcases downstairs?"

"Yes, it's all arranged. Mom, you look so pretty. Dad would be so proud of you."

"Thanks, Sweetheart." Her only thoughts were of leaving Nicky behind. She had to find the strength today to start life without him. There had never been thoughts of laying him to rest anywhere but Middleton. Now with the funeral behind them, life continued.

Walking into the downstairs lobby, it wasn't long before Annie saw her and came running over.

"Jenna, how are you holding up? You left Rosettas before Aunt Joyce, or I could talk to you last night," Annie mentioned giving her a huge hug.

"I know. I'm sorry. Everything was just beginning to be too much for me. After the toasts were given, it's like reality set in, and I just wasn't able to deal with my emotions, much less speak to anyone."

"Oh, I know. It's okay. Aunt Joyce figured you needed to be alone."

"Well, speaking of your Aunt Joyce, she should be here any minute," Bruce stated as he walked up. Why don't we all go in and find a place to sit. I'm starved, and the smell of bacon is calling my name," Bruce grinned, escorting them in the direction of the quaint coffee shop.

It wasn't long before Joyce arrived. It was evident she had been crying.

"Aunt Joyce, is everything alright?" Annie asked, offering her a tissue.

"Oh yes, dear, it was hard saying goodbye to Jerry this morning. He said to offer his apologies. It seems something came up at the last minute. By the way, Bruce, Jerry said he would meet up with you later at the airport. It's so difficult to see him leave again. He reminds me so much of Nicky. Those two boys were more like brothers than cousins. First, it was so hard losing Joan and now Nicky."

The next hour was spent as only a family could, eating and trying to enjoy themselves under challenging circumstances. It would be the last time Jenna and Cameron would spend any time in Middleton.

"Well, folks, it's getting late. These two kids and I have a flight to catch," Bruce smiled, giving Jenna a wink. I don't mean to end our breakfast so soon, but Mac, our new pilot, doesn't like us showing up late at the airport," Bruce interrupted, standing to help Jenna with her coat. It was early spring, but it can still be quite cold in Michigan in April.

Joyce and Annie were now wiping tears from their eyes as they walked around the table to hug Cameron and then Jenna.

"Well, guess we probably won't be seeing either of you for a while. Sure going to miss you both," Joyce said, hugging Cameron so tight he thought he would pass out.

"Aunt Joyce, you know you're always welcome to come to Vancouver. Heck, just let me know in advance, and Bruce will put you in front row seats of any concert. Tony and Annie, you know that goes for you too," Cameron replied, finally free to take a deep breath.

"Oh, thanks, Sweetheart. I can't honestly say that rock concerts are my forte, but I'll keep that in mind. You know I always supported your Dad and Jerry when they were younger. I'm so proud of you. Bruce, you take good care of our boy," she smiled.

"Have a safe flight," Tony added.

As the limo drove out of the hotel entrance, Jenna glanced at Bruce. "Do you think we would have time to take a short detour? Could we possibly drive out to Memorial Gardens? Bruce, I have to visit Nicky's grave before I leave Middleton. There are things I need to say. Just give me a few moments. I promise it won't take long," Jenna asked with tears in her eyes.

"Jenna, do you think that's best? Sweetheart, I know you miss him terribly. But it pains me to see you like this," Bruce sympathetically stated as he reached over to take her hand.

"Yes. Bruce, I need closure before I leave Middleton," Jenna replied, reaching for another tissue to wipe her eyes.

"Mom, I think Bruce is right. What more can be said? Why torture yourself?" Cameron begged, appearing bewildered.

"Oh, Sweetheart, I know. I don't expect you to understand why I need to do this. It won't take long. I know we have to be in Vancouver before 5:00 p.m. You have your whole career ahead of you. I need a few minutes alone to say goodbye to your dad."

As the limo entered the long narrow drive into Memorial Gardens, Cameron decided to walk out to the gravesite with his mom.

"Mom, I will go with you," Cameron whispered, reaching for her hand as he stared deep into her eyes.

"Thanks, Cameron, but I need to go alone. I'm fine, don't worry. Just wait in the car with Bruce."

The limo gradually came to a stop as the flower-covered grave came into view. Exiting the car, Jenna grabbed her scarf to cover her. Then, slowly she walked through the damp grass over to Nicky's grave and knelt.

"Oh Babe, there are so many things to say. Once before, I poured my heart out to you in a letter. Now I find myself again needing to talk with you. Nicky, I loved you the day I first met you in class, when I dropped my pencil. I've always loved you. It was so hard letting you go after our night at the cabin. I came so close to telling you about Cameron. Babe, I loved you enough to let you go back then, and somehow today, I need to find the strength to let you go once again. Nicky, you were everything to me, my safe place, and my whole reason for being. Babe, I'll always love you, always."

Leaning over the flower-covered earth which now held the love of her life, she picked up a single red rose. As tears streamed down her face, she lovingly kissed it. Then, taking a moment, she gently laid it back upon his grave. Slowly she stood, wiping her eyes. Walking back toward the limo, she finally said everything that needed to be said. She was ready to leave Middleton.

Cameron put his arms around her and held her tight as she stepped inside the car. There were no words spoken during the ride out to the airport, only silence. There was nothing more to say.

As the car pulled up alongside the private jet, Bruce noticed two people at the bottom of the steps. Taking another look, he wiped his eyes in unbelief. Kate was standing next to Jerry. Bruce was stunned for a brief moment, as he had remembered seeing a woman dressed in black at the funeral who resembled her. However, he quickly dismissed the thought from his mind that there was even the slightest chance of it being her. Bruce scratched his head, contemplating the dilemma which now faced him. This was undoubtedly the reason Jerry had failed to show up for breakfast. After advising her not to attend, Bruce was anxious to hear why she had decided against taking his advice. After all, he was sure neither Jenna nor Cameron knew anything of her or her past connection to Nicky.

"Hey Bruce, guess we got here a little early," Jerry laughed.

Bruce didn't like surprises or being put on the spot, so he took a moment to gather his thoughts before responding.

"Jenna and Cameron, why don't you both board the plane. I'll be aboard in a few minutes." He had deliberately avoided the introductions.

"I need to speak with Jerry," Bruce added.

"Hey Jerry," Cameron smiled, walking up the steps.

Jenna went over to hug Jerry before she boarded.

"We missed you at breakfast this morning. I hope everything is all right. See you in a few minutes," Jenna smiled, following Cameron onboard.

"Hey, Son. Hello Kate. So what's this all about?" Bruce inquired with a stern look.

"Well, Bruce, Kate saw the news coverage regarding Nicky, and she flew in from New York yesterday to attend the funeral."

"Hey Bruce, nice to see you again," Kate answered, reaching

out to shake his hand. "You seem surprised to see me. I hope you're not upset."

"Well, oddly enough, I thought for a second I saw you yesterday at the graveside services. There were so many people. I wasn't sure." Bruce rubbed his forehead contemplating his dilemma.

"Bruce, please try to understand. You know how much I loved Nicky. I had to come."

"Well, hopefully, Jerry told you that Nicky's wife, Jenna, and his son, Cameron, would be flying with us back to Vancouver this morning."

"Actually, he forgot to mention it, but I'm not here to cause them any more grief. Trust me, Bruce, that's not why I'm here. I spoke with Jerry yesterday after the services, and he informed me that you really could use a stylist with the boys. Bruce, I would love to come back to work for you. Times are truly hard out there right now, and to be blunt, I need a job. You know what a hard worker I am. Besides, there's no one better at hair and make-up than me. I know you came out of retirement to manage Cameron's career. I would love nothing better than to be part of the team again. But, I suppose you could say, I'm begging," she pleaded.

"Okay, only because you've cornered me," Bruce answered, giving her a rather strange look. "I need to get this aircraft in the air and on its way to Vancouver, but there's one condition. I need you to pretend to be Jerry's girlfriend, just until we're back in Vancouver. I don't want to be giving out any details to either Jenna or Cameron as to who you are or your connection to Black Tie Affair or Nicky. Jenna is having a tough time right now dealing with his loss. She's extremely fragile, and she's my main concern, do you understand?" Bruce demanded.

"Yes, Bruce. You can count on me."

"By the way, where are your bags? Are you traveling without luggage?"

"No, you know me—a make-up artist and hairdresser without bags. Jerry already stowed them on board," she laughed.

"Okay, one more thing. I need you both to sit in the back of the aircraft and behave back there. This isn't a social event," Bruce warned them. "Now, let's get this plane in the air. I've got business in Vancouver this evening."

Once onboard and settled in, Bruce went over to inquire if he could get Jenna or Cameron anything before the plane taxied over to the runway.

"Hey, Sweetheart, do either of you need a warm blanket or something to drink before we take off? Oh, I almost forgot, Jerry's girlfriend, Kate, is catching a ride over to Vancouver with us this morning. So they'll be sitting in the back."

"No, but thanks for asking," Jenna replied.

As their private jet lifted off the runway, Jenna took one last look at Middleton. Her mind was instantly flooded with memories. Noticing the tiny cars below reminded her of the early morning Nicky left with Bruce. She had been a passenger in one of those vehicles on her way back to Quebec. Wiping tears that trickled down her cheeks, she only wished she could go back in time. Things could have been different. Maybe she would have told him about the baby she was carrying. Perhaps they would have married and stayed in Middleton. She could only be sure of one thing, her love for Nicky was now strong enough to let him go for the second time, with no regrets.

CHAPTER TWO

Home Alone

The flight to Vancouver had been quiet. Jenna and Cameron had slept most of the way back. Having sat in the back of the jet, Jerry and Kate had remained discreet, trying not to disturb them. However, it was the fear of Bruce which had been their deterrent. Kate was determined not to upset Bruce. He had been her rock when she left Nicky all those years ago in Hollywood, and they had remained close.

As the jet made its final approach before landing, it was easy to see why Jenna and Nicky had settled in Vancouver after getting married. It was beautiful. Being Canadian, Jenna had no desire to stay in Quebec after her mother's passing. Vancouver seemed the perfect place on the Western Coast of Canada to call home. It was closer to Los Angeles, where Bruce had most of his connections in the music industry.

"Mom, we're finally home," Cameron mentioned, gently nudging her awake. In some ways, he hated to wake her. She seemed to be sleeping so peacefully. Now she was going to be faced with the stark reality of starting a new chapter of her life, which no longer included Nicky.

As the plane touched down, Bruce made his way up to their seats.

"Hey kids, how was the ride?" he asked. "Pretty smooth today, wasn't it?"

"Yes, I guess you could say that. Mom slept most of the way back," Cameron said, reaching for one of his bags.

"Felix has the car waiting for us. I will have him drop Jerry and me along with Kate at the hotel. Then he'll take you and Jenna out to the lake house. Unless there's some other place, you would like to go?" Bruce asked. "I've got a meeting later tonight and need to freshen up."

"Thanks, Bruce. I think I would like to go home and sleep in my bed tonight. Cameron is going to stay with me for a few days," Jenna replied as she looked in her compact mirror, trying to straighten her hair.

"Okay, but if there's anything at all you need, give me a call. Oh, one more thing, Cameron, I need you to come into the city tomorrow. We need to take care of a few things, but it can all wait until then. So go home and get some rest. We've got a big week ahead of us," Bruce added.

As the plane taxied over toward the hanger and came to a complete stop, Jenna took a deep breath. So this was it. She was back in Vancouver without the love of her life.

Jerry and Kate waited until Jenna and Cameron exited the plane before they descended the steps and walked over to the car.

"Hey Jerry, don't you think you should introduce mom and me to your girlfriend?" Cameron asked, stepping inside the limo.

"Oh yes, guys, this is Kate. We go way back." He tried nonchalantly to insinuate that Kate had been a girl he had known for a long time, which happened to be very close to the truth. At least it seemed to be working so far.

"It's nice to meet you, Kate. How long will you be staying in Vancouver?" Jenna asked.

"Well, guess it depends. I'm not sure." Finally, Kate offered just enough information to satisfy Jenna's curiosity hopefully.

"Jerry's a great guy. But, of course, I could be prejudiced," Cameron smiled. "After all, he's family and was Dad's best friend as well as a member of Black Tie Affair, but then again, I'm sure Jerry already told you," Cameron smiled.

"Yes," Kate acknowledged, returning his smile. "So sorry to hear about the loss of your father and your husband," she added, staring at Jenna. "I've heard a lot about him. He must have been an awesome musician."

At that point, Bruce eyed her intentionally, giving her a stare. He wasn't going to take the chance that she might let slip her real connection to Nicky. It seemed that Kate had gotten his message loud and clear. She seemed to remain quiet for the remainder of the ride over to the hotel.

It seemed a short drive before the limo stopped under the brightly lit portico of the Ritz Carlton.

"Well, guess this is our stop. Jerry, I've made two reservations. One for you and one for Kate. Just check in with the concierge in the lobby. Okay, kids, this is where I leave you. I have a meeting in about an hour. Sweetheart, have a good evening," Bruce smiled, leaning over to give her a quick kiss. "You've got that brilliant young man beside you," he added as he got out of the car.

"Catch you later, Cameron. See you soon, Jenna. Love you both," Jerry softly spoke, exiting the limo.

When Black Tie Affair was dismantled, Bruce had hired Jerry to work alongside him as an assistant manager of Cameron's band, House of Cards.

Jerry knew this evening was going to be truly hard on Jenna. It would be her first time back at the lake house without Nicky. He was having a hard time keeping his emotions in check. He missed Nicky almost more than life itself and was glad to have Kate with him tonight. He didn't want to be alone.

It seemed that Bruce had disappeared rather quickly after arriving at the hotel. He frequented the Carlton, having a penthouse. Jerry thought this was for the best. It left him and Kate free to figure out their plans for the evening. After receiving their room keys, Jerry glanced at Kate. It seemed they were on the same page.

Stepping into the elevator, Kate giggled, "Really, Jerry, two rooms."

Maybe the idea of Kate being his girlfriend wasn't far off the mark. At least for the night, it seemed to work for him. He had no desire to be alone.

Bruce wasn't born yesterday. Jerry knew that it was Bruce's idea of giving him a way out if he wanted.

"You were reading my mind," Jerry winked. "Which room?"

"Oh, you're sillier than I remember. Just pick one," Kate laughed.

The room was exquisite as they opened the door. French doors opened onto a large balcony revealing dramatic views of Vancouver. The mini bar was fully stocked, and the room contained a cozy king-sized bed. It was beautifully draped in blue silk toile, matching the curtains covering the large windows.

"Wow," Kate laughed again. "Bruce hasn't changed."

"Yes, you know Bruce. The man has class, but we're not staying. At least not now," Jerry replied, putting their bags away. "Let's go down to my favorite little bar. It's the best in Vancouver. What do you think? Are you up for it after the long flight today?"

"Oh, are you kidding? So you don't have to ask me twice," Kate replied.

It wasn't long before they were in a taxi on their way downtown to Jerry's favorite hangout. It was a quaint little pub tucked discreetly between two tall buildings called O'Brian's. Walking in the dimly lit bar, Jerry escorted Kate to a small table near the back. For a brief moment, it reminded her so much of something Nicky would have done. Her eyes moistened as her mind wandered back to the many nights they had shared. Kate had to bite her lip to keep from crying. She had to stay in the moment.

As the waiter came over, Jerry ordered drinks. It seemed they were both on the same wavelength again. Neither of them wished to remain sober. It was one way of dealing with the present. Maybe not the best, but it seemed to be working. It wasn't long before Kate could feel the effects of the alcohol as it coursed throughout her body and down to her toes. Time seemed to fly as they kept their waiter extremely busy trying to keep up with their refills. They spent the evening remembering the many fun times they had shared with Nicky. It was almost midnight when Jerry looked down at his watch. He knew he should get Kate back to the hotel. She was pretty wasted at this point. He only wondered if she would be able to walk out of the bar without assistance.

"Kate, Sweetheart, do you think you can walk?" Jerry asked.

"Well, first, let's see if I can stand," she giggled.

After calling for a taxi, it appeared that luck might be on his side. Kate managed to stand. Now maybe, just perhaps, she could walk out on her own without dropping to the floor. Slowly, he managed to get her outside and into the waiting cab. At this point, she had pretty much passed out.

His only thoughts were getting her back to their room as they arrived at the hotel. As the taxi drove up to the entrance, he had no choice. He would have to carry her. Now his only thoughts were hoping not to see Bruce anywhere near the lobby. Even though it was past midnight, Bruce was known to enjoy a strong drink late at night. The coast was clear. There was no sight of Bruce anywhere as he quickly carried Kate over to the elevator and up to their room.

Unlocking the door, he gently laid Kate down on the bed. Removing her shoes, he put her underneath the warm blankets. She would never remember a thing. Walking over to the mini bar, he pulled out a small bottle of Jack Daniels and mixed it with coke. Taking his drink out on the balcony, he soaked in the views of the evening skyline. A sea of lights emitted from the tall buildings which surrounded him. What a night, he thought. There was finally a beautiful girl in his bed again, and she had passed out. The unfortunate thing was, he knew she had always loved Nicky. It seemed ever since their high school days, Nicky was always the one who got the girls.

Looking up at the abundant stars which twinkled in the night sky, Jerry lifted his glass, "Nicky, here's to you, man."

Earlier that day, as the limo had slowly made its way down the steep mountainous roads to their beautiful home on Bear Lake, Jenna had become apprehensive. She usually loved the views as the highway made its steep descent down to the lake, but not today. How could she? Nicky had built their home to replicate the cabin on the lake where they had spent their last night together. That night would be forever engrained in her memory. Now, living here without him was going to be unbearable. Thank God she would have Cameron staying over for a few nights. Glancing at him, he seemed to be sleeping peacefully.

Driving up to the front entrance, Jenna's thoughts automatically returned to the fateful evening she had come downstairs to find Nicky slumped over in his favorite chair. How was she ever going to be able to do this? How was she ever going to be able to walk inside without him?

"Cameron, Sweetheart, we're home," Jenna whispered, gently nudging him awake.

"Wow, guess I must have been tired. But, Mom, don't forget to disarm the house alarm before you open the front door." Cameron reminded her as he stretched his arms and popped his knuckles.

"Okay, thanks for the reminder." Jenna had always been notorious for forgetting to disarm the security system, always accidentally setting it off. How would she ever manage in this big house alone?

Walking inside, it was much the same as she had left it. It was apparent the maids had been in while she was gone. There were fresh towels in the downstairs bathroom.

"Mom, I'm taking your suitcases upstairs. Why don't you call and have Jake bring the dogs back," Cameron yelled downstairs.

"Okay. That's a good idea." She would need companions for the night. It was her only hope of getting any sleep.

It was only a few minutes before the doorbell rang. Their neighbor,

Jake, had Fritz, their male Yorkie, and Joey, their male Havanese, both attached to leashes with him.

"Wow, Jake, how did you get here so fast? I didn't even call your house yet?" Jenna asked, puzzled.

"Oh, I was walking the dogs down by the lake, and I saw the limo drive up. How are things with you? Jenna, are you okay?"

"Yes, as well as can be."

"How were the services? I hope Bruce took care of things for you and Cameron."

"Yes. There's never a worry with Bruce. I literally couldn't cope without him," Jenna replied, giving the dogs some much-needed attention.

"Wow. They sure missed you."

The dogs were going crazy as usual. Jenna couldn't help but wonder if they missed Nicky as well. But, of course, it would be hard to know for sure. They had always been so attached to her.

"Well, I'll leave you and get back over to the house. Is Cameron here with you tonight?"

"Yes. He's going to stay for a few nights."

"Well, if you two should need anything, anything at all, please call me."

"Thanks. I'm sure we'll be fine. Thanks for watching Fritz and Joey."

"No problem, you know how much I love those two."

Closing the front door, she reached down to scoop Fritz up in her arms. Finally, hopefully, the dogs would be the distraction she so desperately needed.

"Mom, was that Jake?" Cameron yelled, bounding down the stairs.

"Yes. He brought the dogs back home."

"Awesome. Then I don't feel so bad about asking," he smiled sheepishly.

"Asking what, Cameron?"

"Well, I was going to take the jeep and drive back into the city and hang out with the boys for a while tonight. I need to get in some practice before tomorrow. We're going to meet downtown at the Sound Studio. Would you be all right if I left for a few hours?"

Her young son caught her off guard. Sure he would want and need to hang out with the boys in the band. But, she couldn't demand that he stay behind and hold her hand. As much as she might wish to keep him there, she couldn't.

"Okay, but you're coming home later tonight, right?" she found herself asking, almost pleading. "Cameron, no drinking and driving," she sternly reminded him.

"Yes, Mom, don't worry. I won't be that late. I have to meet with Bruce tomorrow. Probably sometime in the morning," Cameron mentioned, walking toward the garage.

"Okay, I love you."

Now she was alone. Hopefully, the dogs would keep her from going insane. Walking out to the back deck, she watched as the sun began to set over the lake. It seemed more vivid this evening. Bright hues of pink covered the late afternoon sky like cotton candy. Once again, her thoughts took her back to many evenings she had shared with Nicky, watching the spectacular sunsets. Now she stood here alone, with only her memories. Staying here without him wasn't going to be easy. He was so much a part of this house, this home. Now she wasn't sure if the world offered her reason enough to stay if it wasn't for Cameron.

Everything reminded her of Nicky as she went back inside. He had worked extremely hard and overseen every aspect of the building of their beautiful home. He had wanted it to be perfect for her, every detail. It was gorgeous, and Nicky had spared no expense. Every inch was to her liking. The lake house was a spacious three-story home. It was built from its outward appearance to resemble a log cabin. It had large redwood beams which stretched outward, forming a stunning entrance. The front of the house incorporated a magnificent wall of windows, which immersed the home in sunlight. They had spent numerous hours talking of future grandkids one day running throughout its enormous rooms. The back of the house included floor-to-ceiling windows, taking in the stunning views of the lake and snow-covered mountains. Now, it felt like it was sucking the life out of her. How could she remain here? It meant nothing to her without him.

Maybe she should take the dogs and go upstairs. There was no reason to wait up for Cameron. As she went upstairs, even the staircase was a work of art. Nicky had paid an outrageous amount to have unique native hardwoods brought in. It was beautiful. He loved this house, and every inch of it was him. Walking into the bedroom, again, it was just as she had left it. Nothing was out of place. Nicky had hired enough help to ensure she never had to lift her hand to do anything, not even cook.

His bathrobe remained folded on his vanity along with his colognes as she walked into the bathroom to get ready for bed. Instantly, she felt compelled to smell each one. Tears welled within her eyes. It felt like she couldn't breathe, as if she had a panic attack. Somehow she managed to get into their huge bed, which seemed to swallow her. Sensing her worries, the dogs immediately jumped up and cuddled next to her. Tonight wasn't going to be easy. Why did Cameron have to leave, especially tonight? Why hadn't he stayed? They could have watched old movies all night long, and she wouldn't have had to close her eyes until morning. Now, she lay there, unable to sleep. Even with the dogs snuggled against her, she felt tormented as thoughts of Nicky kept swirling through her mind. Maybe she was going crazy. She couldn't be sure. Perhaps she needed some warm milk or hot chocolate. There was only one way to find out. Getting out of bed, she went downstairs to the kitchen.

After making a cup of hot cocoa, she walked into the living room. It was too quiet. Now even the stillness of the night bothered her. Turning on the television, she searched for her favorite channel. Then, making herself comfortable on the sofa with Fritz and Joey, she decided to stay up and wait for Cameron to come home. What else could she do, she had tried everything, and nothing worked.

Miraculously, it hadn't taken long. The peacefulness of sleep finally invaded Jenna's petite body. She was only awakened as Cameron gently kissed her on the forehead.

"Mom, I'm home. Time for bed."

CHAPTER THREE

Back to the future

Kate woke up with the worst headache of her life. The night before seemed like a dizzy blur. Looking around the room, she noticed Jerry sitting on the sofa. Beside him was a folded blanket and pillow. It was apparent he had slept on the couch.

"You're awake. How do you feel? We tied one on last night," Jerry boasted.

"Yes. It sure feels like it. My head is still pounding, but other than that, I'm fine. Thanks for being such a gentleman last night and putting me to bed."

"Oh, no problem. I was just waiting for you to wake up before I ordered breakfast. Do you feel like eating this morning, or do you want juice or coffee with some aspirin?" Jerry asked sympathetically.

"Wow. Jerry, it's been a while since anyone has treated me as nice as you."

"Well, it's the least I can do. I sort of feel responsible for last night."

"Are you kidding? You didn't force me to go. But, Jerry, you do remember how much we all partied with Nicky and the boys in the band. I haven't changed. I had a great time."

"Bruce called the room earlier while you were still asleep. He wants us all at the studio this morning. I think he's got something up his sleeve. He asked for you to be there. Do you feel like you can make it?"

"I have to go. I'm not going to start my new job by disappointing Bruce. I can't wait to hear whatever it is that seems so important to him."

"Okay. I'll order toast with coffee and get you some aspirin. Oh, I almost forgot, we'll be meeting with Bruce in about an hour. Felix is arriving to pick us up at 10:00 a.m."

The following morning, Jenna heard a light knock at her bedroom door. Cameron entered with a breakfast tray consisting of scrambled eggs, bacon, and toast, along with a hot cup of coffee. The aroma was enticing. It looked delicious. She could hardly wait to take her first bite, even without much appetite.

"Cameron, what a nice surprise. I never expected this, but I'm so glad you decided to cook. Thank you," Jenna smiled, stopping to take a sip of coffee. "Did you eat?"

"Yes. I had coffee and toast. I knew that Sophie wasn't coming back until tomorrow, and I didn't want you to starve. Anyway, it's the least I can do for leaving you alone last night," Cameron answered, handing her the morning newspaper.

Taking the paper, Jenna wasn't in a hurry to read it. She was sure it would still contain news of Nicky. However, glancing at the front page, she was unexpectedly surprised. In bold print on the front page was a featured article regarding a memorial concert held at the Pacific Coliseum, a tribute to Nicky. Bruce sponsored it, featuring Cameron and his band, House of Cards. Also in bold print was Nicky's band, Black Tie Affair would reunite for the evening.

"Wow. Cameron, you knew, didn't you? Was this the reason for breakfast in bed this morning, to bring me the newspaper?" Jenna smiled.

"Well, sort of, but I wanted to make sure you had something to eat before I left for the studio. Great way to tell you, wasn't it?" Cameron laughed.

"Oh Cameron, I'm so excited for you. Come over here and let me hug you. This is the best news I've had since coming home."

"Mom, you should try to be happy. Please stop being so sad. We're going to get through this, I promise you. David and Jeff and Todd, and the boys are all coming out next week to start rehearsals. Most of them are even bringing their families to Vancouver for the occasion. It's going to be such fun celebrating Dad's career. Oh, by the way, I'm sorry about the mess I left downstairs in the kitchen, but I've got to hurry. Bruce needs us there before 10:30 a.m.," Cameron explained.

"Please don't worry about me. I'll be okay, and I'm going to clean the kitchen. It isn't a problem. I need something to do today, to keep busy. You better get going. You don't want to be late. Oh, please thank Bruce for me and let him know how thrilled I am about the upcoming concert."

"Okay, Mom, I'll call you later to see how things are going," Cameron added, leaning over to give her a quick kiss on the cheek. "I love you."

Wiping tears from her eyes, Jenna felt blessed. Cameron was right. They would get through these difficult days. Finishing breakfast, she set the tray on her vanity. A hot shower would complete her morning.

"Okay, kids, let's get going. Felix is here with the car," Bruce remarked, catching Jerry and Kate just as they walked out of the elevator.

"So, Bruce, what's on the agenda today?" Jerry asked, stepping into the limo behind Kate.

"Well, guess there's no point keeping it a secret at this point. Next week, I've secured the Pacific Coliseum for a memorial concert to honor Nicky. I know it's short notice, but nothing you boys can't handle. I'm reuniting the guys of Black Tie Affair for the evening.

However, the concert will feature Cameron and House of Cards. What do you think?"

"Wow. Does everyone know?" Jerry inquired with a huge grin.

"No, just Cameron. That's why I called the meeting today. Here's the newspaper. Check out the front page. Tickets go on sale today. So Kate, are you ready to get your feet wet again?" Bruce teased, lighting a cigar.

"Yes. I've missed working with a band. It's good to feel like I'm part of something exciting again. I can't wait to see David and Jeff.

"Well, I guess you're going to get another chance. Don't disappoint me," Bruce added. "You've got your work cut out for you. It's going to be long days."

As the limo drove up to the warehouse that contained the sound studio, Bruce's attention was drawn to the long row of impressive cars parked out front. It appeared all the boys were here. As he sometimes referred to them, the kids were young, most not having ever left home before. However, they were all musically talented. Even though they lacked experience, Bruce was determined to hire the most gifted musicians. He would ensure that Cameron had the finest band possible, even if it meant taking them far from home on a world tour. Bruce knew how to sell out venues, and he planned to transform them into one hell of a band. With a bit of publicity and advertising, they would become very well known before even leaving Vancouver.

"Okay, it appears everyone is here. That's what I wanted to see. But, we've got a lot to do, so let's get inside and get started."

Walking inside, Kate felt nervous. She hoped the boys would like her. Kate had always considered her years working with the band members of Black Tie Affair to be her best. She could only hope that Cameron and his crew would feel the same.

"Good morning, glad to see you're all here and ready to get started," Bruce smiled, putting out his cigar. Then, he paused, taking a seat on top of an old desk.

"So I guess you're all wondering why I called you in on such short notice this morning. Well, I know you're all aware of the upcoming concert. It made the headlines of today's paper. Just in case any of you haven't seen it, here it is. Take a look. We're featured on the front page, and tickets go on sale today. The concert is two weeks from today. Black Tie Affair will reunite for a one-time performance, and of course, the evening will highlight House of Cards. I've got the guys from Black Tie Affair coming in this week. Does anyone have any questions?"

"Yes. Bruce, what about the roadies that usually set up. Do you think we're going to have enough guys on hand, considering there's going to be two bands on stage that night?" Drew questioned. Drew Connors was Cameron's lead guitarist. He was twenty-five, a few years older than Cameron. However, Drew was by far the best guitarist Bruce had ever come across since hiring Nicky, and the girls loved him. He was tall with jet black hair, styled into a mohawk. Wearing only a short-sleeve T-shirt and jeans exposed his arms covered in bizarre tattoos. His sculpted muscular appearance made him very popular with the girls.

"Drew, that's a good question. I've already asked the guys who worked for Black Tie Affair if they would like to be part of the memorial. I'm happy to say they're all on board. What I'd like to do today is start working with Hank, our new musical director, on the choice of song titles. He's supposed to be here around noon. Next, I'd like to ask Kate to walk over. Guys, meet Kate Hampton, our new hairdresser and make-up artist. She worked with Black Tie Affair for many years. I'm glad to have her back on board. Kate is the best, and I'm sure you're all going to fall in love with her. Of course, she already knows Jerry, and she's met, Cameron. I'll let you boys make your introductions. Well, I think that does it for right now. I'm going to get a cup of coffee while we wait on Hank to arrive. If you have any questions, you know where to find me," Bruce informed them.

"Hey Jerry, you didn't mention that Kate was coming on board with us?" Cameron asked with a puzzled expression.

"Well, I had no idea until last night. You're going to love her, so will the rest of the guys," Jerry casually replied, walking over to Kate as she talked with Drew.

"Hey Kate, have you met all the boys yet?" Jerry inquired.

"Well, I just met Drew."

The boys were completely the opposite of the band members of Black Tie Affair. Even though the band members of Black Tie Affair wore suits and seemed polished, it had not indicated they were saints. However, House of Cards' band members appeared to be hard-core rockers. It appeared the new generation of rock bands were definitely not inhibited by their appearance. Kate was amused by the fact she was old enough to be their mother.

"Let's walk over, and I'll finish introducing you to the other members of the band," Jerry mentioned, pulling her away from Drew. "Kate, this is Harry Creighton, our drummer. He's wild and crazy. We refer to him as Flame," Jerry laughed.

Harry had fiery red hair, which she determined at one glance had been colored. He was tall and thin with freckles. However, the most notable thing about Harry, other than his hair, was his facial piercings. His lip, eyebrow, and nostril were sporting either a ring or stud. Harry was a very talented drummer, and the band was lucky to have him.

"Nice to meet you. Please don't listen to Jerry. He's the wild one," Harry laughed.

He seemed genuinely friendly and well-mannered. His personality was deceiving and didn't reflect his appearance. However, these guys were members of a rock band, and time would reflect their behavior, she thought.

"Nice to meet you too, Harry. I look forward to working with you," Kate smiled, still thinking his looks might be misleading.

Next, Jerry introduced her to their bass guitarist, Douglas Blackwell. "Hey Douglas, meet Kate."

"Hey, Kate, nice to meet you. You can call me Doug. Glad to have you on board with the band." Doug was short and stout, sporting the unshaven look. He appeared in his early twenties with beautiful green eyes and long brown hair, which he wore pulled back in a ponytail. Doug also had his fair share of tattoos exposed by his sleeveless tank. For a brief moment, Kate was sure she smelled pot. Some things never changed, she thought.

"Wow. Jerry, everyone seems to be incredibly nice. Even though I'll have to admit, I was a bit thrown off by their appearance," Kate stated, walking over to get a cold drink. "Cameron seems to be a non-conformer," she smiled.

"Yes. They're a nice group of boys to work with, but you haven't been on tour with them yet," Jerry laughed. "Things seem quite tame at the moment. Nicky's sudden passing has hit the boys hard. Just wait until you hear them perform. Bruce set Cameron up with the right guys."

The rest of the afternoon was spent in rehearsals. Listening to the band, Kate was back in her element. Finally, as everything wrapped for the day, Cameron invited everyone out to the house as he routinely did. He knew it would be the perfect idea to keep his mom preoccupied, as she had always loved having their home filled with the boisterous sounds of the band members.

Later that evening, the circular drive of the lake house once again looked like the showroom of a costly car dealership. All the guys had arrived except Bruce, who chose to bow out this evening, deciding to turn in early, and Jerry and Kate, who would show up later. Nicky had intentionally built their home away from the city to avoid distractions from uninvited guests. It had been the seclusion he so desperately needed as his health continued to decline.

Thankfully Sophie returned to her duties as their long-time chef. She created a wonderful smorgasbord of everything the Pacific Northwest was known for, smoked salmon, halibut, Dungeness crabs, and her specialty clam chowder.

The boys seem to congregate in the kitchen, helping themselves to the delicious platters of seafood that had been prepared. Then, walking over to the fridge, Cameron grabbed a couple of beers, tossing one over to Harry.

"Hey guys, it's a perfect night for a bonfire. I think there's enough wood stockpiled down by the shore of the lake. What do you think?"

"Oh, you don't have to ask me twice," Harry replied, heading for the door.

"Mom, bring the dogs down and join us."

"Okay. I'll be down as soon as Jerry and his girlfriend arrive."

"Mom, her name is Kate, remember."

"Oh, that's right. Well, you boys go down to the lake and have fun. I'll be down shortly."

With that said, Cameron, along with Harry, Drew, and Douglas, walked outside in the darkness carrying a cooler stocked with beer. It wasn't long before the doorbell rang, announcing Jerry and Kate's arrival.

"Hey Jerry, come in," Jenna smiled, opening the door.

"Hi Jenna, you remember Kate. She flew in with us on the plane after the services."

"Yes, of course. Nice to meet you again. Please come in. Oh, the boys are all down at the lake. Cameron decided to build a bonfire tonight. There are platters of seafood in the kitchen, along with plates and silverware. Please help yourselves to the array of food before you walk down to the lake. I'll be down in a few minutes."

"Thanks, that sounds like fun. See you in a few," Jerry smiled, taking Kate's hand as they walked toward the kitchen.

Jerry and Kate made their way down the steep path to the lake. Tall flames coming from the blazing bonfire were clearly visible. Kate was trying to balance two large plates filled with crab legs as she descended the narrow trail. At the same time, Jerry managed to carry enough drinks to last them for the night, hopefully.

"Hey Jerry," Cameron shouted. "We have a cooler. Come on down and put your drinks inside."

"Hi guys," Kate smiled, taking a seat next to Jerry in one of the weather-beaten Adirondack chairs. "Wow, the seafood smells delicious."

It wasn't long before the flickers from Jenna's flashlight could be seen as she made her way through the darkness down to the lake. Fritz and Joey ran ahead. They were used to the routine. Nicky and Jenna had enjoyed countless nights sitting around the warmth of a bonfire.

"Hey, Mom, come and join us. Would you like a beer?" Cameron asked, taking one of the empty chairs pulling it up near the roaring fire.

"No thanks, Sweetheart, I brought a thermos of hot coffee."

As the guys became boisterous talking about the band and the upcoming memorial, Kate walked over, sitting next to Jenna.

"I've not had a chance to talk with you, but I want to let you know how sorry I am for your loss. I worked with Black Tie Affair as a stylist when Nicky first came onboard with the band. Everyone loved him. He was such an awesome musician. I know you must be extremely proud of Cameron following in his dad's footsteps."

Kate found it hard to keep her life secret with Nicky. She was also mourning the loss of a man she had loved dearly and with whom she had given birth to his daughter. However, she never intended to hurt Jenna by disclosing any parts of her treasured life with her deceased husband.

"Thank you. My life seems surreal without him. If it wasn't for Cameron, I don't know how I would manage," Jenna answered, trying to hide her tears.

Just at that instant and not a moment too soon, the girls heard the sounds of splashing water. Wiping her moist face, Jenna was distracted from her thoughts of Nicky as she gasped with laughter. She caught sight of Harry's freckled backside as he plunged naked into the frigid water. It seemed one of the guys had dared him to go skinny dipping, and he had taken them up on their taunt. If ever any shenanigans were going on with the boys, it seemed always to involve Harry. Now, the dilemma of getting him out of the ice-cold water without clothes had the guys roaring with laughter. Jenna and Kate closed their eyes as Harry quickly grabbed his clothes and made a mad dash up to the house.

"Wow. That was hilarious," Drew laughed.

"Flame, you're crazy," Cameron roared. "Sorry, Mom, I didn't think he would really do it. Guess Douglas owes him a case of beer."

As the night grew colder, everyone moved the party back inside. Once again, the lake house filled with the sounds of laughter and noise of the band members. It was familiar and comforting to Jenna. Their home had always been a place where Cameron enjoyed bringing his friends. Nicky had been such an integral part of these evenings. He had always been the center of attention with his outrageous stories from his years spent on tour. Jenna found herself missing him more than ever tonight. However, the house seemed alive tonight, and she knew it was precisely the kind of evening that Nicky loved. After mingling with the guys and making sure the kitchen was completely stocked with drinks and food, Jenna decided to turn in for the evening. Walking into the living room, she found Cameron, putting her arms around him.

"Hey, Sweetheart, I think I'm going to call it a night and go upstairs," Jenna informed him, quickly kissing him goodnight. "Cameron, don't let the guys drive home. They've all had too much to drink. There are pillows and blankets in the closet and plenty of room for everyone to sleep. See you all in the morning."

"Okay, Mom, thanks for everything. Try and get some sleep."

Walking over to kiss her goodnight, Jerry could feel Jenna's sadness. "Thanks for having us tonight. Try to get some sleep. I'll call you tomorrow."

"Goodnight, Mom, Cameron, and the boys yelled."

Scooping Fritz up in her arms, Joey followed close behind as she made her way up the winding staircase.

Quickly getting changed, Jenna once again found herself in their huge bed, feeling the loneliness of not having Nicky's warm body next to her. It seemed Fritz sensed her dilemma as he came over to snuggle against her under the heavy duvet. Wiping away the tears from her eyes, she took strength in knowing that she wasn't alone. She also knew that Cameron wasn't alone. The sounds coming from downstairs gave her comfort. Listening to the laughter and noise, it wasn't long before she drifted off to sleep.

Waking up the following day to the smell of coffee and bacon cooking, Jenna walked into the bathroom. Turning on the warm water, she showered and dressed, anxious to get downstairs. As she descended the curved steps leading down into the living room, the view made her laugh. The living room now encompassed the sleeping bodies of the boys. It seemed Harry had found a sleeping bag and was mysteriously asleep on the carpet under the grand piano. Cameron was curled up on the sofa. Doug was snoring loudly. He had managed to somehow sleep in Nicky's favorite recliner, and Drew had found a place to rest on the chaise longue which sat beneath the tall front windows. It would be moments like this that let her know that life without him was possible.

Following the smell of bacon coming from the kitchen, she found Sophie busily preparing breakfast.

"Good morning," Sophie smiled. "Can I pour you a cup of coffee?"

"Yes. That sounds wonderful."

"It's so good to have you and Cameron back home. How were the services?"

"It was just as Nicky would have wanted. Bruce kept it private just for the immediate family and close friends. But I'm so glad to be home and away from Middleton. It has always held too many memories for me."

Taking her coffee, Jenna walked out to the back deck. Watching the morning sun as it cast its rays through the clouds, she took in the phenomenal views of the lake. Memories of Nicky and the countless mornings they had shared drinking coffee and discussing their plans for the day invaded her mind. However, she would only enjoy her solitude for a short time. It seemed the incredible aroma of fried bacon coming from the kitchen had finally awakened the sleepy heads in the living room and their appetites. Walking back inside, the guys were anxiously helping themselves to stacks of pancakes, along with bacon and eggs that Sophie had prepared.

"Hey, Mom, Bruce called, and he wants us down at the studio. Guess he's anxious to get started with rehearsals for the concert. Do you want to go hang out with us today?" Cameron asked, ravenously shoveling pancakes into his mouth.

"No, but thanks for asking. I think I'll spend the day at home and later take the dogs out for a long walk," Jenna smiled, filling tall glasses of orange juice for the guys.

"Okay, well, you know where to reach me. Jerry and Kate had the limo pick them up last night. They both wanted me to thank you for having them over last night."

"Oh, that was nice. Please remind Jerry he's always welcome to stop by anytime," Jenna mentioned pouring herself another cup of coffee.

After breakfast, the boys were anxious to drive to Vancouver to the sound studio. It seemed to be their home away from home.

"Okay, Mom, see you later this evening," Cameron yelled, grabbing his keys.

The house was quiet now. Thank goodness Sophie had returned to help fill the empty void. Jenna ran around the living room, trying to restore everything to its original place. Finally, it seemed to give her purpose.

"Oh Jenna, let me take care of this," Sophie smiled, walking in from the kitchen. "I know you must have a lot of things to do today."

"Well, that's just it, I really don't have any plans for today, and the house seems so empty without Nicky," Jenna mentioned as she continued folding the blankets. She wiped tears from her face as she looked around the room, knowing he would never return.

"I'm sure the dogs would love a morning walk. So let me get their leashes," Sophie said, taking the blankets.

"Thanks, that sounds good. I was planning to take them for a walk."

With Fritz and Joey in tow, Jenna made her way down the narrow trail which surrounded the lake. It wasn't long before Joey spotted a squirrel, pulling her closer to explore. Their excitability provided the distraction she needed.

Unleashing the dogs, Jenna was bombarded with thoughts as she watched them running back toward the house. Maybe, it was time to sell. Cameron would be on tour, and remaining here without him almost brought on another panic attack. Finally, her mind was made up. She would drive into Vancouver and talk with a realtor. The beautiful sprawling cabin would no longer be a part of her future but rather a part of her past.

CHAPTER FOUR

Keeping Secrets

Bruce was late this morning. He walked into the sound studio puffing on a Cuban cigar, one of his notorious bad habits.

"Well, guys, I just got off the phone with David Simmons. Jeff and David will arrive this Friday with Todd and the crew. The next two weeks are going to be hectic. Hank will be coming in later this morning to finalize the music for the concert. We're going to open the memorial with the guys of Black Tie Affair, that includes you, Jerry," Bruce smiled, glancing in his direction. "I have arranged for everyone to stay at the Ritz Carlton. I reserved the top floors as of this Friday. Well, I guess that covers my updates for this morning. Why don't you all grab an early lunch? Hank is running later than I expected. I've got a few phone calls to make, so we'll meet after lunch to discuss music arrangements."

After Bruce left the room, Kate walked over to Jerry.

"Hey, let's take a walk downtown and get something to eat," she whispered.

"Okay. But why are you whispering?" Jerry laughed.

"Well, I didn't want Cameron or the guys to overhear our plans and decide to tag along."

"Geez. This sounds serious."

The day was beautiful as they walked outside and down the street—no hint of clouds or rain, which consume most of the calendar for the Pacific Northwest. Stopping in front of Genève's Italian Restaurant, it wasn't long before the aromas drew them inside.

"It smells yummy. Do you feel like pasta?" Kate suggested.

"How could I possibly say no with your expression?"

It wasn't long before they were seated in a booth with a checkered tablecloth enjoying the pasta which Kate craved.

"Okay. Let's have it," Jerry inquired. "It's not like you to exclude the guys. What's going on?"

"Honestly, I really don't know where or how to begin."

"I think you better come out with it. Bruce expects us back shortly."

"Alright," Kate answered, taking a long slow sip of iced tea. "It happened many years ago, just before Nicky and I moved to Hollywood. Remember when he made his first movie, *Life in Spades?*

"Yes."

"Well," Kate paused, taking another sip of tea.

"Kate, come on. We don't have all day. For heaven's sake, what are you trying to tell me."

"Okay, I'll just come out with it. I have a daughter. Her name is Nicole."

"Awesome! Congratulations! So that's what you needed to tell me?"

"Not exactly. Nicole is eighteen and living back in New York with my Aunt Grace. Nicole is the love of my life."

It seemed as if time stood still and everything around her was happening in slow motion as she looked up at Jerry. His quizzical facial expressions gave a hint that he had finally realized the importance of what she was trying to tell him.

The realization hit him like a ton of bricks. Taking his napkin from his lap, he wiped the beaded sweat from his forehead. Remembering how close Nicky had been with Kate, their relationship while on tour, and Nicole's age, it wasn't hard for Jerry to finally realize the implications. But, staring at Kate, words almost failed to come out of his mouth.

"Kate, are you trying to tell me that Nicky is Nicole's father?"

"Yes. I guess I am."

"Does Nicole know? Who knows about this? Does anyone know?"

"Jerry, calm down. You're only the second person I've ever told. The only reason I'm telling you now is that she's flying in this week. I want her to be here for the memorial concert. You have no idea how hard it's been trying to live with this secret all these years."

"So, what are your plans? Are you going to tell her?"

"Not exactly. I felt it would only be right for Nicole to be here for the concert. She knows that I attended the funeral and that Bruce has given me the chance to work as a stylist for the band. However, she knows nothing of the relationship which Nicky and I shared."

"Damn, I'm still blown away. Cameron has a half-sister, and what about Jenna? She's been through too much to be assaulted with this bit of news."

"I know, don't worry. Trust me. I'm not trying to hurt anyone. No one will ever know. That's why I felt I had to tell you before she arrived. Nicole knows that I worked for the band while they were on tour in Europe, but she knows nothing of the short time I spent in Hollywood with Nicky."

"Kate, aren't you forgetting about one person?"

"Oh, you mean Bruce? He knows. He's always known. I don't know what would have happened to Nicole and me if it hadn't been for his help. God bless him. Bruce is a saint. When Nicky passed, he called and informed me about the funeral, even though he insisted that I shouldn't attend. He has met Nicole on occasions like her birthday and holidays. She refers to him as Uncle Bruce.

"So that was just an act that day at the airport when we left Middleton. I mean, you and Bruce had been in contact this whole time?"

"Yes. But there was no way he would have ever wanted anyone to know. Besides, you didn't bother to tell me that Jenna and Cameron would be on that flight. Bruce had no idea I was going to attend the services. He definitely had no idea that I would be at the airport that morning or even ask for my old job back. I think I truly caught him off guard. After we arrived in Vancouver, Bruce cornered me one day in the hallway as I walked over to the elevator. He insisted that I tell you before she arrived. Bruce knew you could handle it and would be a great help with Nicole."

"Geez. This is almost unbelievable. But no worries, your secret is safe with me. I'll be more than happy to show Nicole the city of Vancouver and introduce her to the boys. Man, Cameron has a sister, unbelievable. But, wait just a minute, I have a niece," Jerry beamed.

"Yes, Jerry, but she can't know. Do you hear me? Bruce knew that once you found out who she was that you would be the perfect person to help during her stay in Vancouver, especially now that you and I've become close."

"There's only one more thing."

"What could that possibly be?"

"Jerry, she's the spitting image of Nicky. She's beautiful, just wait until you see her. Nicole has worked with several modeling agencies in New York. She loves modeling. But go figure, she also has a passion for music," Kate added, wiping tears from her face.

"Kate, Sweetheart, don't cry. But, of course, she would be beautiful. She's my niece. I guess this means Uncle Jerry's job will include keeping the boys away."

"Wow. I feel so much better having got this off my chest," Kate mentioned reaching over to take Jerry's hand.

"Well, we better get out of here. Bruce won't be happy if we show up late after lunch. What you've told me will stay just between you and me, and I guess Bruce. Geez, I still find this so hard to believe and the fact that Nicky never knew."

"I know, I never meant it to be this way. It was just the fact that Nicky was not father material back then. Don't worry about Bruce. He knew that I planned to talk with you today," Kate smiled, taking tissue out of her purse to wipe her eyes. "Everyone will know that I have a daughter when she arrives. However, only you and Bruce will ever know that her father was Nicky Spade."

Walking with Kate back to the sound studio, Jerry's thoughts were racing wildly out of control. Nicky had a daughter. Cameron had a sister. Now even his life would never be the same, but it all paled in comparison to the fact that Nicole would never know her dad. So many things might have been different if Nicky had only known.

As they got near the studio, Jerry noticed Jenna's Mercedes parked out front. Undoubtedly she must have gotten lonely at the cabin and decided to drive into Vancouver for the day. Getting closer, he noticed she was sitting inside her car. However, seeing Jerry walk up, Jenna motioned him over to her window.

"Hey Jerry, you're just the person I hoped to see. I haven't gone inside because I didn't want Cameron to know I was here. I've decided to list the lake house for sale. There's no way that I can live alone in that huge house. Especially now, with the band leaving so soon. I'm not sure how Cameron would take the news of me selling the house. So I've decided not to tell him until it's sold. What do you think?"

"Jenna, don't you think he should be involved. That's a huge decision. Shouldn't you tell him before it's sold?"

"I think if it's already sold, he would understand how serious I was. But I don't want you to let him know. So can you please keep this to yourself for now?"

"Yes. No problem. How are you going to arrange to have an open house without him knowing?"

"Well, for one thing, I'm not having a for sale sign put in our front yard, and here's where you come in. I was hoping that you might be able to help. I'll let you know what days the realtor will need to show the house, and then maybe you can arrange a distraction during that time."

"Really, what do you want me to do?"

"Oh Jerry, I'm sure you can come up with something."

"Okay, but just for the record, I'm totally against your idea of not telling him."

"I understand, and I hear you loud and clear. Can I count on you? But, please, Jerry, don't let Cameron know I was here or that we talked."

"Alright, just give me a call. I'll do my best."

"What was that all about?" Kate asked as Jerry walked up the steps to the studio entrance.

"Oh nothing," Jerry mentioned. "Jenna didn't want Cameron to know she had come into the city today."

"That sounds weird."

"Yes. Who knows? Let's just get inside before Bruce realizes we've overstayed our lunch break."

Jerry's mind was once again on overload as he walked inside. Why had Jenna decided to involve him in her crazy scheme? He was convinced this wasn't a good idea and would end badly. However, he felt obligated to help. Keeping secrets was not a game he liked to play, but this seemed trivial compared to what Kate had told him at lunch.

"Hey guys, happy to see you both could make it back this afternoon," Bruce joked. "We've got a lot to do. Jerry, you know you'll be featured as the lead singer when Black Tie Affair performs.

"Bruce, I'm honored to stand in for Nicky. The concert will be the first time the boys of Black Tie Affair and I have been on stage in seven years. After Nicky retired and the band dismantled, it was always a dream to reunite one day. I can't say that I would have wanted it to happen under these circumstances, but I'm thrilled to be performing with the guys again. Frankly, I can't wait to get back on stage with the band."

Things were now being implemented to make the memorial concert a night to be remembered. However, so many things had changed since their last memorial concert in Rome. Life seemed to have a strange way of repeating itself.

CHAPTER FIVE

Night of Remembrance

"Hey, Kate, you should hurry. The limo will be downstairs soon. Have you called Nicole's room to see if she's ready?" Jerry inquired.

"No. Give me just a few minutes to finish drying my hair, and I'll give Nicole a call. On second thought, why don't you call Nicole?"

"Okay, but it's getting late. It's almost 5:00 p.m."

The night of the concert had seemed to arrive sooner than expected. Bruce had scheduled a hectic week of rehearsals, and along with the dinners afterward, it had left little time for Jerry to play tourist guide. Nicole had seemed to settle in with little notice. Bruce introduced her to the remaining band members of Black Tie Affair and Mike, Michelle, and Todd. It seemed everyone had readily accepted her as Kate's daughter without further questions. No one could have known her connection to this night.

"Hey Nicole, your mom asked me to call and see if you were almost ready to go. She's drying her hair, so why don't you just meet us downstairs in the lobby."

"Okay, I'm ready, that sounds fine. I'll meet you both downstairs."

Walking out of the elevator, Jerry smiled, seeing Nicole. She looked beautiful, and even though she was the spitting image of Nicky, no one had bothered to notice a resemblance. Surely it must have been their hectic schedule that worked to keep her identity safe.

As Bruce walked out of the elevator, he beamed like a proud father seeing everyone assembled in the spacious foyer.

"Okay, is everyone ready to go? Wow, I must say you all clean up nicely," Bruce grinned. "I've got three limos arriving shortly. The first one is already out front. Jerry, why don't you and I take the first ride over with Kate and Nicole since Kate needs to set up hair and makeup. Then, Mike, why don't you and Michelle ride over with the boys when they come downstairs. Please let them know the other cars will be arriving shortly. Finally, Todd, why don't you, Jeff, and David ride over with us."

The ride over to the coliseum seemed somber. It was too quiet for Bruce.

"Okay, everyone I know this night is to pay our respects to Nicky, but I'll be honest and just say I hope that everyone lightens up. He would want this to be a night of celebration. No one loved that kid more than me. Heck, I remember the memorial for Alex and Randy back in Rome. Nicky came on stage and made that a night to be remembered. So we're going to do the same for him," Bruce demanded, pouring himself a shot of bourbon."

As the limo arrived at the back entrance of the coliseum, Jerry looked over at Kate and Nicole. He knew that tonight was going to be emotionally hard on Kate. Thankfully, Nicole wouldn't understand the implications of the evening.

"Mom, are you almost ready?" Cameron asked loudly, knocking on Jenna's bedroom door. "The limo will be here soon."

"Yes, son, come in. I'm just trying to decide which heels to wear."

Tears began welling within in her eyes as she looked up at Cameron.

"Cameron, you look so handsome tonight. Your dad would be so proud of you," she stated, taking a tissue from her purse.

"Mom, please don't cry. How do you ever expect me to get through this evening if you're going to be emotional? You have to be strong. We have to do this for Dad. He wouldn't want either of us to be sad," he reminded Jenna as he gently held her in his arms. "Hurry, let's pick out those shoes." Walking downstairs, Cameron caught sight of the limo through the large windows as it parked under the entrance. "Mom, the car is here."

"Cameron, I don't know what I would do without you," Jenna mentioned as she stepped inside the car.

Slowly ascending the mountainous roads, it was quiet. Jenna knew every twist and turn by heart. Even though the darkness of the evening had begun to creep in, there was just enough light remaining from the day to reflect the incredible views. They seemed to haunt her. It had been the one reason Nicky had chosen the location for their home. Now more than ever, she knew she was right in her decision to sell.

"Hey, Mom, would you like a drink? I think it would calm your nerves."

"Sure, that sounds good."

Reaching over to the bar, Cameron opened a small bottle of vodka and mixed it with orange juice.

"I went easy with the vodka, but this should help."

Arriving at the Pacific Coliseum, the line of fans waiting to get inside was incredibly long. However, it seemed the fans had not failed to show up and pay their respects to their favorite rock icon.

"Hey, Sweetheart, how are you holding up this evening," Bruce asked, meeting Jenna and Cameron at the back entrance.

"Oh, I'm fine. Thanks to my handsome son. He takes such good care of me."

"Well, you'll be happy to know the concert is completely sold, as I'm sure you imagined from seeing the long lines outside. It's going to be a great evening. So why don't you come back and hang with the boys? Jerry, Kate, and Nicole, Kate's daughter, are already in the dressing room."

"Okay, I guess I'll go back and say hello to everyone. I wasn't aware that Kate had a daughter?"

"Yes. Nicole came for the memorial. She lives in New York with her aunt.

Sweetheart, you'll have to excuse me. I've got to find Todd, always so much to do right at the very last minute. I've got our usual box seats reserved upstairs for family and friends. I'll meet you there later this evening. Oh don't forget, we've got the Wharf reserved for dinner tonight after the concert. They have the best seafood."

"Thanks, Bruce. Oh, by the way, Annie and Joey couldn't fly out for the concert. It seems Joey's mother has been under the weather, and they didn't want to leave her. Also, Tony and Aunt Joyce weren't able to make it either."

"That's too bad. Nicky's family is going to miss a wonderful tribute to him."

"I know," Jenna smiled as she continued walking down the long narrow hall toward the dressing room.

Entering the room, it was chaotic. Catering had just arrived and set up a drink service of cold champagne and beer. The aroma of fresh flowers infused the air. Two news reporters had somehow managed to find their way inside and were trying to get interviews with a few of the band members. Kate was busily trying to get set up for hair and makeup. Then, noticing a young girl helping her, Jenna decided to walk over and introduce herself.

"Hey Kate, I don't think I've met your daughter. Bruce just told me she came out for the memorial."

"Nicole, this is Jenna Spade, Nicky's wife."

"Nice to meet you," Nicole smiled.

"How long will you be staying in Vancouver?" Jenna inquired.

"Well, I haven't decided. Mom will be leaving to go on tour with the band. So I might go back to New York and continue modeling."

"Great, it was nice meeting you. I'm sure I'll see you later at dinner this evening."

Walking away, Jenna couldn't shake the idea that Nicole seemed strangely familiar. There was something about her appearance which seemed mysterious. She was beautiful, and uncannily, it almost felt as if they had met. Looking deep into her eyes, it gave her goosebumps. Wow, this seemed bizarre. There was no way she had ever seen Nicole, much less met her. However, Jenna sensed an odd familiarity about her.

The following two hours passed quickly as people backstage were busily preparing for the concert. Finally, Jenna made her way upstairs to the box seats where she had sat many times before. Seeing the tables against the back wall filled with an array of seafood, Jenna went over and filled a small bowl with clam chowder. It wasn't long before Michelle walked in. "Hello, I don't think we were introduced. I'm Michelle, Mike's girlfriend. Mike was one of the roadies with Black Tie Affair. He loved Nicky. We both were very sorry to hear of his passing."

"Thank you. It's nice to meet you," Jenna smiled.

"Something sure smells delicious. I think I'll try some."

After getting herself a bowl of chowder, Michelle walked over and took a seat next to Jenna in front of the large viewing window.

"Mike has a lot of good memories of the years he spent traveling with Black Tie Affair. I'll never forget the time when Kate and Nicky stayed at our apartment when Randy and Alex's plane crashed."

"Did you say, Kate?"

"Oh, I'm sorry. Kate did hair and makeup for the band for many years. You didn't know Nicky and Kate were together during his European tour?"

"No. But I guess I do now. You are talking about the same Kate who's working as a stylist for Cameron's band, right?"

"Yes."

Jenna felt like she had been punched in the gut sitting back in her seat. Why, of all times and places, had this happened tonight at Nicky's memorial concert. What a way to start the night. She almost felt ill.

"Jenna, I'm sure they were no more than two ships passing in the night. You know how it is with rock bands. I wouldn't be shocked to find out that Mike hadn't managed to stay faithful all those years.

Still, of course, he's tried his best to make me think otherwise," Michelle said, knowing she had overstepped her bounds by discussing Kate.

Jenna had to stay the course and remain unaffected by this bit of news. She wasn't going to let Michelle make her emotional, at least not now.

"Well, I lost contact with him for many years, and there was no way to know where he was. So when the plane crashed, killing Alex and Randy, I didn't know if he was on board or not. The news media made no mention of who was on the fatal flight until the next day. So I didn't know if he was dead or alive."

"I'm sorry. That must have been brutal. I couldn't imagine not knowing if Mike was in a plane crash."

Just at that instant, Nicole walked in.

"Mom will be up soon. Working with two bands tonight has her extra busy, so Bruce told me to come up and wait here. He said there was food and drinks. Oh, he said to let you know that he would be up later with Mom. So I think you're going to have a little surprise when the boys walk on stage tonight.

"Really, which group of boys? I'm guessing Cameron and House of Cards," Jenna smiled. Once again, Jenna sensed an odd familiarity about her.

"Well, I think I'll let that be a surprise," Nicole answered, surveying the delectable spread of seafood.

The vast auditorium filled up quickly over the next hour. As the fans took their seats, the noise level became extremely loud—two large screens at each side of the stage continually highlighted Nicky's career. The fans were shown unforgettable video recordings of Nicky and the band members of Black Tie Affair. Seeing Nicky at the height of his career sent Jenna to her purse for more tissues. She had missed those years with him. She had always known his dreams were coming true. However, fate had stepped in and stolen the best years of his life from her.

Bruce was beaming like a proud father walking in with Kate once again.

"Well, ladies, are you ready for a great show?" he grinned.

The lights in the auditorium began to dim as the sounds of Jeff playing drums set the crowd of fans on fire. Then, as the guys of Black Tie Affair walked on stage, it was pure pandemonium.

"Good evening, Vancouver. How are you tonight? I'm Jerry Godwin, and we are Black Tie Affair. It's going to be a night of celebration. We hope you enjoy the concert. Stopping for a brief moment, Jerry looked up. "Nicky, this is for you," he yelled, holding his guitar high in the air.

"Hello, Vancouver," David followed.

The guys were definitely in fine form tonight. The band's appearance was clean-cut and downright sexy, dressed in black suits and ties. Noticing that Jenna was reaching for another tissue, Bruce put his arm around her.

"Sweetheart, please don't cry. Tonight is a celebration, please no tears. Nicky had a remarkable career and millions of fans worldwide who loved him. So few people ever get the chance to live out their dreams the way he did. He loved you and Cameron very much."

"Oh, I know. I'm very proud of Nicky and also Cameron. It's just that watching the guys perform tonight is a stark reality of the stolen years that I never got to share with him," Jenna answered, wiping tears from her face.

"Well, Sweetheart, that might be true. Fate is a strange bedfellow. I'm truly sorry those years escaped you," Bruce mentioned, gently hugging her.

The remaining members of Black Tie Affair were energized as they reunited one last time to show their love and respect for Nicky and their amazing fans. Their performance would have made Nicky proud. The passion shown by the thousands of fans who filled the arena was reflected from the stage as the guys gave a stellar performance. Those lucky enough to attend tonight's performance would leave with the memorial concert engrained in their memory forever.

Jenna watched as Jerry and David walked down front after their first song to hand out roses. Later they removed their ties and tossed them to the girls standing in front. Then not to break with tradition, David unbuttoned his white dress shirt and yelled.

"Vancouver, are you ready to party? Let's make some noise and if you feel like dancing, be our guest."

Jenna was mesmerized as she watched their hour-long performance. Then, all too soon, it was over. Next in the lineup was Cameron and his band, House of Cards.

After a short intermission, Jenna was sitting on the edge of her seat. She seemed nervous for Cameron. However, her nerves quickly dissipated as she watched Cameron, Drew, Doug and Harry walk onstage. Surprisingly, they were all sporting bright blue Mohawks. Laughter overtook Jenna at the mere sight of their blue hair. It was Nicky's favorite color. Their wedding colors had been light blue, and even their primary suite at the lake house was painted and decorated in shades of blue. Cameron was the only one of the boys who could have possibly known Nicky's connection. Knowing her son, Jenna was sure it was his idea to make the evening less stressful. Suddenly, Cameron stroked his Mohawk as he looked directly at Jenna and blew her a kiss. Cameron reminded her so much of Nicky. Glancing at Bruce, she smiled.

"Did you know about this?" Jenna laughed.

"Yes, but the boys swore me to secrecy. Cameron knew that watching Black Tie Affair perform would probably leave you a little sad, and he thought this would be just the thing to cheer you up."

"Well, it worked."

Cameron's band dedicated their performance to Nicky. House of Cards had their fans not only screaming out the lyrics but standing waving their hands high in the air, swaying to the beat of the music. The new age of punk rock bands was entirely foreign for Jenna. Even their appearances seemed rogue. But Cameron loved it, and the fans appeared to love it even more. House of Cards captivated the audience for over an hour, performing one hit after another. Cameron and the guys now had two songs at the top of the charts. Their fan base was dedicated, loyal, and a bit crazy, Jenna thought.

As the concert came to a close, the members of Black Tie Affair came back onstage to join House of Cards as they performed the song which Nicky had written and was so well remembered for, *Because of You*. The large overhead screens now projected photos of Nicky performing with Black Tie Affair. It was hard for Jenna to watch as she had to reach for a tissue once again.

"Good night Nicky," Jerry yelled. "We'll miss you."

"So long, Buddy," Jeff shouted, holding his drum sticks in the air.

"Never forgotten," David screamed.

Finally, Cameron walked up to the mike.

"Good night, Dad," Cameron yelled loudly.

Jenna was now definitely needing more tissues. Looking around the room, Kate was sobbing uncontrollably. Nicole walked over to hug her mom as she tried to console her. Bruce had his hands full, trying to comfort the women around him. But unfortunately, he was now having to deal with their emotions.

"Okay, enough tears. Tonight was supposed to be a celebration," Bruce snapped. He had to help them regain their composure.

"Nicole and Michelle, let's get these women out of here and downstairs. The limos are waiting at the back entrance. We'll take them over to the Wharf. The guys will follow soon."

Nicole grabbed Kate by the arm. Then, gently guiding her mom down the hall to the elevator, it was evident she was visibly upset. Michelle walked beside Jenna to make sure she would be okay.

"Geez, I've never seen two women meltdown like this before," Michelle commented as they stepped inside the elevator.

"Yes. Mom and Jenna seemed perfectly fine until the guys began saying their goodbyes. Mom's always been over-sensitive."

Once again, it was quiet inside the car. It seemed there were no words to be said after the concert. However, Nicole thought she should try to engage the women in conversation.

"What did you think of the guys' blue Mohawks? Neat, wasn't it?"

Jenna looked over at her and smiled. "It was Nicky's favorite color."

"Wow, I didn't realize that when I saw mom frantically trying to dye their hair. Guess Cameron is stuck with a new hairstyle now."

Finally, Kate spoke up. "They were planning on doing this before they left to go on tour, but Cameron thought it would be fun for them to have it done for the memorial concert."

"Well, I have to give my son credit. It did make me laugh," Jenna added.

It seemed the women had finally overcome their bouts with sadness and were now looking forward to a great meal and fellowship with the band members and roadies.

Being the first to arrive, Jenna decided to go to the ladies room to freshen up. Kate decided to follow behind her as well.

"Sorry, Jenna, I didn't mean to break down and lose it like that. Nicole always says I'm way too sensitive."

"Oh, that's okay. Did you know Nicky very well?"

It was Jenna's attempt without others around to play detective. After the bomb that Michelle had dropped on her, she needed to know if there were any truths to it.

"Honestly, not very well at all, I'm sorry to say," Kate mentioned.

Jenna found her answer somewhat puzzling. If she had been the stylist for the band, as Michelle had stated, then she would have definitely known him very well. Then, suddenly, it hit her. If Kate and Nicky had been together, it was evident that she would keep quiet about it. Jenna fumed, trying to think of ways to break her silence.

"Well, you seemed rather upset at the close of the concert when Jerry, the boys, and Cameron were saying their goodbyes."

"Oh, as I said before, I'm too emotional," Kate replied, taking a wet towel to wipe her face.

Jenna thought she should back off her interrogation. There were easier ways to find out, and she knew just the person to question.

The guys' limos began to arrive as Jenna walked back into the restaurant's foyer. Then, seeing Cameron stepping out of one of the cars, she had to run outside to meet him.

Touching his Mohawk, Jenna laughed.

"Really, Cameron, blue hair? You certainly knew how to help me deal with my emotions seeing the guys of Black Tie Affair together again on stage."

"Well, I couldn't have you sobbing your eyes out, now could I? So tonight was to celebrate Dad's career."

Taking Jenna by the arm, they walked inside. Tall glass windows surrounded the room, reflecting the harbor lights that lined the wharf. It bathed the restaurant in a warm glow. Jenna and Nicky had shared many romantic evenings at the Wharf. It had been their favorite haunt after concerts at the coliseum. However, tonight it would hold a more somber occasion.

After everyone had arrived and was seated, Bruce stood to give his last toast.

"Tonight was amazing. I'm proud of everyone seated here. I know Nicky was smiling as he watched from above. Thank you for a wonderful tribute and for making it a night to be remembered. Now let's kick off our world tour and take this show back on the road."

Leaving the restaurant that night, Jenna had been subdued by the events of the evening. She failed to corner the one person she had so wanted to interrogate. However, only a few weeks later, she would have her questions answered unexpectedly.

CHAPTER SIX

Far From Home

The days immediately following the memorial concert had flown by too suddenly. As Jenna looked down at her watch, it would only be a few short hours before the limo would arrive and take them out to the airport.

"Cameron, are you packed?" Jenna inquired as she knocked on his bedroom door.

"Yes, Mom, don't worry. I've packed everything."

The reality of Cameron leaving to go on tour had finally hit Jenna. What was she ever going to do alone in this big house? Hopefully, she wouldn't have to stress over the fact for long. Judy Thompson, her realtor, had purposely scheduled the first open house the following day. Jenna felt this would be the distraction she desperately needed after Cameron left. However, most importantly, it would hopefully bring her the buyers needed to get a new start. A new lifestyle that would incorporate the fact she was now single, living alone without Nicky or Cameron.

"Cameron, the car is here," Jenna stated, opening the French doors leading out to their beautiful redwood deck. Cameron was saying goodbye to Fritz and Joey. He loved those two. Now they would become Jenna's constant companions, hopefully easing her back into life once again without Nicky.

Jenna's eyes moistened, stepping inside the limo. It never mattered how many times she had to watch Cameron board the jet that would whisk him away, it never got easier. However, this time, no one would be left standing beside her to hold her and comfort her.

"Please call when you arrive in Hawaii," Jenna insisted, wiping tears from her face.

"Mom, I will. You know you can come over. Bruce will make arrangements for you," Cameron replied, putting on his headphones.

It seemed that Jenna and Cameron had arrived at the airport all too soon. She could see Bruce and Jerry waiting for their car to arrive on the tarmac.

"Okay, son, everyone's on board, and we're ready to get this plane in the air," Bruce smiled.

"Jenna, please don't worry. Jerry and I have just finalized the details of this tour, and it's going to be a fun gig for the boys. Are you sure you don't want to fly over to Hawaii with us for their first concert tomorrow night? We'd be glad to have you along," Bruce suggested giving her a huge hug.

"No, but thanks for asking. I've got some things to take care of tomorrow."

Giving Cameron one last hug, Jenna didn't want to let go. Why did life have to be so cruel? She struggled to keep her emotions inside. She was determined to be strong for Cameron. She wasn't about to let him catch a glimpse of the emotional wreck she would soon become.

"I love you, keep safe and call me."

"Yes, Mom, don't worry. Bruce and Jerry keep a close watch on us. I'll call you when we arrive. Love you," Cameron smiled, kissing her goodbye.

Standing on the tarmac, she watched as the jet lifted from the runway and into the clouds.

"Are you ready to go now?" Felix, their chauffeur, asked as he opened her door.

The ride back home was lonely. Jenna had never felt so alone.

Arriving back at the lake house, Sophie met her at the door with exciting news.

"The realtor just called and left a message on the house phone. She has a client who would desperately like to see the house this evening at 6:00 p.m. So I've cleaned up Cameron's room. Will you be showing it tonight?"

"Yes. As surprising as that is, it's just what I needed to hear."

Perhaps her nights left alone in this huge house would be few.

The young couple who arrived later that evening with Judy fell madly in love with the house. Who wouldn't fall in love with a home that Nicky had so painstakingly been hands-on throughout the building process? Touring through each room, she could overhear the couple's discussion regarding making it their new home.

Later that evening, after waiting for Cameron's call to let her know they had arrived safely, she went upstairs with the dogs. Stopping at the top of the stairs, she looked back, taking in the impressive views of the living area below. It was spectacular with its vaulted ceilings and expansive windows, allowing the spacious room to be inundated with sunlight. Nicky had spared no expense on the décor. It was beautifully decorated with elegant European furnishings. However, after taking a deep breath, she was finally ready to leave, bringing with her only the memories of their lovely home and Nicky's cherished piano. Even though she had been blessed to share many good times here with Nicky and Cameron, it was time to let go.

The phone call from Judy the following day came as no shock. It seemed the couple had made a full-price offer, an offer which she quickly accepted. Judy was determined to hold the open house despite accepting the offer in the rare chance their financing fell through. However, the weather didn't cooperate. Considering the distance from Vancouver and the rain, it seemed to keep most people away.

Things had happened so quickly that Jerry never had to be part of her sudden scheme of selling the house. She was sure he disapproved of her decision to sell without conferring with Cameron. It seemed she would finally get the fresh start in life she desperately needed. Besides having packers brought in, all that remained was searching for a new condominium in Vancouver. A place now shared only with Fritz and Joey, close to shops and the hustle and bustle of downtown.

CHAPTER SEVEN

Surf's Up

Arriving in Hawaii, Jerry and Bruce would be kept busy by the crazy antics of the boys. Even though members of a very well-known rock band, House of Cards, it seemed their maturity level wasn't that of the band members of Black Tie Affair. Bruce was happy with bringing Jerry on in a management position. It appeared that life on tour with the band would be quite different from the previous years with Black Tie Affair. Bruce was sure that Nicky and the guys had not been saints by any stretch of the imagination. However, it now seemed that the guys and their fans could quickly get out of control. Jerry would be just the asset Bruce needed to keep things running as smoothly as possible during their two-year overseas commitment.

After seeing the boys were safely settled into the immense Hilton Resort in Honolulu, Bruce was scheduled to start the day as always by promoting the concert at various media outlets. Finally, leaving them in Jerry's competent hands, he had a full day of appointments.

Hearing a knock on his door, Jerry was suddenly awakened. So much for sleeping in, he thought as he opened the door.

"Hey Jerry, didn't mean to wake you, but it seems like Flame is missing," Drew tried to explain.

"What? What do you mean?" Jerry inquired, not fully awake.

"Well, when Cameron and I got up to order breakfast this morning, Harry wasn't in his room," Drew laughed.

"Have you tried calling his room again?"

"Yes, but he isn't answering."

"Honestly, Drew, this isn't funny. You better hope that Bruce doesn't hear about this. Didn't I tell you guys to stay inside the resort unless I arranged travel and security?" Jerry stated furiously.

"Yes, we all know the rules. I guess Harry just didn't take them seriously."

How difficult could it be to lose a young kid with a blue Mohawk, Jerry wondered to himself. But, knowing that Harry was an avid surfer and passionate over water sports, he had a hunch.

"Did he mention anything about wanting to go surfing?"

"Yes, come to think of it, he did last night, but none of us took him seriously. We had no idea he would be crazy enough to leave the hotel, especially with our first concert scheduled tonight."

"Well, if he doesn't show up by noon, come back and let me know. In the meantime, I suggest you guys stay put. If any of this gets back to Bruce, Harry might be on the next plane back home. Do you understand?"

Jerry wondered if the boys would be responsible enough to endure the commitment of a two-year tour. Bruce worked hard to maintain ticket sales and a sold out status for the concerts. The boys were talented musically, but it would only take a few incidents before Bruce could be in serious trouble if their wild antics hit the tabloids.

Not able to go back to sleep, Jerry turned on the television to the local stations. Unfortunately, there was nothing he could do at the moment. The last thing he needed was the visibility of the boys sporting blue Mohawks as they frantically searched the surrounding area. This wasn't the notoriety the band needed on their first day. Thank God there had been no mention of anything related to Harry on the news so far.

Hearing the phone, Jerry quickly ran over to grab it. It was Kate.

"Hey, Jerry, are you missing one of the boys? Yes, but how did you know?"

"Well, you're not going to believe this, but I was down by the pool a few minutes ago, and I saw Harry with a group of guys who were being rather loud and obnoxious. They actually pushed him into the pool. Don't worry. Harry had on swim trunks. So I walked over to question what was going on. It seems like he took off early this morning to go down to the beach and met up with a group of surfers. So he spent several hours this morning surfing without telling anyone."

"I hope you told him to get his butt up to the room."

"Yes, but I couldn't embarrass him in front of his new buddies. However, I do know how Bruce feels about things like this," Kate snickered.

"Kate, this is serious. Did his so-called new buddies know who he was?"

"Oh, most definitely, they were discussing the fact that they were all going to the concert tonight and were huge fans. I think you dodged a bullet this time. Harry should be on his way up to the room now."

"Okay, thanks. By the way, why don't you come up for a drink? We can get lunch later after I make sure the boys are under control."

"Sounds great. I'll see you in a few minutes after I change."

Opening the door to his room, Jerry saw Harry stepping out of the elevator. Trying to control his anger, he walked over.

"Are you trying to earn your ticket home? What were you thinking? I think Bruce and I have been explicitly clear on the rules regarding your conduct while on tour. Harry, you're a great asset to the band but not irreplaceable. If you continue to act on impulse with these crazy schemes of yours, I'm not going to be able to help you if Bruce should find out. Do you hear me?" Jerry raged.

"Okay. I guess I got a little carried away this morning with the idea of going surfing."

"Look, Harry, I know you're passionate about surfing. We're all very familiar with your stories of being raised in Malibu and living on the beach. Still, you're now under a two-year commitment with the band, and your actions affect everyone. I've told the boys this news can't get back to Bruce. Trust me. Bruce will not take this lightly. Now go back to your room, and stay put until the limo arrives to take you to the convention center this evening. I'm sure you guys can find some video games to play after ordering room service.

"Okay, Jerry, calm down," Harry reluctantly agreed.

Walking back to his room, Jerry needed a strong drink. Damn, this new generation of musicians came with their own set of problems. He was sure none of the members of Black Tie Affair had ever acted so immature. However, he laughed, remembering the dangerous incident at the night market in Taipei.

Hearing another knock at his door, he opened it to find Kate. She looked beautiful, wearing a stunning green halter dress.

"Wow. You look gorgeous. Come in."

"Oh, thanks, Jerry. I was trying to work on my tan earlier at the pool."

"Would you like a drink?"

"Sure, why not. What do you have?"

"Well, let's see," Jerry smiled, walking over to the mini-fridge.

"Looks like we've got several small bottles of rum, vodka, and six bottles of beer along with orange juice and soft drinks."

"On second thought, just a soda for now, please."

Opening a beer for himself and soda for Kate, he walked over to open the patio door.

"Let's sit outside."

Before taking a seat in one of the wicker chairs, Kate smiled, taking in the views of the extraordinary grounds which surrounded the hotel.

Below was an immense array of tall palms and lush foliage. Two sparkling blue pools were free-formed to compliment the spectacular landscape. In the distance was a hint of the sapphire blue waters of the pacific. It was incredible.

"The scenery is breathtaking. I love Hawaii. It's definitely one of my favorite places on earth," Kate mentioned, wiping tears from her eyes.

Surprised to notice that she had suddenly become emotional, Jerry was perplexed. "So beautiful gardens make you cry," he teased.

"Katie, Doll, what's wrong?"

"Wow, I haven't heard those words in a while. You so remind me of Nicky. It's just the memories of the last time we were together in Hawaii. It was here that I found out I was pregnant with Nicole."

"You never told him. Why?"

"Well, his personality seemed to change with the news of his upcoming movie role. I never saw us living in Los Angeles and the fact that he was so willing to accept the script and relocate without even asking if I was happy with his decision."

"Oh, the boys and I thought you were both excited to be working in Hollywood."

"In all honesty, I was just along for the ride at that point in our relationship. Nicky seemed to be spiraling out of control, and even though I tried to get him more involved with the band, it seemed Renee and those around him became more important. He became addicted to drugs during that time, and after I caught him in bed with Renee, well, you know the story. Hollywood was no place to raise a child. So I left, deciding never to tell him about the baby. But, trust me, it was the right decision," Kate recounted with tears in her eyes. "I never stopped loving him."

Going inside for a moment, Jerry returned with a tissue.

Wiping her face, he gently kissed her on the cheek.

"Doll, we all loved him. But life goes on, as hard as it is. Could you ever imagine us back together on tour again after all these years?"

"No, unbelievable, isn't it," Kate smiled, wiping her eyes.

"Now, let's get lunch. We only have a few short hours before the limo will pick us up."

It seemed fate had stepped in to ease the pain of her past relationship with Nicky and began forming a stronger bond connecting them to the present.

There was no mention of the earlier problems with Harry as they stepped inside the car.

"Are you guys ready to deliver a great concert this evening?" Bruce grinned.

"Oh, you bet," Cameron smiled, giving a high five to Drew.

Arriving at the back entrance to the convention center, the line of fans wrapped around the entire block—the appearance of those waiting to get in seemed foreign to Jerry. Not only did they look like kids, but he had never seen so many strange facial piercings and tattooed body parts. Jerry was amazed. Looking at Bruce, he seemed unaffected by the kids' appearance, who waited in line. Clearly, Bruce only related those standing in line to ticket sales, and he was in the business of selling tickets.

Walking down the long corridors to the boy's dressing room, they had finally arrived. As Jerry entered, he stopped contemplating his days with Black Tie Affair. Gone was the vase of roses, racks of men's suits, tables covered in liquor bottles, and the smell of cigarettes infusing the air with smoke. It had been replaced with gaming consoles, video monitors, and a selection of DVD'S. Table tennis had been set up outside in the corridor along with golf carts at their disposal. Catering seemed the only thing familiar to him. It contained a pizza buffet, salads, and enough side entrees to fill the long table.

"Okay, who's up first," Kate asked loudly above the noise.

"Guess I will," Cameron answered, taking a seat in front of the tall mirror.

Kate's job had taken on a more complex role. She now found herself spiking hair into Mohawks and changing the color at the whim of the boys. Their attire was definitely not formal, as had been the case with Black Tie Affair. Dress shoes were now replaced with sneakers. Faded ripped jeans and cut-off shirts, left to expose their strangely tattooed forearms was now the standard form of attire.

"Okay, boys, fifteen minutes to show time," Bruce announced.

Jerry watched as the boys one by one made their way down the long corridor toward the stage entry. It was truly a changing of the guards, he smiled.

The noise level was ear piercing as the boys walked on stage. Harry walked out first, taking his place behind the drums.

"Aloha," Cameron yelled. "We are, House of Cards, and we're happy to be here with you this evening."

"Hello, Honolulu," Drew screamed.

"Are you ready to party?" Doug shouted.

It was pandemonium as the boys opened with their first song, *Colliding Stars*. Beach Balls were being thrown over the heads of the screaming fans and onto the stage. The boys loved the interaction with the fans.

It seemed the boys held their audience captive with their new style of music. Jerry could feel the fans' love and admiration for the band members as he watched their performance. Even though hairstyles and attire might change, the love between a musician and a fan was still magic.

The concert lasted for almost two hours, as the boys delivered one hit song after the other. Then, all too soon, it was over.

Saying their goodbyes, the boys walked to the front of the stage as the screams coming from their fans seemed to go on forever.

"Aloha. Thanks for coming out this evening," Cameron shouted.

"We love you, Honolulu," Drew screamed.

"Thanks for coming," Doug yelled.

Now, it was time to party.

Bruce had finally been convinced to change his routine after each concert. No longer did he reserve the best restaurants in town. Eating out was no longer on the agenda for the band members of House of Cards, even though Bruce still enjoyed a fine meal which he occasionally did after the concerts. Having brought Jerry on as a management team member gave him the freedom to call it an early evening if he wished.

Now Jerry would reserve either a movie theater, theme park, video arcade, or indoor racing arena for the boys. Sometimes the night's activities would depend on the attractions offered by the city where they happened to be performing. Tonight it would be the unexpected premiere of a new movie. Jerry and Kate quickly volunteered to give Bruce the night off.

"Okay, Jerry, I'm going back to the hotel. Take good care of the boys tonight, and I will talk with you in the morning," Bruce stated, walking out of sight down the long corridors.

Arriving at the theater, Jerry had arranged for the boys to enter through a side entrance. Their favorite refreshments awaited them, along with the exciting premiere of a new sci-fi movie. The night was off to a good start. Jerry and Kate sat in the back row to hopefully avoid being the target of thrown popcorn.

Pulling popcorn from her hair, Kate looked over at Jerry.

"Guess your idea of sitting in the back didn't work. Honestly, Jerry, sometimes I think Bruce just hired you to babysit," she said, not amused by the boy's antics. It seemed the movie went on forever, as Kate rubbed her eyes, trying to stay awake.

Resting her head against Jerry's chest, Kate quickly fell asleep on the ride back to the hotel. Gently pushing her tousled black hair away from her eyes, Jerry smiled.

"Wake up, you sleepy head. We're almost at the hotel."

Glancing at the boys, they seemed so young. Jerry, for once, felt old. It appeared his life had taken on warp speed. Kate was right. He felt like a father of rambunctious boys. Exiting the car at the hotel, Cameron and the boys showed no hints of being tired. Drew tripped Doug as he stepped out of the limo, causing him to fall awkwardly out of the car. As the boys laughed hysterically, Jerry knew they were still wired from the concert and movie.

"Okay, here's the deal, no one leaves the hotel tonight. We've got one more concert to perform, and I would like it to be without any incidents. Do you understand? I suggest you go up to your rooms, watch another movie, play video games, or order room service. Whatever, but no one leaves the resort. Have I made myself completely clear?" Jerry warned.

"Yes, Uncle Jerry," Cameron smiled, trying not to laugh. "I'll make sure nothing happens."

Walking away, Jerry felt unsure if his stern warnings had been taken seriously. However, it was late, and he desperately needed a good night's sleep. Kate laughed, giving Jerry a whimsical stare. She knew his advice had probably fallen onto deaf ears as she followed him up to their suite. Their only recourse would be to try and get some sleep and hopefully not be awakened by frantic phone calls.

The following concert went off without a hitch. The fans in Honolulu loved House of Cards. Knowing the boys loved to surf but unaware of the incident in Honolulu, Bruce found a private resort on the north shore of Oahu. Knowing their schedule would be intense, he decided a week of downtime would be just the thing needed to keep these young, energetic boys happy. Their next scheduled performance was in Tokyo. Their short time in Japan would bring with it some unexpected revelations.

CHAPTER EIGHT

Home Alone Two

Back in Vancouver, Jenna, along with the help of Judy, her realtor, and after an extensive search, had finally found the perfect condominium.

Although it was located in a high rise downtown, it allowed her to keep Joey and Fritz and had immaculate gardens surrounding it. A park-like setting offered the outdoor feeling she cherished, and with the help of Judy, she had found and purchased the penthouse apartment in one of the newest complexes downtown. Judy had insisted she let most of the furnishings in the lake house remain for the new owners. Taking only a few sentimental pieces along with the baby grand piano, Judy felt it was her way of helping Jenna let go of her past. Shopping for new furnishing would be the retail therapy she hoped would motivate Jenna in the direction of falling in love with her new purchase and its location. It was an ideal home for Jenna and the dogs.

Behind the complex, tall evergreen trees lined a narrow rocky path that made its way down to the shores of a small pristine lake. The balconies which wrapped the penthouse offered dramatic 360-degree views of the skyline of Vancouver. It was perfect. Perfect in every way. However, the feelings of still being alone haunted her. She was close to downtown shops, restaurants, everything which would typically excite someone over its location.

Jenna felt blessed to have found her new home quickly after Cameron left to go on tour. Now, she no longer had the worries of sleepless nights in their house on the lake, which carried so many memories of Nicky. With the luxury of a quick sale behind her and a new start in life, she should feel elated. However, she didn't. Depression seemed to overwhelm her. Thoughts of Nicky and their life together, even though it had been short, consumed her. Once again, Jenna felt like she was going insane. Judy sensing her dilemma, came by regularly to make sure she didn't become a recluse. When she wasn't busy with her real estate business, she would come by and take Jenna to a movie or dinner in one of the many restaurants located nearby.

Enjoying a glass of chardonnay on the balcony with Judy while taking in the spectacular vistas overshadowed by a vivid sunset in brilliant hues of orange and pink, Judy had an excellent idea.

"Why don't you surprise Cameron and visit him on tour. Aren't the boys supposed to be performing in Japan later this month? I think that would be the perfect vacation, and I'm sure Cameron would love to see you."

"Oh, I don't know, he hasn't been gone that long, and I'm sure the last thing he would probably want is his mother showing up unannounced. But I have to say, I think it might be fun. I've always wanted to go to Japan. Nicky and I traveled to Europe, but we never made it to the Far East. So I'll have to think about it."

"Well, I don't think you should give it a second thought. Just do it. I know a travel agent, she's the best. Her name is Rachel, and she's a client of mine. Here's her card. Give her a call in the morning," Judy insisted, handing Jenna the business card.

"Okay, I'll think about it."

"Guess I should be going. I have a house to show in the morning."

"It's early. Don't you have time for one more glass? Just one more? Jenna insisted. This stuff is good," she smiled.

"Alright, just one more," Judy laughed, getting up to pour herself another glass. "What about you? Think you could use a refill?"

"Okay, I've got nowhere to go, might as well have another."

"Jenna, I know how deeply you loved Nicky, but you're still young. Do you honestly think he would want to know that you're choosing to waste your life away? Let me watch Fritz and Joey for you. Trust me. You won't have to worry about them. I've got three boys who adore dogs, and they'll be well cared for. Please, give some serious thoughts about going to Japan. I'll be expecting a call from you sometime tomorrow to let me know that you contacted Rachel. Do you hear me? I don't mean to come off sounding bossy. I'm your friend. I care about you. Please do this for yourself and Cameron," Judy insisted compassionately.

"Okay, okay, I promise to think about it, now finish your chardonnay," Jenna reiterated with a smile.

Later that evening, as Jenna was getting into bed with Fritz and Joey, thoughts of her surprising Cameron flooded her mind. Maybe Judy was right. She had no reason not to go. Moving had been hard physically and mentally. Perhaps this would keep her from plummeting further into a state of despair. Pulling the dogs close, she tried to sleep. However, her mind was racing with memories of Nicky and the memorial. Lying in bed wide awake, she suddenly sat up. The memorial, how could she have forgotten? She needed answers, and Kate was obviously not going to be truthful. The one person who would have her answers would soon be in Japan. She had to see Jerry. She had to go. Wow, how could she have forgotten? Jenna needed answers, and she was mad that she had almost allowed herself the probability of never knowing. The information Michelle inadvertently leaked out that night was driving her crazy. Jenna knew there was more to this story, and she knew who had the answers.

Calling Judy the following day, she excitedly let her know of her decision to go and graciously thanked her for watching the dogs. Jenna was ecstatic to know she would soon be seeing Cameron, but more than that, she was now on a mission. Checking Cameron's itinerary, she found the number for the hotel and placed a call to Bruce.

After three rings, Bruce answered, "Hello."

"Hello Bruce, this is Jenna."

"Hey, Sweetheart, is something wrong?"

"Oh no, not at all. I was just feeling a little down since selling the lake house and thought a change of scenery would do me a lot of good right now. I was thinking of coming over to Japan and surprising Cameron. What do you think? Think you could find me a place to stay and put up with me for a few days?"

"Are you kidding, you bet, Sweetheart. Do you want me to make all the arrangements for you? We'll be arriving in Japan tomorrow."

"No, but thanks. I've got a travel agent in Vancouver, and she's already booked my trip. However, I could use a hotel room. I'll arrive the evening before the concert—no need to bother picking me up at the airport. I'll find my way to the hotel.

"No problem. I'll get you a room in the hotel where we have reservations and as long as you want to stay."

"Oh Bruce, one more thing, please don't tell Cameron. I want to surprise him."

"Okay, you've got my word. Can't wait to see you."

Jerry knew nothing of what was about to happen. But, against all odds, it now appeared the perfect storm was brewing, and Tokyo would be the epicenter.

CHAPTER NINE

A storm is brewing

As the plane circled Tokyo Bay on its landing approach into Narita Airport, Kate was amazed by the breathtaking scenery below. Kate always felt destined to become a travel agent. Finally, however, fate had stepped in, offering her a career not much unlike her original aspiration.

Reaching over, she tapped Jerry on his shoulder. He had been peacefully sleeping for hours.

"Babe, wake up," Kate whispered. "We're almost on the ground, and I've got something I want to discuss with you before we land."

"Oh yeah, what could that possibly be?" Jerry questioned, wiping the sleep from his eyes as he lifted his seat upright.

"Well, I'm going to hang back at the airport for a while before I arrive at the hotel downtown."

"Why in the world would you do that?" he inquired, looking perplexed.

"Well, Nicole is arriving in a few hours from New York. It seems as if she and Brian have had a major falling out, and I thought it would be just the change she needs to rid him from her life finally."

Brian and Nicole had been friends since high school. However, Kate had never liked Brian. From her earliest memories of him, Brian had always been arrogant and selfish, much like his father, Brian Edwards, Sr., a well-known Investment Banker. Edward, Sr. had been married to his wife, Virginia, for over twenty years. Yet he had no remorse for attempting to become romantically involved with her several years ago even though she had given him no hint or reason to do so. Kate detested them both. This would be the opportunity she had been looking forward to. She had finally found the perfect way to remove both Brian's from their lives permanently.

"I thought she was in love with him?" Jerry questioned.

"I certainly wouldn't call it love, the way he's been neglecting her. You know how many late-night phone calls I've had recently. It upsets me to hear her crying her heart out. So I've made some appointments regarding her modeling career. It seems it would be easy for her to continue with her modeling aspirations in Japan. Distance from Brian is just the thing she needs. Plus, it's a great move to advance her career."

"But Babe, you know we're only here for about a week, then what?"

"Well, the way I see it, if I can find her an apartment and she gets picked up by one of the agents here, it wouldn't be much different than New York."

"Are you kidding? It's a lot different. Babe, it's a totally different country."

"Oh, I know, but she's adventurous like me. It would be a new start for her. No more discussing it. Everything has been arranged. Do you think Bruce would mind if you hang back with me for a few hours while he settles the boys into the hotel downtown?" Kate asked sheepishly.

"I guess not. As soon as we land, I'll walk back and let Bruce know," Jerry answered, giving her a quick kiss.

It was only moments before the plane was on the ground and slowly rolling to a stop near one of the large hangers. Grabbing one of their overhead bags, Jerry walked to the back of the plane to speak with Bruce.

"Hey Bruce, Kate just informed me that Nicole is arriving here from New York in about an hour. So if it's okay, I'm going to wait here with Kate to meet Nicole."

"Oh, that's fine. I didn't know my girl was coming over to Japan?"

Bruce knew of Jenna's decision to come over but was pleasantly surprised to hear of Nicole's arrival.

"Well, I just found out myself. It seems that Kate is trying to get Nicole a modeling gig in Tokyo."

"That sounds fantastic. I'm proud of that girl. Tell her Uncle Bruce will see her later tonight. I've got some great places to take her. Hope she likes Sushi," Bruce smiled. "See you all later at the hotel."

Walking into the airport, Jerry and Kate decided to stop at one of the many shops for coffee. Enjoying their coffee and waiting for Nicole, it seemed the airport was a macrocosm of every nationality. Young and old busily traversing through the many concourses. Finally, the arrival of Nicole's flight was announced. Walking over to get as close as was possible to the arrival area, Kate was anxiously waiting to see her daughter as soon as she'd cleared through customs. It seemed to take forever before Kate finally recognized her statuesque daughter among the crowd of people. Finally, Nicole ran towards her pushing a cart stacked high with luggage.

"Oh, Mom, it's so good to see you," Nicole cried becoming emotional.

"Oh, Sweetheart, it's so good to have you here with us," Kate answered, wiping tears from her eyes.

"Hey Jerry, nice to see you too," Nicole smiled, giving him a huge hug.

"What is it with you women? Tears, always, tears," Jerry winked.

"Oh Jerry, these are happy tears," Nicole laughed, giving her mom another hug.

"Welcome to Japan. Now let's get downtown to the hotel before Cameron and the boys do something I'm not going to like," Jerry smiled.

Finding their way through the massive terminal, they were

quickly in line to board the transit system which would take them into the heart of downtown Tokyo.

Arriving at the Mandarin Hotel, it was one of the tallest buildings on the block. It had a very modern décor with a hint of Asian-inspired furnishings. It was impressive. Walking in through the glass revolving doors, Jerry approached the reception desk. Upon checking in, he discovered that Bruce had already reserved a room for Nicole.

"Well, ladies, guess we're all up on the 18th floor along with Bruce and the boys. Here's your room key," he stated, handing Nicole her key. "You're in room 1820, and we're right across the hall in suite 1823. So let's go up and check it out. They'll bring our luggage up shortly."

Unlocking their door, Kate walked over to the large windows. The views of Tokyo were impressive. Even at dusk, the bright lights emitting from the surrounding buildings seemed to light up the skyline like stars in the skies.

"Mom, if it's okay, I'm going to take a nap. The flight was long, and I feel exhausted. I'll meet you both later this evening for dinner. Oh, if you see Cameron and the guys, don't let them know I'm here. I want to surprise them."

"Okay, hopefully, Bruce doesn't spoil your surprise. We didn't exactly ask him to keep your arrival quiet," Kate smiled, giving her a huge hug. "Sweetheart, I'm so glad you're here," she added. "See you later this evening."

After dinner, Kate fell onto the comfy oversized bed. Nicole wasn't the only one feeling the exhaustion of jet lag.

"Wow, this is comfortable," Kate stated, pulling Jerry down next to her.

Noticing the light on the phone beside the bed blinking, Jerry decided to check to see who would have left a message so soon. Surely it was Bruce announcing his plans for the evening.

Jerry was sure he heard Jenna's voice to his amazement and shock. Listening intently, it was definitely Jenna.

"Hey Jerry, I talked with Bruce this afternoon, and he gave me your room number. So I've decided to come over and surprise

Cameron. Please don't tell him. I'm arriving tomorrow night, just in time for the concert. Oh, I told Bruce no one has to meet me. I'll find my way to the hotel. Thanks for keeping my arrival a surprise. See you tomorrow."

Wow, this not only came as a surprise, it was the worst possible thing Jerry could fathom knowing Nicole was right across the hall. He gasped loudly, putting down the receiver. Why now, Jerry wondered?

"Jerry, you look like you've seen a ghost. Who was on the phone?"

"Kate, you're never going to believe this."

"Believe what? Who called? Is everything okay?"

"Kate, it was Jenna."

"Well, what did she want?" Kate asked, quickly sitting up in bed. "Jerry, you're acting weird. What's going on?"

"Jenna is on her way to Japan. She'll be here tomorrow evening in time for Cameron's concert."

"Oh, that's nice."

"Kate, are you half asleep. You do realize who's in room 1820, right?"

"Oh my, what timing. What are the odds?" Kate giggled.

"Kate, this is serious. What if Jenna starts asking questions?"

"Jerry, relax, lay down and take a nap. You're overreacting, don't be silly."

How could he relax? The perfect storm was brewing, and Japan began to look like ground zero. What was he going to do? He would need to run interference and keep them apart as much as possible. Jenna was brilliant, and he couldn't take the chance that she might begin to ask too many questions. Maybe the fact that Nicole would be busy with appointments would help. Also, there was the fact that Bruce knew. If worse came to worse, Jerry was sure he could count on him to run interference.

Late the following day, when Jerry woke up and glanced at his watch, he couldn't believe the time. He had overslept. It was never easy adjusting to different time zones. Then, hearing a knock at the door, he ran over to answer it.

"Hey, Jerry, is Mom up?"

"I don't think so, but come in. You can wake her. I'm sure she would love to see you."

"Hey Mom, good morning," Nicole whispered, gently nudging Kate awake.

"Oh, Sweetheart, it's so good to see your smiling face. Did you get some rest last night?" Kate asked, sitting up in bed.

"Yes, I was just wondering if you might come over to the room later and help me decide which dress to wear to the interviews today."

"Oh sure, just give me a few minutes to wake up."

"'ll order breakfast," Jerry smiled, handing them each a menu. "What do you girls feel like eating this morning?"

"Anything, I'm starved. I'll have two eggs over easy with toast, bacon, and hash browns," Nicole replied, taking a glance at the menu.

"That actually sounds pretty good. I'll have the same," Kate answered.

"Okay, breakfast will be here in about fifteen minutes," Jerry stated, checking his watch.

Wow, it was morning, and he hadn't had one call from Cameron or the boys. Clearly, it must have been the fatigue of jet lag that had kept them in their rooms during the night. Jerry decided to wait a while longer before checking on them. Let sleeping dogs lie, he thought.

"Honey, I think I'll jump in the shower real quick before breakfast arrives," Kate smiled, kissing Nicole on the cheeks.

It was only minutes before Kate walked out of the shower in her bathrobe, wearing her wet hair pulled up in a turban.

"Now, there's a vision of beauty," Jerry winked.

"Oh Jerry, what a sweet thing to say to Mom," Nicole blushed.

It was evident that Jerry had strong feelings for Kate at this point in their relationship. Nicole couldn't have been happier that her mom had an awesome job working with House of Cards, but she also seemed to be extremely happy with Jerry in her life as well.

Hearing another knock at the door, let them know that breakfast had arrived. Sitting down to eat almost felt like a family affair—something that Nicole and Kate had never experienced until now.

"Well, girls, I've finished eating, so I've got to run over to Bruce's room and see what's on the schedule for today. The concert is at 8:00 p.m., so if you girls have things to do today, go ahead. Oh, don't forget Bruce is going to need you at the convention center no later than 6:30 p.m.," Jerry mentioned, finishing his coffee.

"Okay, Babe, see you later this evening. Nicole and I have a few appointments to make today," Kate explained, giving Jerry a quick kiss.

"Good luck," Jerry winked as he walked around the table to kiss Nicole on the forehead. "One look at you, and you'll have them eating out of your hands," Jerry added.

"Wow, no wonder you like this guy," Nicole smiled. But, of course, she had no way to know that Jerry was already family.

As he walked toward the door, he hoped to propose to Kate one day in the not-so-distant future. Nicole would then know her connection to him, and he would be promoted from uncle to stepfather if Kate's answer was yes.

Hearing a knock at his door, Bruce yelled, "Just a minute."

"Good morning Jerry, you're up bright and early," Bruce grinned as he opened the door.

"Well, you know how it is with different time zones. I never seem to adjust before we're out of the one-time zone and into another. I just wanted to stop by and see what's on the agenda for today. I haven't heard from the boys."

"Oh, hopefully, they're still sleeping. Would you like a cup of coffee?"

"Sure. I just finished one, but I won't turn it down."

"Okay, come in and sit down," Bruce answered as he poured them each a cup from the carafe. "As you know, we have three performances at the convention center. I'm going to be doing my publicity rounds today, giving away a ton of free tickets. The concerts are almost sold out. After all the advertisements today on the local news and radio, I'm sure we'll have no problem hitting the mark. I will need the boys down at the performing arts center, or convention center, early this evening. As usual, I will be giving a few lucky fans a photo opportunity with the boys, so I'll need them to arrive early. Make sure they get there by 4:30 p.m., don't disappoint me," Bruce added.

"Oh, don't worry about that, they'll be there. But, Bruce, I wanted to talk with you about something before I leave," Jerry said, taking a sip of coffee.

"What's on your mind this morning?" Bruce smiled, reaching over to pour himself another cup.

"Well, you know that Nicole is here, and I'm sure you're aware that Jenna is coming in tonight."

"Yes, Jenna called me."

"Bruce, maybe I'm being paranoid, but did it ever cross your mind that Jenna might suspect something regarding Nicole."

"Oh, that," Bruce smiled.

"Well, I guess I can't say it's never crossed my mind. Why do you have reason to believe that Jenna suspects or knows something?"

"Guess it's more of a gut feeling. I don't know. I have no specific reasons or anything like that for thinking Jenna might be suspicious. But, the day Kate told me in Vancouver, it came as quite a shock. Kate told me of your connection to Nicole. I have to say, Bruce, it was nice to hear that you were always there for Kate and Nicole. I know you helped Kate through some difficult days after she left Nicky."

"Well, after what Nicky did to her, I felt somewhat responsible for Kate and the baby. There was no way I would stand by and let Kate walk away with all the responsibilities of a newborn and no job. So I've always stayed in touch with them and tried to see them whenever time permitted. I've considered it a privilege to watch Nicole grow up and be a part of her life. Nicole thinks of me as her Uncle Bruce, you know. She's a beautiful girl. She looks a lot like Nicky, don't you think?"

"Yes, Bruce, she does look a lot like Nicky, too much. That's what bothers me. Jenna isn't stupid, you know. Heck, when I introduced Nicole to Cameron, it gave me goosebumps seeing them together.

They're almost a reflection of each other. But, Bruce, it isn't just her looks. Nicole has so many of Nicky's quirks and mannerisms. So weird, isn't it?"

"Yes, son, reckon it is," Bruce chuckled.

"Bruce, be serious. Do you know the implications if Cameron should find out? He's the lead singer. Do you really want to chance him walking off stage one night or, even worse, refusing to show up at all, depending on how he takes the news? Bruce, I don't have to remind you that you are in the business of selling tickets. The way I see it, House of Cards could crash and burn if Cameron held any resentment toward his dad or even Nicole perhaps."

"Jerry, Jenna wasn't in Nicky's life during that time. So I don't really see the implications of everything you're saying. However, I definitely agree that we shouldn't bring any of this into the open. This secret is best kept just between the three of us at this time," Bruce sternly suggested pouring himself another cup.

"Well, Bruce, I think you forget one important fact. Jenna was always in love with Nicky. She never stopped loving him. She loved him enough to let him go, deciding not to tell him about the baby she was carrying the day he left. Can you even fathom a bond of love that strong between two people? I know that even though Cameron wasn't told who his dad was until just before the concert in Quebec, Jenna had instilled a lot of respect for Nicky in Cameron's eyes. Do you want to jeopardize this whole tour? I'm telling you, call it a hunch or whatever. I have a bad feeling about this. If Jenna spends any time with Nicole, she's going to sense an air of familiarity. I'm afraid Jenna already has. Well enough said, I know there's a lot to do before the concert this evening. Oh, one last thing before I go check on the boys, we're agreed to both keep this a secret, right?"

"Yes, son. Why would you even doubt my intentions to either Kate or Jenna or even Nicole for that matter?" Bruce now looked irritated as he finished his coffee.

"Well, I didn't come by this morning to get you upset or worried. I just wanted to remind you of our dilemma and ask for your help if needed. Trust me. I'm going to desperately try and keep the girls apart as much as I can. Nicole is going to be rather busy this afternoon. She has several interviews in regards to her modeling career. Kate is going with her, so that should take care of each day. However, their time together at the concerts each evening worries me the most. I'm sure Jenna is simply coming over to spend time with Cameron. I'll just keep my fingers crossed she doesn't have another reason for her visit," Jerry mentioned finishing his coffee.

Jerry had at least made Bruce aware of his worries walking toward the door.

"Okay, son, see you later. Don't worry. I think you're all worked up over nothing. But if you need me to lay to rest any rumors or if Jenna does get suspicious, let me know. Just make sure you have my boys there early tonight for photos," Bruce reiterated, closing the door.

Walking down the hall toward the boy's suite, Jerry didn't share Bruce's confidence that Jenna wouldn't discover the truth. However, knowing he was about to see Cameron this morning, he had no thought of Cameron ever suspecting anything unusual about Nicole. Guys were usually the last to notice or have a fifth sense regarding such matters. Even though Nicole and Cameron could easily pass for twins, he was sure none of the boys had taken notice of their familiarities.

It seemed the boys were in no hurry to answer the door as Jerry repeatedly knocked. Then, finally, Drew came to the door.

"Wow. You guys really are still sleeping. I didn't hear from any of you last night."

"Hey Jerry, come in. Well, what did you expect? That was a long flight, not to mention the change in time zones."

"We ordered room service and pretty much were out like light bulbs last night," Cameron mentioned. "All of us except Harry, who decided to play video games all night. What's up, early for a visit, isn't it?"

"Well, not really. Have you looked at the time?" Jerry stated, pulling back the drapes allowing the morning sun to flood the room instantly.

"Wow, man, that's pretty bright," Doug yelled. Can't a guy just get a little sleep around here?"

"I'm afraid you would sleep the day away if I didn't stop to check on you. At least some of you, that is," Jerry remarked, looking surprised at finding Harry still snoring under his covers. "It looks like Mr. Trouble over there is still fast asleep."

"Yep, you know Harry. He never sleeps at night," Drew laughed.

"Who wants to order room service?" Cameron suggested.

"I will," Doug answered, passing around the menu. "Just let me know what everyone wants, and I will call. Jerry, would you like anything?"

"No thanks, I've already had breakfast this morning, and I've just come from Bruce's room where I drank way too much coffee. By the way, you guys have a photoshoot with some fans this evening before the concert. So there's not going to be any time today for sightseeing."

"Awe, you're kidding, right," Harry spoke up.

"Oh, look who's awake now," Jerry laughed.

"Thought I heard the word breakfast," Harry yawned.

"Okay, Flame, what do you feel like this morning? Think we've all decided on pancakes and sausage," Doug informed him.

"Oh, that sounds fine. Make sure room service sends extra orange juice along with that order."

"Okay," Doug said, reaching for the phone.

"So Jerry, if we're not leaving the hotel today, just what do you suggest we do all day?" Harry inquired.

"Well, the way I see it, you have your choice of the weight room, sauna, pool, or you could just make it a marathon day of playing video games. I believe there's a room downstairs set up for movies which I could reserve. Just think about it and let me know," Jerry mentioned, walking over to draw the drapes. "I'm going back to my room to change clothes and head down to the weight room if any of you want to join me later. If not, I'll check back with you guys around 3:30 p.m. Bruce has a photo session arranged for you guys this afternoon with some fans. He needs everyone there by 4:30 p.m., and it's already getting late," Jerry stated, glancing at his watch.

You guys don't have but a few hours to kill anyways before the limo arrives. Still, no one leaves the hotel for today. Do you understand?" Jerry reminded them.

"Okay, see you later," Cameron smiled, closing the door.

Wow, that seemed to go over too easy, Jerry worried. These kids with their colored Mohawks were members of a punk rock band, and he wasn't so sure they could be trusted. Either way, he wasn't going to sit inside their room and babysit them all day. He had things to do. Jerry had too much nervous energy after talking with Bruce earlier. There was only one thing to do, work out for a few hours.

Opening the door to their suite, Jerry was surprised to find Kate and Nicole still getting dressed.

"Unbelievable, you're still here. Aren't you going to be late for those interviews?"

"No. We still have a little time. Nicole can't seem to decide on which dress and heels to wear."

"What's wrong with what she has on?"

"Oh Jerry, that's a typical answer coming from a guy," Kate smiled, walking over to give him a quick kiss. "What brings you back to the room so early?"

"I just came to change clothes. I'm going down to the weight room and get in a little exercise."

Walking out of the bathroom in a pair of gym shorts, Jerry was finally ready to hit the workout room.

"Kate, don't forget to allow time to find each office and traffic. It's a madhouse out there. Have you seen the traffic on the streets below? Wait just a minute. I have an idea. The guys are staying in for today, so their limo is available. Let me call Bruce and get you girls a ride for today. At least I won't have to worry about you getting lost, and I'll know for sure you'll be back at the hotel in time for the concert. Oh, speaking of the concert, I almost forgot to tell you. This evening, Bruce has arranged a photo session with the boys and some lucky fans. He's going to need you there a lot earlier than 6:30 p.m. Bruce wants everyone there by 4:30 p.m."

"What did you say? Jerry, I scheduled one of Nicole's interviews for 4:00 p.m."

"Sorry, Doll, I think you better call and reschedule."

"Jerry, this was important," Kate looked up, giving him a menacing stare.

"Oh, Mom, it'll be okay. Don't worry. We can just reschedule, and besides, I'm really anxious to see the guys this afternoon and find out what their plans are for later tonight," Nicole smiled as she slipped on a different pair of heels.

"Okay, Sweetheart, I guess I'll reschedule. But, Jerry is right about one thing, we better hurry. That doesn't leave us much time today," Kate stated as she fastened a long set of pearls around her neck.

"Now that you girls have everything all straightened out, I'm headed down to the gym. Good luck with those interviews," Jerry winked, looking at Nicole. "Oh, I almost forgot, Bruce, said to give him a call when you're ready to be picked up." With that said, Jerry was out the door.

There were only a few hours left in the day. Due to jet lag fatigue, everyone had decided to sleep in. Today for the guys at least, it would simply be one of staying inside the hotel, forgoing any opportunity at the moment of becoming a tourist in Tokyo. Kate and Nicole would be the first to mingle with the locals absorbing the ambiance and culture of the diverse city.

After working out for over an hour, Jerry was covered in sweat and desperately needed a shower. Grabbing his gym bag, he decided it was time to head back to the room and clean up. It appeared that no matter how hard he had tried, nothing seemed to work to relieve him of his worries over Jenna's arrival. Even while spending thirty minutes on a stationary bike, his mind was racing with possible scenarios. Maybe Bruce was right. Perhaps he was worried over nothing. However, knowing Jenna as well as he did, he couldn't be sure of anything. The only thing he knew for sure was that he didn't want to be the one to bring more tragedy into Jenna's life. He couldn't break her heart and tarnish her love and respect for a husband she had not so long ago laid to rest.

Stepping inside the elevator gave him more time to reflect on his impending dilemma. Jerry ranted his frustrations to Nicky as if he were there.

Nicky, how could you do this and leave me to clean up your past mistakes? Man, how could you?

Unlocking the door to the room, Jerry quickly showered and dressed for the concert. Now, he needed a drink. Walking over to the mini bar, he found it filled with tiny bottles. These bottles would never suffice. This evening required more, much more. Calling for room service would be a waste of time, so he immediately decided to go down to the bar located adjacent to the hotel reception desk.

Taking a seat at the bar, it wasn't long before a young man came over.

"Good evening, sir, what can I get you," the waiter inquired, setting a cocktail napkin in front of him.

"I'd like a tall glass of Jack Daniels, straight with no ice."

"I'll be right back with that."

Returning with his drink, the bartender set the glass on the bar. Taking a sip, it seemed to burn all the way down to the pit of his stomach. Quickly, he took another drink, a much longer drink. This time it tasted smooth. He finally began to feel the relaxing effects of the alcohol. Unbuttoning the top button on his white dress shirt, Jerry loosened his tie. Wow, this was just what the doctor ordered, Jerry thought to himself as he finished off his first glass—catching the bartender's attention.

"I'll have another, please, make it the same."

Just at that moment, Jerry felt someone gently place their hand on his shoulder. Turning around, it was Bruce.

"I figured you might be here. Son, how are you holding up?" Bruce smiled, taking a seat on the stool next to him.

"Oh, I'm fine," Jerry replied, as another drink was set in front of him.

"Let me guess, Jack Daniels, right?"

"Yes."

As the bartender approached, Bruce grinned.

"I'll have the same, JD straight, no ice."

"Jerry, listen, I can't say I truly know what's going to happen tonight when Jenna arrives. But son, this is a situation of Nicky's own making. Do you understand? Sorry that you seem to be caught in the middle of things, especially since you and Kate are now together. We both know that Nicky was on a path of self-destruction while in Hollywood, which is why I stepped down as manager. I loved that kid. We all did. But there was no way I was going to stand by and watch him self-destruct. I know Nicky was family to you, but son, you're not responsible for your cousin's actions or mistakes," Bruce stated, taking a long sip. "Wow, this is smooth," Bruce smiled.

After sitting at the bar for almost an hour, Bruce looked down at his watch.

"Well, as relaxing as this has been, I think we better get out of here. I've got to get down to the convention center, and you need to go upstairs and make certain the boys are ready to leave. We've got a sold out concert to take care of this evening," Bruce grinned. "Oh, I almost forgot. I have Jenna booked into suite 1836. It's next door to Cameron and the boys. She should be arriving soon. Hopefully, she didn't have any flight delays. I just wanted to give you a heads up. No reason for panic," Bruce added.

Jerry was lucky. He had managed to make it back to the room before Kate and Nicole returned. But, not wanting to wait around for their arrival, he decided to walk down to the guy's room and make sure they were ready for the limo to pick them up.

Knocking at their door, Cameron answered.

"Hey Jerry, come in. You don't even have to ask. We're all ready for tonight's photos with the fans."

Taking one glance around the room, Cameron was right. Surprisingly, they were all dressed and ready for photos. Jerry laughed, checking out their brightly colored spiked Mohawks, tattooed body parts, and facial piercings. Gone were the days of suits and ties. The only ones wearing suits now were him and Bruce.

"Okay, boys, meet you down in the lobby in about twenty minutes.

I've got to run back over to my room and check on a few things. See you downstairs."

Unlocking the door, he saw Kate and Nicole.

"So, how did it go this afternoon with the job interviews?"

"Oh Jerry, I'm so proud of Nicole. It went really well. I wouldn't be surprised if she receives a callback tonight. They loved her portfolio. Her photos are amazing," Kate smiled, giving Nicole a huge hug.

"Well, congratulations in advance. They'd have to be blind and crazy not to see how beautiful our girl is," Jerry winked. "Are you both ready to ride over in the limo with the guys? I told them to meet me downstairs in the lobby."

"Thanks, Jerry. Yes, Mom and I are both ready. Oh, I almost forgot the boys have no idea I'm here," Nicole laughed.

"Well, I guess they're in for a pleasant surprise," Jerry winked, knowing Nicole wasn't exactly the only surprise for the evening.

As Jerry closed the door, Nicole and Kate walked toward the elevator.

"Hey Kate, hang back for a second. I just wanted to remind you that Jenna might be downstairs," Jerry whispered, not wanting Nicole to overhear their conversation.

"Oh, that. That's what you wanted to tell me," Kate scoffed. "What is it with you and that girl? Sometimes I think you're infatuated with Jenna. Do you think when Nicky died, it somehow left you in charge of her happiness?" Really?" Kate added abrasively.

"Wow, where did that come from? Katie, Doll, you have to know by now that I love you. So, how can you say such vile things?"

Stopping in her tracks, Jerry now more than ever reminded her of Nicky. Hearing him use those words of endearment melted Kate's heart. Nicky had often lovingly referred to her with those exact words. Maybe somewhere deep inside, Kate did hold a resentment toward Jenna.

"Oh, I'm sorry. Really, Jerry, I am. I think I'm tired from running around to all those appointments today with Nicole. We tried to get in as many as we could in such a short time. Don't worry. I don't plan on stirring up any problems tonight."

Kate felt remorseful for lashing out at Jerry. Surely she was losing it. He hadn't deserved those unkind words. Jerry had been exceptionally good to her since they had met the day of Nicky's funeral. She now had a man in her life, a good man. Jenna was now the one who was alone, except for Cameron. Wow, she had to remember to show a little empathy toward Jenna.

"Oh, it's okay. I'm sure you're tired. You're still exhausted from the long flight, and then today, you were extremely busy helping Nicole. Don't worry, Babe," he winked, giving Kate a tight squeeze and a rather lengthy kiss.

"Hey, come on, you two love birds. Don't we have a concert to go to?" Nicole laughed as she held the elevator door open for them.

Stepping out of the elevator, the guys came running over the minute they saw Nicole.

"Wow. We didn't know you were here," Cameron smiled.

"No way. You're really here," Drew exclaimed.

"Man, what an awesome surprise," Harry yelled, attempting to pick Nicole up and twirl her around.

"Okay, Harry, she isn't a porcelain doll. Put her down, for heaven's sake," Jerry insisted.

"Wow, I can't believe it. You're actually here," Doug smiled.

"Thanks, guys. I'm happy to see you too," Nicole giggled.

"All right, enough of the formalities. We have a limo waiting outside," Jerry informed them.

"Geez, I guess we weren't the only ones happy to see her," Kate whispered into Jerry's ear as she stepped inside the car.

Arriving at the massive Tokyo Center for the Performing Arts, the lines of fans waiting to get in wrapped the length of three city blocks.

"Wow, Bruce was right. It does appear that we're sold out for this evening," Jerry stated.

"Jerry, you're crazy. Didn't you see the huge marquee out front? I don't know how you could've missed it," Cameron laughed. "It had our three concert dates and times listed."

"Yes, Jerry, across the bottom in brilliantly lit lettering were the words sold out. Drew chuckled as the limo drove into the back entrance. "I don't know how you missed that one."

Wow, he probably shouldn't have had those last two drinks earlier. Oh well, it was still hours before the concert. Depending on how the evening went, he had hidden a few small bottles in his suit pockets, just in case. Jerry had to be prepared for anything, he thought.

Walking inside, the boys immediately jumped into golf carts waiting for them near the back entrance.

"Hey Nicole, hop on," Harry insisted.

"Oh, okay, where are we going?"

"Who knows?"

"Follow us. We'll try and find the directions to the dressing room," Cameron suggested.

The boys quickly disappeared out of sight on the golf carts, taking Nicole with them.

"Jerry, do you think that was a wise decision to let them disappear like that?" Kate questioned.

"Well, I don't see how it could hurt. The boys are simply having a bit of fun before the concert. I'm sure they can't get lost, where could they go. Also, there are too many security guards around here."

Making their way through the labyrinth of concrete hallways, Jerry and Kate finally arrived at the dressing room. Seeing a line of golf carts parked outside the doorway, Kate felt relieved to know they were all inside.

As Jerry opened the door, Harry laughed.

"Hey, what took you so long?" he teased.

"Well, we old folks needed the exercise."

Looking around, Mr. Sato, the sponsor for the Japanese engagement of the tour, had beautifully furnished the boys' dressing room. Entrées of Japanese cuisine, shrimp teriyaki, spicy red snapper teriyaki, vegetable fried rice, and vegetable tempura, along with many more delicacies, all sat exquisitely arranged on long tables. An abundance of fresh flowers filled the room, and seven elegantly wrapped boxes sat on top of an ornate credenza. The room was quite large, containing an imposing dressing area. There were six brightly lit mirrors with matching chairs, along with a luxurious red sofa sitting along the back wall.

"Wow, very impressive," Kate smiled as she walked in.

"Yes, I'd say," Jerry added.

It was only minutes later the door opened, and Bruce walked in. However, he wasn't alone.

"Oh, Mom," Cameron screamed excitedly, running over to give her a huge hug. "You came. No one told me," he smiled, curiously staring at Bruce and Jerry.

"Well, your mom insisted we didn't tell you," Bruce explained.

"Yes, some things are better-kept secret," Jerry mentioned looking Jenna straight in the eyes. He was sure she had not picked up on his subtleties due to her emotions of seeing Cameron.

"Cameron, it's so good to see you too," Jenna smiled with tears in her eyes. "Wow. They take good care of you boys," she stated, wiping her eyes.

Looking around the room, it didn't take Jenna long to recognize Nicole standing next to her mom. Jenna immediately walked over.

"I didn't know you were here," Jenna asked considerately with a somewhat surprising appearance.

"Oh, Mom paid for me to come over. Unfortunately, things were not working out for me in New York, so she arranged for me to have interviews at several of the large modeling agencies in Tokyo. I'm so excited over the possibilities."

"Are you thinking of relocating?"

"I certainly hope so. Things seemed to go well today. I'm keeping my fingers crossed that I receive a callback."

"Well, good luck. I'm sure any of the agencies would be lucky to have you."

"Oh, thanks."

Hearing a loud commotion in the back of the room, Jenna turned around to watch as Harry anxiously ripped open one of the gift boxes.

"Wow, guys, it's a man's kimono," he announced.

Hurriedly, he tried it on.

"Man, it seems to fit perfectly."

Harry proudly danced around the room, showing off his new attire.

"Cameron, come over and check it out," Harry suggested. "There are gift boxes for each of you, even Jerry, Kate, and Bruce."

"Okay, let's see what we have here," Cameron grinned.

Opening his box, it contained another stylish kimono.

"Just what I always wanted," Cameron smiled quickly, trying it on.

At that point, Jerry, Kate, and the boys all anxiously ripped open their boxes to reveal elegant kimonos. Each one was elegantly made of blue silk with gold embroidered dragons. They were exquisite. Excitedly they all tried them on, except for Bruce. Walking over to open the credenza, he pulled out two more gift boxes—one box each for Nicole and Jenna.

"Here you go, girls," Bruce smiled. "I knew Mr. Sato specifically made the kimonos for Jerry, Kate, and the boys. So when I found out you both were coming over, I went downtown and had these personally made for you both. I hope they fit. I've arranged for the photographer who will be taking the photos of the band to come earlier and take a group photo of us wearing the kimonos. Great publicity idea, don't you think," Bruce grinned, trying his on.

"Oh Bruce, it's beautiful. I love it," Nicole said, pulling her kimono out of the box and putting it on. It fits perfectly. "Wow, maybe I should have worn this to my interviews today," she laughed, proudly modeling it for everyone. Thank you."

"Sweetheart, you look stunning," Kate stated, kissing her daughter.

Next, Jenna opened her box. Quickly trying it on, she smiled.

"Thank you, Bruce, it's lovely."

"Oh, Mom, you're gorgeous," Cameron winked as he came over to check her out.

Kate looked around the room and laughed. The boys looked hysterical with their blue Mohawks and wearing, of all things, blue kimonos. She had to give Bruce credit. He never missed a great photo opportunity with the band. But, when it came to publicity stunts, Bruce was on his game. The kimonos were by far one of his best.

Just at that moment, the photographer walked in, ready to take a group photo.

"Everyone, this is Jim. I've asked him to come by early and get our group photo." Bruce announced.

"Hello. I think I'll have each of you stand in front of the draped tables. Squeeze in close, look this way, and smile," Jim instructed.

After taking several photos, Jim walked over to Bruce.

"These look great. Call me. I'll be back when you're ready to have the photos taken with the band and their fans."

It just so happened that Jenna had been standing next to Jerry as the photos were taken.

Whispering in his ear, Jenna took the first opportunity to let him know that she needed to speak with him.

"I want to talk with you. I'll meet you in the bar at the hotel later tonight after the concert."

Jerry felt the blood drain from his face. Jenna had taken no time at all to put him on notice.

"Okay, guys, I think we all looked pretty spectacular. The photos will be great advertising in tomorrow's newspapers," Bruce mentioned taking off his kimono.

It was only a short time before there was a knock on the dressing room door. Mr. Sato walked in with the fans chosen to take their photos with the band.

"Good evening, Bruce," Mr. Sato bowed. "Good evening, Mr. Sato, please come in. We've been waiting for you," Bruce bowed in respect for his culture.

"I see you've brought some special fans with you tonight," Bruce smiled.

"Yes. They are anxious to meet the band and even more excited to have photos taken with the band members."

"Great. Let's get started by making some introductions," Bruce grinned, walking over to get the boys together.

After thanking Mr. Sato for the beautiful kimonos and introducing him to the guys, they were ready for the photo session with the fans.

Eagerly the fans lined up to have their pictures taken with the boys. Jim took photos individually and together. Bruce also instructed Jim to take even more photos with the band wearing their kimonos.

Wow, this will look fantastic in the tabloids, Bruce thought. After years of working with rock bands, Bruce was at the pinnacle of his career as a band manager. He was famous for selling out venues and the publicity required to keep them in the headlines as sold out.

"Now that the meet and greet and photo sessions are over, let's eat," Bruce suggested walking over to sample the delicious array of Asian-inspired cuisine.

After Jenna's suggestion of meeting him later, Jerry had utterly lost his appetite. There was only one thing on his mind, trying to keep Jenna and Kate apart.

"That sounds great, Bruce, but I need to check with one of the roadies about a lighting problem before the concert tonight. So, Kate, why don't you join me?"

"What? I'm starved."

"Oh, I wasn't aware we had a problem," Bruce inquired. Then the insinuation of what Jerry had said hit him.

"Okay, son, you do what you need to do. I'm starved. Jenna, why don't you help me sample this amazing buffet."

"Nicole, get yourself something to eat. I'll be right back," Kate mentioned.

"Jerry, what the heck, you're starting to annoy me again," Kate whispered. "You know there's no problem with lighting. So what's going on?"

"Well, when we were having our photos taken, Jenna asked me to meet her later tonight at the bar in the hotel. I knew she was beginning to get suspicious regarding Nicole."

"Jerry, you're just being paranoid. There's no possible way she could have figured out Nicole's relation to Nicky unless someone said something to her. Nobody knows but you and Bruce. I don't understand why you are freaking out. You're starting to act crazy," Kate added, infuriated. "Trust me. No one knows."

"Well, I'll let you know later tonight after I talk with her. Let's walk outside and find a place to eat. I'm starved too."

Buying rice and steak teriyaki from a local street vendor, they sat outside enjoying the cool evening air and the unique city's diversification. Finally, glancing at his watch, Jerry realized it was getting late.

"We better go back inside. You've got a lot of mohawks to retouch before the boys walk out on stage," Jerry laughed.

"Yes. You're right about that. I hope the boys keep their original blue color, at least for tonight. I'll have more time to recolor their hair tomorrow."

"Okay, let's get going," Jerry insisted.

Bruce and Jenna were sitting on the sofa drinking coffee as Jerry and Kate entered the dressing room.

"Where's Nicole and the guys?" Kate quickly asked.

"Oh, after they ate, they took the golf carts to explore the complex, and Nicole went with them," Bruce explained.

"Do you think that was a wise decision? First, I need to make sure they're ready," Kate asked frantically.

Just at that instant, Kate heard brakes squealing.

"I don't think you have to worry about that," Bruce laughed. "I think they're back. Oh, since you girls are all here now, I forgot to mention that I've reserved box seating for you tonight," he grinned. "I'll have one of the security guards take you up and show you where they're located before the concert starts."

"Thanks, Bruce," Jenna smiled, hugging him.

"Yes, thanks, Bruce, that's sweet of you considering Nicole is here tonight," Kate smiled.

"Oh, I have to take care of my girls."

"Thanks, Uncle Bruce, but Jerry promised he would let me stand down front near the stage tonight. I want to be as close to the guys as I can get. I was looking forward to that," Nicole begged.

"Yes, Bruce, Nicole can't be stuck in box seats tonight. That's for old folks," Harry laughed.

"Oh, thanks, Flame, you're calling me old. I'll remember to glue your hair to your head tonight," Kate laughed.

"Kate, I just meant that the guys and I want her down front tonight. We feel like she's one of us," Harry added.

"Yes, that's right. Nicole needs to be in the front," Cameron added.

"Yes, Bruce," Doug and Drew chimed in.

"Okay, okay, I know when I'm outnumbered," Bruce grinned. "Well, Jerry, I guess a promise is a promise, but you need to be with her or have security standing beside her. Do you understand?"

"Yes, Bruce, I'm not about to let anything happen to Nicole. But, don't worry, she'll be fine. She can't experience what it feels like to be at one of the guy's concerts if she's sitting in box seats," Jerry suggested.

"Thanks, Uncle Bruce, I love you," Nicole said, quickly giving him a huge hug and kiss.

"I think you better, thank Jerry. He's the one I'm holding responsible for you tonight.

"Thanks, Jerry, you're the best," Nicole said, running over to hug him.

It was almost time for the concert to begin, as Jerry found the perfect spot for Nicole to watch the boy's performance.

"Nicole, this is Larry. He's part of our security team. He's been with the band since Bruce came back on board to manage House of Cards. I'm going backstage, so I've asked Larry to take care of you," Jerry informed Nicole talking loud enough to be heard.

"Hi Nicole, nice to meet you," Larry smiled, trying to talk above the screaming fans. "It's fun being part of the crowd, but just in case things start to get out of control, don't worry, this is what I get paid for. So just enjoy yourself and forget I'm standing here. This is the best part of my job," Larry laughed.

Pandemonium set in as soon as Harry began his warmup on the drums. It seemed the entire building was vibrating from the screaming fans.

Nicole got goosebumps as the boys walked on stage. Then, she found herself completely absorbed in the moment as she raised her hands and began screaming out the guys' names as, one by one, they walked on stage.

"Good evening, Tokyo," Cameron yelled, sporting his blue mohawk.

"Tokyo, we're so thrilled to be here," Drew shouted.

"Is everyone ready to party?" Doug screamed.

Instantly, flames shot upward from the edge of the stage, sending the fans into a screaming frenzy. A rainbow of intense neon lights pulsated with the beat of the music as fireworks flashed brilliantly across a giant screen behind the stage.

House of Cards opened with one of their number one hits, *Wicked Star*. The fans reacted, dancing in the aisles with hands held high. However, Nicole loved every minute of it, especially when Drew looked her way and blew her a kiss. She felt completely absorbed in the moment. Then, watching as the guys performed one hit song after the other, she felt fortunate to be so close to them.

Nicole seemed to drift in and out of an unconscious rhythmic state immersed in the music. Looking around, the fans standing next to her were jumping as they waved their hands high into the air shouting their love to the guys while they kept colored beach balls floating overhead.

House of Cards was at its best tonight. Suddenly, fans began to push and shove their way closer to the front.

Tapping Nicole on the shoulder, Larry knew it was time to get her out of the mosh pit for her safety.

"Nicole, we're leaving. Hold tightly to my hand, don't let go."

"Oh, do we have to leave now? Can't we just stay until the guys walk off stage?"

"I promised Jerry that I would watch over you, and the concert is coming to a close. I've got to get you out of here now. Just follow me, and I'll take you back to the guy's dressing room. I have a golf cart parked outside this exit."

It wasn't long before Nicole was waiting for the boys to arrive.

"Man, what a wild crowd," Cameron said as he opened the door.

"Yeah, but it was hella fun," Doug laughed.

"Oh Nicole, you're here already. What did you think?" Drew winked. "Think you can watch two more performances of us going crazy on stage."

"Are you silly? I loved every second. I can't wait for the next two concerts."

"Where's Harry?"

"Oh, he's coming. He was having problems trying to get his golf cart started, so we left him behind," Drew laughed hysterically.

"Great concert," Bruce grinned.

"Cameron, you guys were awesome, and the fans loved you," Jenna smiled, walking over to hug her son. "I'm so proud of you."

Hearing the sound of brakes squealing outside the door, it seemed Harry had finally arrived.

"Thanks, guys. That wasn't funny," Harry stated with a scowl.

"Okay, now that we're all here, I've reserved a great place for dinner. I know you boys usually do your own thing, but tonight is special. We have Jenna and Nicole with us. The limo is waiting, so let's eat. I'm starved," Bruce announced, holding the door open for everyone.

It seemed Bruce was spot on as usual. He reserved a beautiful Japanese restaurant located in the heart of downtown Tokyo. Although it was located in the middle of the sprawling metropolitan area, it was impressive, with lush gardens at the front entrance containing a well-lit path and Koi ponds. Again, it seemed Bruce never disappointed. After dining on the best cuisine Tokyo had to offer, everyone was finally ready to call it a night.

It appeared jet lag still had a firm hold on the boys and Nicole as they instantly began falling asleep on the ride back to the hotel. Even Kate nodded off with her head lying on Jerry's shoulder.

"Jerry," Jenna whispered. "Don't forget, I want to talk with you. I'll meet you at the bar inside the lobby. Give me just a few minutes to say goodnight to Cameron and the boys when we arrive. Oh, I suggest you come alone."

"Wow, this sounds serious," Jerry replied, trying to downplay the implications.

"Well, let's just say it's long overdue. I wanted to talk with you the night of the memorial, but things were just too hectic that night."

"Okay, I'll meet you as soon as Kate and Nicole are settled in for the night."

Jerry was nervous. He did realize this conversation was way overdue, but why did it have to fall on his shoulders. *Damn you, Nicky, he thought to himself.*

It seemed all too soon they had arrived back at the hotel.

"Hey Mom, I'm going to play video games with the guys for a while. So if you happen to call my room later, you'll know where I am."

"Okay, Sweetheart," Kate replied, stepping inside the elevator.

Unlocking the door to their room, Jerry opened the mini-fridge to pour himself a drink. Kate fell onto the bed.

"Aren't you going to remove your clothes?" Jerry teased.

"Yes. I'm exhausted tonight. Guess it's the stress of taking Nicole to all those interviews today."

"Well, I've got to meet Jenna down in the lobby at the Hamasaki Bar in a few minutes. She's like a dog with a bone. She's not going to let this go."

"Do you want me to go with you?"

"Thanks, but she specifically asked me to come alone. Honestly, I don't know how to tell her about Nicole. The last thing I want to do is hurt her."

"Jerry, you're reading too much into this. Simply tell her the truth. She's a big girl. She can handle it."

"Yes, but you don't understand she's family. Nicky and I were always very close."

"Jerry listen to me, be honest. If I were her and wanted answers, I would be more upset if you lied to me or tried to cover things up."

"Okay, I'll be back. I'll let you know what happens if you're still awake."

"Oh, I'll probably be asleep. We'll talk in the morning. Love you."

Walking into the bar, Jerry could see Jenna sitting at one of the small tables near the back, enjoying a glass of wine. So this was it. What would he say?

"Hey Jenna, great concert tonight, wasn't it? Nicky would be so proud of Cameron and House of Cards."

"Yes. There's no doubt about that. I'm truly proud of Cameron. I'm having another glass of wine. What would you like?"

"Oh, I'll have my usual Jack Daniels, straight up with no ice."

It appeared that even before the young waiter walked over to take their orders, Jenna was feeling the effects of the wine. After his drink arrived and Jenna's glass was refilled, he took a long slow sip. Jerry was waiting for her first question. He wasn't going to offer any information willingly, just in case he was wrong about her reason for being here. Sitting back in his chair, he braced himself.

"Jerry, something has been bothering me since the night of the memorial. I guess you could say two things. First, let me say that I know how much you loved Nicky. I've never loved but one person in my entire life, and it was him," Jenna hesitated, taking a drink. "I had to come. You're the only person I can trust to tell me the truth."

"Jenna, what is it that's bothering you? Why would you come halfway around the world to ask me anything?" he questioned, dreading the dilemma which now faced him.

"Jerry is Nicole Nicky's daughter?" Jenna asked straight away without hesitation.

"Wow, Jenna," he paused, reaching across the table to take her hand.

Hesitating for a brief moment, "Yes." He had not planned to prolong the agony of his answer.

"I knew it. Jerry, the first time I met her, there was such an air of familiarity surrounding her," Jenna replied with tears in her eyes. Reaching for her purse, she grabbed tissues to wipe her face. "Nicole resembles him so much. Even her personality is a total reflection of Nicky," Jenna cried softly.

"Jenna, Nicky loved you. You have to know. So please don't

take this so hard. I hate Nicky for leaving me to take care of his unfinished business.

"Jerry, I feel like I can't breathe. I think I'm having a panic attack. I've got to get out of here."

"Okay, Doll, where do you want to go?"

"Anywhere, outside. I need some fresh air."

Hurriedly leaving enough money for the bar bill and tip, he pulled out Jenna's chair as she fell into his arms. Having noticed her condition when he walked in, he was afraid that not only was she drunk, but she might not even remember a word he had said.

"Jenna, Sweetheart, are you alright?"

"I feel a bit dizzy."

"Jenna, hang in here. I'm taking you up to your room. There's no way you can leave the hotel like this."

Scooping Jenna into his arms, he carried her over to the elevator. Reaching their floor, he quickly found her room key and opened the door. Walking inside, he gently laid her down on the bed and ran into the bathroom to wet a towel.

"Jenna, you have to be strong," he mentioned sympathetically, wiping her face. "Let me get you something to drink."

Opening the mini-fridge, he found a bottle of water.

"Sit up. It would help if you drank this. I think you had too much wine before I arrived."

"Thanks, Jerry. I'm a little better now," Jenna replied, sitting up. "Let's go sit outside on the balcony."

"Are you sure you feel like sitting outside? It's really late."

"Yes. I need some fresh air."

The night air was refreshing as they walked out to the balcony. First, Jerry took Jenna's hand. Then, sitting next to her, he waited for the questions to begin.

"Doesn't this cool breeze feel refreshing," Jenna mentioned looking up at the dazzling skyline of twinkling lights. "Jerry, I want to know everything. Do you understand? I don't care if it takes the rest of the night. I love Cameron dearly, but I came here to talk to you. I need answers."

"Okay, but let me ask you a question?"

"What was it that made you suspect Nicole was Nicky's daughter? I know you said you sensed an air of familiarity about her, but come on, there has to be more than that."

"Alright, to be perfectly honest, at the memorial concert, Michelle said that Kate and Nicky had stayed at their apartment in Frankfurt the night the boy's plane crashed. It hit me as odd because Nicky never mentioned Kate or the fact they'd had an ongoing relationship. When I approached Michelle to ask questions, she simply tried to avoid the topic. She dodged any direct questions by letting me know that guys, especially Nicky, who traveled with a rock band, were notorious. Jerry that isn't Nicky. I know she wasn't telling me the whole truth. Believe me. Women have a fifth sense when it comes to these matters. How long had Nicky known Kate? As I said before, I came here to get answers."

"Okay, just know that it isn't my intention to hurt you by anything I tell you. I can only start from my earliest memories of Kate. I received a phone call from Bruce and Nicky a few days after the boys' plane went down. Bruce called and offered me a position with the band. He remembered me from the talent contest in Middleton when he discovered Nicky. Well, not only did he remember and invite me to join Black Tie Affair, he flew back to Middleton the next day to get me. That was the first time I met Kate. It seemed she was with Nicky at that point. By the way, Kate was the stylist for the band. She worked with the guys from their European tour in London. However, Nicky later told me he first met her in Dublin," Jerry stated, getting up to grab a few beers. "Can I get you something to drink, maybe orange juice?

"No thanks, but can you bring my wrap. It's lying over the sofa? I'm starting to feel a slight chill."

Walking back outside with beer for himself, he gently wrapped the shawl around Jenna. I brought you some tissues. Knowing you,

you're probably going to need them," Jerry smiled, giving her a quick kiss to the forehead.

Jerry continued, "They had been together for quite a while before I came over. Jenna, it did appear they were in love. But you have to know that Nicky said he had written you postcards and even made phone calls trying to reach you after leaving Middleton. He never stopped loving you, I'm sure of it. But let's face it, no man, especially Nicky Spade, would've ever become a monk and stayed single for long. Jenna, as the lead vocalist for Black Tie Affair, girls were crazy over him. He was brilliant. Nicky was finally living his dream. Kate just so happened to share the world he lived in. I guess a simple explanation would be the fact, she was simply there," Jerry mentioned stopping to take a drink.

Noticing Jenna wiping her eyes, he handed her one of the tissues.

"Doll, he loved you. But, Jenna, I'm sure he thought he would probably never see you again. He had no way to know where you were or anything about you for that matter."

"Oh, I know Jerry, and I feel like I was robbed of all those years with him. I knew deep inside the day he left Middleton that fate was pulling us apart. I knew he was restless and would never stop chasing his dream to become a solo artist. I tried to find comfort in the fact that I was carrying his baby," Jenna cried softly. "Jerry, you have to know that I never stopped loving him, never. My dad hated him for leaving me, especially when he found out I was pregnant. He convinced my mom and grandmother to hide the postcards and not let me know about his phone calls," Jenna replied, wiping the myriad of tears flowing down her face.

"Jenna, I wished things could have turned out differently for you both. I know how much you loved him. Trust me, that was easy to see, but I had no way to know that you were pregnant with Cameron when you left," Jerry continued handing her another tissue. "After the tour was over, Nicky was offered a movie contract. Kate went with him to Hollywood as his stylist and make-up artist. That's when things changed, according to Kate. Nicky quickly let himself get involved with the Hollywood lifestyle, including cocaine. Kate hated the person Nicky had become. But worse than that, she found him in bed with his co-star, Renee Ricci. You can only imagine the nightmare Kate went through. On the other hand, Nicky wasn't aware that she was pregnant with Nicole. She never told him," Jerry said, reaching for another beer.

"So Doll, that's pretty much it. Kate left Nicky and the band at that time. None of us knew about her being pregnant with Nicole or even where she went, for that matter. However, I later learned from Kate that Bruce knew, and he continued to support her and Nicole. Oh, I almost forgot, Bruce, stepped down as manager of the band during that time. He said he couldn't stand by and watch the so-called train wreck that Nicky had become. William Kirkland took over the management of the band. He committed us to a two-year contract overseas with options to extend the tour. I hate to say this about Nicky, but their drug use got out of control when David returned. Jeff and I tried to cover for those two as long as possible. I loved Nicky. I just can't say I loved the person he had become at that time."

"Wow, Bruce has always been one of a kind. He's been like my rock since Nicky passed," Jenna mentioned, wiping her eyes.

"Yes, Bruce is the essence of the word, gentleman. You never have to worry about Cameron. He would never allow anything to happen to our boy."

"Okay, Jerry, one more thing before we call it a night."

"Yes, what could that be, and it isn't exactly night. The sun is already coming up. See it on the horizon between those tall buildings," Jerry pointed out.

"What about you and Kate? You're in love with Kate, aren't you?" Jenna questioned, attempting a smile.

"You sure know how to change the subject. Yes. Is it that easy to see?"

"Jerry, I know you. But, do you honestly think that I or anyone else, for that matter, can't see how crazy you are about Kate?"

"Okay, the ruse is up," he chuckled. "Yes. I've fallen in love with

Kate. Jenna, I hope you don't hold that against me. I hope you won't hate me or think any less of me because I've fallen in love with her."

"Jerry, as hard as this might be for you to believe, I don't have a problem with it. I really can't blame Kate for falling in love with Nicky. I'm sure that was easy. It was easy for me," Jenna added, wiping away more tears.

"Jenna, Doll, please stop crying. I feel so bad. You've cried the entire night."

"I can't help it. I think tears are cathartic. It's the emotions of finally letting go. Kate was part of Nicky's life. I had to know."

"You girls and your emotions."

"Jerry speaking of girls, what about Nicole? Who knows? Does anyone know other than you, me, Bruce, and Kate? What about Cameron? Jerry, Cameron has a half-sister. You're a great uncle. Wow. There's a lot of repercussions to what you've told me tonight. How does Kate want to handle the fact they're brother and sister? I don't think I'm ready or prepared to let Cameron know about Nicole, at least not yet."

"Don't worry. You're both on the same page as far as telling either of them. Kate doesn't want Nicole to know either. So it'll be kept a secret just between the four of us for now."

"Jerry, I want you to let Kate know that I don't hate her. Give us some time to figure this all out. She's Nicole's mother, and Nicole is Cameron's half-sister. So we're all family, now aren't we?"

"Jenna, I think that's a wonderful way to look at things. The way I see it, none of us asked to be in this situation that we now find ourselves in. We're all adults here, and I think we should put Cameron and Nicole's needs first. Although, I do think they should be told in the future. I love Cameron, and I love Nicole."

Think it's about time we go in," Jerry suggested feeling the warmth of the morning sun. "I think we've about covered everything. I can't remember the last time I stayed up all night talking. Geez, I feel like I've been invited to a weird all-girls sleepover. I'm tired, and it's going to be a long day. I promised the guys to take them sightseeing."

"Thanks, Jerry," Jenna smiled, reaching over to give him a quick kiss. "Thank you for filling in that part of Nicky's life. I can go back to Vancouver having all my questions answered now. I truly wish you and Kate the best. Life is short. I want you to be happy," Jenna smiled.

"Wow. Now that's what I wanted to see. I've waited all night to see that smile return. Jenna, I love you. You and Cameron are family, and I always want us to remain close. I think you'll like Kate. Who knows? If I do ask Kate to marry me and she accepts my proposal, I think you two could become best friends," Jerry winked.

"Doll, let's go inside. I've got to get a few hours of sleep."

Unlocking the door to their suite, it was early morning. Getting into bed, Jerry slipped under the covers next to Kate. He hoped to get into bed and asleep before she woke. However, Kate was awake.

"Jerry, do you know what time it is?" Kate questioned, turning to face him.

"Yes. It's morning."

"Jerry, for heaven's sake, it took you all night to explain my relationship with Nicky. Maybe I should have gone with you to speed things up. How in the world could you have stayed out all night?" Kate furiously questioned.

"Kate, let me explain. First, I went down to the bar, and as I walked in, Jenna was already sitting at a table near the back. She was drinking a glass of wine as I walked over. I'm sure Jenna had probably already had a glass or two before I arrived. So as I ordered a drink, she ordered another refill. By this time, Jenna already seemed intoxicated to me. To make a long story short, she directly asked me if Nicole was Nicky's daughter. What was I to do? I told her the truth, not wanting to beat around the bush. I guess it was finally hearing the words come out of my mouth, which sent her into a panic attack. She said she couldn't breathe and had to leave. Well, there was no way she could go anywhere. I wasn't even sure she could walk at this point. What is it with you girls and alcohol? I even had to carry you back to our room one night, remember."

"Jerry, get on with it. Who cares. It's not important."

"Okay, just trying to explain. Well, Jenna was extremely dizzy, so I literally had to carry her back to her room and lay her on the bed. I wet a hand towel, warmed it under the water, and tried to revive her. I made her sit up and drink some water. It must have worked because she asked me to go with her outside on the balcony to get some fresh air the next minute. So we sat outside in the cool night air for what seemed like hours."

"You mean until the sun came up. I can't believe my relationship with Nicky took all night for you to recap," Kate frowned.

"Kate, don't give me a hard time. Jenna is family to me. What else could I have done? Explaining Nicky Spade to anyone isn't exactly easy, and then trying to explain your relationship with him, what do you expect?" Jerry laughed.

"How did she begin to discover that Nicole was Nicky's daughter?"

"Well, you and I both know how much Nicole favors her Dad. But it's actually more than that. Nicole shares his mannerisms and quirks. Odd, isn't it? Jenna sensed something familiar when she was around her. Unexplainable at first, until Michelle mentioned something to her at the memorial."

"What did Michelle say that made her start putting it all together?"

"She let it slip at the memorial concert that you and Nicky had spent the night at their apartment in Frankfurt when the boy's plane went down. So naturally, Jenna asked her if you two were together. Of course, Michelle said no, but I'm sure she probably realized that she had said too much by that time. So Michelle tried to cover her tracks by making Jenna think that perhaps both Nicky and Mike were Casanovas because they traveled with the band. I'm sure that irritated Jenna. But, on the other hand, she knew Nicky well enough to know that he didn't look elsewhere when he was in a relationship. So that combined with Nicole's appearance was pretty much how she began putting the pieces together."

"Wow, poor girl, no wonder Jenna came all the way to Japan to get answers. Having just lost Nicky, I'm sure this must have been eating away at her. I probably would have done the same. Well, did you explain how our relationship broke up and why I've never told Nicole about her father?"

"Yes, she needed to know the truth about Nicky's addictions. I dreaded telling her about how he spiraled out of control after he arrived in Hollywood."

"Doll, it's over. She knows everything now. I'm tired. I need to get a few hours of sleep before I take the boys sightseeing later today."

"Jerry, I love you. I know what you did was hard, but she deserved to know the truth, and she needed to hear it from you. Come over here and let me kiss your face off," Kate laughed, sitting up in bed. "Babe, I love you. Get some sleep. Oh, I almost forgot, one more thing and this is important. Did you ask her not to say anything to Cameron?"

"Yes, Babe, don't worry. I'll leave that one up to you and Jenna. Now, let a man get a little sleep," Jerry replied, kissing her.

"Sleep, is it?" Kate laughed, kissing him passionately.

"Well, maybe not," Jerry winked, pulling her next to him.

House of Cards performed for the next two nights in front of sold out crowds. Nicole received a call back the following day, finally getting her dream job with one of the best fashion houses in Tokyo. It seemed apartment hunting never became necessary as the agency provided housing for their girls.

Jenna also got the answers she came for, which gave closure to her life with Nicky.

Tokyo turned out to be therapeutic in many ways.

CHAPTER TEN

Bangkok
Walking in his father's footsteps

Arriving in Bangkok, everyone was both physically and mentally exhausted. Tokyo had been cathartic. However, Kate left her daughter behind, and Cameron once again said goodbye to his mom.

"Okay, gang, we're booked into the Hilton. I've reserved rooms for each of you. I figured you boys might enjoy the luxury of having your own space. So, Jerry, I've booked you and Kate into a suite," Bruce mentioned as the Lear Jet rolled to a stop on the tarmac.

"Thanks, Bruce," Cameron smiled.

"Great. I won't have to listen to Harry snore tonight," Drew laughed.

Getting into the limo, they were soon on their way downtown.

Driving past a large sign, it announced their concert. It was brilliantly lit, giving the dates and times.

"Wow, another billboard," Harry spoke up. "Bruce, you're good. That's amazing."

"Well, how do you think I keep your concerts sold out? It takes a lot of work and advertising," Bruce grinned, lighting a cigar. "Oh, one last thing before we arrive at the hotel, I thought you guys might want to order room service for dinner tonight. It's late, and we have a lot to do tomorrow."

Arriving at the hotel and receiving their room keys, the boys quickly disappeared to check out their rooms. First, however, Bruce headed in the direction of the lounge for a quick drink.

"Wait up Bruce, Kate and I will join you."

"Great," Bruce added, leading the way.

The hotel was impeccable. Twin dragons covered in gold sat guarding the entryway. Colorful paper lanterns hung from the ceilings as they walked farther inside, and lush foliage surrounded a large bubbling fountain.

"Would you both prefer a table or sitting at the bar?" Bruce asked.

"Oh, I'd definitely prefer a table, if it's okay with you guys," Kate suggested.

"Sounds good, a table it is," Bruce answered, finding an open spot.

After being seated, a young girl came over to take their drink orders.

"I'll have a glass of wine, riesling, if you have it," Kate smiled.

"'ll have Jack Daniels, straight no ice," Jerry stated.

"I'll have the same, JD, straight no ice," Bruce added.

"Wow, this place is gorgeous," Kate mentioned looking around.

"Well, you know Bruce, the man has class," Jerry grinned.

"Thanks, Jerry, I try," Bruce laughed. "By the way, since the boys are not here, how did things go with Jenna? I know you were worried. Did she corner you for answers?"

"Yes, Bruce, she did. I had a long talk with her the other night."

"I'll say it was a long talk," Kate reminded him. "It took all night," she mentioned taking a sip of wine.

"How did she take the news about Nicole?" Bruce inquired.

"A lot easier than I thought, but maybe her being inebriated helped."

"What? She was drunk?" Bruce laughed. "That doesn't sound like my girl."

"Well, sort of, let's just say she had a little too much wine. Yes, Kate is right. I had to take her up to her room. Jenna thought she had a panic attack, but I think it was the wine. I brought her a warm towel and water, and then surprisingly enough, Jenna wanted to sit outside on the balcony. But all in all, it was a good talk, long but good. She knows that Nicole is Nicky's daughter, but we all agreed not to let Cameron or Nicole know. At least not yet, as I told Kate, that's better left to her and Jenna. When the time is right, I know they'll let the kids know. So let's just say Jenna got the answers she came for."

"I love that girl, and I loved Nicky. It's too bad she had to learn of this so soon after Nicky's passing." Bruce grimaced.

"Well, I know this may sound strange, but I think in some weird sort of way, it probably helped give her closure," Jerry added, finishing his drink.

"Guess we better be going. Tomorrow is going to be a long day. There's always a lot to do on the first day in town. I've got a lot of promo work to do, and I know you're going to take the boys sightseeing. See you both in the morning," Bruce suggested leaving the tab and tip on the table. "Oh, I think we're both up on the eighteenth floor. I have the boys on the twelfth floor."

Unlocking the door to their room, it was stunning. Red silk curtains draped the patio door. The kingsize bed was covered with a matching silk duvet, and ornate furniture made out of mahogany complimented the décor. It didn't take Kate long before removing her shoes, pulling back the blankets, and lying down.

"Doll, you're sleeping in your clothes again," Jerry laughed.

"Oh Jerry, I'm tired. The wine has me so relaxed."

"Well, maybe I can help you with that," he teased, unzipping her dress.

Turning out the lights, Jerry had other things on his mind.

Waking up the following day, Jerry rolled over, kissing Kate awake.

"Babe, wake up. It's getting late," he reminded, glancing at the clock. "It's almost 9:00 a.m. We've got a long day today, and you get to play tour guide. So since our first concert isn't until tomorrow evening, I figured today we would take the boys out and show them the sights of Bangkok."

"Okay, but order coffee, lots of coffee."

"Sounds good, but how about a little breakfast to go with it. I'm starved," Jerry mentioned.

"Alright, I'll have a poached egg with toast."

After having a leisurely breakfast, showering, and getting dressed, Jerry was ready to check in with the boys. Calling down to Cameron's room, he quickly answered the phone.

"Good morning, Jerry," Cameron answered.

"Cameron, please let Drew, Harry, and Doug know to meet Kate and me down in the lobby no later than 10:30 a.m. The limo will be picking us up for a day of sightseeing. Make sure the boys order breakfast, dress casually, and they might want to bring their cameras. I'll see you shortly."

"Okay, thanks, Jerry. I know the guys are excited. I've already checked out one of the brochures. There are several places we want to go. So don't worry, I'll have them in the lobby by 10:30 a.m."

Watching the boys as they walked out of the elevator, Kate laughed.

"Now I'm not sure, who's going to be watching whom today? But you guys are going to stand out. I don't think I've ever gone on a sightseeing tour with a more diverse bunch," Kate laughed. "You guys are going to have everyone staring at you."

"Jerry, I want to visit the statue of the Emerald Buddha and the Grand Palace," Cameron mentioned, stepping inside the limo. "Dad described those places to me, and they sounded so neat. He loved Bangkok."

"Okay. We'll go to the Grand Palace and visit the Wat Phra Kaew, which houses the Emerald Buddha."

Exiting the limo almost necessitated security. Curiosity seekers instantly ran up for autographs and to have their photos made with the guys. However, Jerry and the boys were accommodating when signing various souvenirs and stopping for photos.

Kate took snapshots of the guys and Jerry and a few fans in front of the temple that contained the green Buddha. Then, looking through the camera lens, she laughed.

Harry, always being the life of the party, took the opportunity to pose doing the Egyptian walk. He held one arm horizontal, with his arm bent at the elbow facing up while his other arm was at his side bent at the elbows facing downward.

"Harry, your crazy, wrong tourist attraction. Guys, you look hilariously out of place in front of the temple, with your spiked purple Mohawks, your facial piercings, tattoos, and ripped faded jeans. I can only imagine what some of the locals must think. But of course, I know your fans adore you. That's plain to see after all the pictures I've had to take of you posing with them."

After spending hours walking around the compound, it was beginning to get late.

"Okay, everyone back in the car, let's go eat. Bruce recommended a great place to eat. How does that sound?" Jerry asked.

"Awesome," Drew smiled.

"Cameron, how do you feel, knowing your dad also toured these same historical places with Black Tie Affair? You might say you've actually walked in his footprints today."

"Well, it does seem weird, knowing that Dad has been here. But you know what? I'm proud to be following in his footsteps," Cameron smiled. "Kate, can you make sure Mom receives copies of our photos?"

"Oh sure, no problem. I'm sure Jenna will love these."

Parking in front of a small restaurant located on one of the side streets, its outward appearance seemed unremarkable, effortlessly blending in with the local surroundings. However, it contained numerous mosaic murals that depicted the local culture inside.

Walking in, they were ushered to a long table in a small adjacent room. It seemed Bruce had made a private reservation allowing them to enjoy the restaurant's ambiance while enjoying the local cuisine without interruption from those around them. The manager had prepared Thai delicacies, which were immediately brought out. These included Gang Keow Wan (a Thai green curry), Gai Pad Pongali (chicken, onions, tomatoes, and peppers in a delicate Thai yellow curry paste), Gang Jued (a clear vegetable soup containing garden vegetables), Kao Na Phet (roasted duck) along with Kao Niew Moo Yang (grilled pork skewers and sticky rice). The guys and Kate enjoyed the Thai delicacies.

"Okay, I hate to end this lovely evening, but we have our first concert at the Coliseum tomorrow night. So let's call it a night and get some rest."

Kate fell asleep leaning against Jerry's shoulder on the ride back to their hotel.

Upon their arrival, the boys soon disappeared as was usual for them.

Unlocking the door, Kate immediately walked over to the bed, pulled back the duvet, and laid down.

"Sleeping in your clothes again," Jerry teased. "Wow, Doll, what is it with you and getting in bed with your clothes on," he laughed.

"Oh, I'm tired, and the wine at dinner has me so relaxed, as usual."

"Well, don't worry," he winked. "I think I can help you with your clothes. Then, kissing Kate passionately, he unzipped her dress. Jerry, as usual, had other things on his mind, which didn't include sleep.

The following morning arrived early, as the room filled with the warmth of the sunlight. Jerry woke first. He laid awake for almost twenty minutes, staring at the beautiful woman peacefully sleeping next to him. His mind was filled with thoughts of sharing the rest of his life with her. Contemplating his next move, it instantly became obvious. He would shop for an engagement ring. Knowing how much Kate loved to visit popular tourist destinations, he had a perfect idea. He would ask Bruce to reserve a cabana for them on the beach in Phuket. The band was due for a bit of downtime after Bangkok. It would be the perfect time for him and Kate to hang back for a few days while Bruce continued with the boys to their next destination, Taiwan.

"Wake up, sleepyhead," Jerry smiled, kissing Kate awake. "Let's order breakfast. What sounds good?"

"Coffee," came her usual answer as she rubbed her eyes.

"Jerry, can't you for once sleep in, just a little," she smiled.

"Well, not today, but hopefully soon. We have a few down days on the schedule after the concerts here in Bangkok," he winked.

After eating, Jerry jumped in the shower and got dressed. He was a man on a mission.

"Hey Doll, I've got to run over to Bruce's room. I want to catch him before he leaves to do his publicity rounds today."

"Okay, guess I'll take a shower and get dressed."

Knocking at Bruce's door, Jerry's mind was again replaying the details of taking Kate to Phuket.

"Good morning Jerry, come in. You're up bright and early this morning. Come in and sit down. I'll pour us some coffee."

"Bruce, I was hoping I would catch you here. I know you'll be busy today, but I have something I want to discuss with you. If you have the time."

"Sure, son, what's on your mind?" Bruce questioned, handing him a cup of coffee.

"Oh, thanks. Well, this morning I had a brilliant idea, or at least I think it's brilliant. But, of course, you know that I've fallen in love with Kate."

"Yes, son, that's pretty plain to see. So why do you think I gave you two love birds the same suite?" Bruce laughed.

"Well, I've given it some serious thought. I'm going to buy an engagement ring today. I don't want to wait. I'm not getting any younger, and besides that, I'm madly in love with Kate."

"Jerry, that's wonderful. Congratulations," Bruce smiled.

"Well, don't congratulate me just yet. I still have to ask Kate. Hopefully, she'll say yes. However, that leads me to the reason I came by this morning."

"What could that be?" Bruce smiled, taking a sip of coffee.

"Well, I was wondering," Jerry paused, taking a much longer sip of coffee.

"Son, I suggest you spit it out. We haven't got all day."

"Bruce, do you think you could reserve Kate and me a cabana on the beach in Phuket? I thought it would be the perfect location to ask her to marry me."

"Of course, I would be thrilled. What day did you have in mind?"

"Well, I thought perhaps after the boys finish their performances here in Bangkok. I know we're all scheduled for a few down days between here and Taiwan."

"That would actually work out. I'll take the boys and get them settled in Taipei. You and Kate can stay behind and then fly over afterward. Would you like a reservation for three days, or are you thinking longer?"

"No, two days would be great. I don't want to leave you hanging with the boys. Sometimes they can be a handful. So two days would be perfect."

"Okay, you've got it. I'll make the arrangements. Just leave everything up to me. I love that girl and Nicole. What about Nicole? Does she know?"

"No, I'm not telling anyone yet. So please, don't say anything. We'll let everyone think it's a spur of the moment mini-vacation."

"You've got it. The best Phuket has to offer. I'll check on reservations today while I'm downtown doing my publicity rounds."

"Thanks, Bruce. What time do you want the boys to arrive tonight?"

"Oh, I think as long as they're there by 7:00 p.m., everything should be fine."

"Thanks again, Bruce. I really appreciate it. Guess I'll go check on the boys."

"No problem. I'm sure Kate will say yes. I can't say I didn't see this one coming. I've known for a while that you two seemed awfully fond of each other," Bruce grinned, closing the door.

Taking the elevator down to the boy's rooms, Jerry felt elated. Now he just had to find the time today to shop for a ring.

Knocking at the door, Cameron answered.

"Hey Jerry, come in. What brings you here so early?"

"Well, it isn't that early. I just left Bruce's room."

"So, what's up?"

"I've got a few errands to run downtown. I just wanted to check in with you all before I left. By the way, Bruce needs everyone at the coliseum by 7:00 p.m. this evening. What were you and the guys planning to do today?"

"Oh, we haven't discussed it this morning, but last night we were thinking of renting mopeds and going to the beach."

"Okay, that sounds like fun, but you're not going by yourselves. I'll have Kate chaperone you guys. You'll only have a few hours to do your exploring this afternoon. Let me call the room and see if she's available."

Hearing the phone ring, Kate immediately answered.

"Hey Kate, I've got a few errands to run downtown, and the boys were thinking of renting mopeds and maybe going to the beach this afternoon. Do you think you could chaperone and keep them out of trouble? Oh, and Bruce needs everyone at the coliseum by 7:00 p.m. this evening, so you're not going to have a lot of time. What do you think? Are you up for it?"

"Are you kidding? I'd love to. Can't you come along? It would be so much fun."

"Babe, sorry I can't. I've got a few things to do, but have fun. Just make sure you have the guys back in enough time to shower and dress for tonight's concert."

"No problem. Jerry, have them meet me in the lobby in about an hour, and don't worry."

"Thanks, Doll. Oh, the limo is available to get you to a moped rental. See you later tonight."

"Okay, Cameron, you guys are all set. Call the boys, get them up and dressed. Kate will meet you in the lobby in about an hour. You should have time to order breakfast or something to eat before you leave. Oh, one last thing, no shenanigans today. Please, don't give Kate any problems. Do you understand?"

"Oh Jerry, we'd never do that," Cameron laughed.

"Right. I have a hard time believing that one," Jerry laughed. "Well, I'm out of here. See you guys later tonight. Oh, have fun."

Kate was in her element as a tourist guide, and her favorite mode of travel was by moped. Memories of Paris and Nicky flooded her mind. She only wished Jerry could have gone with her today.

Hailing a cab, Jerry was finally excited to be on his way downtown. Asking the driver for information regarding jewelry purchases, especially diamonds, he was surprised to learn of the notorious scams in Bangkok. His recommendations included either China Town or a shopping mall. Jerry decided the mall would best fit his needs, and the cabbie vowed to come back later to get him.

It didn't take Jerry long to pick out a high-quality diamond. He wanted a rather simplistic yet elegant ring. Deciding on a three-carat heart-shaped solitaire, he had finally found the perfect one. Now, he could only hope that Kate would fall in love with his choice.

Arriving back earlier than expected to the hotel, he put away his treasure and decided a nap was in order. The traffic had been horrible. He could only hope that Kate and the boys were not held up on the same congested streets. Having second thoughts about having sent her out by herself with the boys, he must have had a moment of insanity. If she didn't make it back in time, Bruce would make his life intolerable.

However, it seemed he had only been asleep for about an hour when Kate walked in. Looking over at his watch, it was only 4:00 p.m.

"Wow, you're back early. I was beginning to think I should never have sent you out alone with the boys."

"Well, you probably shouldn't have. It was scary. The traffic was horrific. But worse than that, we got lost. Normally traffic doesn't bother me. I lived in Paris every summer until I started working with the band, and I always traveled by moped. However, today, I learned that Bangkok is definitely not Paris," Kate shrugged.

"What happened?" Jerry laughed.

"Geez, Honestly, I don't know where to start. Well, it started at the moped rental. The boys wanted individual scooters, which was my first mistake. I suggested they double up, but they were determined to each drive a moped. Big mistake," Kate laughed. "Of course, Harry drove off without putting on his helmet, leaving the rest of us behind. At that point, I'm sure he had no idea where he was going or the direction to the beach. The traffic, as you know, was unbelievable, and by the time the boys and I finally got on the road, we had no idea where Harry had disappeared. I panicked. There was no way to communicate with the boys, so I tried to motion them to stay behind me. Jerry, it was awful, really awful," Kate frowned.

"What Doll? Do I really want to hear this?"

"Well, I think you should. But, I'm sorry, you have to."

"Kate, what happened?" Jerry asked curiously.

"Let's just say we found Harry. It seems like he lost control of his moped, but I think he was probably going too fast, and that caused him to lose control."

"What do you mean, he lost control?"

"Okay. Harry had an accident."

"Kate, we're in a foreign country. Do you even realize the implications?"

"Well, I guess it's a little too late to worry about that once it's already happened."

"Babe, give it to me straight. How bad was it, and for heaven's sake, please tell me he didn't injure someone," Jerry asked furiously, pacing the floor.

"No. Thank God. It wasn't that bad. Jerry, sit down. You're making me nervous."

"Making you nervous, what the hell Kate," Jerry grimaced, lighting a cigarette.

"Jerry, you haven't smoked in ages."

"Well, I guess I do now," he insisted angrily.

"Listen, it's not that bad. Harry's moped hit a corner market stall filled with fruits and vegetables. No one was hurt, but of course, fruit and vegetables rolled everywhere, all over the road. Surprisingly, the owner, Mr. Aromdee, was pretty nice, considering the fact that he was horrified by Harry's appearance. He kept calling Harry an ugly American."

"Did he know Harry's prominence or the fact he's performing at the coliseum tonight?"

"Oh no, not at first, which was a good thing. However, as soon as I arrived with the boys, they didn't help matters by advertising that they were all members of a punk rock band from the states. Strange, but in a weird way, the boys thought it might help. But you and I both know, they just made matters worse. So anyway, to make a long story short, I had to think quickly on my feet," Kate grinned.

"So, Kate, what exactly does that mean? This isn't funny, you know."

"Well, let's just say I promised a lot of free tickets to the concert tonight. So I asked if he or his family would like to come as our guest. Thank goodness, he wasn't interested at all, but he said he had granddaughters who would love to come."

"So, Babe, what did you use for tickets?" Jerry fumed.

"Well, I simply wrote your name as assistant manager for the band on a piece of paper. Then, I told him to have his granddaughters present it to the security at the entrance tonight."

"You did what?" Jerry exploded.

"Oh Jerry, how many granddaughters could he possibly have?"

"Wow, let me think. How about half of Bangkok? I don't know. Really, Kate, you couldn't think of anything better than that."

"Geez, Jerry, I'd like to see what you would've done. I didn't exactly plan for this. Anyway, the boys helped me pick up most of the fruit and vegetables and everything. I gave him what cash I had on me. I kept apologizing and saying that it was just an unfortunate accident. You should be thanking me," Kate demanded.

"Thanking you for what? Thanking you for the fact that half of Bangkok might show up tonight expecting free tickets?" Jerry swore under his breath as he lit another cigarette.

"Oh Jerry, don't be so dramatic."

"I'm going downstairs right now. I'm talking with Flame."

"Just try not to let Bruce know. The police weren't called, so there will be no incident report. Thankfully the moped wasn't damaged. Seriously, it wasn't that bad. I'm sure you can talk with security tonight and work something out with his granddaughters. I'll be doing hair and make-up, so there's no way I can stand by the door waiting for them to arrive," Kate snickered.

"Oh, don't worry, guess I'll come up with something."

Jerry had to get out of the room before he lost it. He was going down to talk with Harry and the boys. As the elevator door closed, Jerry started laughing. He wasn't sure if it was nerves or just trying to envision the whole scene. Hopefully, he had dodged another bullet, at least as far as Bruce was concerned. But, of course, that was unless half of Bangkok did show up.

Hearing a knock at the door, Harry hesitated to open it.

"Okay, Harry, I know you're in there."

"Alright, I'm coming. Wait just a minute."

"Hey Jerry, come in and sit down."

"What the hell were you thinking? Why is it when something crazy happens, your name always comes up first? Harry, I thought you learned a lesson back in Hawaii. I want to keep you. You're one hell of a drummer. But if you continue to create problems and Bruce finds out, you'll have your ticket back to the states. Do you hear me? Do you understand?" Jerry furiously demanded.

"Yes, Jerry, I promise. But, man, I'm sorry, really I am. I guess I got a little too excited over driving a moped. I was just going to circle the block while Kate and the guys waited to get their scooters, but the traffic pinned me in, and I couldn't turn around. I think I was probably going a little too fast and lost control."

"Pinned you in? Harry, for heaven's sake, you were driving a scooter, right?"

"Yeah, but Jerry, the traffic was bad, really awful. I'm sorry."

"Harry, you have to know, I do appreciate your honesty and your apology, but that's not going to keep you here? You've got to stay out of trouble. I don't know what's going to happen tonight. Kate promised his granddaughters free tickets. What would you do if you had to pay for those? You better hope he doesn't have a lot of granddaughters if you know what I mean. Bruce cannot find out about this. You were fortunate the local police weren't involved, that no one was injured, and the moped wasn't damaged."

"I know Jerry. Trust me, nothing like this will ever happen again. I promise."

"I want to believe you. I really do. I'm going to talk with Cameron, Drew, and Doug. I'll need you guys dressed and in the lobby no later than 6:30 p.m.," Jerry stated, getting up to leave. Wow, Jerry was sure this was by far the ridiculous story he had ever heard, unbelievable.

"Okay, Jerry, see you later."

After making his rounds to the boy's rooms and laying down the law, Jerry returned to his room. Walking in, he found Kate crying.

"Babe, don't cry. I'm sorry. I didn't mean to get so upset. I was simply freaked out at first. But it could have been a lot worse," Jerry mentioned putting his arms around her.

"Oh Jerry, I'm so sorry. I had no idea something like that was going to happen," Kate replied, wiping her eyes with the back of her hand.

Taking a tissue, Jerry wiped her face, softly kissing her.

"I know you did the best you could. It wasn't your fault, none of it. I just had a serious talk with Harry. Hopefully, he learned a lesson this time."

"Why don't you lay down and close your eyes for a while," Jerry smiled as he took her hand, pulling her toward the bed. We've still got a little time before we have to leave. I'm sure you could use a little rest, especially after the story I just heard," he laughed, removing her shoes and putting her under the covers. I'll order something to eat. What would you like?"

"A salad sounds good. Make that a grilled chicken salad with extra dressing and iced tea."

"Okay. I think I'll order a burger with fries. Are you sure you don't want a burger?"

"Yes. I'm sure. Oh, make sure I have plenty of time to shower and dress if I fall asleep."

"Alright, get a little rest. We've got a long night ahead of us."

Hearing a knock at the door, the food had finally arrived. Noticing that Kate was sleeping peacefully, Jerry decided to eat alone without waking her. He couldn't help but laugh every time he thought of Kate's dilemma with the boys, especially Harry's idiotic explanation. Then, looking over at her, Jerry smiled. Hopefully, within a few short days, she would make him the happiest he had ever been by simply saying yes.

"Babe, it's time to wake up," he mentioned as he lovingly nudged her awake. "I put your salad in the fridge. After that, you'll have just enough time to eat and shower. The boys are supposed to be meet us down in the lobby at 6:30 p.m."

Pulling him down onto the bed next to her, Kate laughed.

"Jerry, surely I just had a bad dream, or did it all really happen?"

"Doll, I think it all really happened," Jerry reminded, gently kissing her awake.

"Wow. I better jump in the shower," Kate panicked, glancing at the clock.

"We still have a little time. I'll get your salad out of the fridge."

"Not now, Jerry Godwin," Kate laughed, referring to him by his full name.

"What's the Jerry Godwin about," he smiled.

"Oh, you'll find out," Kate smiled, pulling him toward the bathroom.

"We're getting a shower."

"What are you crazy?" he laughed.

Like two kids at play, they were both quickly standing under the warm water, fully clothed. "What is it with you and clothes," he winked, removing her wet garments.

"Well, Babe, consider it our memory of Bangkok, in case we're both fired tonight by Bruce. If half of Bangkok does show up for free tickets, we might as well have a little fun on our last night," Kate laughed as things got steamy.

The guys were dressed and ready as they walked out of the elevator.

"Well, at least it appears you guys can do something right," Jerry smiled. "Ready to give Bangkok the most outrageous rock concert ever," he grinned, stepping inside the limo.

"You bet, Jerry," everyone answered.

As usual, there were long lines of fans waiting to get in as the limo arrived at the back entrance. Jerry couldn't resist the urge to tease Kate.

"Wow, Kate, I wonder how many of those girls might be Mr. Aromdee's granddaughters," he winked.

"Oh Jerry, you're mean," Kate scolded.

Walking in, once again, golf carts were waiting for their arrival. This time they all hopped on, including Jerry and Kate. After driving only a short distance, they found Bruce talking with one of the guys from the sound crew.

"Right down this hallway and to the left," Bruce directed, watching them drive up.

Opening the door, they were not to be disappointed. Food, fresh flowers, and soft music filled the room.

"Let's eat," Cameron mentioned.

"Yes. We're starved," Drew stated, walking over to check out the mouth-watering buffet.

It didn't take long before the boys sat with their plates filled to overflowing with a tasty array of Thai delicacies.

"Guess we should eat something since I didn't get to eat my salad earlier," Kate smirked, glancing at Jerry.

"Yes, Doll, you never know it might be your last meal. So better get something to eat," he added.

"Jerry, stop it," Kate demanded, jabbing him in his upper arm.

"Okay, boys, as soon as you're finished eating, its hair and make-up," Kate suggested.

"Who wants to be first?"

"Guess I will," Drew answered.

"Kate, if Bruce asks where I am for the next hour or so, you better come up with something good. Something believable. I've got to go and talk with the security guys who are working the entry doors tonight. I need them to let me know if or when Mr. Aromdee's granddaughters arrive. I don't want Bruce to hear anything about this."

"Okay, Jerry, I understand. Good luck."

"Alright, Drew, are you ready? What did you boys decide on hair color for tonight? I think as late as it is now, you should stay with purple for tonight's performance. But I can always change your hair color tomorrow," Kate suggested.

"That's fine with me. I'm sure the guys won't have a problem with it."

Jerry nervously made his way to the front doors. Seeing Larry and the guys standing nearby, he took the opportunity to make them aware of his situation. The guys laughed till their sides hurt, listening to Jerry's explanation of the earlier incident.

"Okay, Jerry, don't worry. No one is getting through these doors tonight unless they have a ticket or have proved to be Mr. Aromdee's granddaughters," Larry stated.

As the doors opened, everything seemed to be going smoothly. However, no girls had shown up yet with a piece of paper from Kate having his name on it. After almost an hour of waiting, it seemed the girls perhaps were going to be no show after all. Hopefully, all the worry and getting upset was for nothing. However, only minutes later, four beautiful Thai girls approached Larry. They had in hand the signed paper from Kate. Larry immediately called Jerry over.

"Wow, so you girls are Mr. Aromdee's granddaughters?" Jerry smiled.

"Yes. Thank you so much for the tickets. We are huge fans of House of Cards. It's a dream come true to come to the concert tonight."

Jerry would feel like an idiot for inquiring, but he had to make sure.

"Are there more of you?" he asked nervously.

The girls looked at each other strangely, completely not understanding the question.

"More?" they asked.

"I mean, are you the only granddaughters of Mr. Aromdee? The only ones coming to the concert tonight?" he asked again.

"Yes, my name is May. These are my sisters, Ploy, Arisa, and Pim. Why do you ask?"

"Oh, never mind," Jerry replied, feeling immense relief.

"Larry, why don't you take these lovely girls down to the front? I'm sure they would like to be near the stage because they are huge fans. Oh, and stay near them. We don't want anything happening to them since they are our guests and will be standing in the mosh pit."

"Sure, Jerry. Girls, just follow me. The concert is almost ready to start," Larry informed them as he led them in the direction of the stage.

Wow, Jerry took a deep breath. It was over. Finally, he could relax. He could hardly wait to get backstage and let Kate know.

Harry walked on stage, taking his place behind the drums. As he began his intro, the fans started screaming out the name of the band and the guys. The noise level would probably have registered on the Richter scale as Cameron, Drew, and Doug walked on stage.

"Hello, Bangkok," Cameron shouted, holding his guitar high in the air.

"Good evening, Bangkok," Drew yelled. "It's so good to be here."

"Bangkok, are you ready to party," Doug screamed.

It was pure chaos as the flames shot upward from the front of the stage. As the fire began to dissipate slowly, it would only be moments later that fireworks would start to emerge on the giant screens behind the band. Colored lights crisscrossed the stage and vast audience. Bruce always ensured the fans enjoyed every moment of the concert. He figured it was his job to sell out the arenas and coliseums, and as long as the boys delivered one hell of a concert, things were fine in his world. Thankfully the guys had never let him down. It was a mutual love fest every night between the band and their devoted fans.

House of Cards kept the fans energized with their music for almost an hour and a half. As usual, it was pure pandemonium as the concert came to a close. No one wanted to leave. Ending with their last song, *Dark Riot*, the guys walked down to the front of the stage to say goodbye.

"Goodnight, Bangkok," Cameron shouted.

"Bangkok, we love you," Drew screamed.

"Thanks for coming out to party with us," Doug yelled.

"We love you, Bangkok," the guys all screamed in unison.

Jerry met the boys as they walked off stage.

"Hell of a concert tonight, boys. It was truly awesome."

Jerry was extremely relieved the night was over, walking back to find Kate.

"Well?" Kate asked as Jerry walked up.

"Doll, we're still employed," Jerry laughed. "Now, I need a drink."

"Whew, can't say that I wasn't a little nervous," she smiled.

"Alright, gang, what's the plan for tonight," Bruce inquired, entering the dressing room. "Oh, by the way, great concert tonight," he grinned.

"Well," Jerry stated, giving the boys a stern warning look. "I think they've decided to stay in for the night."

"What?" Harry freaked.

"Okay," Cameron mentioned, not daring to confront Jerry by asking why.

"Well, if that's what you boys want to do," Bruce mentioned.

"The limo is already at the back entrance. Let's go back to the hotel," Bruce suggested.

"Sounds good to me," Jerry grinned, staring at all the sad faces.

Arriving back at the hotel, the guys reluctantly made their way up to their rooms. None of them dared approach Jerry about going out later that evening.

Bruce always looked forward to a good drink after the concerts.

"So how about a nightcap," he asked, glancing at Jerry.

"Actually sounds pretty good."

"How about you, Kate."

"Sure, I definitely wouldn't turn you down."

Walking into the bar, Bruce was always predictable. Finding an empty table, Jerry pulled out a chair for Kate. As the waiter came over, the drinks never seemed to change, just the location of the bars.

"Great concert tonight, wasn't it?" Bruce grinned, taking a sip of JD.

"Yes, I'll say," Jerry mentioned picking up his drink.

"So Bruce, I forgot our schedule. Where are we booked next?"

"Oh, that would be Taiwan, but we're going to have a few down days before we play Taipei."

"Wow, guess I'm looking forward to that," Kate spoke up, taking a sip of wine.

"How's our girl doing back in Tokyo?" Bruce inquired.

"She's fine, Bruce, thanks for asking. Nicole has fallen in love with Tokyo."

"Well, I'm glad to hear that. Tell her Uncle Bruce says hello and sends his love the next time you talk with her."

"Sure thing," Kate smiled, taking a drink.

"Well, kids don't mean to cut this short, but I think I'm ready for bed," Bruce mentioned, finishing his drink.

"No problem. We won't be long behind you. It's been a long day," Jerry smiled.

"Okay, see you two tomorrow," Bruce said, standing to leave.

"Wow, well, everything turned out alright tonight," Jerry winked, reaching over to take Kate's hand.

"Yes. I knew it would. You panicked for nothing," Kate added.

"Mr. Aromdee only had four granddaughters. Can you believe it? They were not only nice, but they were also huge fans of the band. I let Larry take them down front to the mosh pit but made him keep an eye on them. Sure wouldn't have wanted anything to happen to them."

"Oh, you were convinced half of Bangkok would show up," Kate scolded.

"Okay, Babe, let's never mention this incident again."

"Fine with me, I'm getting tired. Are you finished with your drink?"

"Yes, let's go up to the room," Jerry smiled, grasping her hand.

The band finished their engagement in Bangkok without further incident. Bruce and the guys took the Lear Jet to Taiwan, while Jerry and Kate remained behind until the following day. Kate had no idea of the surprise which Jerry had arranged with Bruce's help.

Waking up the next morning, Kate began asking a lot of questions. However, Jerry's mind was fixated on only one question. Hopefully, her answer would be yes.

CHAPTER ELEVEN

Cabana Eighteen
The Question

Waking the following day, Kate had no idea of Jerry's plans. She only knew they were given a few days off to relax before the next scheduled performance in Taipei.

"Babe, are you finished packing?" Kate asked.

"Yes, almost. I just need to get my suit out of the closet and packed away in the suitcase."

"Okay, so where are we going? I know Bruce already left with the boys this morning on their way to Taiwan."

"Well, let's just say I have a surprise mini-vacation planned for us."

"Great. Where?"

"Well, if I told you, it wouldn't be a surprise. Trust me. You'll find out soon enough."

Closing the door, they were soon in the elevator and on their way down to the lobby.

Stepping outside the elevator, Kate heard someone calling Jerry by name.

"Mr. Godwin, your taxi is here," the valet said, picking up their suitcases."

"Thanks, right on time," Jerry answered, checking his watch.

"Wow, Babe, guess you do have it all planned," Kate smiled, stepping inside the cab.

"No more questions," he winked.

Almost an hour later, they arrived at the harbor. After depositing the luggage at the gateway, the cabbie quickly sped away.

Jerry looked up and smiled.

"Doll, we're taking a ferry boat ride. How does that sound?"

"Well, Jerry, where to would be my first question?"

"Here are the rules. You only get one question each day," he winked.

"We're going to Phuket."

"Wow. I've always wanted to visit Phuket, and when I found out we were coming to Thailand, I was hoping we could go. But I had no idea Bruce would give us a break between schedules. I figured it was several hours away and would be out of the question."

"So, does that mean you're excited?" Jerry winked.

However, once onboard and out on the open water, Kate wasn't so sure about the mode of transportation. The ferry encountered choppy seas, making her queasy. It seemed Bruce hadn't bothered to check the weather conditions.

"Jerry, I think I'm getting a little nauseated," Kate mentioned.

"Oh no, guess I hadn't exactly planned on that. Okay, let's get something to drink. I'll try and find you something for your seasickness."

About an hour after taking something for motion sickness, Kate began to feel somewhat better.

"Hey Babe, do you feel like eating? The food actually smells delicious?"

"Okay. I'll try."

Sitting by the window, Kate finally enjoyed the magnificent view. Watching as white caps crested the rolling waves, they dined on bowls of rice covered in chicken, onions, tomatoes, peppers, and yellow curry paste.

Glancing at Jerry, Kate smiled.

"Wow, Babe, I didn't mean to spoil your surprise getaway."

"Sweetheart, don't worry. Perhaps it would have been better to fly down, but I thought this would be a little more exotic. Knowing how you love to experience the local culture of every place we visit, I thought you would love traveling by boat."

"You're right. I'm usually up for experiencing everything our locations offer. That's what attracted me to working with Black Tie Affair. Also, I love living out of a suitcase."

"Well, I think you'll enjoy the rest of our trip. We should be arriving in about two hours. Hopefully before dark."

Once back in port, a limo from the resort arrived to pick them up.

"Okay, so what's next?" Kate smiled.

"Remember, you only get one question for today."

Unfortunately, it was dark upon their arrival. However, Jerry thought it could work in his favor to cloak their beautiful surroundings until morning discretely.

Stepping inside the car, Jerry quickly poured Kate a drink from the bar.

"Here, it's just what the doctor ordered," he laughed, handing her a vodka with orange juice.

"Wow, I think you're right. It's yummy plus relaxing, just what I need after stepping off the boat."

The limo entered the long narrow drive, which curved through tall palms and lush tropical foliage. Stopping under the stunning entrance, it was open to the night sky. Tall stone columns held honed wooden beams across the vaulted portico. Exiting the car, the chauffeur carried their luggage inside.

The foyer was exquisite, with modern décor and marble floors. Massive sliding doors were open to the back entrance. It revealed a lighted pathway down to the beach and the relaxing sound of waves gently rolling ashore.

Walking up to the reception desk, Jerry checked in, receiving the keys to their cabana.

"Babe, this place is gorgeous."

"Sir, if you'll meet us outside, your transportation is waiting. I'll have the suitcases brought out momentarily," the concierge replied.

"What? We're not staying here?" Kate frowned.

"Well, not exactly."

Waiting outside was an extra-long golf cart with two rows of seats.

Their luggage was immediately stored behind them as they stepped inside.

"You're in cabana 18. It's just a short drive down the beach. It's by far the best we have to offer and the most secluded."

The driver was right as they stopped in front of their cabana. It was the farthest from the main entrance and included a private pool and hot tub.

"Is there anything I can assist you with?" the driver asked as he unlocked their door, placing their luggage inside.

"No, but thank you," Jerry mentioned handing him a generous tip.

"Oh Jerry, I can't believe we have this all to ourselves."

"Doll, only for you," he smiled.

Walking out to the back patio to check out the pool, Jerry pulled her close, stopping to kiss her passionately.

"So Babe, the hot tub looks pretty amazing. What do you think?" he winked.

Sitting in the warm water under the evening sky, Kate looked up.

"Wow, the stars appear to be out in abundance tonight."

Kate's mind flashed back to the night in Paris when she and Nicky sat outside on the balcony under the stars and made their wish.

Putting his arms around, Nicky held her close.

"Babe, you know I've fallen in love with you. I love you more than you could know."

Before he could even kiss her came the response he had wished for.

"Jerry, I love you, too," Kate smiled, kissing him intensely.

Kate had no idea of the treasured box Jerry had secretly hidden within his luggage. If she only knew the real reason for their visit to Phuket. His heart was pounding.

"Babe, thanks for bringing me here. It's so romantic," Kate smiled, wiping tears from her eyes.

"Doll, here you go again with the waterworks. What is it with you?"

Jerry was most definitely Nicky's Italian counterpart.

Trying to erase her memories of Nicky, she had to keep him in the past. She needed to live in the present moment, which now included Jerry. She loved Jerry. There was no room for doubt.

"Guess I'm too emotional, you know that. But I can't help it. Guess it's why girls cry at movies or while reading a good book. It's part of our DNA. What makes us female," Kate smiled.

"Sweetheart, I love you and your silly quirks," Jerry winked. Then, taking his hand, he gently wiped her eyes.

Pulling her up from the hot tub, he carried her inside.

"Babe, I'm dripping with water."

"Hush," he softly whispered, laying her on the bed.

Wiping her entire body with warm towels, he covered her with kisses. Kate thought it was possibly the most romantic gesture she had ever experienced.

Turning off the lights, Cabana Eighteen was quickly the most sensual place on earth tonight. It held inside its walls two people madly in love.

As the morning sun rays flooded their room, Jerry was the first to wake. Staring at the beautiful woman who shared his bed, he couldn't take his eyes off her. This gorgeous girl who now slept so peacefully beside him with her black hair tousled over the pillow, draped only in satin sheets, took his breath away. In only a few short hours, hopefully, she would change his world forever. His heart raced, trying to imagine how he was going to make it through the next few hours. Finally, deciding to wake Sleeping Beauty, he leaned over, combing back her gorgeous long hair with his fingers. Softly kissing her face, she slowly woke from her slumber.

"Wow, Babe, what a night," Kate exclaimed, rolling over to kiss him.

"Yes, Doll, if these walls could talk," Jerry laughed.

Was it possible for two people to be so happy, so in love?

Sitting up in bed, he contemplated his dilemma of where to ask the most important question of his life, maybe over dinner later that evening or on the beach. However, his heart told him it most definitely would happen on the beach. After all, that was his reasoning for bringing Kate to Phuket.

"I'm starved," she smiled.

"Okay, I'll order breakfast. What would you like?"

"How about scrambled eggs, potatoes, bacon, and toast. Oh, don't forget coffee, lots of coffee."

"Wow, Babe, you must be starved," he teased.

It wasn't long before there was a knock at the door.

"Breakfast," the voice announced.

Eating on the patio, it overlooked the spectacular views of the azure blue water.

"So, Sweetheart, what would you like to do today? I was thinking of taking a ferry over to Ko Phi Phi. It's a small archipelago of six islands. I've heard they have the best snorkeling and gorgeous beaches. What do you think? Think you're up for it?"

"Sounds like fun, as long as it doesn't require a long ferry ride."

"It's only about three hours each way, what do you think? So we'll just make a day trip over and back. We only have one night left in Phuket. Then we're scheduled to leave out of Bangkok for Taiwan."

Jerry knew Bruce had already made the arrangements for a day trip which included snorkeling. He just needed to know that she was on board for the adventure. He hoped to arrive back later that night for a late dinner and stroll along the beach. It would be the surprise ending to a beautiful day. After eating, Jerry called for their ride down to the port at Ao Chalong Bay.

"Kate, just pack a small bag for the day. Babe, you're only going to need your swimsuit and a cover for the trip," he winked.

Walking outside to catch their ride, Jerry wasn't exactly shocked to see Kate pulling an oversized carry- on which looked as if it hardly closed.

"Geez, Doll, I told you a small bag," he smiled. "Really, Kate, all you needed was a swimsuit, cover, sunscreen, and your sunglasses."

"Jerry, clothes are a hard decision. I don't expect you to understand. For heaven's sake, I'm a stylist, remember," Kate laughed.

Arriving at the port, Bruce arranged a surprise that Jerry hadn't even been aware of. Handing over their tickets, they were amazed to find they were going on board a private yacht. Bruce had hired a luxury cruiser for their day trip over to the islands.

"Wow, Babe, Bruce is a class act. He's one of a kind," Jerry stated.

"I'll say, this is unbelievable," Kate smiled.

They were soon out of the bay and on their way. Kate went below to change. Now that she had a changing room, she was happy to have brought so many outfits. Emerging from below, Kate wore a tiny red halter bikini with her long dark hair pulled back into a ponytail. She took his breath away.

"Wow, Babe, okay, and yes, never listen to me." He had quickly become a blubbering idiot. "You're stunning," Jerry whistled.

"You're making me blush. Stop it," Kate laughed.

Today turned into one of those days you could only dream about, except for one thing, it was entirely real. Thanks to Bruce, the man was a genius.

Touring the islands of Phi Phi, they were taken ashore on a Dinghy that was kept on board the yacht. Hand in hand, they strolled along endless beaches of pure white sand, and at one point, they decided to take a swim through the crystal blue waters back to the yacht. Their day included snorkeling to view the habitats of some of the most beautiful fish on earth and a visit to James Bond Island. Unable to go ashore, they slowly drifted by, enjoying the scenic beauty of the tall limestone rock formations, some of which were covered in green vegetation. The beauty of the islands and the color of the water had to be seen to be appreciated. Words would never be enough to describe their detailed beauty. The day had been unbelievable, but now it was time to begin their journey back to Phuket.

The staff had prepared an extravagant dinner to be served on deck, slowing the boat to make their dining experience more pleasurable. Then, losing the sun from the day, they ate outside under the stars.

Kate walked out in an exquisite turquoise halter dress, with a thin flowing chiffon overlay and matching blue turban.

"Wow, Doll, I didn't think we were dressing for dinner," Jerry winked. Kate was exquisite, and her face radiated from the tan she had acquired.

Pulling out her chair, Jerry gently kissed her.

He was at a crossroads. The ring was with him all day, stored safely in his bag, and he had planned to propose back on the beach in Phuket. But somewhere in his heart, it seemed more surreal here. Slowly drifting with the gentle waves, it would be an unforgettable memory. His decision was finally made. They would enjoy the delicious array of food that had been brought out and set before them, along with wine. After dinner, he would ask for a bottle of champagne to be brought out. He could only hope by some slim chance there was one onboard. Putting down his fork, he excused himself to walk inside and check with the staff about the possibilities of having champagne onboard. Once again, it seemed Bruce had stepped in as if to read it his mind. The crew laughed, handing him a large bottle of the best French champagne money could buy.

"It's compliments of your friend, Mr. Weber," they happily informed him. "Now there's one more surprise. He's arranged to have fireworks after your meal. We have prepared everything for this special moment, with his good wishes. You must have a special connection to this gentleman. He was very strict on how his instructions were to be carried out, even to the song which he wants playing in the background during the fireworks."

Jerry laughed. It seemed Bruce knew him probably better than he knew himself. How would he ever be able to repay his extraordinary kindness?

"Okay, I'm going outside," Jerry informed the staff. "After my future fiancee finishes her meal, I'll take her to the upper deck. As soon as you see us leaving the table, give us a few minutes. I'm thinking about ten minutes at least, and then you can begin the fireworks."

"Oh sir, there is something more. Our staff will be putting lit candles abundantly throughout the stateroom and rose petals on the bed in the shape of a heart. Mr. Weber thought you might like to stay on board tonight, returning to Phuket early in the morning. Is that your desire?"

Wow, Bruce was a pro. As old as he might be, the man had exceptional taste. Once again, Jerry laughed, thinking of Bruce. Wherever he was tonight in Taipei, Jerry was sure he was smiling.

"Yes, most definitely, we'll stay the night. How could I ever disappoint my good friend, Bruce?" Jerry smiled.

Walking back to finish dinner, Kate was inquiring about his sudden disappearance.

"Jerry, is something wrong?"

"Oh, Babe, not at all. I was just checking on dessert," Jerry winked.

"How was dinner? Did you enjoy it?" Jerry asked, noting that she had almost finished eating.

"Yes. It was wonderful. How could it not be, sitting here with you under the stars in the middle of the ocean," Kate smiled.

"Well, how about dessert? The staff said they would serve us on the upper deck. Would you like to go up now?" Jerry asked, reaching for Kate's hand. It was his way of getting her up the steps to the top deck without asking too many questions.

"Yes, that actually sounds nice."

Following close to Jerry, Kate held tight to his hand as they made their way to the upper deck. Standing underneath a canopy of twinkling stars, they were exposed to the brilliance of the night sky. The gentle ocean breeze blew Kate's dress snugly against her body, exposing her slim frame. Pausing to stare at her, she took his breath away. Then reaching inside his jacket, Jerry was shaking. Trembling, he took her hand, looking straight into her eyes. He had never loved her more.

"Kate, remember the first day we left to make this trip, you had questions, and I told you that you only got one question a day," Jerry winked.

"Well, tonight, I have one question for you?"

Kate started crying, expecting what might be coming next.

Pulling the diamond ring from his pocket, he got down on one knee and opened the tiny box.

"Kate, Sweetheart, will you marry me?" Jerry asked.

"Yes. My answer is yes!" Kate exclaimed.

Then, placing the ring on her outstretched finger, it fit perfectly.

"Oh Jerry, it's beautiful. I love you," Kate cried, throwing herself into Jerry's outstretched arms.

Kissing passionately, they only stopped for a brief moment to watch as the fireworks exploded overhead. The fireworks shot upward into the night sky, displaying various colors and patterns as they slowly drifted back down toward the water.

"Jerry, how in the world did you arrange all of this," Kate questioned as they held each other in a tight embrace.

"Oh, it wasn't me. I would love to take credit for everything. It was Bruce, can you even believe it?"

"Yes, yes, I can. That man means the world to me. It's so fitting that he had a part in this. Bruce is the father I never had."

Just at that moment, *Because of You*, the song that made Black Tie Affair famous, filled the air.

"Wow, Babe, can you believe it. That song has always meant so much to me. Nicky wrote it for the boy's memorial concert in Rome."

"Yes, Doll, I know it pretty well. I think I've performed it at least a thousand times," Jerry winked.

Being held in Jerry's arms under the stars watching the fireworks, Kate never wanted the evening to end. It was sheer magic.

"Jerry, I love you so much," Kate cried as tears gentle cascaded down her face.

"Kate, you've made my world complete tonight. I was beginning to doubt if I would ever find that one special person. Someone who could share this crazy world that I live in," Jerry smiled, holding her in his arms.

"Well, Sweetheart, Bruce has arranged for us to spend the night in the stateroom below. Are you up for it?"

"Is that a question you even have to ask?" Kate wept, gazing at the ring on her left hand.

"Oh, Nicole, I almost forgot about her."

"We'll call Nicole in the morning. Right now, we're going to check out the stateroom," Jerry winked, scooping Kate into his arms.

Jerry carried her down the steps and through the main cabin toward the impressive bedroom below.

Walking inside, the smell of lit candles and fresh flowers infused the room.

"Oh, wow, look at the bed," Kate smiled. It's covered in rose petals forming a heart.

"Jerry, this is unbelievable. Is this really real?"

Walking over to the bed, Jerry gently laid Kate on top of the sprinkled rose petals. Beside the bed sat a Magnum of Moet & Chandon White Star Extra Dry Champagne and two fluted glasses. Popping the cork, Jerry filled the glasses. Then, handing a glass to Kate, he made a toast.

"Doll here's to you, the love of my life, soon to be my wife," Jerry toasted with tears welling within his eyes.

"Now, Babe, look who's crying now."

"Babe, I'll love you forever. Here's to our wedding day," Kate said with tears streaming down her face.

After downing several glasses of the sparkling drink, Kate began to feel dizzy.

"Geez, Jerry, I've had so much champagne that being on a yacht in the middle of the ocean isn't a worry," Kate smiled.

Pulling back the impeccable duvet, Kate once again was fully clothed.

"Wow, Sweetheart, I think we should break your tradition of sleeping in your clothes," Jerry laughed.

Carefully untying her stunning turquoise halter, he gently kissed her neck.

However, Kate was out like a light bulb from the champagne. Jerry slipped into bed next to her. With unexpected tears gently caressing his face, he had the love of his life next to him. She had said yes.

CHAPTER TWELVE

Love is in the air

As the plane made its final approach into Taipei International Airport, Jerry had to wake the beautiful girl who slept peacefully with her head rested against his chest.

"Babe, we're almost here," he whispered, gently pulling her long hair away from her eyes.

"Oh no, it's over."

"Yes. I'm afraid it's back to work for both of us. We can't stay on vacation forever," Jerry frowned. Besides, I can't wait to see Bruce. There's no telling what those boys have been up to while we were away."

"Holding out her left hand," Kate smiled. "I can't wait for everyone to see my exquisite souvenir."

"Sweetheart, I love you," Jerry winked, taking a closer look at the ring she wore on her left hand. He now felt completely confident with his purchase.

Once inside the terminal, they quickly found the Mass Rapid Transit System, taking them into Taipei. Sitting next to the window for the ride downtown, Kate began to wonder why it seemed that Bruce had put Taiwan on their schedule after Bangkok. It seemed an odd order to her.

"Hey, Babe, was there any particular reason Bruce chose Taiwan to be our next stop on the schedule?"

"Oh, I really don't know. It probably had more to do with availability dates than the actual location. Who knows, Bruce hands me the schedule, and most often, I just glance at it before putting it away in my briefcase. However, I do know that we are staying at the Grand Hotel."

Later arriving at the hotel, it was magnificent. It had classic Chinese architecture and was supported by red columns with gold roof tiles. Located midway up the Yuanshan, it appeared like a majestic fourteen-story palace.

"Wow, this place is incredible," Kate gasped, stepping out of the taxi.

A massive red-carpeted staircase with an oversized vase of flowers sitting at the entrance welcomed them as they walked inside. It was stunningly decorated with Asian-inspired furnishings. On the wall, an enormous mural depicted various colored dragons. Checking in with the reception desk, they soon had their room keys.

"Bruce has us booked into a suite on the sixth floor. It appears that he and the boys are on the same floor. As soon as we're settled, I've got to check in with the boys. So let's go up and check out the room. The concierge will bring our bags up in a few minutes."

The room was impressive as they entered their suite. Modern furniture and décor filled the space with aspects of Asian accents. In addition, the large windows gave a unique view of the Keelung River.

"Doll, I'm going to check on the boys and see if Bruce is in his room. I won't be gone long."

"Take your time. I think I might just take a nap before dinner," Kate smiled.

Catching Jerry before he walked out the door, Kate gave him a quick kiss. However, it quickly became hot and passionate.

"Wow, Sweetheart, on second thought, maybe I'll just wait until later."

"Jerry, go to work," Kate laughed.

Knocking at Cameron's door, he answered.

"Hey Jerry, how was Phuket?" Cameron asked.

"Maybe I should wait and let Kate answer that one."

"Okay. So what happened?" Cameron teased.

"Well, I proposed on our last night. Thank God she said yes. It was unbelievable. The best two days of my life."

"Congratulations, man," Cameron laughed. "Actually, I already knew. We all knew. Bruce can't keep secrets. On the flight over from Bangkok, he let us in on his plans."

"So everyone knows?"

"Yes. But we're all happy for you both. It wasn't like we didn't see it coming. It was easy to see that you two were in love. So when's the big day?"

"Oh, we haven't planned that far ahead yet. First, I want to check the band's schedule with Kate. Then, maybe we'll all fly to Hawaii. It's one of Kate's favorite places, or maybe Paris. Kate spent every summer in Paris before she signed on as the stylist with Black Tie Affair."

"Well, wherever you decide, I'm sure it's going to be beautiful. I just happen to know of a great rock band for the reception."

"Funny Cameron, I just wanted to stop by and see how things went while we were away. Did Flame behave himself?"

"Yes. Don't worry, Jerry, things have been great, except for one small detail."

"Okay, what happened?" Jerry panicked. "I just knew it. I knew something would probably happen as soon as you guys left Bangkok."

"Oh, it's nothing like that, nothing major. It seems that you're not the only one who's fallen in love," Cameron laughed.

"What?" Jerry asked. "Let me rephrase that, "Is it one of the boys?"

"Yes. It's Doug, and maybe it's time you stop referring to him as a boy. He's twenty-three."

"That's beside the point. What happened? Who is she? Where did he meet her?"

"Calm down, Jerry. I don't think you have a monopoly on falling in love. Well, you know how much Bruce likes to eat at great restaurants."

"Yes. Get on with it."

"While you were gone, we naturally had to placate Bruce by eating wherever he recommended. So the first night, we all went out to this great place on the Danshui River. I think it was called Chun's Chinese Restaurant. To make a long story short, she was one of the servers. Flame and I kept noticing that she took her sweet time getting his order. Every time she came over to our table to refill our glasses or inquire if we needed anything, they kept staring at each other. By the end of the night, it was easy to see that something was going on between those two. So as we were leaving, I saw Doug write down the name of the hotel where we were staying. He slipped it into her hand. Of course, it was definitely none of my business, so there was no way in hell that I would mention it to Bruce.

Here's where it gets weird, it's not like Bruce ever wants to eat at the same restaurant twice. So guess where we ate last night, Chun's Chinese Restaurant. Bruce kept raving about their sumptuous array of local delicacies, so naturally, we weren't going to dispute restaurants with the boss. Now I'm not saying he did this to appease Doug. Who knows, maybe Bruce really did fall in love with the food at their establishment. However, Doug fell in love, and it wasn't with their menu," Cameron laughed.

"Cameron love is a pretty strong term."

"Well, Jerry, go figure, she's in Doug's room."

"What?" Jerry freaked out.

"Oh, Jerry, come on. Are you trying to make me think you guys were saints as members of Black Tie Affair? I've heard wild stories from Dad. He told me Bruce's policy was that he considered the guys consenting adults. If their relationships didn't affect the concerts and they kept it low-key and out of the tabloids, Bruce stayed out of their affairs."

"Okay. I guess you've got me there," Jerry paused.

How could he dispute what Cameron was saying? If he only knew the truth about Nicky and the girls who were in and out of his bed after leaving Middleton. Nicky's affairs while living in Hollywood were not only notorious, they were legendary. It was Déjà vu, as he remembered his days as a member of Black Tie Affair. However, this was definitely a discussion for another day. A much later day, hopefully.

"So, what's her name?"

"It's Alondra. She's cute and actually really nice."

"So I guess the main question is, does Bruce know she's in his room?"

"Yes, but here's the deal, Jerry. You can't let Bruce know what I'm about to tell you, do you understand?"

"What? There's more?"

"After we left the restaurant the other night and came back to the hotel, Doug left to meet Alondra at a local bar downtown. It was late at night, and I'm sure no one recognized him. However, the boys and I were talking about it. We don't want Doug to get into trouble. We can't snitch on him, so maybe you could bring up the fact that he doesn't need to be wandering around Taipei at night."

"Oh, you don't have to worry about that. I'll be discreet. He'll never know that we talked."

Remembering back to the night Nicky was slashed at the Ta Lat night market, Jerry couldn't take any chances with Doug.

"Well, I'm back now, so let me know what you guys would like to do while we're in Taipei. I should go and see if Bruce happens to be in his room. I need to check with him about our schedule. So don't worry, our talk will not leave this room."

Jerry knew there would never be a reason to bring up Doug's relationships, especially since Bruce was aware she was staying in his room. But Cameron was right. Bruce did stay out of the guy's private lives. Bruce had managed so many rock bands over his expansive career, and it was simply par for the course.

Hearing a knock at his door, Bruce quickly answered.

"Well, I guess congratulations are in order," he stated, patting Jerry on the back as he walked in. "Come in and sit down. How was Phuket?"

"Oh Bruce, it was amazing. Kate and I could never thank you enough for everything you did. We truly appreciate your kindness."

"Oh son, it was nothing. I hope everything went as planned."

"It was incredible. I don't know how you pulled it off. The private yacht and fireworks were spectacular."

"Well, I had to do something for my favorite couple. So I'm thinking Kate's answer was yes.

"Yes, Bruce, it was. Sorry I didn't mention it when I first walked in. I couldn't imagine my life right now if her answer had been no.

"Well, I don't think that would've ever happened. I see the way she looks at you. I'm very happy for you both. Okay, let's talk business. We have two concerts here in Taipei. I'll need the boys dressed and at the sports complex early tomorrow evening. I've got my publicity rounds to make tomorrow. As usual, I'm going to let the radio stations give a few lucky fans a chance to have their photos made with the band."

"Okay. Sounds great," Jerry smiled, leaving. "Thanks again, Bruce. Kate and I will never forget what you did for us. Speaking of Kate, I guess I better get back to the room. I told her I wouldn't be long, and I know you probably have things to do."

"Oh, by the way, I found a great little Chinese Restaurant. Perhaps, we can all eat there later tonight," Bruce grinned.

"Alright, I'll check with the guys. See you later this evening," Jerry grinned, closing the door.

He could never imagine Bruce eating more than once at the same restaurant. Wow. Three times had to set a record.

Unlocking the door, Kate lay peacefully sleeping on the king-size bed. Walking over, he gently kissed her awake.

"Wow, Doll, I just knew something would happen while I was away."

"Really. We were only gone for two days. But, seriously, Jerry, you're telling me those boys managed to stir up trouble in such a short period. Don't tell me it involved Harry again?" Kate yawned.

"No, and I guess it wasn't exactly trouble."

"Okay, so what happened?"

"Well, it seems Doug met someone while we were gone and that someone is now sleeping in his room."

"Does Bruce know?" Kate laughed.

"Yes. It seems they met at a Chinese Restaurant where Bruce took the boys to have dinner one evening. She was the server, and if you're to believe Cameron's spin on things, it must have been love at first sight."

"So does this someone have a name," Kate giggled.

"Yes, it's Alondra."

"That's actually a pretty name. But, Jerry, you do realize these boys are not exactly boys. You should have seen this one coming. They're not monks. Surely, you haven't forgotten what it was like being a member of Black Tie Affair. I know you came on board after Randy and Alex's tragic accident, but those two always had girls in and out of their rooms. Unfortunately, as a result, two young girls died in that crash."

"Oh, I know, and that was terrible. I don't know how Bruce does it. I suppose I'm beginning to see things from a different perspective."

"Well, Jerry, the best advice that I can give you is to learn from Bruce. As a manager, he's always stayed out of the band members' personal lives except for the use of hard drugs. He's not paying you to be their father, just to make sure they arrive on time and give a stellar performance. Have you decided where we're going to have dinner this evening?" Kate smiled, changing the subject of their conversation.

"Maybe we should check out Chun's Chinese Restaurant. If Bruce has eaten there more than once, it's got to be great. I'll call over to Cameron's room and see if the guys are ordering in tonight."

Just as he was about to pick up the phone, it rang.

"Hey Jerry, it's Nicole. Is mom there?"

"Yes, is everything alright?"

"Yes. I just need to talk to her."

"Okay, just a minute. Kate, it's Nicole."

"Hey, Sweetheart, are you okay?"

"Yes, Mom, but I've been giving a lot of thought about my career in modeling. As much as I love what I do, I miss being with everyone. I miss the excitement of being around the guys. So please don't be mad, but I've already given my notice. I'm arriving in the morning."

"Wow, Sweetheart, you've caught me off guard with your decision to give up modeling. Are you sure you want to give up on a career that you've just started?"

"Yes. Mom, I don't expect you to understand. We'll talk tomorrow. I have to go. Oh, don't bother coming to the airport. I'll get a taxi to the hotel. Love you."

"Love you too, Sweetheart, see you tomorrow."

"So, what was that all about?" Jerry inquired.

"You're not going to believe this, but Nicole has decided to quit her modeling career. She'll be here tomorrow."

"Geez, that sounds awfully sudden. Do you think she's really given this enough thought?"

"Well, if you ask me, I think there's something else going on. Guess we'll know more tomorrow."

"Yes. I suppose we will. Let me check to see if the guys want to eat out or stay put for the evening."

Calling Cameron's room, it seemed the boys had decided to order room service. They were not the least bit interested in returning to Chun's for the third night in a row. However, knowing that it had strangely become Bruce's favorite place to eat, Jerry decided to invite him.

Walking inside Chun's later that evening, its location on the river along with its impeccable Asian décor created a unique ambiance. Large windows reflected gorgeous views of the river, candles sat glowing on each table, and vibrant paper lanterns hung exquisitely from the ceilings.

"Bruce, it's beautiful. No wonder you like coming here," Kate smiled.

"Well, just wait until you taste the cuisine. I love the Gongbao Chicken. Its stir-fried chicken with chili and peanuts and also their Peking duck is fabulous."

"Think I'll have Dimsum," Jerry mentioned. "What looks appetizing to you?" Jerry asked, glancing at Kate.

"Oh, I think I'll have the Xiaolongbao steamed dumplings stuffed with pork."

After consuming their sumptuous meal, the conversation quickly became one of talk about the guys and Nicole's sudden decision to leave modeling.

"Bruce, after talking with Cameron this afternoon, I'm sure you're aware of the girl whom Douglas has supposedly fallen in love with. I believe her name is Alondra," Jerry inquired.

"Yes. Doug met Alondra in this restaurant. But I don't think they're that serious, probably more of an infatuation. Doug is experiencing a new culture, and Alondra just happens to be beautiful and exotic. I can't say that I blame

"Well, you do know she's staying in his room?"

"Yes, son, I do know about that. But you know, from working with me in the past, I stay out of the boys' personal lives. So I figure that's best left to them."

"All right, I just wanted to touch base with you concerning her staying in the hotel."

"Bruce, I got a rather peculiar call from Nicole this afternoon. She's decided to quit modeling after only a few short weeks, and she's arriving in the morning. So I'll need to get her a room here at the hotel," Kate mentioned.

"I've already taken care of it. Nicole is booked into the suite right across the hall from the boys."

"How did you know?" Kate asked, completely baffled.

"Oh, Nicole called me earlier this afternoon as well," Bruce smiled. "She told me about her decision to quit modeling and even asked for my advice. You know how much I love that girl."

"So what did you tell her? What kind of advice did you offer?"

"Slow down. I'm sure there's a little more to this story than you know."

"Yes. I kind of sensed that. I am her mother, for heaven's sake."

"Well, Sweetheart, just because you're someone's mother doesn't always mean they come to you for advice. But, I guess since we're all here together, you and Jerry should know."

"Know what?" Kate demanded.

"That she's in love with Drew. She's been in love with that boy since she met him at the memorial concert."

"What? That's impossible. I'm sure I would know if my daughter was in love with someone."

"Well, you seem pretty surprised. But, listen, Kate, I've known about this for a while but figured it wasn't my place to tell you. Drew is a great guy. Sure he's a little older than the other boys but very grounded, and he's got a great work ethic."

"So, does everyone know? Jerry, did you know?" Kate asked, perturbed.

"No, Babe, I swear. This is the first I've heard about this."

"Yes, Kate, all the boys know. Do you really think they could pull that off without the guys noticing?" Bruce laughed. "Nicole actually stayed in Tokyo longer than I expected, don't be so upset. If memory serves, I do believe you and Nicky fell in love not long after you first met. Look, Sweetheart, what I'm trying to say is that sometimes I think you and Jerry consider these boys to be just that, boys. These guys are young men. Young men fall in love with beautiful girls," Bruce laughed, pushing back his chair from the table. Nicole is gorgeous," he winked. "Did you honestly think for one second that one of the guys wouldn't notice?" Bruce grinned, relighting his cigar.

"Well, I guess I never gave it much thought."

"I think the best advice that I can give you is to let her tell you in her way. Don't be upset because you weren't the first one to know. I've been giving a lot of thought to Nicole and her future. Kate, she's a lot like you. She is very independent. She loves the madness of being connected to the guys on tour. Let's face it. Not everyone loves the nomadic lifestyle as we do. Living out of a suitcase, in different hotels and countries isn't everyone's idea of a great life. Kate, I'm not getting any younger, and neither are you or Jerry. I think Nicole would make one hell of a great manager for any band. So if she's interested, and believe me, I think she is, Jerry and I will start introducing her to what it takes to keep this show on the road, so to speak. After all, you have to remember who her father was," Bruce smiled. "Jerry, what I've said here doesn't take anything away from the awesome job you're doing and will continue doing. Trust me. There's plenty of work to go around. So Kate, when are you going to show me that ring of yours," he laughed, putting down his cigar.

Getting back to their room later that night, Kate fell onto the bed, pulling Jerry down next to her.

"So, what did you think of what Bruce said at dinner this evening?"

"Well, as I've always said, Bruce is very insightful. He's been in this business for a long time, and you don't get to where he's at unless you're able to read people very well. He's astute, and if he thinks Nicole has what it takes, then I think you can take that to the bank, literally speaking."

"Alright, it's just that all of this has happened so suddenly."

"Sweetheart, I know, but kids do grow up, and we have to let Nicole find her path in life. After all, I believe you started out wanting to be a travel agent, right," Jerry winked. "So the way I see it, she gave up modeling to follow her guy around the world, and perhaps one day she just might wind up filling Bruce's shoes. Now that's something to think about," he grinned. So stop your worrying and come over here and let me put that smile back on your face."

Turning off the light, the worries from the day gently faded away.

Waking up as their room was brightly infused with the morning sun, Jerry kissed her awake.

"Morning, Babe, it's getting late. I think we better get up, shower, dress, and order breakfast. Nicole will be arriving today."

"Geez, I almost forgot about Nicole. Why don't you order breakfast while I jump in the shower?"

"Okay, so what sounds good this morning?"

"How about two eggs sunny side up, toast and coffee."

"Alright, did Nicole say what time she would arrive?"

"No. She didn't give any specifics."

"Well, I was just wondering. I thought I would check with the guys to see if they would like to venture out of the hotel today. Maybe she would like to go along if her flight arrives in time. Also, don't forget the guys have a photoshoot before the concert tonight."

Kate's hair was wrapped in a turban as she walked out of the shower, and her face was covered entirely in a green facial mask, leaving only her eyes and mouth exposed.

"Wow, Doll, you're stunning in green," Jerry winked, walking over to kiss her. "Babe, do you think you can eat with that goo all over your face?"

"Jerry, it isn't goo. It just happens to be a great way to reduce wrinkles and moisturize your skin."

"But Babe, you don't have wrinkles."

"Well, after yesterday and being so stressed, I'm not taking any chances," Kate smiled, taking a sip of coffee.

After a leisurely breakfast, Jerry decided to check on the guys.

"Doll, I'm going over to Cameron's room. Suppose I should check on them and make sure Doug didn't leave the hotel again."

"Okay. Hopefully, Nicole will be here before long."

Hearing a knock at his door, Cameron quickly walked over to open it.

"Hey Cameron, thought I'd check to see if you guys would like to go downtown or visit one of the markets today before the concert?"

"That sounds good, but isn't Nicole arriving today?"

"How did you know?"

"Well, perhaps it's the fact that Drew and Nicole talk almost every night on the phone for hours or the fact that he left the hotel this morning to meet her at the airport."

"He did what? When did he leave?" Jerry fumed.

"Oh, early this morning, he came by my room about 6:00 a.m."

"Hell, first it was Doug disappearing late at night, and now you're telling me Drew left early this morning. Do you guys want me to lose my job?" Jerry freaked. "As soon as Drew returns, get all the guys in your room. We're going to have a meeting of the minds. Let's just hope that he doesn't get recognized. He has no security with him. If the paparazzi discover him and photos get out, Bruce will kill all of us. Cameron, I'm not trying to vent at you, really I'm not. It just seems that Doug and now Drew seem to be looking for trouble. I'll be back as soon as Nicole arrives."

There was no place to go. It was too early to go down to the bar in the lobby. So Jerry figured he would go back to the room and raid the mini-bar to help erase his fears.

Opening the door, he heard squeals of laughter. Drew was standing with his arms around Nicole. She was hysterical seeing Kate.

"Hey Nicole, it's so good to have you back," Jerry mentioned walking over to give her a quick kiss. But, drew, I need to speak with you at once, outside," Jerry demanded.

Jerry's anger was visceral, closing the door.

"Look, Jerry, I know what you're going to say. I know I broke the band's protocol by leaving the hotel without security or informing you, and I know how upset you must be. Still, I had to meet Nicole at the airport."

"No, Drew, you didn't have to meet her. Let's get this straight. You chose to meet her. What is it with you guys lately? I come back from Phuket, and you guys are making up your own rules. Listen, I know how it feels to be in love, but the band's policy is very clear about security while on tour. Maybe something could have been worked out if you had just come and asked. Bruce could've arranged the limo. You wouldn't have had to take public transportation. So I'm assuming you weren't recognized."

"Well, not exactly," Drew smiled, stroking his Mohawk. I think I'm pretty much a dead ringer as a member of House of Cards. But airport security stepped in and kept the girls at a distance until we could make our escape into a taxi."

"Damn, you got lucky this time. I'll give you a few minutes with Nicole. Afterward, I'm calling a meeting in Cameron's room, and we're going to get a few things straight, do you understand?"

"Yes, Jerry," Drew agreed, following him back inside the room.

"Congratulations, I just saw Mom's ring. It's gorgeous," Nicole beamed as she ran over to give Jerry a giant hug. Mom was just telling me how Uncle Bruce arranged the private yacht and fireworks. It sounds so romantic."

"Your mother has made me the happiest guy on earth," Jerry winked.

"Well, you've certainly got my blessings," Nicole smiled, giving him another hug.

"Kate, Drew, and I will leave you girls alone to catch up on things. I've got a meeting with the guys. It shouldn't take that long," Jerry explained, giving Kate a quick kiss. "Come on, Drew," Jerry demanded.

"Jerry, please don't give Drew a hard time. It's my fault. I begged him to meet me at the airport," Nicole sheepishly grinned.

Knocking once again at Cameron's door, he instantly answered.

"Great, it appears everyone is already here. Look, guys, I'm trying to keep my cool and not lose it right now. When you signed up for the tour, I thought Bruce had made it explicitly clear what the ground rules were. Also, each of you signed a contract stating the rules while on tour and out of the country. I'm going to refresh your memory regarding the rule that says no band member is to leave the group without security or informing Bruce or myself. You are highly visible with your Mohawks, tattoos, and facial piercings. Also, there's the fact your photos as members of the band are plastered everywhere. I know you're all grown adults and over the age of twenty-one, and I'm not trying to treat you like children. That's not my intent. Bruce hired enough security to hopefully not encounter any problems while out of the country. So from this point on, if you feel the need to escape, you better damn well let one of us know. Also, while I have everyone here, a word of warning about the night markets in Taipei, they're not a safe place to be. Years ago, we were here with Black Tie Affair, and Nicky almost lost the vision in his eye. Hell, his decision to chase after a kid who had stolen his wallet almost cost him his life. Without him knowing, the kid had a machete. He came darn close to dying that night. I'm sure Cameron is familiar with that story. So enough said, let's have some fun today. Did any of you have any particular places you wanted to visit while in Taipei, like the Lungshan Temple?"

"Well, actually, as crazy as this may sound, we had planned on staying in today. However, we want to go to the Ta Lat, the night market, before leaving. So we have to visit there. We've heard all the stories, now we have to leave our mark there," Flame instantly interjected.

"Okay. I'll schedule a limo to take you guys before we leave. Even though you know the dangers, it can be arranged with security. That's it for me. I'm going back to my room. Oh, before I forget, Bruce needs you to arrive early tonight. There's another photo opportunity for fans."

Opening the door to his room, Jerry found Kate and Nicole sitting on the sofa chatting away.

"So did you read the boys the riot act," Kate smiled.

"Oh, no, Jerry, I hope you didn't. But, really, it was my fault," Nicole frowned.

"I had to remind them of the rules, that's all," Jerry laughed. "So what have you girls been up to? Nicole, it's good to have you back."

"Thanks, Jerry. I'm excited over the fact that you and Mom are getting married. So Mom, when is the big day?"

"Well, we haven't exactly set a date yet. Whenever the band's schedule opens up, I guess."

"Nicole, tell us about your relationship with Drew. That took us by surprise," Jerry inquired.

"I know. We hadn't meant not to tell anyone. The guys have known since the beginning."

Just at that moment, there was a knock at the door.

"Hey, Jerry, is Nicole still here?"

"Wow, your timing is impeccable. Come in. We were just discussing your relationship with Nicole."

Walking over Drew, took a seat on the sofa next to Nicole.

"Well, to be honest, I loved her the moment I first saw her. I know that might sound corny and unbelievable, but just look at her. She's gorgeous."

"Drew, you're making me blush. Stop."

"Babe, I don't mean to make you blush, just speaking the truth."

"Mom, it's mutual. I couldn't stand to be away from him. I hope you're not mad at me for giving up on my modeling career so soon. I'm in love with this crazy guy," Nicole smiled, leaning over to kiss him.

"Nicole, if you're both happy, then Jerry and I are happy. We only wish the best for you."

"Thanks, Mom. We are truly happy."

"Thanks, Kate. I'm totally in love with your daughter."

"Well, I suppose that makes us one big happy family now, doesn't it?" Jerry retorted.

"Listen, Jerry, Mom and I were the only family we had except for Bruce and my aunt. I always wanted brothers and sisters. I'm so happy that you and Drew are part of our lives."

"Wow, Jerry, now that you and Kate are engaged, maybe there's still a chance of Nicole finally having those sisters and brothers," Drew laughed.

"I don't think so, Drew," Kate laughed. "After all, we have you guys to look after."

"Yes, and that can be a bit much," Jerry added. "Well, if the guys are staying in for the day, why don't we go downtown and find a place to have lunch."

"Oh, that sounds nice," Nicole agreed.

"Drew, before I forget, what do you know about Alondra?"

"Who's Alondra?" Nicole asked.

"Oh, she's Doug's girlfriend. Well, he met her the first night Bruce took us to Chun's Chinese Restaurant. She was our server that night. All I know is that Doug is crazy over her, and she's been staying in his room. She seems nice, and the boys and I like her."

"Well, if she's planning on accompanying him to the concert tonight, he should let Bruce know."

"Oh, I'm sure she will. They seem inseparable right now."

"Let's go eat. I'm starved," Kate suggested. "You can talk shop later."

Later that evening, everyone was dressed and ready to go to the Sports Complex. Stepping out of the elevator, Alondra held tightly to Doug. She was petite and thin with long dark hair. Her Asian complexion was stunning. She was pretty, but it appeared she felt shy and out of place.

"Hi, I'm Alondra," she smiled timidly.

"It's nice to meet you. I'm Nicole. I'm sure Doug told you my mom, Kate, is the stylist for the band. She's engaged to Jerry Godwin, the assistant manager for the band. They should be down in a few minutes. I'll introduce you to them."

"Thanks. Do you work with the band?"

"Oh no, well, at least not yet," Nicole mentioned.

It wasn't long before Jerry, Kate, Cameron, and Harry stepped out of the elevator, making their way over to where Drew, Nicole, Doug, and Alondra were standing.

"Mom and Jerry, this is Alondra. She's with Doug."

"Nice to meet you," Kate smiled.

"Okay, gang, we should be going. I'm sure the limo is waiting. Bruce needs you guys there early tonight. He's arranged another photo opportunity with you."

Shortly arriving at the back entrance to the Sports Complex, the long line of fans waiting to get in covered two city blocks.

"Wow. You have a lot of fans," Alondra gasped. "You are very popular in Taipei. We love your music."

Thankfully, golf carts waited for them as they entered through the large steel doors.

"Okay. This is great. Everyone take one of the carts and follow Kate and me," Jerry suggested.

"Jerry, do you know which direction leads to the dressing room?" Kate questioned as they sped away.

"No, but how hard can it be. We'll simply follow the hallways until we find it," Jerry laughed.

Stopping one of the security guards, he assured Jerry and the gang they were going in the right direction.

"Just at the end of the long hallway," he pointed.

Walking inside, the aromas of cooked food, along with the smell of fresh flowers, permeated the room. It wasn't long before Bruce walked in with the photographer and six fans whose names were chosen to win a photo with the band.

"Okay, guys, please come over and let me introduce you to our special guests."

After making the introductions, the fans eagerly took turns having their photo's taken with the guys. Bruce had extra T-shirts on hand with the band's logo on them. He made sure each fan left with an extra souvenir.

"Let's eat," Bruce announced after the room was vacated.

"Well, it's nice to have two young ladies with us tonight," Bruce smiled, glancing at Nicole and Alondra. "I'll have Jerry take you both down front to the stage before the concert starts. Larry, one of our security guards, will be close by if things get out of hand."

The display of love and affection was evident between Doug and Alondra as he explained the progression of the concert.

"Wow, Jerry, it does appear that Doug is fond of her," Kate whispered.

After Kate finished hair and make-up, the guys only had a few minutes until showtime.

"Okay, guys, go out there and give them one hell of a concert. After all, that's why we're here," Bruce grinned, lighting one of his smelly cigars.

Walking Nicole and Alondra down the long narrow corridor, Larry escorted them in the direction of the mosh pit.

"This is exciting," Alondra giggled.

"Yes. The guys always give a stellar performance. They're very talented," Nicole smiled.

Harry walked out and took his place behind the drums. Only moments later, the guys walked out. Flames shot upward from the edge of the stage. The fans were always ecstatic at this point.

"Hello, Taipei," Cameron shouted.

"Good evening, Taipei," Drew yelled, holding his guitar high in the air.

"We're so happy to be here," Doug added, screaming out his affection for the fans.

The concert would not disappoint this evening. As usual, an incredible display of fireworks was shown on giant screens that covered the stage's backdrop.

Fans began screaming their affections to the guys as Cameron led into their first song of the evening.

Nicole blew a kiss toward Drew as he made eye contact with her. She was madly in love with this crazy guy sporting a Mohawk, wearing ripped jeans, black boots, and a sleeveless T-shirt.

The guys performed for over an hour and a half, their usual time spent on stage. It was mayhem as their fans screamed and danced with raised hands high into the air with the rhythmic beat of the music. It was hypnotic. However, as always, it seemed the concert was over too soon.

"Good night, Taipei," Cameron screamed.

"Thanks for coming out," Drew yelled.

"We love you, Taipei," Doug shouted.

"So what did you think of the concert," Nicole asked Alondra as the boys left the stage.

"It was fun," she laughed.

"Well, let's see if we can manage to get through the crowd. Then, we'll go backstage to the dressing room."

Seeing their dilemma of maneuvering through the immense crowd, Larry came over to ease their transition out of the mosh pit. Then, finally, they were safely backstage. Walking into the dressing room, Alondra anxiously ran over to Doug wrapping her arms around him, hugging him intensely.

Drew came over and quickly kissed Nicole.

"So, Babe, see what you've been missing," he teased.

"Not any longer," Nicole smiled admiringly.

"Boys, that was a great concert tonight," Bruce announced, walking into the dressing room puffing away on another cigar. So let's all celebrate at Chun's Chinese Restaurant. The limo is out back," Bruce grinned.

"Wow," Kate giggled. "If I didn't know Bruce Weber, I'd almost say he was drunk," she laughed. "Jerry, you don't think he's beginning to get Alzheimer's, do you? Did you hear him say that he wants to eat at Chun's again?"

Staring at each other, they both laughed hysterically.

"Seriously, Jerry, I think this makes four times in a row Bruce has eaten at Chun's." Kate laughed so hard she buried her head against Jerry's chest to hide her embarrassment.

"Well, Doll, I don't know about Alzheimer's, but the food wasn't bad, that's for sure. I could eat there again," Jerry winked.

"Oh Jerry, you're crazy, you're turning into Bruce. You better not light up one of those Cuban cigars," Kate insisted.

The evening turned into an unforgettable night at Chun's. Everyone seemed to be enjoying themselves, especially Bruce.

House of Cards played their last concert in Taipei to a sold out crowd the following night. The guys managed to visit the night market without incident. Their time in Taiwan, even though short and problematic, seemed pleasurable. It appeared love was in the air, placing the guys under its spell, making them willing to risk everything.

CHAPTER THIRTEEN

Shock and Awe

Arriving in Manila, the flight seemed long and tiring. As the Lear Jet slowly rolled to a complete stop, Jerry woke Kate.

"Wow, Jerry, I was in the middle of a wonderful dream," Kate yawned, stretching her arms.

"Well, Babe, guess you'll have to continue that at the hotel," Jerry laughed, reaching overhead for their bags.

Stepping inside the limo, Bruce enthusiastically announced the resort he had secured for their stay in Manila.

"Kids, you're going to love this place. I've managed to reserve an entire resort. It's beautifully tucked away on a small secluded island. Each of you will have a private cabana on the beach where you can go to sleep listening to the soothing sounds of the waves washing ashore. You'll also be able to walk directly out your door every morning and enjoy a refreshing swim in the warm waters. I figured you could use a little privacy and no better place to enjoy it but on a private island," Bruce grinned, lighting a cigar.

"Geez, Bruce, I think you've finally found us the perfect accommodations," Kate stated excitedly.

"Well, no need to thank me. Just enjoy yourselves. You've all earned it. I might say," Bruce replied, pouring himself a shot of bourbon.

The limo stopped outside the intricately wrought iron gates guarding the resort. As the gates opened, it revealed a long narrow bridge that led over to the island. Its seclusion gave privacy to all who were fortunate to stay here. It was paradise at its best. Surrounded by the sparkling azure blue waters of the Pacific and tropical foliage, it included a grove of tall Queen Palms that led to the main lobby. As the limo parked underneath the entrance, it was breathtaking. Bubbling fountains and Koi ponds filled with colorful fish bordered the entry. It showcased the double doors made of carved mahogany.

Walking inside, Bruce checked everyone in and handed out keys.

"You're all together on the north side of the island, but each of you has your own cabana. The extra keys are for the electric carts you saw parked outside as we drove up. They're for your use here on the island. The resort comes with various amenities such as tennis, pool and hot tub, sauna, spa, indoor theater, and even kayaks if you feel daring. Here's a brochure for each of you, it gives the locations. A restaurant that includes a full-service bar is located inside the main entrance, and of course, there's room service. So you kids have fun. Our first concert is tomorrow night at the coliseum. Jerry will be in touch with you. Oh, one last thing, don't forget the sunscreen," Bruce laughed. Getting sunburned will not stop your performing tomorrow night."

"Wow," Cameron grinned, staring at the guys. "We've got our own playground," he laughed.

"Well, guys, Kate and I are going to take one of the carts and check out our cabana. You're all welcome unless the *do not disturb* sign is on our door," Jerry winked, glancing at Kate.

Kate gave him a menacing glance. Jerry reminded her of Nicky.

"Doll, it's a joke. You boys have fun. You can't get lost. After all, it is an island," he laughed. "I'll check in with you tomorrow morning."

"Nicole, which cabana are you in?" Kate questioned.

"Well, the key says number six, but I might hang out with Drew?"

"Babe, leave them alone. Don't be a nuisance," Jerry winked.

Walking inside their cabana, it was immaculate. Stark white sheets were impeccably turned back to compliment the tropical print duvet. A wicker tray sat midway on the bed. It contained a bottle of champagne, two fluted glasses, and a note from Bruce. It read *Congratulations. Have fun. No worries.*

"Wow, Bruce is a class act," Jerry grinned. "What a guy. I'm sure he figured there would be no need to stress over the guys while we're here."

"Yes. Bruce is one of a kind. You have to love that man," Kate smiled.

"Babe, come over here, and let's have a toast."

Popping the cork, he poured them each a glass.

"Here's to a great time, but more importantly, here's to your becoming Mrs. Jerry Godwin," he winked.

After finishing the champagne, Jerry pulled Kate toward the bed.

"Remember our night on the yacht? I believe you fell asleep on me after I proposed. So Doll, I believe you have some *making up to do,*" Jerry teased.

Jerry had indeed slipped the *Do not disturb* sign on their outside door without Kate noticing.

"What a night, Doll," Jerry grinned, sitting up in bed the following morning.

"Wow, Jerry, it's late. We slept in," Kate mentioned.

"Yes, and it feels great," Jerry smiled, pulling her closer for a kiss.

"Doesn't it seem odd that we haven't heard from Nicole or the guys?" Then, suddenly it hit her.

"Jerry, you didn't?"

"Didn't do what?" he asked, quickly, sliding underneath the covers. He had to hide his laughter. It was killing him.

"Really," Kate shrieked, pulling back the covers to expose him.

"Jerry," she screamed, making a mad dash to open the door.

The sign hanging on the doorknob was there for the whole world to see.

"Oh Doll, come over here and give me another kiss. I think it was kind of funny," Jerry laughed.

"Jerry Godwin, how am I going to explain that one?" Kate freaked.

"Explain what, that we're newly engaged, that I love you, and that we wanted to be alone. Really, Babe, you worry too much."

After ordering breakfast, Kate jumped in the shower.

Walking out in a white robe and wet hair, she found Nicole and Jerry sitting at the table drinking orange juice.

"Geez, Mom, really the sign. Drew and I walked over last night to see if you and Jerry wanted to take a stroll along the beach. But I guess you were both busy," Nicole laughed hysterically, choking on her juice. "Sorry, Mom, I had to tease you. I couldn't resist."

"Oh that, well you can thank Jerry. I wondered why no one stopped by. I can't believe he did that. Honestly, Jerry, how embarrassing."

"Oh, Mom, lighten up. Drew thought it was hilarious. Don't take life so serious," Nicole snickered.

"I just came by to see if you had any plans for today before the concert. Drew went kayaking with the boys."

"Sweetheart, why didn't you go?"

"Oh, I thought I would just lay out by the pool and work on my tan. Would you like to join me?"

"Sure, let me change," Kate smiled, rummaging through the clothes in her suitcase. "Okay, I found my swimsuit."

"You girls relax and enjoy yourselves. Then, I need to grab the keys to the cart parked outside and check on Bruce. I need to find out what he has planned for the day."

Walking over, he kissed Kate and Nicole lovingly on their cheeks.

"If Bruce doesn't have something for me to do, later, I'll come over to the pool," Jerry mentioned, closing the door.

"Okay, Mom, get changed. The day is wasting. We only have a few hours before the concert tonight."

Nicole whistled as Kate walked out of the bathroom wearing her turquoise halter bikini.

"Wow, Mom, you look stunning."

"Thanks, Sweetheart. Do you have your swimsuit with you?"

"Yes. I've got it on. I tied my crochet sarong to cover it."

"Well, Jerry took the cart, so we'll have to walk over," Kate smiled.

"Oh, that's fine. We could use the exercise."

Finally arriving at the pool, they pulled two lounge chairs next to each other as Kate drew her long black hair into a ponytail.

Within minutes, the resort concierge came over to inquire if drinks were needed.

"Can I get you, ladies, something cold to drink?"

"Yes. Two bottles of water would be wonderful," Kate smiled.

"Wow, Mom, is this the life or what?" Nicole mentioned reclining in her lounge chair to take full advantage of the sun.

"Yes, Sweetheart, it truly is. Tell me more about Drew. Are you really in love with him? Where do you see this relationship going?"

"Mom, I'm seriously in love with him. Why all the questions? We've talked about marriage, and it's something we both want."

"Well, I just needed to hear you say that he's the one."

"Yes. There's no doubt. Why do you think I couldn't stay in Tokyo? I missed him so much."

"Nicole, I'm happy for you both," Kate answered, wiping her eyes.

Kate was beginning to let her emotions creep in. Thoughts of Nicky not ever having known his beautiful daughter, never getting to walk her down the aisle brought tears to her eyes. Quickly putting on her sunglasses, Kate had to hide her emotions.

Knocking at Bruce's door, it seemed to be taking him a long time to answer. Finally, after knocking three times, Bruce opened the door, still wearing his pajamas and robe.

"Bruce, are you alright? You do realize what time it is, right?"

"Ah, yes, son, I must have been exhausted last night. Come in and sit down. I'll order us some breakfast."

"Bruce, what was on your schedule for today? Weren't you supposed to do some publicity rounds today at the local television and radio stations?"

"Yes. What time is it?"

"Bruce, it's noon. I just asked you a few minutes ago if you knew the time. Listen, I'm going to order your breakfast. I'll grab your briefcase and make a beeline straight down to those offices for you right now. I'll send Kate over to check on you while I'm gone. Quickly calling room service, Jerry ordered a huge breakfast for Bruce. I'm leaving now, but breakfast is on its way."

Driving the cart like a maniac, Jerry raced to the pool to talk with Kate. Then, seeing Nicole and Kate together, he ran over.

"Jerry, what's wrong? You're white as a sheet?" Kate gasped.

"Kate, it's not me. It's Bruce."

"What do you mean it's Bruce?"

"Something's wrong with him. He's still in his pajamas, and I had to knock three times at the door before he finally answered. I need you to stay with him until I get back. I've got to run over to the cabana and get dressed. I'm going to cover his publicity appointments downtown. It shouldn't take that long."

"Jerry, I'll ride with you to our room. I need to change clothes."

"Okay, let's hurry. Nicole, you just enjoy the sun and pool. There's not anything you can do at the moment. I'll give you an update on Bruce as soon as I get back. Oh, one last thing, please don't say anything to the boys about Bruce. I don't want anyone to hear about this, at least not right now. Do I have your word on that?"

"Yes, Jerry, for heaven's sake, you and Mom get going. Don't worry. I'm not going to say anything."

"Oh Jerry, what do you think is wrong?" Kate questioned impulsively.

"I have no idea, but I'm worried he might have the beginning stages of Alzheimer's. But, listen, I'm no doctor, so don't worry. Let's just get through these next few hours and the concert tonight.

Dropping Kate off at Bruce's cabana, Jerry called for a taxi. He was soon on his way downtown to the city center of Manila. He quickly found each office by checking the addresses in Bruce's day planner. In rapid succession, Jerry visited each one. Discussing the details of the concerts and leaving enough promotional materials behind, Jerry felt confident he had covered for Bruce. However, he had one last stop to make before going back to the resort. Jerry went straight to the coliseum. Things seemed to be progressing normally for the night's concert as he walked inside. After completing a thorough walk around the vast complex and talking with the roadies who always traveled with them, it seemed everything was right on schedule. However, seeing Larry in the distance, he went over to check with him."

"Hey Jerry, you're here early," Larry inquired, appearing puzzled.

"Oh, I was just in the area, so I thought I'd drop by and see how things were progressing for the concert."

"Things are fine. We're expecting a sold out crowd tonight."

"Great. That's what I wanted to hear. I hate to run, but I've got a few things to do before the concert tonight. See you later this evening."

"Okay, Jerry, see you tonight."

Hailing another taxi, Jerry was soon back at the resort. Thankfully traffic hadn't been a problem this afternoon, which tremendously worked in his favor.

Arriving back at the resort, Jerry raced over to Bruce's cabana. His heart was racing, not knowing what he would find. Knocking at the door, Bruce answered immediately.

"Hey Jerry, come in. Kate and I were just finishing a carafe of coffee. Would you like for me to order another?"

"Oh, no thanks. Bruce, how are you feeling? You seem to be doing much better right now. You had me scared earlier."

"I'm fine. I took a couple of sleeping pills last night. Unfortunately, I might have taken too many."

"My God, Bruce, how many did you take?" Jerry panicked.

"Oh, just a couple. Don't worry. I'm fine. You don't have to worry about me. Trust me. I'm fine," Bruce reiterated. "Kate told me you took my briefcase and did the publicity rounds for me. Thanks, son, that was awfully nice of you. I didn't mean to get everyone so worried."

"Kate, did he eat breakfast? How long did it take him before he began to feel better?"

"Jerry, he ate everything without any problems. After he ate, it seemed like he began to feel better. He's going to be alright," Kate smiled.

"Yes, Jerry, my nurse says I'm going to live," Bruce laughed, lighting a cigar.

"Bruce, really, do you think you need that stogie?"

"Well, son, I can't honestly think of a reason not to, and believe me, it's not a stogie. I wouldn't smoke those cheap cigars. If it's not Cuban, I won't bother to light it," Bruce laughed. "You kids, get out of here before this old man kicks you out. The limo will be here at 6:00 p.m. You have my boys ready."

"Okay, Kate, guess we're out of here. See you at 6:00 p.m. We love you, old man," Jerry laughed.

"Wow, those are words I don't hear very often. Now, don't get mushy on me," Bruce smiled.

On the ride back over to their cabana, Jerry wiped tears from his eyes.

"Babe, don't worry. He's going to be alright. Maybe it was the fact he might have taken a few extra sleeping pills last night."

"Oh, Kate, you didn't really fall for that story, did you? I don't believe for one minute that he took any sleeping pills. Bruce is smarter than a fox. He's trying to cover everything for some odd reason. Did you see a bottle of sleeping pills laying around anywhere?"

"Honestly, I didn't check. Why would I when he says he took some."

"Why, because he's lying, that's why."

Walking inside the cabana, Jerry threw himself onto the bed.

"Now look who's sleeping in their clothes. Jerry, you need to take off your jacket. It will get wrinkled."

"I'm not going to sleep, no time for that. I'm stressed about Bruce."

"Well, Babe," Kate said after checking the time. "I can help you with that," she smiled, removing his belt.

"Okay, Doll, don't start anything you can't finish," Jerry winked.

"Oh, don't worry about me," Kate giggled.

Glancing at the clock, it was 5:00 p.m. "We better get ready," Kate mentioned, jumping out of bed. "Do you want me to order coffee?"

"Yes, that sounds good. Add a couple of sandwiches to go with that. I'm starved. I skipped lunch earlier today."

Quickly getting showers and dressed for the evening, Jerry and Kate quickly consumed their sandwiches and coffee.

"Jerry, I don't want you to worry about Bruce. But, listen, Babe, if anything, and I do mean anything should happen to him, we'll get him the best medical care this world has to offer. I love him like a father. We all do. That man has taken such good care of us," Kate said with tears streaming down her face.

"Now look who's crying," Jerry winked. Then, taking his napkin, he lovingly wiped her face.

"Doll, I don't know what I would do without you, now let's get over to the lobby."

As the limo parked under the portico, everyone was dressed and excited. Finally, stepping inside the car, they were on their way downtown to the coliseum.

"So, how's everyone tonight? What exciting things did you boys and girls do today?" Bruce inquired. "Looks like you all took my advice and lathered up well with sunscreen," he added.

"The guys and I went kayaking. We were surprised at the number of dolphins we saw," Cameron mentioned.

"We tried to get Nicole to tag along, but she wanted to hang out by the pool," Harry grinned.

"Well, not all of us are water enthusiasts," Kate insisted with a smirk.

"Geez, look at that crowd," Harry exclaimed as the limo drove into the back entrance.

"Yes. It's sold out for tonight and tomorrow," Jerry added.

As usual, they were met by security and a long line of golf carts. Taking a cart, each of the guys, including Nicole, sped away.

"You know it's funny to me how the guys get on those carts and speed away each time without having any idea where the dressing room is located," Jerry laughed. "Bruce, hop on the back. We'll give you a ride."

"Okay. I won't turn you down."

It wasn't long before they saw the line of golf carts parked outside the doors that led to the dressing.

"Well, looks like they found it after all," Bruce grinned.

The room was brightly furnished with modern décor. An oval glass coffee table sat in front of a long sofa. Fresh flowers and a delicious array of seafood, salads, adobo, and pinakbet, Pilipino favorites, were beautifully arranged on a long narrow credenza.

"Okay, who wants to go first for hair and make-up?" Kate asked.

"Guess I will," Drew said, taking a seat in front of the tall lighted mirror.

"So I heard you and Nicole spent some time at the pool today."

"Yes, we were working on our tans," Kate smiled.

"Kate, I wanted to talk with you and Jerry later tonight. I don't want Nicole to know, but I have an engagement ring. It belonged to my mother."

"Oh, Drew, is this for real? Are you seriously thinking of proposing?"

"Yes. That's why I wanted to sit down and talk with you and Jerry before I proposed."

"Well, okay, come over to the cabana later tonight," Kate whispered, quickly catching sight of Nicole as she walked inside the dressing area.

Wow, so many things had happened today, and now it was beginning to look like a rather long night ahead after talking with Drew.

After finishing hair and make-up, Kate walked over to the sofa and sat next to Nicole.

"Hey, Sweetheart, is Jerry going to let you stand in the mosh pit tonight."

"Well, I don't know. I forgot to ask."

"Let me find Jerry. I'll ask if Larry is available to stand near you."

"Thanks, Mom. I love you."

Opening the doors which led outside the dressing room, Kate found Jerry in the hallway talking with Cameron.

"Jerry, Nicole wants to know if she could stand in the mosh pit tonight."

"Let me ask Larry. First, I want to make sure he's available. He might be working in a different area."

Stopping one of the roadies who walked past, Jerry inquired about Larry.

"Hey Lee, have you seen Larry?"

"Yes. Lee just went outside to take a smoke break."

"Okay, thanks," Jerry replied, walking outside to find him.

"Hey Larry," Jerry yelled.

"Yeah, man, what can I do for you?"

"Nicole wants to watch the concert from the mosh pit. Would you be available to stand nearby?"

"Yes, that shouldn't be a problem. Is she ready to go right now?"

"Yes. I think so. Wait here, and I'll get Nicole. Thanks, Larry."

"No problem," Larry answered, putting out his cigarette.

Walking back inside, Jerry found Nicole.

"Okay. It's all set. Larry is outside waiting to walk you down. He'll be close by if you should need him."

"Thanks, Jerry, you're the best."

"Okay, Mom, see you after the concert."

"Have fun."

"Oh, I will," Nicole smiled.

After Nicole left the room, Kate grabbed Jerry by his arm.

"You're not going to believe this, but Drew is coming by the cabana later tonight. He wants to talk with us about proposing to Nicole," Kate whispered in his ear.

"Wow, today is full of surprises. How do you feel about it?"

"Well, Jerry, they seem to be in love. So I'm going to give him my blessings," Kate replied as a tear trickled down her face.

"Babe, don't cry. For heaven's sake, haven't we had enough tears today," he reminded her with a kiss.

"Okay, boys, time to go," Bruce yelled, opening the door.

The roar coming from the coliseum grew louder and louder as Bruce walked with his boys to the back of the stage.

"The fans were shouting out the guy's names as Harry took his place behind the drums.

Moments later, Cameron, Drew, and Doug walked onstage.

"Good evening, Manila," Cameron shouted.

"Manila, we love you," Drew yelled.

"Manila, are you ready to party?" Doug screamed as the flames and light show began.

The crowd was in a frenzied state as the lights lowered in the massive coliseum allowing only the brilliance coming from the flames to light the stage.

"We'd like to open with one of our newest hits, *Starburst*," Cameron announced.

Nicole was in a daze watching the guy's performance. She found herself conforming to those around her as she screamed, danced, and waved her hands high into the air. The energy felt in the mosh pit was like nothing else on earth. She had no way to possibly know the DNA pulsing through her veins had been inherited from her famous father.

It always seemed the concerts were over far too soon. As the hour passed fleetingly, time was impossible to tell. It seemed to stand still.

"Good night, Manila," Cameron shouted.

"Thanks for coming out to party with us," Drew yelled.

"We love you, Manila," Doug screamed.

Nicole ran to catch up with Drew.

"Wow, Babe, that was awesome," Nicole smiled, giving him a quick kiss.

Finally, everyone was back in the dressing room.

"Great concert tonight. It was spectacular," Bruce added. "Is everyone ready to return to the resort? The limo is waiting."

It was quiet on the short ride back to the island. Kate was asleep as usual with her head resting against Jerry's chest.

"Why don't we have a few drinks before retiring tonight?" Bruce suggested. "I asked the staff to keep the bar open late tonight."

"Well, I suppose we could all use a nightcap," Jerry agreed.

"That's what I wanted to hear. So you boys can sleep in tomorrow."

"Sleep in. Are you kidding with all these amenities," Harry laughed.

Glowing candles sat on each table as they entered the dimly lit bar giving the interior a warm ambiance.

"So what will it be, boys?" Bruce asked, walking up to the bar.

"I'll have a San Miguel," Doug spoke up.

"Make that four," the guys chimed in.

"I'll have my usual, Jack Daniels, straight no ice," Jerry stated.

"Yes, and I'll have the same as this young man," Bruce grinned.

"Okay, ladies, what are you both drinking tonight?"

"I'm thinking a glass of red wine. Nicole, what would you like," Kate asked.

"Oh, I'll have the same a glass of wine."

"Red or white?" the bartender inquired.

"Make that red also," Nicole smiled.

The resort had incorporated a long wooden pier from the restaurant. It extended over the water and was well-lit, providing a fun place to hold parties or large groups. Tables with matching umbrellas sat scattered around the deck.

"Hey everyone, let's take our drinks outside to the deck. It's a beautiful evening. Let's take advantage of all those twinkling stars and the full moon," Bruce suggested.

Taking his advice, everyone followed him outside. Jerry and the guys pulled several tables together.

"I'd like to make a toast. I've been fortunate to travel the world more than once with some of you, and it never gets any better than being here this evening. We're family. We work hard, and we play hard. So here's to each of you," Bruce toasted as he raised his glass.

Sitting outside under the stars, listening to the waves gently rolling ashore, it was serene. The boys had another round of San Miguel, and Bruce and Jerry had another tall JD with no ice. Finally, after two more glasses of wine, it seemed the girls were falling asleep. Once Jerry finished another round, he suggested that Kate and Nicole might like to call it a night.

"Well, as great as this has been, I see two ladies that are just about out for the night. I think Drew and I should see them to their cabana before we have to carry them," Jerry laughed.

"Okay, good night. See you tomorrow," Bruce grinned, lighting a cigar.

"So boys, are you up for another round," Bruce inquired, glancing at Doug, Cameron, and Harry.

"Maybe just one more," Doug mentioned.

Bruce felt like a proud father, enjoying the evening with the boys and a Cuban cigar. However, the thoughts of Nicky, along with Randy and Alex, were never far from his mind. After another round of drinks, Bruce suggested they finally call it a night.

Jerry and Drew had to carry the girls out to the parking lot. Stopping for a moment, Drew whispered that he would stop by in the morning.

Reaching their cabana, Jerry carried Kate inside. Laying her on the bed, he gently removed her shoes, putting her under the warm blankets deciding not to wake her. He smiled as he thought of Kate's past experiences with ouzo and the fact that Nicky had carried her back to their hotel room on more than one occasion. Even though she had not encountered the strong drink tonight, it seemed she had a low tolerance to alcohol. Getting in bed next to her, Jerry softly pulled Kate's long hair away from her face. Fate was a strange bedfellow. It seemed unbelievable that Nicky was gone. However, what seemed surreal was that she now shared his bed.

Waking up to the warmth of sunlight filtering through the curtains, Jerry noticed Kate was still sleeping. He decided to get up without disturbing her. He called for room service to order breakfast, including a large carafe of hot coffee, orange juice, and aspirin.

It wasn't long before Sleeping Beauty had awakened.

"Do I smell coffee," Kate asked, sitting up in bed.

"Well, good morning, Sunshine. How do you feel? I've ordered breakfast. Do you feel like eating?" he smiled.

"Wow, Jerry, you've cooked."

"Doll, I'm very domesticated, just wait. You'll see," he winked.

Pouring a cup of coffee, he took it over to the bed.

"Well, Babe, maybe you are domesticated," Kate smiled, taking a sip.

"Kate, I believe Drew is supposed to be stopping by this morning. Being as you and Nicole weren't exactly ambulatory last night, there were no further thoughts of him discussing his proposal with us last night."

"I know Drew wants to propose to Nicole, and he has his mother's ring. So I suppose if this is what they want, we shouldn't stand in their way."

It was only moments later they heard a knock at the door.

"Hey Drew, come in. We were expecting you," Jerry mentioned opening the door.

"Hate to come over so early, but Nicole is still asleep. So I figured this would be my best chance to sneak away before she woke up."

"Would you like a cup of coffee?" Jerry asked.

"Actually, that sounds great."

Grabbing her robe, Kate walked out to the table. The aroma coming from the breakfast cart made her hungry. Kate lifted the silver tops from the serving dishes exposing bacon, eggs, and hash browns.

"Would you like breakfast?" Kate mentioned.

"Oh no, thanks. I'll order when Nicole wakes up. Besides, if I ate now, she would wonder why I wasn't hungry."

Jerry poured Drew a cup of coffee as everyone sat around the table.

"Well, I'm sure you both know why I'm here. Kate, I would like to propose to Nicole tonight. Jerry, this is where you come in. I want to propose to her during our concert. Do you think it would be possible to have my proposal flashed across the large screens tonight while we're on stage? It would be an unforgettable moment, and I know Nicole would love it. If we could somehow capture her surprise and have her come up on stage, I believe she would be thrilled, and the fans would love it as well. Do you think Bruce would mind?"

"Wow, I think Bruce would love the idea, and you're right. The fans would love it. So I'll go over and talk with him, and I'll even go down to the coliseum and talk with Larry and the boys so it can be arranged for tonight. Are you sure this is how you want to propose?"

"Are you kidding? I've talked it over with the boys, and they think it's rad."

"Rad, is it?" Jerry laughed. "Okay then, let's make it happen."

"So, Mom, what do you think? Guess I can call you Mom now."

"Oh, Drew, I think it would be romantic. You certainly have our blessings, and yes, you can call me, Mom," Kate answered with tears in her eyes.

Getting up from her seat, she went over to give Drew a giant hug as tears ran down her cheeks.

"I didn't mean to make you cry," Drew mentioned handing her a tissue.

"Oh, you'll get used to that or maybe not. I'm still learning how to deal with it. The girls cry over everything, and I do mean everything," Jerry winked, staring at Kate.

"Well, I don't mean to rush off, but I want to get back to the cabana before Nicole wakes up. Jerry, will you let me know as soon as you get the approval from Bruce?" Drew asked, taking his last sip of coffee.

"Yes, kid, you've got it. Welcome to the family."

"You're going to make Nicole very happy tonight. I can't wait to see her reaction when she realizes what's happening. Trust me. It's going to be a huge surprise."

After Drew left, Kate grabbed even more tissues.

"Jerry isn't this the most romantic thing you've ever heard," Kate smiled, wiping her eyes.

"Well, Doll, I thought a private yacht in the middle of the ocean and fireworks might have topped your list," Jerry smiled.

"Oh, Babe, get over here," Kate replied, kissing him passionately.

"Geez, Doll, you're not making it easy for me to get out of here."

"Oh, it's still early," Kate laughed, pulling him toward the bed.

Knocking at Bruce's door, he answered immediately.

"Glad to see you're not wearing your pajamas," Jerry teased.

"Come in. What brings you over so early this morning."

"Let's sit down, and I'll give you all the details, but first, do you have any coffee?"

"Yes, son, I do. Sit down, and I'll pour us a cup."

"So, what's on your mind?"

"Well, Drew came by our cabana this morning."

"Why so early?"

"He needed to come by without Nicole knowing, and she just happened to be asleep," Jerry explained, taking a sip of the hot brew.

"Okay," Bruce questioned, sitting down the warm carafe.

"Bruce, here's the deal. Drew wants to propose to Nicole tonight."

"Wonderful, you know I love that girl, and I think a lot of Drew. They make a cute couple. I'm extremely happy for them."

"Well, Bruce, it's not the fact that he wants to propose tonight, but rather how he wants to propose. He wants to propose during the concert. Drew wants us to put his proposal on the screens and ask Nicole to come up on stage. What do you think? Is it possible to arrange it for tonight's concert?"

"Wow, not only would it be possible, the fans would love it. Talk about public relations for the band. It would be an unbelievable moment," Bruce smiled, lighting a cigar. I couldn't possibly think of a better proposal."

"Well, Bruce, guess you would see it from that standpoint," Jerry laughed.

"So, does that mean it's a go for tonight?"

"Oh, son, it most definitely does. Do the boys know?"

"Yes, everyone except Nicole. Can you even imagine? She has no idea?"

"Great. I'll go down to the coliseum early this afternoon and arrange everything. But, you know, Nicole will need to be standing in the front. Maybe in the mosh pit area."

"That won't be a problem. I can't keep Nicole out of there when Drew is performing on stage," Jerry laughed. "Alright, I guess that does it then," Jerry added, finishing his coffee.

"Don't worry about a thing. Please let Drew know it's not going to be a problem. Oh, one last thought, at what point in the concert does he want to propose? Can you ask him and then get back to me? I'll need to let the crew at the coliseum know."

"Yes. I'll give you a call before you leave to go downtown. Thanks, Bruce, I think you've just made two kids very happy," Jerry smiled.

Stopping by Drew and Nicole's cabana, Jerry hoped Drew would be the one to answer the door.

It seemed luck was on his side.

"Hey, Jerry, come in," Drew answered.

"Oh, I can't. Is Nicole here?"

"Yes, but she's in the shower."

"Great. I was stopping by to let you know that I just left Bruce's cabana, and it's on for tonight. First, however, he wants to know at what point in the concert you want to pop the question, so to speak?"

"Well, I'd like to play through a couple of songs first. I don't want Nicole to suspect anything."

"Okay, got it. Would you say maybe after your fourth song?"

"On second thought, why don't we make it the middle of the concert?"

"That actually sounds perfect. I'll let Bruce know. Just make sure the boys are aware of what we're doing. I almost forgot I'll make sure Nicole is standing in her favorite spot."

"Thanks, Jerry. I really owe you, man."

"You just make our girl happy, and by that, I mean a lifetime commitment. Do you understand?"

"Yes, Dad, got it," Drew smiled.

Just at that moment, Nicole walked out of the shower.

"Hey Jerry, what's Mom doing later?"

"I'm not sure. She hasn't mentioned anything particular."

"Well, will you ask her if she wants to lay out by the pool again today?"

"Sure, Sweetheart. See you guys later."

Arriving back at the cabana, Kate came running over.

"Okay, what happened? Does Bruce think he can pull this off tonight?"

"Are you kidding? Bruce sees this as one of the biggest public relations opportunities ever. I almost think he would stage this. It's perfect," Jerry laughed.

"Really. Oh, Jerry, my little girl is getting engaged tonight," Kate cried as tears welled within her eyes. She knew that Nicky would never be there to witness his daughter's proposal or walk her down the aisle.

"Doll, please, no more waterworks. You're killing me with these emotions of yours."

Jerry would never connect with Kate's emotions because Nicky wouldn't be there to share in his daughter's life.

"Oh, I almost forgot. Nicole wanted to know if you wanted to go to the pool later."

"That sounds nice. I'll walk over. So what are you going to do this afternoon?"

"I'll probably go to the coliseum early with Bruce. I want to make sure everything goes as planned for tonight. So if you come back to the cabana and I'm not here, you'll know where I've gone. Kate, Please make sure the guys arrive on time."

"Okay, but I don't think you're going to have to worry about that one. I'm sure they'll be ready in plenty of time, especially tonight," Kate smiled.

Changing into her swimsuit, she grabbed her sunglasses along with her beach bag.

"I'm going to walk over to Nicole's and see if she's ready to go soak up some rays," Kate smiled, quickly kissing Jerry goodbye.

"Have fun, Babe. See you later this evening."

Spreading out their towels and reclining their lounge chairs, it was time to relax.

"So, where are Drew and the boys this afternoon?" Kate questioned.

"They're playing tennis. It appeared Drew had a lot of nervous energy for some odd reason. So the boys came by, and they decided to go over to the tennis courts. He's been acting kind of weird today."

"Oh, I'm sure it's nothing. You can only imagine the pressure the boys are under having another concert tonight."

"I guess you're right. Mom, I'm so happy to be here with you, Jerry, especially Drew. I've missed everyone."

"Sweetheart, we're all thrilled that you're back too. We are truly blessed to be together. Traveling the world with the band doesn't feel like a job. It feels like a huge road trip," Kate laughed.

"I don't think I could be any happier than I am right now," Nicole smiled.

Hearing those words spoken by her daughter melted Kate's heart. Nicole had no idea of the surprise which waited for her later that evening. After being in the sun for a few hours, Kate suggested they go in, shower, and start to get ready.

"See you later, Mom," Nicole smiled, opening the door to her cabana.

"Okay, Sweetheart. Jerry went down to the coliseum a little early today with Bruce. So I'll meet you in the lobby in about an hour.

Later, walking into the lobby, Kate was relieved to see the boys had shown up on time. It seemed everyone was in a festive mood and anxious to get on their way. However, it did appear that Drew was a little apprehensive.

"Does anyone want a drink for the ride downtown?" Drew inquired.

"What do we have to work with?" Cameron questioned.

"Well, we have orange juice, pineapple, scotch, vodka, tonic water, bourbon, soda, and San Miguel," Drew laughed, listing their available options.

"Beer sounds good," Harry stated.

"Yes. Pass us a San Miguel," Cameron added.

"Kate, would you and Nicole like something to drink?" Drew asked.

"Actually, I think that sounds nice. I'll have a vodka and orange juice," Kate replied.

"Babe, would you like something?" Drew asked.

"Well, if everyone is having a drink, I'll have the same as Mom."

"Okay. Let's toast to a great concert," Drew announced.

Entering the back of the coliseum, the line of fans waiting to get in wrapped the entire complex.

"Wow, we have the best fans on earth," Harry remarked.

"Yes. There's no doubt about that," Cameron added.

Arriving at the coliseum, Jerry met them at the entrance.

"Seems like you've already got the party started," Jerry grinned, seeing them step out of the limo with their drinks.

The boys and Nicole each grabbed a golf cart and sped away in the direction of the dressing room, leaving him and Kate behind.

"Well, Doll, are you ready for tonight?"

"Jerry, I'm nervous. I'm already drinking," Kate laughed.

"Sweetheart, you're not the one getting engaged. Give me your left hand, just what I thought. You're already engaged," Jerry laughed.

"Jerry, honestly, I don't know what I would do without you," Kate smiled, giving him a quick kiss.

Entering the dressing room, everyone was inside, including Bruce.

"Well, kids, ready for a great show tonight," Bruce grinned.

The dressing room was again filled with fresh flowers and every delicacy imaginable from the local restaurants. Tonight the bar was fully stocked.

"Does everyone have something to drink? I want to make a toast," Bruce announced.

"Here's to one hell of a night in Manila. An unforgettable night, I might add."

"Geez, Jerry, what's wrong with Bruce tonight? Don't you think he's acting kind of strange," Nicole laughed.

"Oh, you know Bruce. He gets excited over the most ordinary things," Jerry mentioned. "But, he's one hell of a guy."

"I know. You've got to love that man. I don't know what Mom and I would have done without him."

Kate was busy with hair and make-up as usual. However, as Drew sat down in the chair, she took a moment to whisper words of encouragement.

"Drew, I know you're going to make Nicole very happy tonight. I just want you to know how much I love you both."

"Thanks, Mom," Drew whispered.

Kate was trying desperately to keep her emotions in check.

"Kate, I'm ready to take Nicole down to meet Larry. He's going to stand next to her tonight in the mosh pit. I just thought I would come over and let you know before we left the room," Jerry smiled.

"Thanks."

"Nicole, Sweetheart, I hope you enjoy the concert tonight. I love you so much, see you afterward," Kate smiled, quickly kissing her precious daughter.

Making their way down the long narrow hallway, Nicole glanced at Jerry.

"Call me crazy, but isn't everyone acting a little weird tonight?" Nicole snickered.

She had caught him off guard with her question.

"Oh, it's our last concert here. Everyone is simply relaxed from staying in such a luxurious resort for the past few days," Jerry answered at a loss for words.

After Jerry left the dressing room with Nicole, Bruce offered one last toast with the boys.

"Attention, everyone. It's almost showtime. But before we go, I think we could all use a glass of bubbly. Popping the cork on a magnum of champagne, Bruce filled six glasses. Okay, everyone, please raise your glass. Drew, here's to you and Nicole and a night you'll never forget. May you both be blessed with a lifetime of happiness," Bruce toasted.

"Okay. Let's go. There'll be more champagne after the concert."

Walking toward the stage, the guys were all teasing Drew. He seemed to be getting more nervous and anxious by the moment.

"Now, don't get tongue-tied and forget your lines," Doug taunted hysterically.

"Doug, he's not in a play, for heaven's sake," Cameron grinned.

"Now, don't get nervous, and pee your pants," Flame roared teasingly.

"Do you have the ring?" Cameron asked.

"Yes. It's in my pocket."

The fans screams resonated as they got closer to the stage. The excitement and energy reflected from the crowd encouraged the boys to perform their best and give their fans the best hour and a half of their lives.

Harry walked out first and took his place behind the drums as the girls went crazy shouting out the guys' names.

It was chaotic as the boys entered the stage.

"Good evening, Manila. How are you?" Cameron yelled, holding his guitar high above his head.

"Hello, Manila," Drew shouted.

"Manila, how are you this evening? Are you ready to party?" Doug screamed.

It was pure mayhem as the lights lowered and the flames danced upward from the stage. The roar was deafening as the light show began.

"We would like to open as we did last night with our newest single, *Starburst*," Cameron announced.

Afterward, Cameron focused the fan's attention on Harry. He performed a drum solo. Harry's talents as a musician were evident as his fans shouted his name in recognition of his abilities.

The coliseum rocked with the music of House of Cards as thousands of fans screamed and shouted the words to each song. The night was amazing. The fans in the mosh pit waved their hands enthusiastically into the air, dancing to the beat of the music. The air seemed tangible, almost electrified, filled with energy radiating from the fans.

The concert was midway when Jerry tapped Larry on his shoulder without Nicole seeing him. Nicole was immersed in the music and hadn't noticed.

"Okay, Larry, take Nicole's hand and be ready to lead her out of the mosh pit and onto the stage."

The lights in the coliseum lowered as the guys started to sing, *It Must Be Love*. The large screens flashed in bold lettering, **Nicole, will you marry me?** An overhead spotlight focused brightly on Nicole's blushing face as a hush fell over the entire coliseum. Realizing it was for her, the fans began to cheer. Nicole was mesmerized, completely frozen, holding her hands over her mouth until Larry escorted her toward the stage. Drew walked over to meet her. Then taking her hand, Drew led Nicole to the center of the stage. Nicole felt paralyzed as Drew took the ring from his pocket, bending down on one knee in front of everyone, repeating the four magic words.

"Nicole, will you marry me?" Drew asked, lovingly staring into her beautiful eyes.

"Yes! Oh, yes!" Nicole exclaimed, stunned at seeing the gorgeous antique ring.

Drew picked up his lovely bride-to-be, twirling her in his arms kissing her passionately. At that point, it was sheer pandemonium. The cheers coming from the fans were ear-piercing as they gave their approval. Then, finally, leading Nicole backstage, the entire audience began to clap.

Harry instantly picked up the beat to their next song as Drew walked back on stage to the roar of his amazing fans. The concert continued.

Walking backstage, Nicole was met by Bruce, Jerry, and Kate.

"Congratulations, Sweetheart," Kate cried.

"Congratulations, Baby," Bruce grinned, wiping tears of joy from his eyes.

"Yes, congratulations, Nicole," Jerry smiled, giving her a quick kiss. "Welcome to the family." Nicole was still unaware that she had been a family member since birth.

Their stay in Manila had been one of worry and elation. Finally, however, the stage was set for change—changes that would affect everyone.

CHAPTER FOURTEEN

Changing of the Guard

Nicole sat next to the window taking in the sights below as the Lear Jet began its descent into Auckland, New Zealand. Drew was still sleeping with his head supported between two pillows. Looking over at him, Nicole decided to let him sleep. It would be several minutes before the plane taxied to a stop.

As the jet rolled to a stop, Nicole could see the limo parked on the tarmac. Easing the pillows from under Jerry's head, it startled him awake.

"Hey, what's going on?"

"Babe, we're in New Zealand, time to wake up," she smiled.

"Okay, gang, I've reserved several suites at the Fairmont," Bruce announced, reaching to open his overhead compartment.

Most of the boys were still asleep as Jerry made his way up the aisle to wake them.

"Okay, boys, naptime is over," he remarked, gently tapping them on their shoulders.

Entering the limo, it appeared Harry had become their unofficial tour guide as he kept stating amazing facts about New Zealand.

"Guys, did you know that Sir Edmund Hillary was born in Auckland, and the people refer to themselves as Kiwis.

"Thanks for the remarkable info," Doug laughed.

Arriving at the hotel, it was gorgeous. It was uniquely located at the intersection of two busy streets. Walking in the décor was modern but emphasized Polynesian furnishings.

"Here are your room keys. Kate, you, and Jerry, along with Nicole and Drew, are on the sixth floor. Cameron, Doug, and Harry, you are on the tenth. I've reserved the penthouse if any of you would like to check it out later," Bruce grinned. "Does anyone care to get a drink before going up?" he asked, lighting a cigar.

"Thanks, but I think Kate and I are going up to our room."

"Thanks, Uncle Bruce, but Drew and I are going up with Mom and Jerry," Nicole added.

"Yes, we've got a couple of video games we've been waiting to play," Flame grinned as the boys made their way to the elevator.

"Okay, if no one wants to join me, I'll be down in the bar. If anyone needs me, you know where I'll be," Bruce smiled, puffing away on his notorious cigar making his way to the lounge.

Entering their room was exquisite. A beautiful four-poster bed covered in a green floral duvet sat between two wicker nightstands. Oversized wooden planter boxes containing lush greenery sat near the patio doors. Along one side of the room was a large rattan wall unit encompassing a fully stocked bar.

"Wow, is this room impeccable or what?" Kate stated, pulling Jerry toward the king-size bed.

"Yes, you know Bruce, either go extravagant or go home," Jerry laughed.

Taking off their shoes, they climbed into bed. Resting his head on the pillow, Jerry quickly fell asleep. Staring at the love of her life, Kate for once decided to let Jerry sleep. Pulling back the covers, it wasn't long before she too began to fall asleep. They were awakened about an hour later when the phone in their room rang.

"Hey, Jerry, are you and Mom dining in tonight?"

"Well, we haven't exactly given it much thought. We pretty much fell asleep after unlocking the door."

"I'm sorry. I didn't mean to wake you."

"Oh, that's no problem," Jerry answered, glancing at his watch. "It's only 7:00 p.m. It's still early. Why don't you both come over? I'll wake your mom and see if she would like to go out for dinner."

"Okay, that sounds great. See you in a few minutes."

Turning over, he lovingly kissed Kate awake.

"Doll, Nicole, and Drew are coming over. Would you like to dine in this evening or go out for dinner?"

"Actually, Jerry, I'm exhausted. Why don't we order in and eat on the balcony?"

"Okay, that sounds good. Hopefully, Nicole will agree."

Hearing a knock at the door only moments later, Jerry walked over.

"Hey, guys, come in."

"Geez, your room is as nice as ours," Nicole mentioned surveying the room.

"Well, you know your Uncle Bruce. He takes care of everyone."

"Hey sweetheart, would you mind if we ordered in tonight. I'm still a little tired from the flight. I thought we could order in and eat outside on the balcony," Kate mentioned.

"That sounds nice. Do you have a menu from the restaurant downstairs?"

"Yes. Take a look."

After ordering roast lamb and seasoned vegetables, they decided to add dessert, Pavlova, a meringue-type dessert topped with cream and fresh fruit. Sitting outside, they enjoyed the ambiance of the evening, along with the local cuisine. Topping off their meal with glasses of pinot noir and sauvignon blanc, it was the perfect ending to a beautiful day.

"Wow, I'm so relaxed from the wine," Nicole yawned. "I think we should call it an evening."

"Okay, Sweetheart," Kate smiled, hugging her. "See you in the morning," she added, walking Nicole and Drew to the door.

As the morning light filtered through the curtains, Jerry turned over in bed to face his gorgeous fiancee, kissing her awake.

"Hey Doll, guess we better get the day started. Why don't you order breakfast while I jump in the shower?" Jerry suggested.

"I've got a better idea," Kate smiled seductively. "We'll both jump in the shower and order breakfast afterward."

"I like the way you think. I can't argue with that," Jerry winked, reaching for Kate's hand pulling her out of bed and toward the shower.

After enjoying a leisurely breakfast, Jerry noticed the time.

"Well, Babe, it's almost 10:00 a.m., and as nice as this morning has been, I should go over and talk with Bruce. First, I need to find out what's on the schedule for today. Afterward, I'm going to check in with the guys. Did you have anything special planned for today?"

"Not really, but if you're free later, maybe we can go downtown and have lunch."

"All right, that sounds great. Hopefully, it won't take long.," Jerry smiled, giving her a quick kiss.

It appeared Bruce was in no hurry to answer as Jerry knocked on his door. Jerry's mind quickly replayed the previous encounter finding him in a questionable state of health. Waiting a few minutes longer, Bruce finally opened the door.

"Hey Jerry, what brings you by," Bruce asked, still in his bathrobe.

At this point, Jerry was horrified. There was no room for doubt this morning. They were in trouble. Whatever was wrong with Bruce had to be dealt with, and the sooner, the better.

"How are you feeling? Is everything alright?"

"Oh, I'm fine."

"Bruce, do you know what country you're in and what day of the week it is?"

Jerry quickly devised a litmus test, trying to determine the seriousness of Bruce's condition.

"Come in, son, let me pour you a cup of coffee."

There was no hint of a carafe of coffee or the evidence to prove that Bruce had even ordered breakfast as Jerry surveyed the room.

"Bruce, have you had breakfast this morning?"

"Well, come to think of it, I'm not sure."

"What country are we in?" Jerry asked once again.

"Oh, we're in Thailand," Bruce paused, scratching his head.

"Bruce, I'm going to order breakfast and get some coffee. Come over and sit on the sofa while I make the call."

Picking up the phone, Jerry immediately called Kate.

"Kate, I need you to get dressed and come up to Bruce's penthouse. But, hurry, he's not well. He's not even dressed, and he thinks we're still in Thailand."

"I'll be right there. Don't panic."

Waiting for Kate, Jerry ordered breakfast and hurriedly found Bruce's briefcase. It was déjà vu all over again. Thank God Bruce was organized. His day planner was the first thing he spotted once he opened the briefcase. Taking a glance at today's date, his list of publicity rounds was in order. Hearing a knock at the door, Jerry rushed over.

"Good morning, breakfast," the young man stated, pushing a food card laden with everything imaginable for breakfast.

"Thank you," Jerry smiled, handing him a generous tip.

"Bruce, breakfast has arrived. I've ordered eggs, hash browns, bacon, and toast along with coffee. I'll pour you a cup of coffee."

Hearing another knock at the door, hopefully, it was Kate.

"Hey Kate, come in. We've got a hell of a problem on our hands," Jerry whispered.

"What do you think is wrong?"

"As I mentioned before, I'm not sure, but my guess would be Alzheimer's or a form of dementia. Either way, this isn't good. I'm going back to the room and get dressed. I'll make his publicity rounds, and then we'll need to get Bruce seen at a clinic. Why don't you see if he'll eat breakfast while I'm gone? If you need help with him before I get back, I suppose you'll have to call Cameron or one of the guys. The concert for tonight and tomorrow has to go on as scheduled. In the meantime, we'll do the best we can. Everything hinges on the diagnosis we get. Anyways, I've got to run. I hate to leave you like this, but I've got to get to the radio and television stations. These appointments are paramount. With any luck, I won't be gone long," Jerry grimaced, running for the door.

"Okay, don't worry about Bruce. You take care of his publicity rounds, and I'll do my best to take care of him."

Quickly getting dressed, Jerry hurried down to the lobby and arranged for a taxi. He only needed to contact four offices. It wouldn't be that difficult. Thankfully Bruce was organized, and he had accompanied Bruce on enough of these meetings to feel confident. If there had to be a changing of the guards, so to speak, Jerry knew he was more than capable of stepping into Bruce's shoes.

Leaving his last appointment at the local radio station, Jerry looked down at his watch. It had only taken him two hours to complete the list. He felt assured the public relations aspects of the concert were completed as Bruce would have wanted. Thankfully, Bruce had left several free tickets in his briefcase to give away. Bruce was a genius when it came to PR Campaigns. Now, Jerry only worried about what he would find once he arrived back at the hotel. As the taxi weaved in and out of traffic, Jerry began to think of what life would be like without Bruce for the first time today. His eyes moistened. Bruce wasn't only a father figure, he was the magic that made bands famous. He was the glue that held everything together. There would never be another Bruce Weber. Arriving back at the hotel, Jerry wiped his eyes. Racing toward the elevator, Jerry prayed for good news.

Knocking at the door, Kate quickly answered.

"How's he doing?" Jerry asked frantically.

"Not good. I've made arrangements with the concierge to have a doctor come up to the room. He should be here soon. He still seems confused and sort of dazed," Kate whispered.

"I'm so worried about him."

"I know, but try not to worry. Let's just wait and see what the doctor has to say."

Hearing another knock at the door, Jerry hurried over to open it.

"Hello, I'm Dr. Reid. The hotel concierge asked me to check on Mr. Weber."

"Yes, come in. Mr. Weber is sitting on the sofa. Bruce, this is Dr. Reid. He's come by to take your vital signs."

"Oh, I don't need a doctor. Trust me. I'm fine."

"Well, let's let him make that decision."

After a quick but thorough evaluation, Dr. Reid asked to speak with Jerry outside.

"Have you noticed this before? Has he seemed to be confused or disorientated at other times?"

"Yes, not long ago, he answered the door in his pajamas and seemed unaware of the time and his schedule for the day."

"Well, it's hard to make a clinical diagnosis without further tests. However, after speaking with Mr. Weber and asking him a few simple questions, he seems to be displaying classic symptoms of early dementia or Alzheimer's. Still, as I said, I would need to run further tests. How long will Mr. Weber be in Auckland?"

"We have two concerts at the sports arena. We are scheduled to leave on Sunday. Australia is our next stop on this tour."

"I would like to admit him to the local hospital for a complete evaluation. Then if further tests confirm my initial diagnosis, I would suggest you fly him back to the states. He would need to be under the care of a doctor who specializes in treating these illnesses. I've given him a mild sedative, so he will feel more comfortable while we move him to the local hospital. Would you like to transport him, or would you prefer that I call for an ambulance?"

"Oh, I think we can handle that. I sure hate to hear your initial diagnosis. Bruce is the manager of our band, House of Cards. I don't have to tell you that he's vital in arranging the intricate details of our schedule."

"Well, I don't mean to be the bearer of bad news, but you might want to consider a temporary replacement, depending on the outcome of the tests. I'll know more in a few days. But, first, let's get Mr. Weber checked into St. Mary's Hospital. I'll be around to see him later this evening."

"Okay, thank you for coming to the hotel. We'll have Mr. Weber at the hospital within the hour."

Closing the door, Jerry immediately asked Kate to speak with him outside on the balcony. Again, Jerry felt like he had an out-of-body experience. He had always known somewhere in the back of his mind that this day might come. Jerry knew that age might sooner or later become a deterrent regarding Bruce's abilities to manage the band, but how could he have ever been prepared.

"Oh babe, it's not good," Jerry whispered. "Dr. Reid wants Bruce admitted to St. Mary's Hospital for some further tests, and we have our first concert tonight. He even suggested that we should think of a replacement in case the tests confirm his suspicions."

"Jerry, please don't panic. Nobody knows this business better than you, except for Bruce. You can do this. You've already taken care of the public relations for Auckland, and you've been trained by the best, don't let him down," Kate stated. "Jerry, you're more than capable, and you have a great team. The boys, Larry, and the roadies are the best in the business. I love you. I'll be right by your side," Kate smiled, wiping tears from her eyes. "Oh Jerry, I love that man. Do you even know how much he means to Nicole and me?" Kate reminded him as tears flooded down her face.

"Doll, I know. Trust me. I know. We need to get back inside before Bruce starts to suspect something more than we're willing to discuss right now. I need you to be strong. I'm going to the boy's room and informing them that we're admitting Bruce to the hospital. I'll be right back, why don't you arrange for a taxi while I'm gone. The doctor has given him a sedative, so just stay with him until I get back," Jerry suggested, taking the back of his hand to wipe tears from Kate's face.

Hearing a knock at the door, Cameron answered.

"Hey Cameron, I need you to get the guys together. I've got some things to discuss with you, and I don't have a lot of time. It's important," Jerry stated as he walked in."

"Well, you're in luck. Harry and Doug are sitting outside on the balcony having lunch. We just ordered room service. Can I order something for you?"

"No, there's no time. I'll call Drew and Nicole to join us."

"Okay. You seem worried. Is everything alright?"

"I'd rather not go into any details until everyone is here, but it concerns Bruce. Why don't you go outside and ask the boys to come inside while I call Drew and Nicole."

A short time later, Drew and Nicole knocked at the door.

"Hey, guys, come in. Guess something has come up," Cameron mentioned.

"I hate to be the bearer of bad news, but we're admitting Bruce to St. Mary's Hospital this afternoon. Bruce has been very disorientated today. He couldn't remember what country we were in or the correct day of the month. I called a doctor to his room earlier, and the doctor suggested admitting Bruce so that he could run some tests at the hospital."

"Oh no, not Uncle Bruce," Nicole cried. "Where's Mom? Does she know?"

"Yes. Kate's with Bruce. Listen, we don't really know much now, but I'm afraid it's not looking good. The doctor suspects dementia or the beginning stages of Alzheimer's. Sweetheart, I know you're upset, but we're going to get him the best medical care possible. Do you understand?"

"Yes, Jerry, but we can't lose him. We just can't. He means everything to mom and me," Nicole answered, visibly upset.

"Drew, why don't you get Nicole something to drink."

"Listen, guys, here's the deal. I know how much everyone in this room loves that man. Believe me. He's been a father to all of us. He's taken care of us in a way that no other person on earth could," Jerry stated, becoming slightly emotional. "We are family. Do you remember Bruce's toast the other night? It seems surreal thinking back to what he said," Jerry recollected as he paused to wipe his eyes. "One thing is for sure. We're not going to let him down. First, we're going to do the two concerts here in Auckland. Then I'll decide whether to postpone Australia or keep it on the schedule as planned. But, right now, I have to get back to the penthouse. Kate and I are going to check him into the hospital."

"Jerry, I'm coming with you," Nicole insisted.

"Listen, Sweetheart, the best thing you can do is remain here with Drew and the guys. We don't want to upset Bruce by everyone showing up. Just stay here. We probably won't have any definite answers until tomorrow or the next day. You can come and visit him later. I need you guys to hang here at the hotel for the rest of the day. The limo will arrive at about 6:00 p.m. to take you over to the sports center. I'll try to be back before then. If not, I'll meet you at the arena. Just keep him in your prayers. I know how much you all love him, so don't worry. We will make sure that he gets the best medical care possible. I'll call as soon as we get him checked in and let you know his room number. I've got to run. Drew, please take good care of our girl."

Taking the elevator up to the penthouse, Jerry could only imagine how the boys must be feeling. He knew the anguish and worries they must be experiencing. However, he was determined to keep the show on the road.

"Kate, how's Bruce? Did you call for the limo?" Jerry inquired, walking in.

"The hotel arranged transportation, and we're ready to go. Bruce is still unsure of what day it is or even where he's at. However, I did get him to eat some of his breakfast."

"Hey Bruce, we're going to take a ride over to the hospital. How are you feeling?" Jerry asked sympathetically.

"Why? Who's sick? Are the boys okay?" Bruce asked, holding onto Jerry's arm.

"Yes. Bruce, everyone is fine. We just want to make sure that you're alright."

Getting Bruce admitted wasn't much of a problem. He had always made sure the band had excellent health coverage. They had been lucky in the fact that he could only remember a few times anyone in the band had actually been sick.

"Kate, after Bruce is in a room and I've spoken with his nurse or the doctor, we're leaving for the sports arena."

"Jerry, I've got an idea. Nicole can do hair and make-up for the guys tonight. She'll be great at it. Remember, she's been working in the modeling industry for several years now. I want to stay here with Bruce, at least until the concert is over. Afterward, you can stop by and pick me up. How does that sound?"

"Are you sure?"

"Yes. I wouldn't feel right leaving Bruce. Besides, I want to talk with his doctor. Here's the phone number of the hospital. You can call me later."

"Okay, if you're certain Nicole can handle make-up and hair."

"Oh, I'm sure, now get out of here. I know you're nervous about tonight's concert, but everything is going to be fine," Kate assured him.

After giving Kate a quick kiss, Jerry glanced at Bruce. It appeared he had fallen asleep.

Finally arriving at the sports arena, the line of fans waiting to get in was already getting long. The two concerts in Auckland were sold out. Looking at all the fans patiently waiting to get inside, Jerry knew there was no one in the business better than Bruce when it came to filling seats. He was brilliant. Walking in, Jerry decided it would be best to call a meeting before the boys arrived to inform everyone about Bruce's condition.

"Hey Larry, I'd like to get everyone together for a moment before the guys get busy setting up for the concert."

"Okay, let me grab a microphone, and I'll make an announcement," Larry suggested.

"Can I please have everyone stop what they're doing and come down to the front of the auditorium? It shouldn't take that long," Larry stated.

Jerry knew these guys loved and respected Bruce. A lot of these guys had traveled with Bruce for years. Their hard work and loyalty were a tribute to how much they loved their job. Bruce had never failed to treat them with mutual respect and admiration for their hard work. Handing the microphone to Jerry, everyone, including Larry, wondered what was on his mind.

"Hey guys, the reason I called everyone together is to inform you about Bruce. He was admitted to St. Mary's Hospital this afternoon. To sum things up quickly, when I went to his room this morning, it was obvious that Bruce was confused and disorientated. He couldn't even remember what country he was in or the date."

"Jerry, think we've all been there," Stan joked, lighting a smoke.

"Well, Stan, I wish that was the case with Bruce. But, unfortunately, I think it's a bit more serious. After an initial evaluation by the doctor, he seemed to think it might possibly be the onset of dementia or Alzheimer's. A few weeks ago, I stopped by his room to go over the schedule, and he was still in his pajamas and had forgotten to make his publicity rounds. Then today, once again, I found Bruce confused and completely unaware of his surroundings, and worse yet, he had forgotten to eat. So Bruce has been admitted for tests. If his diagnosis turns out to be as dire as the doctor suggested, then we'll get him back to the states and under the care of a specialist. As of right now, I'm going to fill in for Bruce. So if you need anything or have any questions, just get in touch with me. The band is going to complete its commitment in Auckland. Then, afterward, I'll decide whether or not we continue to Australia or reschedule. I'll know more tomorrow after the doctor runs some tests. So let's get to work and put on a great show for the good people of Auckland. I'll give you an update tomorrow. Thanks, everyone."

"Jerry, is there anything the guys or I can do?" Larry asked.

"No. But as Bruce would say, the show goes on. So just continue with the phenomenal job, and thanks for asking. Just keep him in your prayers. The boys should be arriving soon, and Nicole will stand-in for Kate tonight. She wouldn't leave Bruce."

"Wow, this must be hitting Kate pretty hard. Bruce has always been like a father figure to Kate. She really loves that man."

"Yes. I know. It's going to be an adjustment, but one thing is for sure, we're not going to let Bruce down. We owe him that much."

"You're right about that. Well, I better get back to work. I certainly hope you have better news from the doctor tomorrow," Larry mentioned, taking a pack of cigarettes out of his pocket.

Walking down to the dressing room, it seemed odd knowing that Bruce wouldn't be coming in later. The room was exceptional. It had an oversized brown leather couch in the corner with a mirrored coffee table sitting in front. Two pinball machines were against the back wall, which would keep the boys busy before going on stage each night. Fresh flowers and a long table prepared for catering completed the ambiance. Noticing a phone, he decided to check in with Kate.

"Hey Kate, how's Bruce?"

"Well, he seems to be a little better right now. But, you know Bruce, he already wants to get out of here, and he's giving me the third degree about making him stay here tonight. He was determined to come down to the sports arena until his doctor came in and told him he was staying put."

"You did remind him that he's scheduled for tests tomorrow?"

"Yes. The doctor informed him that he was scheduled for a scan. They've taken blood and urine samples. Dr. Reid said he should know more about his condition tomorrow afternoon. I've tried my best to keep Bruce calm. He's upset that he can't attend the concert tonight, but he knows you and Nicole have things covered. Have the boys or Nicole arrived?"

"Not yet, but they should be here any minute. Do you want me to stop by the hospital after the concert?"

"Actually, he'll probably be asleep by then. So why don't I just meet you back at the hotel? We'll come back in the morning."

"Okay, Babe, if anything changes or you need me, just call or leave a message with Larry or one of the guys. I'll see you later at the hotel."

"Hope the concert goes great," Kate replied. "Love you."

A light knock on the dressing room door indicated that catering had arrived to set up. The aroma was mouthwatering, as large trays containing roasted lamb flavored with rosemary and various sundries of seafood were deliciously arranged. Mussels, oysters, and scallops, along with fish and chips, completed one end of the table. Kiwis and other local fruits and hokey pokey, a creamy vanilla ice cream sprinkled with honeycomb pieces, were kept refrigerated until the band arrived.

"Hey, Jerry, how's Bruce?" Nicole asked as the boys walked in.

"He's resting comfortably. But you know Bruce, he was demanding to be let out of the hospital to come over to the arena. Your mom is staying with him for a few hours tonight. She wouldn't leave him. Which reminds me, she wants you to step in and do hair and make-up for the guys tonight. I had Larry go over to the hotel and pick up her cosmetic kits. Think you're up for it?"

"Oh, are you kidding? Drew, you're up first," Nicole laughed.

"Babe, I'm not sure I liked the sound of your laughter. Do you know what you're doing?"

"Oh please, with my years of experience as a model. I think I've learned a few tricks by now. So let's see, which color of lipstick would look best," Nicole laughed.

"Nicole," Drew screamed, sitting down in front of the tall lighted mirror.

"Just relax. You guys are in good hands tonight," Nicole smiled.

"Wow, pinball," Harry yelled, totally forgoing the spread of local cuisine, which had been beautifully arranged.

After the guys were ready and everyone had a chance to eat, Jerry called them together.

"Okay, I want you guys to go on stage tonight and give Auckland one hell of a concert. Even though Bruce isn't here with us tonight, we're not letting him down. We owe him. We're going to finish our commitment, and then I'll decide what happens next after I confer with the doctor. Now, go out there and make him proud."

"You got it, Jerry. We would never let him down," Cameron smiled.

"Yes. No worries," Harry insisted.

Jerry felt proud walking with the boys down the long narrow hallway toward the stage. He knew he had the best guys in the business standing beside him. There was no way even one of them would ever let Bruce down.

"Alright boys, it's up to you now," Jerry smiled.

Walking on stage first, Harry took his place behind the drums. He played his usual intro for the guys. However, tonight seemed surreal and intense as he was committed to giving the fans a great concert.

Next, Doug, Drew, and finally Cameron walked out to the roar of the crowd.

"Hello, Auckland," Cameron shouted.

"Auckland, how are you this evening?" Drew yelled.

"Auckland, we love you," Doug screamed.

The concert was incredible. Nicole found her usual spot in the mosh pit with Larry beside her for protection. It appeared the guys were determined to give their fans a show to remember. They were united in the fact that Bruce deserved their very best.

At the close of the show, Cameron, Drew, Doug, and Harry walked to the front of the stage. After pouring out their love and affection to their amazing fans, they gave a shout-out to Bruce.

"Here's to Bruce, we love you, man. Get well soon," they yelled in unison.

Jerry was proud of the guys as they walked off stage. He knew they would never let Bruce down, even though they were young and somewhat naïve. The boys each possessed exceptional musical abilities and would be committed to keeping the show on the road. They had learned from the best. Now, Jerry was anxious to check on Bruce. Once back inside the dressing room, Jerry made a call over to the hospital.

After a few rings, Nicole answered.

"Hey, Babe, how's Bruce?"

"He's sleeping comfortably. The doctor informed me they would be running tests on him early in the morning, so I'll get a taxi and come over to the hotel. I want to make sure that I'm awake and here tomorrow when he goes in for the tests."

"Listen, Sweetheart, don't bother with a taxi. The guys and I are ready to leave the arena. We'll have the limo driver stop by the hospital and pick you up. Give us about twenty minutes."

"Okay, thanks. I'll be waiting in the lobby."

Watching as the limo drove up to the entrance, Nicole hurried outside.

"Thanks. How did the concert go tonight?" she inquired, stepping inside the car.

"Oh, it was phenomenal," Drew smiled.

"So, Sweetheart, how did it go with make-up and hair tonight?" Kate questioned.

"Oh, Mom, do you even have to ask. I would never let you down. Just ask the guys," Nicole laughed.

"Yes, well, she tried to make Drew wear lipstick," Harry laughed.

"Really, that's hilarious. But, Jerry, I'm so worried about Bruce," Kate whispered, laying her head gently against his chest.

"I know, Doll, please don't worry. We'll be here early in the morning," Jerry answered, kissing her on the cheek as he lovingly combed through her long locks with his fingers.

"Guys, I know it's our usual routine to go out and have fun after the concerts, but tonight I think we should go back to the hotel. Knowing that Bruce is in the hospital, I simply don't feel like partying tonight.

"Jerry, don't worry, that's fine with us," Cameron interjected. "After all, I think we all feel the same way. So we'll just order room service and watch movies."

As the limo arrived back at the hotel, the guys were silent and appeared in a somber mood.

"I don't want any of you to worry or stress over Bruce. Kate and I will be going to the hospital early in the morning. I'll let you all know more tomorrow after Dr. Reid runs some tests," Jerry stated, walking into the hotel lobby.

"See you tomorrow," Nicole smiled, giving her mom a tight squeeze as they stepped outside the elevator and walked over to their room. "Oh, Mom, please don't forget to call and let us know about Uncle Bruce in the morning."

"Of course, Sweetheart, don't worry. Get some sleep. I'll see you tomorrow."

Walking into their room, Kate fell onto the bed as she pulled the blankets over her. Jerry could hear the sound of muffled cries as he walked over to close the drapes.

"Doll, you have to be strong. Please don't cry," Jerry pleaded, pulling her into his arms. "Babe, I know how much Bruce means to you. We won't know anything until tomorrow, so please don't do this to yourself." Laying down beside Kate, Jerry for once fell asleep fully clothed.

Waking to the sound of his alarm, Jerry drowsily reached over to push it off.

"Wow, Babe, guess your bad habits are rubbing off on me," Jerry grinned, gently kissing Kate awake. "The alarm just went off. We better get dressed and over to the hospital."

Hearing the word hospital, Kate jumped up.

"Geez, Jerry," she smiled. "Now look who's sleeping in their clothes," she teased.

"Yes. I know. You're a bad influence, Kate Godwin."

"You just called me Kate Godwin."

"Guess I did," Jerry winked. "I've been thinking a lot about us the last few days. I think it's about time we make everything official. What do you think?"

"Oh, Jerry, your right. I don't want to wait. Life is too short. Let's do it," Kate agreed.

Walking into the hospital and taking the elevator up to Bruce's room, Kate began to let stress consume her once again.

"Jerry, I'm so worried," Kate stated, grabbing hold of his arm.

"Let's just wait and see what Dr. Reid says," Jerry replied, kissing her sympathetically on the forehead.

Entering Bruce's room, it was empty. Jerry decided to walk over to the nurse's station and inquire about Bruce.

"Miss, could you please tell me if Mr. Weber is still having tests?"

"Yes. He should be back in his room in about an hour. So you can wait for him in his room, or there's a waiting room on the next floor," the young nurse smiled.

"Okay. Thank you."

"Kate, why don't we go down to the hospital cafeteria and get breakfast."

"Alright, but I'm not really hungry."

"Well, I think we both could use a cup of coffee," Jerry insisted as he reached for Kate's hand, leading her over to the elevator.

An hour later, they walked back into Bruce's room. Finding him asleep, they quietly sat down and waited for the doctor to make his rounds. It seemed like an eternity before Dr. Reid finally walked in.

"Dr. Reid, do you have any tests results back on Mr. Weber?" Jerry asked quietly.

"Yes, as a matter of fact, I do. Let's walk outside."

Taking Kate by the hand, they followed Dr. Reid out into the hallway.

"The initial tests confirmed my original diagnosis. However, I want to follow up with further tests tomorrow to confirm. Unfortunately, his illness seems to have progressed further than I'd originally expected. I'll know more tomorrow. Mr. Weber is very ill. He has advanced Alzheimer's disease."

"Oh no," Kate cried in shock.

"What does this mean? How long does he have?" Jerry asked in disbelief.

"Well, I never like to talk in terms of time left. I'm a man of faith, and I've been a doctor long enough to know that isn't exactly my call. I would say maybe two years, maybe more with good medical supervision. It's is a vicious disease," Dr. Reid answered, putting his arms around Kate. "I'm sorry. I would advise getting him back to the states and under the care of a good doctor. Many great facilities provide wonderful care for Alzheimer's patients. He can be released tomorrow as soon as you've arranged for his travel back home. It seems you both love him a lot. As I said, I will keep him another day to do further tests and for observation. I'll write a few prescriptions, which can be picked up later at the nurse's station. You can pick those up before you leave. Do you have any questions? Again, I'm truly sorry," Dr. Reid added sympathetically.

"No. But thank you," Jerry replied, catching Kate as her legs went limp.

Noticing his dilemma, one of the nurses brought over a cup of water and a wet towel for Kate and helped her into a chair that sat nearby.

"I think the news hit her pretty hard," Jerry said, wiping Kate's face with a wet towel, quickly reviving her.

"Oh Jerry, I'm so sorry. What happened?"

"You simply fainted, but are you feeling better?"

"Yes. How embarrassing. I can't believe I went out like that."

"Well, Doll, we've both been given some dreadful news about Bruce, and it isn't great. So I should get you back to the hotel."

"No. I'm fine. I want to go in and see Bruce."

"Are you sure you're up to it? We don't want to give him any reason to worry."

"Yes. I'm not leaving the hospital without seeing Bruce."

"Okay, if you're sure."

Walking into Bruce's room, it seemed he was awake and eating breakfast.

"Alright, which one of you is responsible for putting me in here," Bruce laughed.

"Glad to see that you're awake and sitting up," Jerry smiled.

"Yes, but I'm ready to get out of here. So how did the concert go last night?" Bruce inquired.

"Everything was fine. The guys put on a great show. You don't have to worry about them."

"Hey Bruce, how are you feeling?" Kate asked, walking over to his bed.

"I'm fine, especially seeing your sweet face. Weren't you in my room last night?"

"Yes. I stayed with you while the guys performed at the arena."

"What about hair and make-up? Who took care of that?"

"Oh Bruce, don't worry. Nicole did a great job."

"Man, it appears that I've created quite a problem for everyone," Bruce frowned.

"No. I don't think so. You had to come in for some tests. You'll be getting out soon," Kate remarked, checking to make sure Bruce had eaten most of his meal.

"Bruce, we're both glad that you're feeling better. I've got to go back to the hotel. Kate is going with me. We just wanted to check on you this morning and ensure you had everything you needed to keep you comfortable. We'll try to stop by before the concert. Behave yourself and don't give the nurses a hard time," Jerry teased, taking Kate by the hand.

"We love you. I'll be back later to check on you," Kate mentioned.

"Oh, you two get out of here before I have a couple of those cute nurses throw you out," Bruce grinned.

Before they left, Jerry walked over to the nurse's station.

"I know the doctor said he would be able to leave the hospital tomorrow when transportation is arranged. Well, we'll be leaving on Sunday. We have a private jet at the airport. So if you can just keep him comfortable until then, that would be great."

"Oh sir, don't worry, that's what we get paid to do," the nurse smiled.

"Here are a few tickets to our concert at the sports arena, if any of you are fans of House of Cards," Jerry grinned.

"Are you kidding," one of the younger nurses stated, immediately running over to grab one.

"Thank you," she smiled excitedly.

Walking down to the elevator, Kate began crying.

"Jerry, Bruce seemed to be his ole self again. Maybe this whole thing is just a huge mistake," Kate said, wiping her eyes.

"Oh, Babe, I only wish that were the case. I hate seeing you like this. As much as it pains me to say this, I'm sure the doctor gave us the truth. Those tests don't lie, and we've both witnessed his episodes."

Arriving back at the hotel, Jerry held to Kate as they took the elevator up to their room.

"I'm going to order lunch and ask Nicole to come over and stay with you. I need to meet with the boys. I've got a hard decision to make, so just take it easy until I get back. Nicole should be here soon." With that being said, Jerry closed the door.

Knocking at the door, he was surprised to find that everyone was inside, including Nicole, as Cameron opened the door.

"Nicole, would you mind staying with your mom while I talk with the boys?"

"Yes, not a problem. Is she okay?"

"Well, she fainted earlier at the hospital. Don't worry, she's fine. I'd just feel better if you were with her."

"Yes. I'm going right now."

After Nicole left the room, Jerry asked the guys to sit down.

"I don't know how to say this, but you boys aren't kids anymore, so I'm going to give it to you straight. Bruce is very sick. According to his doctor, he's probably only got a few years left. The bottom line is that Bruce will no longer manage the band. I certainly wasn't ready to hear such terrible news regarding Bruce. However, there's one thing that I am sure of without a doubt. I'm ready, willing, and able to step into Bruce's shoes and keep this show on the road. So please don't worry, the band is and will always be in good hands. I wanted to stop by to discuss the idea of us all returning to Vancouver with Bruce. We'll just take a short hiatus from our world tour. I'll start rescheduling our tour dates immediately. We were supposed to be in Australia on Monday, but I'm going to be in touch with them today and let them know of our dilemma. Cameron, I'm going to call Jenna and have her check on facilities in Vancouver for Bruce. We're the only family he has, except for his nephew, Jeff, and we're not about to let him lack for anything. So as soon as everything is arranged, we'll continue with our world tour. Do any of you have any questions?" Jerry frowned, rubbing his forehead.

"Yes, Jerry, I think we're all agreed to whatever you ask. We want the best for him," Cameron stated.

"Oh my God, Jerry, not Bruce," Harry insisted, becoming emotional.

"Listen, Harry. I know that you're all attached to Bruce. I've not informed you about the prior episodes that Kate and I have dealt with because I didn't want to worry you until I knew we had something to be concerned about. Look, I'm not saying you guys have anything to fear regarding your careers, but Bruce isn't getting any younger. He's one hell of a guy. I think we can all agree on that. What he's done for each of us and the band is truly unheard of these days. He's been a hands-on manager in every aspect of keeping this show on the road. We owe him a great debt. He took a chance on all of us. We need to make sure he's in good hands before we continue. Do you all agree?"

"Yes, Jerry, whatever it takes," Drew agreed, getting a drink from the mini-fridge.

"Are we still performing tonight?" Doug asked.

"Yes. We're going to fulfill our commitment in Auckland."

"Hey Cameron, is there anything strong to drink in your room?" Jerry asked.

"Beer, a bottle of wine, and some bourbon."

"Bring over the bourbon and a couple of glasses."

Opening the bottle of bourbon, Jerry poured them each a shot.

"Here's to Bruce and one hell of a concert tonight," Jerry toasted.

"We'll I need to run over and check on Kate. The limo will arrive at 6:00 p.m. make sure you're dressed and down in the lobby. I might go to the hospital with Kate before the concert tonight. So if I'm not down in the lobby when the limo arrives, I'll catch up with you later at the arena," Jerry said, walking toward the door.

"Hey Jerry, would you ask Nicole to come back over to Cameron's room?"

"Yes. No problem."

Jerry found Kate and Nicole sitting on the couch as he entered their hotel room. It seemed Nicole was trying to comfort her mother.

"Hey, girls, is everything okay?"

"Yes, Mom was telling me about Uncle Bruce. I just find it so hard to believe. Is it really true? Does Uncle Bruce really have Alzheimer's?"

"Yes, I'm afraid so. Nicole, Drew wanted me to ask you to come back over to Cameron's room."

"Okay. Take good care of Mom. She's really worried."

"I know. Don't worry, Sweetheart. I wouldn't let anything happen to her or you, for that matter. I love you," Jerry smiled, giving her a quick kiss on the cheek.

After Nicole left, Jerry sat down on the sofa beside Kate.

"Kate, I just talked with the guys, and we've all decided to go back to Vancouver with Bruce. We're going to take a thirty-day hiatus from our world tour. We owe him that. I want to make sure that he has everything possible as far as his health is concerned and a great care facility before continuing the tour. But there's one more reason," he mentioned taking her by the hand. "Kate, what do you think about us getting married while we're in Vancouver?" Jerry questioned, waiting pensively for her answer as he stared into her beautiful blue eyes.

"I thought you'd never ask," Kate teased with tears streaming down her face.

"Doll, please don't cry. I love you. I thought perhaps you might want Bruce to walk you down the aisle. He should be well enough to do that, and I think he would be honored. However, if we waited, no one would know for sure if he'd still be able," Jerry suggested wiping tears from her face.

"Jerry, nothing could be more perfect. I couldn't want anything more," Kate answered, wrapping her arms around him giving him a tight squeeze. I don't know what I'd do without you," she cried.

Picking her up, he carried her over to the bed.

"It's early. But all I want right now is to feel the warmth of your body next to mine for the next few hours," Jerry winked.

The boys performed one hell of a concert later that evening. Stopping by the hospital afterward, it seemed the nurses who worked the evening shift were more than delighted to see the boys walk in. After that, everyone crowded around Bruce's bedside, showering him with love as only a family could.

The next day as the Lear Jet lifted into the clouds, Bruce thought they were going to Australia. But, little did he know, he was on his way back home?

CHAPTER FIFTEEN

Taking Care of Business

As the plane touched down in Vancouver, Jerry glanced at Bruce. He was sure that Bruce had probably not remembered his talk with the doctor before leaving the hospital. Surely, Bruce didn't even know they had arrived in Vancouver. However, Jenna was meeting them at the airport, and hopefully, he would recognize her.

"Hey Bruce, how are you feeling?"

"Oh, I'm fine, son, smooth ride today."

"Yes, it was," Jerry remarked, reaching for his bags.

"Bruce, we've just arrived in Vancouver."

"Vancouver, what in the world are we doing back in Vancouver?" Bruce questioned, appearing agitated and confused.

"Do you remember being admitted to the hospital in Auckland?"

"Well, sort of, but we're supposed to be in Australia."

"Yes, I know, but you had some tests while you were in the hospital, and it appears you're going to need closer medical supervision. So I decided to bring you home to Vancouver, and having Jenna look after you was the best possible answer. We all love you and want the very best for you. Jenna has made all the arrangements."

"Jenna, did you say Jenna?"

"Yes. Jenna's meeting us inside the terminal."

"What about the tour? Please, don't tell me you canceled the tour?"

"Bruce, I would never do that. If you've taught me anything, it's the fact that the show must go on. *So* I've rescheduled the tour dates. We're not excluding any of our scheduled venues, just postponing them until you're settled."

Bruce looked perplexed, rubbing his forehead.

"Don't worry. You've trained me well. The guys and I would never let you down. We're family, remember."

Walking down the steps from the plane, Jerry saw Jenna running toward the jet.

First, she greeted Bruce, then Cameron.

"Hey Bruce, welcome home," Jenna smiled, wrapping her arms around him, then giving him a huge hug. "How are you feeling? It's so good to see you."

"Sweetheart, what's going on? Has Jerry gotten you involved in this wild scheme of his?" Bruce inquired.

"Well, let's leave that to the doctors. It's just so good to have you home."

Seeing Cameron exit the jet, Jenna was thrilled.

"Hey, honey, it's so great to see you," Jenna exclaimed, running over to hug Cameron. "How's life been on tour so far?"

"Oh, Mom, it's fantastic," Cameron smiled. "That is until Uncle Bruce got sick."

"I know, but don't worry. He's in good hands now," Jenna smiled, hugging him repeatedly.

"Okay, Mom, that's enough," Cameron blushed.

As everyone stood on the tarmac getting reacquainted, it felt right. Jerry finally felt confident he had made the right decision.

"Alright, let's load up," Jerry suggested herding everyone in the direction of the limo. "I've booked everyone into the Ritz Carlton for the night. Bruce will stay in the penthouse. He's familiar with his surroundings there. Everyone has their own suite. Jenna, do you and Cameron prefer to stay in the hotel, or would you rather have the limo take you downtown to your condominium?"

"Condominium, what condominium?" Cameron yelled. "Jerry, you knew about this?"

"Oh, I think I'll let your mom handle this one," Jerry laughed, staring at Jenna. "I told you it wasn't a good idea, remember."

"Well, honey, home isn't exactly where we lived before," Jenna explained.

"So, Mom, what else did you get rid of? How about Fritz and Joey?" Cameron asked sarcastically.

"Sweetheart, let's discuss this later. I don't think everyone in the car wants to hear why I sold the lake house. The dogs are fine."

"Yes, and I don't want to be dragged into the middle of this," Jerry interjected.

Driving under the brilliantly lit entrance of the Carlton Hotel, everyone exited the car except for Jenna and Cameron.

"Jerry, I'll be over in the morning. I've got some brochures I want to show Bruce on assisted living facilities in Vancouver. They're phenomenal care facilities, and I think they're perfect," Jenna whispered to Jerry as he stepped out of the limo.

The limo was quiet at first after everyone exited the car at the Carlton. Finally, Cameron had waited long enough. He was determined to know why his Mom had sold their home without him knowing.

"Okay, Mom, let's have it. Why on earth would you have ever sold the lake house? Dad had it built specifically for you, every detail. I literally can't believe this," Cameron steamed.

"Well, honey, if you'll give me a chance, I'll explain it all to you. Please don't hate me or get upset. There was no way on earth that I could have lived in that huge house after your dad passed and you left. Trust me. It was a beautiful home, and I treasured it. However, it has nothing to do with the house. It was the fact it held too many memories. Can you even imagine me in that huge house alone with only the dogs? Honey, I couldn't do it. I tried," Jenna stated, wiping her eyes.

"Oh, alright," Cameron finally answered, putting his arms around her. "Don't cry. It's just the fact that I was initially shocked when I heard. I hope you got a good price for the house, and what about Dad's piano?"

"Yes, I did, and don't worry about the piano. I still have it. It's not exactly a condominium. It's the penthouse in a new building downtown. I think you're going to love it. I have the most spectacular views, and there are trails nearby for the dogs. I'm truly happy living downtown," Jenna reminded him with tears in her eyes. "Oh honey, I still miss your dad more than you could know. It's so hard to believe he's gone, but I'm so excited that you're here now. I know the dogs are going to go crazy when they see you."

Arriving downtown at Jenna's new address, Jenna and Cameron exited the limo as Cameron grabbed his bags.

"One thing is for sure. You're definitely in the middle of town. You certainly have a lot to do here."

"Yes, you're right. I eat out a lot, and I love browsing through the shops, but I still get lonely."

"Well, not tonight. I'm home. So let's go up and see this new place," Cameron smiled.

Jenna and Cameron stayed up late that evening. But, more importantly, they reminisced about Cameron's younger days and their days with Nicky.

Walking into their suite at the hotel, it almost felt like being back home.

"Wow, in a weird way, Vancouver feels like home," Kate remarked.

"Yes, it does for me as well, but it's because I've spent so much time here. We've made so many records downtown at the Warehouse," Jerry mentioned falling onto the bed.

"So, Babe, you're sleeping in your clothes," Kate teased.

"Oh, I don't think so," Jerry winked, pulling her down next to him. Then, removing his shirt, he turned out the lights.

Drew and Nicole felt worlds removed from the last time they

were in Vancouver upon entering their suite. But, even though only gone for six short months, they were now engaged.

"Do you feel like going out for dinner, or would you rather stay in this evening?" Drew questioned.

"Oh, after that long flight, this bed is looking rather comfortable," Nicole giggled. "Let's order in. I'm tired," she suggested taking off her shoes.

"Sounds good to me," Drew smiled, removing his shoes. Then, slipping into bed, he pulled Nicole next to him. "Wow, Mrs. Connor," Drew teased, checking out the beautiful engagement ring on her left hand.

"Well, not yet, but soon," Nicole smiled. "I think Mom and Jerry will beat us to the altar."

"I've been thinking about this for a while. Why don't we make it a double wedding? What do you think?" Drew questioned.

"Wow. Honestly, I've not given it a thought, but since you've brought it up, I think that would be amazing. But Babe, I think Mom and Jerry are planning to get married while we're in Vancouver."

"So, are you saying it's too soon?"

"No, are you kidding? I think it would be spectacular," Nicole smiled. "Mom and I can shop for our dresses together. We can do it all together. I need to make a list right now," Nicole smiled, jumping out of bed to find pencil and paper.

Drew had opened Pandora's Box. There would be no turning back. What had he done?

"Oh, Drew, I don't think I'm going to be able to sleep tonight. I've got so much to get done, and in such a short time."

"Oh, I think I can fix that."

Quickly getting out of bed, Drew walked over to where Nicole sat with her list. Then, pulling back her beautiful black hair, he gently kissed her on the nape of her neck.

"Babe," she paused. "Okay, it can wait," Nicole laughed, kissing him passionately.

It seemed Doug and Harry were anxious to check out available movies as soon as they walked into their suite. They decided to share a room. Sleep wasn't in their plans for the night, having slept on the plane.

"Let's order room service," Doug suggested. "How does pizza sound?"

"Great, make it a deluxe with everything included," Harry added.

Checking out the mini-fridge seemed to hold just what they needed to complement their pizza. Finding six bottles of Viking Lager, they were set for the night. They would order more as needed.

Hearing a knock at the door, it seemed pizza had arrived. The overwhelming aromas coming from the pizza made them ravenous. Taking slices of pizza and bottles of beer, they walked outside to the balcony to eat.

"Man, does it seem surreal that we've been to so many different countries in the past few months?" Harry mentioned.

"No, it doesn't seem real, but I can honestly say that I've enjoyed every minute of it," Doug grinned, taking a sip of lager. "Especially Taiwan," he smiled. "I haven't told anyone yet, but I've kept in touch with Alondra."

"What? You're joking?" Harry laughed.

"No. Alondra might come to Vancouver if we're here for a while."

"Wow, this sounds serious."

"Well, it's too early to know for sure, but I'm hoping she can arrange it."

"Man, a lot has happened in such a short time," Harry smiled.

"Wow, Bruce, I still can't get over the fact that he's been diagnosed with Alzheimer's. He's been our rock since we left here."

"That's for sure, but Jerry is definitely ready and experienced to take over as manager. We all like him, and getting along with him is a great asset to any band. It's just going to be sad leaving Bruce behind."

"Yeah, man, I can't stand to think of that right now. So let's get back inside and check out those sci-fi movies," Harry suggested.

As Bruce entered the penthouse, it seemed vaguely familiar to him. His world was evolving and not in a good way. Slowly he walked around the rooms taking note of everything. He could never be prepared for what lay ahead of him. Forgetting your existence, your reason for being wasn't typical. Especially after his life, it seemed the worst thing possible. If there were a good part, it would be the fact that he would probably never know or remember his life as it started to slip away from him.

Sitting down, Bruce poured himself a shot of Jack Daniels. Thankfully he had never married. He couldn't imagine imposing this type of cruelty on others. After his second drink, he decided to turn in for the night. Hopefully, the peacefulness of sleep would invade his body, taking away the thoughts of what lay ahead.

Waking as the morning light streamed in through the curtains, Jerry noticed the time. It was only 9:00 a.m. early by any standards of a rock star, but there was a lot to get done. Jenna would be arriving shortly. They had planned to visit the different facilities with Bruce. Deciding to let Kate sleep in for a while longer, he quickly jumped in the shower, dressed, and ordered breakfast.

Hearing a knock at the door, Jerry ran over, expecting breakfast.

"Hey, Jerry, is Mom up?" Nicole asked.

"No. I was letting her sleep a bit longer. I've ordered breakfast. Why don't you go over and do me the honors of waking her this morning," Jerry smiled.

"Mom, sleepyhead, wake up. I've got something I want to discuss with you and Jerry," Nicole stated, gently nudging Kate awake.

"Wow, Nicole, such a pretty face to see so early in the morning, but for heaven's sakes, Sweetheart, what brings you over this early?"

"Mom, first of all, it's not that early. It's already 9:00 a.m., but that's beside the point. I've got something to ask you, and it involves Jerry too."

"Yes. What can that be?" Jerry smiled quizzically.

"Well, Drew came up with an idea last night. The second I heard it, I haven't been able to think about anything else."

"Man, this seems serious," Jerry snickered.

"We want to have a double wedding with you both while we're here in Vancouver. What do you think?" Nicole asked enthusiastically.

"Guess I never really thought of it. Jerry, what do you think?" Kate asked.

"I think," he paused for a few moments teasing Nicole. "Yes. Why not?" he laughed. "However, Doll, it's really not up to me. What do you think?" Jerry asked, giving Kate an amused kiss.

"Well, I think it would be lovely."

"Wow, Mom, we can shop for our dresses together. Can you even imagine the fun? I'm so excited. Okay, I've got to run back to my room and finish my list," Nicole stated, racing for the door.

"Wow, we have lists now?" Jerry inquired. "This sounds expensive."

"Honey, don't you want to wait and have breakfast with us?"

"No, but thanks for asking. Drew's already ordered breakfast. Love you guys," Nicole beamed, quickly closing the door.

"We're all going through such a difficult time right now. I think a double wedding is exactly what we all need," Kate suggested. "Besides, did you see how happy she was? I think you've just made her day," Kate smiled.

"Babe, I won't argue that fact with you. But, unfortunately, it seems I'm outnumbered. Have you given any thought to a venue?"

"Jerry, stop talking like a band manager and referring to the location as a venue. I'm sure we'll find the right place. In fact, Jenna might happen to know of a church or outdoor setting which would be perfect."

Hearing another knock at the door, it seemed breakfast had arrived.

As the cart was pushed inside their room, the aroma smelled divine.

"Would you want to eat outside on the balcony?" Jerry asked.

"Yes. That sounds wonderful. Let me grab my robe and slippers."

Sitting outside in the fresh morning air, it seemed the day was getting off to an incredible start until Jerry remembered what his day entailed.

"Doll, do you want to go with Jenna and me to check out the Alzheimer's facilities today?" he asked, refilling their cups with coffee.

"No. I think maybe fewer people with him today might be better. What do you think?"

"You're probably right. It shouldn't take that long. Maybe we can check out a few venues later this afternoon."

"Jerry, it's our wedding, not a gig," Kate laughed.

It wasn't long before there was another knock at the door.

"Man, this place is beginning to feel like Grand Central Station," Jerry laughed.

"Hey Jerry, I hope I'm not here too early. I wanted to come over and check on Bruce and see if you were ready to take him to visit some of the places that I found," Jenna smiled.

"Yes. Come in. We're just finishing breakfast outside on the balcony."

"Oh, I didn't mean to interfere with breakfast."

"You're not interfering at all. Come outside and have a cup of coffee."

"Thanks, that sounds good."

Grabbing another cup from inside, Jerry followed Jenna outside to the balcony.

"Good morning Kate, how are you? Are you rested after the long flight from Auckland yesterday?"

"Yes. But I'll have to admit it was rather tiring. So how did Cameron take the idea of your moving into the condominium last night?" Kate questioned.

"Oh, it went better than expected. After I reminded him what my life was like after losing his dad, he understood."

"Well, I'm glad that went well. I knew he was upset in the limo about the fact that you sold the lake house."

"Yes, he was at first, but he's a good son. So much like his father," Jenna smiled.

"Can't say I didn't warn you about that one," Jerry chimed in.

"Okay, Mr. Know It All," Jenna teased.

"This may not be the right time or place," Kate hesitated.

"However, since you brought up Nicky, I think we all need to talk. Nicole wants to have a double wedding while we're here in Vancouver."

"Oh, that sounds wonderful," Jenna smiled, taking a sip of coffee.

"Well, that's not exactly where this conversation is going," Kate paused again.

Jerry looked puzzled.

"I guess I will just come out with it. What do you think of us finally getting the kids together and telling them about their father? The fact that they're siblings. I want Bruce to walk me down the aisle if it's possible. I truly believe in my heart if Nicole knew that Cameron was her brother that she might want to have him walk her down the aisle," Kate stated, wiping tears from her eyes.

"Wow, you're right. I didn't see that coming," Jenna responded.

Kate glanced at Jerry, who appeared confused and bewildered.

"Jenna, I didn't mean to bombard you with all of this when I know that you're concerned and busy helping Bruce. But I honestly don't want to start my married life with unfinished business from my past. What do you think? Can I count on you?" Kate asked as tears flooded her face.

"Yes, of course," Jenna paused with tears streaming down her cheeks.

"Nicky was such a huge part of our lives. We owe it to him as well as the kids," Kate added.

"Of course we do, and you're right. It's the perfect time," Jenna suggested wiping her face.

"Wow, guess this is where I walk inside and try to find you both some tissues," Jerry smiled, once again carrying on a conversation with Nicky.

"Nicky, how could you? I'm left here alone with two crying women, still trying to clean up your life. Thanks, bro, let's just hope your son and daughter don't hate you after this," Jerry thought to himself as he walked inside.

Coming back with tissues in hand, Jerry found the women crying as they consoled each other. It seemed they were having a weird sort of female bonding episode.

"Seriously, is this what I'm to expect with three women in my life. It was bad enough with you, Kate. Now I'll be dealing with Nicole and Jenna at holidays, birthdays, and family gatherings. I should buy stock in Kleenex," Jerry teased.

Finally, they stopped sniveling. Then, glancing at each other, Kate and Jenna began laughing so hard it was unbelievable.

"Geez, Jerry, guess Nicky left you a bunch of blubbering idiots," Jenna laughed.

"Come over here, you handsome hunk," Kate laughed, giving him a hug for the Kleenex.

"Yes, Jerry, what would we do without you?" Jenna added, taking a tissue. "Well, I think we've got a huge wedding to plan."

"Not today. We've got Bruce to think about. We better get going. The day is wasting away, and we need to check on him. See if he's even had breakfast or out of his pajamas," Jerry mentioned.

"Before I go, do you want to be married inside a church or outdoors?" Jenna inquired. "I'll need to know to check on locations. Also, when did you want to speak with our kids," Jenna smiled as a single tear rolled down her face.

"What about tonight?"

"Really, that soon?" Jenna appeared surprised.

"Well, it's not actually that soon. How old are they?" Kate reminded with a smile. "Besides, what are we waiting for? We need to tell them to find out if Cameron will walk his sister down the aisle."

"Okay, why don't you, Jerry and Nicole, come over to the condo later tonight, say about 7:00 p.m. What about Drew? Don't you think he should be involved?" Jenna questioned.

"I think he should. If I'm allowed to make any suggestions," Jerry mentioned. "After all, he's marrying Nicole. What better time to get immersed into our family problems."

"Yes. I think you're right," Kate smiled.

"Alright, see you all later tonight. If anything changes, let me know. Guess it's time to deal with poor Bruce," Jenna frowned, walking inside toward the door.

"Doll, I don't know exactly how long this will take. Just pray that Bruce will happen to fall in love with one of the facilities," Jerry remarked, giving Kate a quick kiss at the door.

Taking the elevator up to the penthouse, neither knew what to expect when Bruce answered the door.

Knocking over four times, Bruce finally answered. Still, Jerry wasn't surprised to find him this way in his nightclothes.

"Bruce, it's almost noon, and you're still in your pajamas," Jerry smiled.

"Oh, I wasn't expecting guests. Come in."

"Have you had breakfast?"

"What?" Bruce looked confused.

"Have you had anything to eat this morning?" Jerry insisted.

"No, not yet. Why are you hungry?"

"Bruce, we've had breakfast. Never mind, I'll order you something. How about bacon and eggs," Jerry suggested calling room service.

"Jerry, I wouldn't even bother to ask him. Just order anything," Jenna mentioned. "Bruce, you need to get dressed. We've come by to take you to visit assisted care facilities. I think you're going to like what you see, so you need to get ready. The limo will be here in less than an hour," Jenna smiled.

"Alright, where did you say we're going?"

It was not one of Bruce's better days. Jerry could never be prepared for his continuous decline as vicious as his illness might be. His cognitive skills could vary greatly. However, would there ever be a suitable time? Their stay in Vancouver was going to be short. It was imperative a place be secured for him before the overseas tour continued.

As soon as breakfast was delivered, Jenna lovingly made sure Bruce had eaten enough to get him through the better part of the day. Jerry helped get him dressed. Finally, they were ready to leave the penthouse.

"Okay, Bruce, we're going down to the lobby."

Getting him inside the limo was no problem, but Jerry began to wonder just how much of the day he might remember. As sad as it was to entrust his care into the hands of a professional, Jerry couldn't leave Vancouver without at least knowing he had found the perfect place.

Stopping at the first assisted care facility, the outside appeared nondescript and almost an institutional compound. Glancing at Jenna, Jerry frowned.

"This place is definitely not right for him. Just look at it. Would you really want to see him in this place?"

"You're right. Let's not bother to take Bruce inside. However, the brochure had depicted a much better view," Jenna pointed out.

Jerry could only hope they got better driving to the next facility.

"Jenna, did you thoroughly check on everything available?"

"Yes. I did. Do you honestly think that I would put Bruce in a facility like the one we just left?"

"Well, it was on your list," Jerry moaned.

"Let's take a look at the next one before you start complaining."

Driving into the entrance of the second facility, Crestwood, it appeared much improved. It had individual cottages surrounding the main building and was gated.

"This looks much better," Jerry finally smiled.

Taking Bruce inside, the staff was friendly and courteous. It seemed for all intent and purposes to be a nice place.

"So, what do you think?" Jenna asked as the staff walked them through the main complex, cottages, and adjoining grounds.

"I like it, but I'd like to see more."

After thanking the staff for their time, Jerry helped Bruce back inside the limo, and they continued with their search.

"I think you're going to like this next place. But, of course, it's definitely not on the cheaper end of the scale."

"Well, the price doesn't concern me. Bruce has worked extra hard all of his life. Trust me. Money isn't going to be a problem."

Arriving at the third facility, Haven Wood, it was a high-rise facility and by far the nicest. Walking inside, its grand entrance and immaculate lobby felt welcoming and serene. It contained a large comfortable seating area surrounded by lush greenery, a waterfall, and a baby grand piano. Soft music played in the background as they approached the desk.

"Hello, we have an appointment to tour your facility this afternoon. We have Mr. Bruce Weber with us. He's a potential resident."

"Okay, just a moment while I call for someone to give you the tour. I think you'll find that our facility will meet all of his needs. We're only two blocks from the local hospital, and we provide many different programs for our residents. Some of them are located within our facility, and others we provide buses to transport our residents as needed."

After taking a lengthy tour, Jerry decided it finally felt right. Each unit covered the gap between living independently and in a skilled nursing home. It provided 24-hour staff, housekeeping, laundry, as well as transportation.

"Now, what I've shown you are the assisted living quarters, but we also provide a more confined unit with bedrooms only, sharing living and dining facilities when needed."

"So, what do you think?" Jerry asked, looking at Jenna.

"I like it. Bruce is highly sociable, so I think he would fit in fine. I'm sure he would love attending the different functions they offer."

"Okay, I guess we've agreed. We're ready to fill out the application. Our attorney has provided all the necessary paperwork. I think you'll find everything is in order. When would it be possible for Mr. Weber to move in?" Jerry inquired.

"As soon as we can process his paperwork, it usually takes a few days. So let's walk down to the office and get everything started."

Walking into the office, Jerry ensured everything was documented and signed. Bruce seemed somewhat aware that Haven Wood would soon become his new home. After everything was filled out correctly, Jerry and Jenna decided to take Bruce out to dinner at one of Vancouver's best restaurants, The Roadhouse.

Later returning to the hotel, they made sure Bruce was in for the night and arranged an aide to stay with him. It would ensure he got his meals on time and provide the necessary help he would require.

Looking down at his watch, it was almost 5:30 p.m.

"Okay, now that's taken care of, I guess we should think about getting the kids together. Let's go back to the hotel and see if Kate has made arrangements with Nicole and Drew. Will Cameron be available tonight?"

"Yes. I think so. As far as I know, Cameron was just going to hang out and keep the dogs company until I came home."

Unlocking the door, Kate was in the shower. Hearing them walk in, she quickly dressed, wrapped her hair in a towel, and opened the door.

"How did it go with Bruce?" Kate asked anxiously.

"Well, Babe, you'll be relieved to know that we found an extremely nice facility, Haven Wood."

"So Jenna, what were your impressions?"

"Oh, the same as Jerry, I think he'll like it. It's very nice, and they offer a lot of amenities."

"Thank goodness that part of your day is over. Nicole and Drew are coming by around 6:30 p.m. I told them we'd been invited to see your new condominium. Hope that was alright?" Kate asked.

"Yes. That's great. I actually need to be going. I'll stop by one of the restaurants near our building and order dinner for everyone, so don't eat before you come. Hope you like Chinese food?"

"That sounds delicious," Kate mentioned.

"See you in a few hours. Let's just keep our fingers crossed and pray that tonight goes well with the kids," Jenna mentioned walking to the door.

"No worries," Jerry added.

"Think I'm going to blow dry my hair. Are you going to change before we leave?"

"Yes, but first, I'm going to pour myself a stiff drink. I really need it. Today was hard knowing that Bruce will be admitted to Haven Wood. Kate, please shoot me if you ever feel the need to put me away," Jerry laughed. After a day like today, I'm still faced with talking with the kids. Wow, doesn't a man ever get a break?"

"What? You, get a break? Aren't you now the manager of some famous band," Kate teased. "I don't think you're going to get away from stress," she smiled, rubbing his back. "Just drink your Jack Daniels and let me go blow dry my hair."

Hearing a knock at the door, Jerry looked down at his watch. Sure enough, it was already 6:30 p.m. Where had the time gone?

"Jerry, get the door. I'm looking for my earrings."

"Hey guys come in," Jerry smiled.

"How did it go with Uncle Bruce today?" Nicole questioned.

"Great. We found a nice facility called Haven Wood."

"Jerry, that sounds like the name of a horror movie. Are you sure it's a good place?" Nicole snickered.

"Yes. You watch too many scary flicks."

"Okay, guess I'm ready," Kate smiled, walking out from the bathroom.

"Oh, Mom, you look so pretty."

"Thanks, Sweetheart, you do too."

Walking over to the elevator, Jerry inquired about Doug and Harry's plans for the evening.

"So, what are Doug and Harry up to this evening?"

"Oh, I think they're in the middle of a movie marathon. Those guys have been watching sci-fi movies all day. Later they said they might go down to the gym," Drew mentioned as they entered the elevator.

"Really, the gym?" Jerry laughed.

Stepping inside the limo, the girls looked beautiful. However, Jerry was nervous.

"My, you ladies look nice tonight. Does anyone care for a drink?" Jerry asked, pouring himself a shot of bourbon.

"Guess it wouldn't hurt," Drew remarked. "Here's to our double wedding," he toasted.

"Oh Babe, that's sweet of you," Nicole smiled, giving him a quick kiss.

"Would you girls care for a drink?"

"No, thank you, we'll leave that for you boys," Kate answered, hoping it wouldn't be needed.

Soon arriving downtown, the limo parked in front of the towers where Jenna lived.

"Wow, this is really nice. No wonder Jenna loves it here," Nicole smiled.

The doorman let them in. However, not recognizing them as tenants, he inquired about their visit.

"Good evening, may I help you?"

"Yes. We're here to see Jenna Spade."

"Great, just pick up the phone, and it will connect you with her apartment."

"Hi Jenna, we're down in the lobby."

"Great. Take the elevator up to the top floor. Oh, that's the 28th floor, penthouse."

"Wow, Jerry, we need a place like this," Kate grinned.

"I'll say mom," Nicole snickered.

"Well, it's not in the cards for a while," Jerry laughed. "Remember what you told me earlier. Something about me being the manager of some famous band. Wasn't that your exact words?" he winked, pulling her close.

Drew laughed. "Yes, but I think I heard one of them is getting married first," he smiled, leaning over to kiss Nicole.

"Hey, don't forget about that new manager. I heard he's also getting hitched," Kate laughed.

"Okay, kids, we're almost there. Act civil," Jerry insisted.

The penthouse was magnificent, and the views were breathtaking as Jenna opened the door.

"Come in. Let me show you around. Cameron will be out in a moment."

The living room came alive with a wall of windows that led out onto a wraparound balcony. The millions of lights sparkling from the nearby high rises made you question where the buildings ended and the night sky began. It was luxuriously furnished. Nicky's baby grand piano sat showcased in front of the tall windows.

"Follow me. I'll show you the kitchen."

Walking in, it was state of the art. A huge granite island sat in the middle, surrounded by gorgeous cherry wood cabinetry. A sizeable professional stove highlighted the kitchen with its enormous arched range hood towering above. The windows gave a hint of a mountain range in the distance.

"Something smells yummy," Nicole smiled.

"Yes. I've had Chinese food brought up for us tonight. Hope you're hungry."

Just at that moment, Cameron walked in.

"Did I hear someone mention food?" he inquired.

"Hey, man," Drew smiled. "So, what did you do today?"

"Oh, I just hung around the apartment with the dogs and tried to catch up on some of my favorite television programs. I heard there's going to be a double wedding?" Cameron grinned.

"Yes. It appears news travels fast around here," Drew mentioned. "What do you think? How does being our best man sound?"

Kate eyed Jenna when she heard Drew's announcement. But, of course, there was no way for him to know the implications of that question, at least not this early in the evening.

"Well, why don't we go into the dining room? Cameron, why don't you take everyone over to the table. I'll uncover the warming trays. Kate, would you like to help me in the kitchen?"

Seeking the privacy of the kitchen, Jenna wondered if Kate had caught the implication of Drew's statement.

"Wow, did you hear what Drew asked Cameron?" Jenna whispered.

"Yes. It's funny. Drew has no idea that Cameron will be walking his sister down the aisle," Kate answered.

After bringing all the warming trays to the table, everyone enjoyed a delicious meal of almond chicken, pepper steak, beef and broccoli, and fried wontons along with fried rice. It seemed everyone was enjoying not only the food but each other's company as well.

"When we're finished with dinner, we'll have coffee or drinks in the living room," Jenna stated. Also, I want to box up some of the leftovers for Doug and Harry. I know those boys love Chinese food."

Clearing the table, Jenna once again asked for Kate's help.

"Kate, I hate to ask, but could you please help with the coffee?"

"Yes. No problem." Kate followed Jenna back into the kitchen.

"I'm sorry. Honestly, I didn't need any help. I'm just getting nervous," Jenna whispered.

"Don't be nervous. Let's just get this over with."

Deciding to check on Jenna and Kate, Jerry walked into the kitchen.

"Are you both okay? It seems like you've both kept disappearing into the kitchen all night."

"Why has it been that noticeable?" Jenna questioned.

"Yes, sort of, and don't be silly, the kids don't drink coffee. You're both beginning to act weird. So let's just get them all into the living room and get this show on the road, as Bruce would say."

"Jerry, easy for you to say, you're not their mother," Kate frowned.

"Alright, guess you've made your point, but if you two keep hanging out in the kitchen, it's not going to get the job done. So I'll go and suggest we all move into the living room. Then you two better get on with this. Forget the damn coffee. It would help if you had brownies. Kids love brownies."

"Jerry, honestly, do I look like Suzy Homemaker. I don't do brownies," Jenna laughed.

"Whatever, then grab some fortune cookies or sodas? Heck, I don't care, just no coffee. You're both beginning to act like you've attended too many old ladies' coffee klatches," Jerry laughed.

"Okay, go back in and keep your cool. We've got this. Take the kids into the living room. Geez, this is getting out of control, and we haven't even said anything to anyone yet," Jenna insisted.

"Alright, I'll give you both just a few minutes to get your act together."

"Jerry, get out of here. You're only making matters worse," Kate demanded. "Let us handle this. We know what we're doing?"

"Okay, but if this goes wrong, don't blame me."

Jerry encouraged the kids to relax in the living room while walking back into the dining room.

"Hey, if you're all finished, let's go into the living room. I think the girls are going to bring out some cookies and sodas."

"Thank goodness, who drinks coffee?" Cameron frowned.

"Yes. That's for old folks," Drew added.

"So, did everyone enjoy dinner this evening?" Jenna asked, bringing out a tray of cookies and cold drinks.

"Yes. Thank you, it was delicious," Nicole answered.

"I'll just set this tray on the coffee table. Help yourselves," Jenna reminded once again.

"Where's Mom?" Nicole wondered.

"Oh, I think she went to the bathroom. She'll be right out," Jenna smiled, noticing a seething scowl from Jerry.

"Here she comes," Jenna mentioned.

After Kate walked into the living room and sat down, things got unusually quiet. Kate took Jerry's hand, trying to keep calm and collected.

"Kids, there's a reason for us having you all here for dinner this evening, and I'm at a loss where to start," Jenna began.

"Mom, what's going on? Jerry, what's this all about?" Nicole insisted.

"Well, Sweetheart, I think this is better left up to your Moms," Jerry contended.

"Jerry, you just said moms. Did you mean Mom?" Nicole asked again.

"Well, sort of, I think they both have some things to tell you, but it should come from them?"

"Okay," Cameron paused. "What's going on? Since there are two Moms here, I guess that indicates something about Nicole or me."

"Oh honey," Jenna paused. "What if I told you that you had a sister. What if I told you that you were sitting next to her," she stated with tears in her eyes.

"What?" Cameron looked utterly confused.

"Nicole, Sweetheart, you're sitting next to your brother, half-brother, that is," Kate added, wiping her eyes.

"What?" Nicole asked, completely shocked, glancing at Cameron.

"Is this a joke?" Cameron demanded.

"No. I'm afraid we're telling you both the truth," Jenna cried.

"Jerry, are they lying?" Nicole insisted.

"No. Sweetheart, what they're telling you both is true."

"So, how long have you both known about this?" Cameron questioned with the hint of a smile.

"Not long. Actually, Japan was when everything came out in the open," Jenna informed them.

"So, what you're both trying to tell us is that Nicky was also my father," Nicole questioned in a state of total confusion and unbelief.

"Yes. That's right, Sweetheart," Kate answered as tears rolled down her face.

"Well, we're all adults sitting here, to ask how is crazy. But that leaves the questions of why and when?" Cameron inquired.

"Can we just leave it right here for now? Just know that you both were conceived out of love," Jenna added, wiping her eyes.

"The worst part for you, honey, is that you never really got to know your father. He would have loved you dearly," Kate cried, entirely losing her composure.

Jerry put his arms around her, "Kate, please get a hold of yourself. It's over, they both know. Everything is going to be alright."

"What if she hates me now?" Kate cried into his chest as he held her close.

"Mom, I don't hate you. I really don't," Nicole answered, running over to put her arms around Kate.

"Wow. I'm shocked, and I find this all truly unbelievable," Drew mentioned staring at Cameron. "Man, you never had any idea about this?" he asked.

"No. How could I? But you know what?" Cameron paused. "Nicole does look an awful lot like Dad," he smiled.

"Oh, Sweetheart, she does, doesn't she?" Jenna implied.

"Mom, it's okay. It would help if you didn't worry either. Everything is going to be fine," Cameron insisted.

Walking over to Nicole, Cameron put his arms around her. Tears welled within his eyes, giving his sister a huge hug.

"So, Sis, what do you think? Think you can handle a brother like me?" Cameron smiled with tears in his eyes.

"Oh, Cameron," Nicole hesitated with tears streaming down her face. "I already love you," she cried.

"What the hell? I'm crying now," Jerry laughed, wiping tears from his eyes.

Drew walked over as the three of them huddled together for a moment.

"Hell, I'm most definitely going to need stock in Kleenex now," Jerry laughed.

"Jenna walked over to hug Kate. We did it," she cried.

"We did. We did," Kate reiterated, still sobbing.

"Cameron, would you walk me down the aisle?" Nicole questioned.

"Oh, you didn't even have to ask," Cameron replied, giving Nicole another hug.

"Guess I'm going to need a new best man," Drew mentioned.

He was the only one still somewhat in control of his emotions. However, he felt his eyes moisten as he looked over at Nicole and Cameron.

"Well, this has been a long night," Jerry informed everyone.

"Yes. It has," Jenna confirmed.

"I think Kate and I should call it a night, along with Nicole and Drew," Jerry suggested looking down at his watch.

"So we'll figure out who's who as far as family connection go tomorrow. I think I've just become an uncle again," Jerry snickered.

"Does it even matter at this point? We're all family, and that's all that matters," Jenna finally smiled as she hugged Nicole. "Today has been one of those memorable days in life. We've all been blessed through someone who isn't even here."

Hearing the words which Jenna spoke, Kate looked around at everyone.

"Oh, I don't know about that. I kind of think Nicky somehow knows," Kate smiled as tears filled her eyes.

Secrets had been revealed uniquely, as only a family could.

CHAPTER SIXTEEN

Wedding Bells

The previous night had been traumatic for everyone involved. Jerry was happy to know that one hurdle standing in the way of his marriage had been overcome. However, today held another major mild stone in their lives. Bruce was moving into Haven Woods.

"Wow, Babe, that was quite an evening last night," Jerry mentioned pushing off his alarm clock.

"Yes, it was. I can't even begin to tell you how relieved I am that it's finally behind us. No more keeping secrets," Kate smiled, sitting up in bed as she pulled her hair back into a ponytail. "I'm starved. Let's order breakfast."

"Sounds good to me. What do you feel like eating this morning?"

"How about pancakes and sausage? Let's mix things up a bit."

"Oh, I thought that was what we did last night," Jerry laughed.

"Jerry, you're crazy, but I love you silly," Kate giggled, giving him a hug and a quick kiss.

"So, what's on your agenda for today?"

"Oh, Jenna and I are moving Bruce over to Haven Wood this afternoon."

"Is there anything I can do to help?"

"No. I think we're going to keep things low-key and easy. The last thing we need is for Bruce to decide at the last minute he's not going? What are your plans for today?"

"Well, Nicole and I are going shopping for our wedding gowns today. I can't even begin to tell you how excited she is?"

"So, Doll, you're not?" Jerry questioned with a frown.

"Jerry, you're being silly again. But, of course, I'm excited. How could I not be? I just meant that Nicole is much younger and into fashion. She has so many bridal magazines in her room she could open her own boutique. Nicole's going to be the most beautiful bride ever. I can't wait to watch as she tries on different styles of gowns today. I wish you could come along."

"Doll, I would love nothing better than watching my gorgeous girls model bridal gowns, but it's moving day for Bruce," Jerry smiled, picking up the phone to order room service.

"Too bad, I've heard they've got some pretty sexy lingerie in those stores," Kate snickered.

"Now, who's teasing who?" Jerry winked.

After enjoying their pancakes, it was time to get the day started.

Hearing a knock at the door, Jerry walked over to answer it.

He was surprised to see Jenna with Nicole.

"Hey Jerry, I ran into Nicole as I stepped inside the elevator. She informed me that she and Kate are shopping for wedding gowns today. Too bad you're not able to join them. It sounds like a lot of fun."

"Yes. I'm sure I would love it. Maybe I could even keep them within their budget," Jerry winked, glancing at Kate. "Then again, probably not, so I think we should get upstairs and see if Bruce is ready to go. You girls have fun," Jerry mentioned giving them each a quick kiss.

"I wish I could tag along. I would love to spend the day with you both, searching for the perfect gowns. However, Jerry is right. We need to make sure Bruce has an easy transition into Haven Wood. I can't wait to hear all about your search when we get back."

"Give Bruce our love and let him know that he's in our thoughts and prayers today. Let him know that Nicole and I will be over to see him tomorrow," Kate insisted as she closed the door behind them.

Jerry was relieved, knowing that someone had stayed with Bruce overnight as they entered the elevator up to the penthouse. Hopefully, there would be no surprises this morning. Louie Higgins, one of the CNA's from Haven Wood, had graciously offered to come over and stay with Bruce.

Knocking at the door, Louie answered immediately.

"Good morning. Is Bruce ready to go?" Jerry smiled.

"Yes. I think we've got everything ready, and Bruce had breakfast," Louie mentioned.

"Hey Bruce, how are you feeling this morning. Are you excited about moving over to Haven Wood?" Jenna inquired.

"No. I feel like I'm being abandoned," Bruce frowned.

"Oh Bruce, please don't feel that way. You're loved and respected by all of us. We want the best for you. Right now, Haven Wood offers you the comfort and care you need, and you're in good hands. Remember, I'll not only stop by often to see you, but on better days when you feel like getting away, I'll come and take you out for the day. Trust me. We're not just dumping you there. Plus, there's going to be a wedding, a double wedding," Jenna stated.

"Oh, who's getting married?" Bruce asked, totally confused.

"Remember Kate and Jerry, also Nicole and Drew."

As Jerry opened the door, Bruce paused for a moment, looking back at the penthouse. He was finally ready to go. So much had happened since he had left Vancouver.

Walking into Bella's Bridal Boutique, Nicole felt like a kid in a candy shop.

"Good morning. May we help you?" Anita smiled. "So, who's the lucky bride?" she inquired.

"Well, I suppose you could say we both are," Kate replied. "My daughter, Nicole, and I are having a double wedding."

"How wonderful. We don't get many mother-daughter brides these days. How soon is the wedding?"

"The end of this month, we don't have much time. Hopefully, you have some gowns available, which wouldn't require ordering."

"Yes, we always keep a specific number of gowns in stock which would only require altering unless there's something specific you have in mind. Please come with me and let me show you what we have. What is your price limit?"

"Well, we don't actually have a set price. We're just hoping to find gowns that we fall in love with."

"Great. Let me open dressing rooms for you."

"I would love to try on a heart-shaped gown," Nicole stated.

"I think I would like to see something fitted with a small sleeve, to cover my upper arms, maybe lace with no sequins."

"Okay. Give me and my assistant, Brandy, just a few minutes to pull what we have. Would either of you like something to drink?"

"No, thank you, not at this moment," Nicole smiled.

It wasn't long before Brandy walked in with several gowns. She had found five gowns with heart-shaped bodices and classic A-lined silhouettes. They were adorned with beautiful sequins for Nicole. She also pulled four lace empire gowns for Kate with V-necks and off-the-shoulder sleeves, which were stunning.

"Wow, Mom, where do we start," Nicole laughed.

"Well, I think we should try them all on. You never know which one might just surprise you."

"Okay," Nicole giggled.

Brandy worked with Nicole, while Anita helped Kate. It only took a few minutes before they walked out of the dressing rooms.

"Oh, Sweetheart, you look stunning," Kate smiled. "I think that's the one."

"Mom, it's only the first gown, but I do love it," Nicole mentioned admiring her profile in front of the full-length mirror. "Mom, you look gorgeous. Do you like it?"

"Well, I'm not sure. I want to try on one of the other gowns."

After almost an hour, it seemed they had both finally found gowns which would be fitting for their special day. However, Nicole asked for their dresses to be held for the day, as she still wanted to look further. It seemed after looking through the bridal magazines, Nicole wasn't ready to settle for just any off-the-rack gown. So, leaving Bella's Boutique, they continued to the next shop.

Next, walking into Elite's Bridal Boutique, Kate hoped Nicole might find that special gown. But, after hours of trying on heart-shaped dresses of silk, satin, organza, lace, tulle, and two glasses of champagne, it seemed Nicole was still indecisive.

"Sweetheart, I think we should take a short time out and get something to eat. What do you think?"

"Oh, I guess you're right, but I want to stop at The Bridal Gallery before we call it a day."

After enjoying lunch at the Wharf, Kate was hopeful that Nicole would finally find her perfect gown at The Bridal Gallery. But she had decided to return to Bella's Boutique for her purchase. Now it left Nicole still searching for her unique dress.

Walking into The Bridal Gallery, they were immediately met by an eager sales lady who inquired about the date of the wedding, styles, and price. Afterward, they were ushered into the dressing room.

"Nicole, it appears they offer the most gowns in stock that we've found so far. So, honey, I sure hope you find what you're looking for."

After only a few minutes, the attendant returned with several gowns in tow. However, it seemed luck was on their side. Nicole beamed, glancing at the first gown she saw. It was the one. Kate knew it by the look on Nicole's face.

"Oh, Mom, I think this is my gown."

Anxiously trying it on, Nicole looked stunning. Standing in front of the mirror, watching as her daughter modeled the heart-shaped, silk A-line gown brought tears to her eyes. It was embroidered with seeded pearls and Swarovski crystals and carried a hefty price tag of over fifteen thousand dollars. However, after spending all day hunting down the perfect gown, Kate was happy to write out the check.

"Mom, it's gorgeous. They'll only have to make a few alterations, and then it will fit perfectly. I love it," Nicole smiled, twirling around in front of the large mirrors.

"Sweetheart, you look like a princess," Kate smiled as the attendant brought over a long matching veil.

Leaving the gown with a seamstress, they hurried over to Bella's Boutique to purchase Kate's lace empire gown. It beautifully fit her slim body, accenting her sensual curves. Styled with off-the-shoulder see-through sleeves, it was gorgeous and came with a more affordable price tag of only seven thousand dollars. It was perfect and needed no alterations.

"Wow, we did it," Nicole laughed, stepping inside the limo for the ride back to the hotel. "I think Drew and Jerry will love the gowns. What do you think, Mom?"

"Oh, honey, I'm sure they will love what we've chosen. I was going to treat us to a massage with pedicure and manicure, but it has gotten rather late, so I'll schedule it for another day."

Arriving back at the Ritz Carlton, Kate was anxious to see Jerry and find out how his day had gone with Bruce.

"Sweetheart, do you want to come over to our room," Kate asked, stepping outside of the elevator.

"Thanks, but I'm going back to our room. I've been gone all day, and I want to see Drew. Love you, Mom, it was fun."

"Honey, today was unforgettable. I love you," Kate smiled, giving her daughter a huge hug and kiss.

Unlocking the door, Kate could see Jerry sitting outside on the balcony smoking a cigarette. He had practically quit smoking, so evidently, today must have taken a toll on him. Desperately wanting to know about Bruce, she walked out to inquire about the move.

"Hey Babe, how did it go today?"

"Doll, you're back. Did you girls find what you were looking for?"

"Yes, but how's Bruce? Was it hard admitting him to Haven Wood?"

"Kate, it was the hardest thing I've ever done. Even Jenna was becoming emotional as we left. Do you think we made the right decision placing Bruce in Haven Wood?" Jerry questioned, lighting another cigarette.

"Yes, Babe, I do. You must be stressed. You're smoking again."

"Doll, a man's got to do, what man's got to do," Jerry grinned.

"Jerry, please don't take this so hard. I know it wasn't easy. You made the right decision. We're the only family he has, besides Jeff and no one even knows where he's at these days, so someone had to stand in the gap and do the right thing, even if it was hard. They will take great care of him at Haven Wood. You and I both know that he couldn't live alone anymore. Once we're all back on tour, there would have been no one to care for him other than Jenna. That's a lot to ask of anyone, especially since she lives alone and would have no one to help her. Let's order room service and watch a movie. No more thinking about it for tonight," Kate insisted.

"Okay. I guess you're right. So are you going to show me that dress of yours?"

"What? No way. You don't get to see it until I walk down the aisle. Besides, we left them at the boutiques. Nicole's dress is being altered, and mine is being steam pressed."

"Were they expensive?"

"Jerry, what kind of question is that. Does the price really matter if it makes us happy? Let's just say that we're both thrilled to have finally found the perfect gowns and leave it at that," Kate giggled.

"So how much did this little piece of happiness cost?"

"Well, Nicole's cost more than mine. I'm thinking about fifteen thousand."

"What," Jerry exclaimed, putting out his cigarette. "My first car cost less than that."

"Listen, Jerry, how do you put a price on happiness? Besides, we can afford it. You've just stepped into the management position with the band."

"Well, when I heard Nicole state she was making out a list, all I could think of was dollar signs."

"Babe, we're having a double wedding, so it makes sense it might be a little more than your average wedding. But think of the memories we'll be creating for our family and the amazing photos."

"Oh, I almost forgot. Jenna left some brochures inside for different venues. She wanted you and Nicole to take a look at them, and if you find one that you're interested in, she said she would be happy to arrange a tour."

"Great, then let me go inside and get them. Did you happen to browse through them?"

"No. I figured I'd leave that up to you girls."

Walking inside, Kate was anxious to see what was available.

"Wow, it looks like we've got several choices. A winery, golf course, Paradise Valley Resort, St. Michael's downtown, Mountain View Lodge, and the Cliff House."

Walking back out to the balcony, she carried with her all the brochures.

"Okay, this might surprise you, as a lot of them offer great amenities, but I want to get married in a church. I've always dreamed of a big wedding, and to me, a church is a perfect place to start our lives. St. Michael's is gorgeous. It will hold a lot of people. The stained glass windows inside are magnificent, especially the depiction of angels above the altar. It's so large it has two main aisles leading down to the front, and at dusk, the ambiance from glowing candles would be breathtaking. We could hold the reception at the Cliff House. It has an enormous ballroom and isn't that far from downtown. What do you think?"

"It sounds good, but you need to talk with Nicole. After all, it's her wedding too," Jerry mentioned, lighting another smoke.

"Yes. You're right. I would never make that decision without consulting with Nicole. So why don't you put that smelly cigarette out, and let's go inside and order room service? We'll order a bottle of wine. That should help you forget about Bruce and Haven Wood."

"Doll, I think it would take a lot more than a bottle of wine."

"Well, we'll order two bottles," Kate laughed. "Let's catch up on the latest movie rentals that should help."

After enjoying a delicious dinner of steak teriyaki, rice, and steamed vegetables along with red wine, Kate fell asleep on Jerry's shoulder before the end of their first movie.

"Babe, time for bed," Jerry whispered, turning off the television.

Early the following day, the light creeping into the room woke Jerry. Looking at the clock, it was only 6:00 a.m. However, his mind was consumed with things that needed to be done, none of which included the wedding. Stepping into Bruce's shoes, there was much to do. Jerry mentally attempted to map out the band's schedule for the following month, sitting up in bed. But first, he desperately needed a cup of coffee before any serious amount of work would ever get started. Then, calling down for room service, he ordered breakfast.

Hearing a knock at the door, breakfast along with a much-needed carafe of coffee had arrived. Pouring himself a cup, Jerry grabbed his briefcase. It wasn't long before the aroma of hot coffee had awakened Kate.

"Geez, Babe, you're up bright and early. How long have you been up?"

"Not long, thought I'd get a little work done. I've ordered breakfast."

"It smells yummy. Guess I must have fallen asleep with my clothes on again," Kate laughed, looking down at her wrinkled skirt.

"Yes, why break a bad habit," Jerry winked. "I think you were exhausted, and after the wine, you were out like a light bulb."

"So, what are your plans for the day?" Kate asked, pouring herself a cup of coffee.

"Oh, I'll probably stay in and make a few phone calls. I need to get things organized for the tour to resume next month, and I need to check in with the guys. What are your plans?"

"Well, I want to confirm with Nicole my idea of using the church. Then if she approves, I'd like to meet with Jenna and go down to St. Michaels today. But, first, we need to find out if the church will be available, there's still so much to do for the wedding. Do you think we'll have time to send out invitations?"

"Guess it depends if the church will be available and if you can reserve the Cliff House today. But, of course, that also depends on Nicole's approval."

"Yes, first things first. I need to call over to Nicole's room after breakfast. I forgot to tell you. She's having three of her close friends from New York come out for the wedding. She asked Tiffany, Alicia, and Robin to be her bridesmaids."

"So, Doll, who are your bridesmaids?" Jerry snickered.

"Jerry, don't be mean. I'm going to ask Jenna. Hopefully, she'll be honored."

"Oh, I'm sure she'll be delighted."

"So who's going to be your best man and groomsmen?"

"Babe, that's easy. Who do you think? I will ask Cameron to be the best man, and the guys will be my groomsmen. Drew and I will have to figure this double wedding thing out. Maybe the priest will have an idea as to the formalities."

"Yes. It's going to be a little different from a typical wedding."

It wasn't long after breakfast that Kate called Nicole's room.

"Hey, Sweetheart, how are you this morning?"

"I'm fine, Mom. How are you? Bet you were tired last night after checking out all the boutiques yesterday?"

"Yes, honey, I was. I fell asleep while watching a movie last night. The reason for my call is that I wanted to ask you about the location for our wedding ceremonies. Jenna left some brochures here with Jerry yesterday. After looking at them, what do you think about St. Michaels Church? It's a magnificent older church, and the stained glass windows are amazing. I can just envision it at dusk lit with candles. It has two main aisles and will hold a lot of people. What do you think?"

"Mom, it sounds like you've already got it all worked out," Nicole laughed. "Yes, of course, just let me ask Drew. I'm sure he shouldn't mind. After all, it is a church."

"Oh, one last thing, the brochure for the Cliff House looked spectacular for the reception afterward. They have a huge ballroom. It would be perfect for cocktails and dinner after the ceremony. Their menu is phenomenal, but we should go over and sample the main courses. I don't mean to take charge of everything, but if we can decide on a few of these things today, there would still be enough time to send out invitations."

"Oh, Mom, please be my guest at arranging everything. Drew

and I aren't really hung up on all the details. We just want to get married," Nicole snickered. "After finding my dream gown yesterday, I'm happy. Besides, I know how particular you are and your ability to organize things. We would be honored for you to handle all the details. Why don't we come over to your room after breakfast, and we can look at the brochures."

"That sounds great. When are the girls coming out."

"I'm not sure yet. I'll probably call them today if we get things reserved and have a definite date. See you in a few minutes."

"Okay, Sweetheart, I love you."

Overhearing some of the conversation, Jerry was curious about Nicole's thoughts.

"So, Babe, what did Nicole think of your ideas? It seems to me like you're running the show."

"Oh Jerry, it's not that at all. Nicole has never been very organized. If I left everything up to her, we would probably be getting married sometime next year. Time isn't a luxury we have right now. It usually does take a year to plan a wedding. However we've only got a month, that's not much time. So I've got to get everything organized. I need to make a list. We need to decide on our dinner menus, including hors d'oeuvre, drink service, two wedding cakes, flowers, bridesmaids' gowns. I'm starting to get nervous. There's so much to get done."

"Babe, relax, come over here and sit on my lap. Look at me, Doll, I love you," Jerry said, gently caressing her face. "I don't give a damn about all that stuff, do you understand. We can get married in city hall for all I care. I love you. I just want to marry you," he reminded, kissing her passionately.

"Wow, that was some kiss," Kate giggled. "What would I do without you?"

"Oh, so you stopped worrying for a moment," he winked.

"You and Nicole are a lot alike. She just reiterated those same feelings about Drew. She said they just want to get married."

"She's a smart girl."

Hearing a knock at the door, Kate ran over to answer it.

"Hey guys, come in. Would either of you like some orange juice?"

"No, thanks, Mom, we just had breakfast. Where are the brochures?"

"Oh, over on the sofa table. So Drew, what is your opinion about getting married at St. Michael's?" Kate questioned.

"I think it would be awesome. Nicole told me all about it. She mentioned you had a brochure on the Cliff House."

"Yes. The brochures are on the table. I think the Cliff House offers the largest room for dinner and dancing. If I get the reservation, I'll need you both to go with me to sample their menu. Also, you'll need to decide on the flavor and style of your wedding cake. Oh, one more thing, flowers. What type of flowers and décor would you both like at the reception?"

"Oh, Mom, it doesn't matter to us."

After going through the brochures, everyone agreed. The ceremonies would be held at St. Michael's, and the Cliff House would host their reception. Nicole and Drew decided to go with Kate to order their wedding cake and sample the menu, but Drew thought it best left up to the girls regarding the other details like flowers.

"Mom, thanks for everything. Drew and I have made plans today to look at wedding bands. So I guess we'll be on our way. Love you," Nicole mentioned hugging her and Jerry before she left.

"Okay, Sweetheart, you guys have fun. I'll let you know what I find out today. Talk with you this evening."

Closing the door, Kate walked over to Jerry.

"Rings. I almost forgot. We need to pick out our wedding rings."

"Babe, is that something you want?" Jerry grinned.

"Jerry, don't tease me. You know we have to pick out our wedding rings."

"Okay, let me get some work done today. Call Jenna and see if she's available to go down to St. Michael's with you and to the Cliff House and I promise tomorrow we'll go look at rings," he winked.

"Okay, that's a promise. Don't forget," Kate reminded, giving him a quick kiss.

"Doll, somehow I don't think there's the slightest chance of that happening," Jerry laughed.

Picking up the phone, Kate called Jenna and arranged to meet her at the church around 1:00 p.m. Afterward, they would continue to the Cliff House.

Later that evening, Jerry met Kate and Jenna downtown at the Wharf for dinner. It appeared that St. Michaels would indeed be available, and reserving the Cliff House hadn't been a problem. Kate finally felt confident the venues were taken care of. The ceremonies would take place on Saturday, August 1st, 5:00 p.m., with the reception to follow immediately afterward. Finally, the announcements were ready to be put in the mail. Now, Jerry and Kate had to take care of their wedding bands. Also, the florist, cake, bridesmaids' dresses, and the guys' tuxedo rentals were the few remaining details of the wedding.

The next few days kept them extremely busy. Then, finally, Nicole's friends were arriving from New York. Nicole and Drew had arranged to meet the girls at the airport the following evening.

Waking up to another busy day ahead, it seemed Kate was the first one up this morning.

"Jerry, did you remember to reserve suites at the Carlton for Nicole's bridesmaids?" Kate asked, waking up early.

"Yes, as a matter of fact, their rooms are on the same floor as Nicole and Drew's. I believe Nicole agreed to pick them up this evening, so I made arrangements for the limo to be available."

"Thanks. I think we should reserve a restaurant tonight. It would be nice after the girls arrive to get everyone together. I'll let Jenna and Cameron know as soon we decide where we would like to eat. Maybe if Bruce feels up to it, he could join us."

"That sounds great. I need to get all the boys together tomorrow. They have a final fitting for their tuxedos. I don't want to chance waiting till the last minute with those guys. Something would invariably come up to prevent one of them from being available," Jerry grinned.

"Yes. You better play it safe and get that taken care of tomorrow," Kate called out from the bathroom where she was getting dressed.

"Oh, Babe, I forgot, I finalized the plans for the kids' honeymoon. I went by the travel agent yesterday. Their two weeks in Paris are arranged. They leave the next morning. Don't you think we should tell them?"

"No. I want it to be a surprise. Nicole has wanted to see Paris for eons. She's going to be so excited. We'll give them the tickets and itinerary at the reception," Kate answered, turning off the hairdryer for a moment.

"So, Doll, I have a little surprise for you. I think you should come out and give me a huge thank you."

"Really, maybe you should come in here and tell me why I owe you a big thank you," Kate laughed.

"Well, I'll only tell you that I booked our honeymoon trip while I was downtown."

"Oh, I thought we agreed to wait until later."

"Well, let's just say that I got a bargain and couldn't turn it down."

"Okay, Babe, I give up. Where are we going?" Kate snickered.

"That's all you get to know until we arrive at the airport. It's a surprise. I think you're going to love the location," Jerry grinned, walking up behind her kissing her softly on the neck. "Anyway, our trip back to Vancouver has been stressful, and I think we could use some downtime."

"Babe, you have to tell me if it's someplace warm. Then, I'll need to purchase some things to add to my trousseau."

"Let's just stick to that list of yours. I don't remember seeing a wardrobe on it," Jerry laughed. "Besides, Doll, it's a honeymoon, and I don't exactly think a wardrobe tops my list," he winked. Maybe just a swimsuit and sunglasses."

"Oh, so are you are hinting it's someplace warm," Kate giggled.

"Guess you'll find out at the airport," he winked. "I'm going to order breakfast. Is it your usual?"

"Yes. I'll be right out. I'm almost finished with my hair."

Get me to the church on time

The day of the wedding had finally arrived. It was happily chaotic as the last-minute preparations were underway. Jerry and the boys managed to dress quickly and were already at Saint Michaels awaiting the arrival of the women, who were already running late. Jenna was busily helping Kate with her dress and hair as Nicole was across the hall with her bridesmaids. It seemed that using two rooms had made the preparations more manageable.

Helping Kate into her wedding gown, Jenna's mind was flooded with memories of Nicky and their wedding. Watching as Kate adjusted the lace veil which adorned the beautiful dress, Jenna's eyes moistened. How would she ever get through the day? Memories of Nicky were never far from her mind. Grabbing a tissue, she wiped her eyes.

"Oh Jenna, I'm so sorry. When I asked you to be my maid of honor, I never thought it might be difficult for you. I know you miss Nicky terribly. Please don't cry. He loved you very much."

"I know. I just feel so lost without him. However, I'm very happy for you, truly I am. I only wish that he was here today."

Hearing a knock at the door, Kate ran over to answer it.

"Hi Kate, Nicole needs a safety pin," Tiffany smiled.

"Come in. There's a small box of pins on the table. Are you girl's almost dressed and ready to leave for the church?"

"Almost, Robin and Alicia haven't finished with their hair and makeup. Nicole suggested that you and Jenna take the first car over. We'll follow behind you as soon as the girls are ready."

"Okay, but hurry, we shouldn't keep the guys waiting. Jenna and I are almost ready, so we'll be leaving shortly. See you, girls, at the church."

"Thanks for the pins."

Tiffany was surprised to see the girls huddled outside the bathroom.

"What's going on? I told Kate we would be ready soon."

"Oh, you're not going to believe this," Robin laughed.

"Believe what?" Tiffany inquired, looking puzzled by the girls' strange behavior.

"Well, we'll let Nicole tell you," Alicia giggled.

"I'm pregnant," Nicole stated, waving a plastic test strip in her hands. "I had a hunch, but I wanted to know before I left for the church."

"Wow, congratulations. Does Drew have any idea you were going to take a pregnancy test?"

"No. Trust me. No one knows. You guys can't tell anyone, not even Mom. So promise me you won't say a word," Nicole pleaded.

"Alright, we're all sworn to secrecy," Tiffany promised. "I just need to know one thing. Was it the results you were hoping for?"

"Tiffany, don't be so meddlesome," Robin demanded.

"Oh, it's okay. Yes, I was hoping it would be positive. I can't wait to tell Drew. But first things first, we've got to hurry. I'm getting married," Nicole beamed.

The excitement from the girls quickly quieted, hearing a knock at the door. Nicole hurriedly hid the test strip as the girls tried to keep their emotions in check.

"Hi Tiffany, I just wanted to come over and give my beautiful daughter a hug before I left for the church," Kate smiled.

"Hey, Mom, you look stunning."

"Oh honey, so do you. I love you, and I wish you and Drew all the happiness in the world."

Hugging her gorgeous daughter, Kate wiped tears of happiness from her moist face.

"Mom, don't cry. Your mascara will run," Nicole mentioned grabbing a tissue. "I love you too. Jerry is one lucky guy. I'll see you at the church."

"Okay, Sweetheart, I love you," Kate replied, closing the door.

"Wow, that was close," Nicole giggled. "I want to tell Drew before I let Mom and Jerry know."

In the few remaining minutes before the second limo arrived, the girls frantically gazed into the mirrors, ensuring their hair and makeup were perfect. Nicole seemed to be glowing as they stepped out of the elevator and made their way to the hotel entrance.

It seemed Jerry's nerves were finally getting the best of him. He walked outside the church to lite a cigarette.

"Hey man, do you have a lighter?" Doug inquired, walking over.

"I thought you quit smoking."

"Yes, I did, but weddings make me nervous."

"That's funny, and you're not even getting married. So how's Bruce holding up?"

"He's sitting inside talking with Cameron. I think he'll be fine walking Kate down the aisle. It seems to be one of his better days."

"That's good to hear. I was worried."

"Kate will be happy to know that he's actually excited about escorting her. He loves her as if she was in own daughter."

"I know. Bruce has always been a father figure to all of us."

Time seemed to be standing still as Jerry lit up another cigarette. Glancing at his watch, he was becoming apprehensive. The girls were running late, and the church was filled with guests whom he was sure by now were beginning to wonder if the ceremony would ever get underway.

Watching as the first car arrived at the church, his fears were somewhat abated as Nicole and her bridesmaids stepped out.

"Where's Kate and Jenna? Didn't they ride over with you?"

"No. We were running a little late. Mom and Jenna stopped by our room earlier, so I assumed they were already here," Nicole smiled.

"Oh, their car probably took a detour because of the road construction, and I'll bet they're stuck in traffic," Tiffany stated. However, our driver knew about the road work and took the side roads."

"Yes. I'm sure Kate and Jenna will be here in a few minutes. But, Jerry, you look nervous," Nicole laughed. "How's Drew holding up?"

"Fine, he's inside with Cameron and the boys. I had to come out and have a cigarette. Oh, there's a dressing room all set up for you girls. It's to the left as you enter the church. Think I'll stay out here and wait for your mom."

"Okay. See you inside," Nicole smiled, giving Jerry a comforting hug.

Finally, after what seemed like an eternity, Harry walked outside to find Jerry nervously smoking like a chimney.

"Where's Kate and Jenna? Drew and Nicole are getting a little concerned."

"I'm not sure. I suppose they are stuck in traffic," Jerry grinned as he reached into his pocket, pulling out an almost empty pack. I'm nearly out of cigarettes. Tell Drew to hang loose. I'm sure they'll be here any minute."

"Alright, I'll let him know. I think you should put those things down and come inside. Kate's not going to want you smelling like cigarettes on your wedding day," Harry laughed.

Why hadn't they just eloped or married in a quick civil ceremony? Jerry's mind was now contemplating all the what if's. He had not even wanted a huge wedding. However, he loved Kate and wanted to ensure her dreams of their special day were to her liking in every possible way, especially with Nicole and Drew sharing their vows alongside. As every second passed, Jerry was falling deeper into a state of panic. They were almost an hour late. Trying to remain calm, the last thing he needed was for Nicole to sense his uneasiness. Taking a deep breath, he tried to calm himself. Finally, Jerry saw the priest slowly walking down the steps in his direction. Unquestionably, he had also come out to inquire about Kate and Jenna's whereabouts.

Putting his arm around Jerry, he paused, "Son, I just received a call from the Presbyterian Hospital downtown. It seems there's been an accident. I'm so sorry. Their car was hit head-on by a construction vehicle on Highway 50. It's serious, and Jenna was airlifted to Presbyterian. I'm truly sorry. It seems the congestion on the roads due to ongoing construction was extremely bad. I'm sure their driver was attempting to pass a few cars to get them here on time. Noting their attire, the personnel at the hospital attempted to call all the local churches to see if they had scheduled a wedding for today. That's how they reached me. I haven't told anyone inside yet. I wanted to inform you first. Son, again I'm so very sorry. How can I help?"

"Oh, God! God, please don't take Kate from me, not now, not today, Jerry screamed. Father, I have to get to the hospital right now."

"Son, I'm going inside and make an announcement. Maybe you should go inside and let the wedding party know. Nicole is in the dressing room, and Drew is in the vestibule, pacing the floor. Please try and remain calm. There isn't any other word on their condition except I was informed it's very serious."

"Father, how can I? How can I go in there and give Nicole and Cameron the worst news of their life?" Jerry cried out.

"Son, God will give you the strength. He will give you the words which will comfort them."

Wiping the tears from his eyes, Jerry desperately tried to regain his composure as he walked up the steps. Then, entering the huge doors, he immediately saw Drew.

"Hey Jerry, what's going on? Where Are Kate and Jenna? Nicole is starting to go crazy."

"Drew, there's been an accident. Kate and Jenna have been taken downtown to the Presbyterian Hospital. It's serious. I have to tell Nicole and Cameron."

"Oh no," Drew gasped. "I can't believe it. I'm going in with you to talk with Nicole."

"Okay, but we've got to keep her as calm as possible. We also have to inform Cameron, and then I'll need the boys to take care of Bruce while we get to the hospital. I don't want him to find out about the accident. I'm sure you guys can come up with some reason the wedding had to be canceled at the last minute. Have Harry and Doug take him back over to Haven Wood before they come down to the hospital."

With that said, they entered the dressing room.

"Hey, Jerry, where's Mom? Doesn't she know she's getting married today," Nicole laughed, taking a sip of mimosa.

"Don't worry, Jerry. We're not going to let Nicole get drunk. Just a little something to keep her calm," Tiffany giggled.

"Nicole, I don't know how to say this. There's been an accident, and Kate and Jenna have been taken to a hospital downtown. I'm afraid it's serious," Jerry stated, catching Nicole just before she hit the floor. Mimosa spilled down the entire length of her beautiful gown and all over the floor.

"Drew, run to the bathroom and wet some towels," Jerry demanded.

Thankfully Nicole was only out for a short time. As Drew held her in his arms, she repeatedly asked about Kate.

"Sweetheart, we don't really know a lot about the accident. Jerry went to find Cameron and asked someone to take us all over to the hospital. Please try not to worry."

Just at that moment, Cameron ran into the room. Rushing over to Nicole, he put his arm around her.

"Oh Nicole, I just heard," Cameron said frantically. "Come on. Let's go. Jerry has a car waiting to take us to the hospital. Tiffany, you and the girls, wait here. One of the ladies from the church will take you back to the hotel. I'm sure you'll want to change clothes. Just wait for us there."

Putting his arms around Nicole, Drew held her tightly as they hurried outside and down the steep flight of steps into the waiting car.

Soon arriving at the hospital, they were quickly ushered into a large waiting room. However, it was only moments before one of the doctors who attended to Kate and Jenna walked in.

"I'm Dr. Reese. I have some good news. Ms. Hampton has been upgraded from serious to stable condition. She's a fortunate young woman. She has a mild concussion, fractured leg, and two broken ribs. She's still unconscious, but you can go in and see her in a few minutes. She's in intensive care for the night. However, I expect her to be moved downstairs tomorrow. Unfortunately, Mrs. Spade is in critical condition. She's on life support in the intensive care unit, and I would ask that only two of you go in right now. We'll keep you updated. Do you have any questions?"

"Yes. Can you tell us exactly what happened? We were told they were in a head-on collision," Drew asked impatiently.

"I don't have all the details regarding the accident, but the medical crew aboard the helicopter which flew them over to Presbyterian said it was horrific. The driver of their car was killed instantly. It seems there was a lot of traffic congestion on the road due to construction, and it appears the driver may have tried to pass another vehicle. There was only one person in the cement truck who hit them. Unfortunately, he was also killed instantly. I'm truly sorry to give you such terrible news this afternoon. If you should need anything, one of the nurses on the unit will be happy to help you."

"Jerry, I've got to go in and see Mom," Cameron cried with tears streaming down his face.

"Do you want me to go in with you?" Jerry asked sympathetically.

"No. You take Nicole in to see Kate. I'll be fine."

Walking into the room, flashbacks of Jenna's hospitalization with her aneurysm flooded his mind. Her petite body rested again on the stark white sheets of the hospital bed. Despite the plastic tubes that connected her to the machine keeping her alive, she was beautiful. This time there were no bandages, and her long blonde hair lay tousled upon the pillow. Except for the machines, Jenna simply appeared to be sleeping. Tears filled Cameron's eyes as he gently reached over to take her hand.

"Oh, Mom, I'm here. I love you. Please be strong. You have to fight. Do you hear me? Mom, just like before, you can do this. You have to. I'm not letting you go. Do you hear me?" Cameron cried. "Mom, I lost Dad. I can't lose you too."

Pulling a chair next to Jenna's bed, Cameron sat down. Wiping the myriad of tears flowing down his face, it seemed surreal that he found himself once again encouraging her to fight for her life. She had won this battle once before, and he was certain she would be strong enough to win again. Just one more time, he said to himself.

Nicole trembled as Drew took her hand. Then, following Jerry, they walked into Kate's room.

"Oh, Mom, we're here. Can you hear me? Mom, I love you. I love you," Nicole cried softly. "Oh Jerry, do you think she can hear us?"

Seeing that Nicole was having difficulty standing, Jerry ran over to grab a chair before she fainted. Drew grabbed her arm, and together they eased her into a chair. Jerry went into the bathroom to wet a towel just in case she passed out again.

"Nicole, Sweetheart, are you alright?" Jerry asked, wiping her forehead.

"Yes. I'm just so worried about Mom. I'm fine."

Seeing that Nicole was stable, Jerry walked over to Kate's bed.

"Babe, I'm here. You're going to be fine. Do you hear me? I love you so much. The doctor said, you're going to be okay. Please, if you hear me, open your eyes. I love you."

Taking her hand, he waited for her response. However, there was nothing.

"Babe, I'm not leaving until you open your eyes. Do you understand? Please wake up. Nicole, Drew, and I are here with you. Jerry's eyes filled with tears as he lovingly swept Kate's gorgeous black curls away from her face and behind her ears. Babe, today was supposed to be our day. I can't live without you. I'm not leaving you," Jerry whispered as tears streamed down his face. "Nicole, if you and Drew want to go back to the hotel, I will stay with Kate. I'm not leaving."

"No, Jerry, I'm not leaving either."

"Nicole, it's okay. She's going to be fine. You heard what the doctor said. She's going to be alright. Don't worry," Drew added.

"I don't care what you say. I'm not leaving. Do you hear me?" Nicole demanded.

"Okay, Sweetheart. Whatever makes you feel better," Jerry agreed.

One of the nurses walked in to check on Kate.

"I'm Beth, a Registered Nurse in the ICU. Is this your mom?" she smiled, glancing at Nicole.

"Yes."

"Well, I'd say she's a lucky young woman. From what I was told about the accident, we usually don't get many survivors. Let me check her vital signs," Beth smiled. "Her vital signs are good. Her blood pressure is stable. If she continues to do well through the night, she'll be moved into a room downstairs tomorrow. Let me have some chairs brought in for you and a couple of blankets."

Once Nicole was settled into one of the chairs with a warm blanket, Jerry felt safe to leave her with Drew.

"I'm going to Jenna's room. But, first, I need to check on Cameron. I'm sure he's by himself, and I don't want to leave him alone."

"Okay, Jerry, don't worry about Nicole. I'm not leaving either," Drew smiled.

Walking into Jenna's room, Jerry stopped for a moment. His legs almost buckled beneath him. Seeing the machines which were keeping her alive, he felt sick. He would do anything to turn back the clock, if only for twenty-four hours. Seeing Cameron so distraught, he felt nauseous.

"Cameron, I'm sure she's going to be alright. She's a fighter. She's been through worse, and she fought her way back. Please, try not to worry," Jerry whispered, knowing he doubted his own words.

"Jerry, I'm really worried. I can't lose her. I just can't. I lost Dad. I can't lose mom two," Cameron cried softly.

"I know, Cameron. We all need her. She's going to pull through." Trying to find words of encouragement, Jerry gave him a huge hug and slowly walked over to Jenna's bed.

"Hey, Sweetheart, we're all here. Jenna, you can do this. You've got to be strong. We all love you. You can't leave Cameron and all of us. Do you hear me? Do you understand? You've got to come back to us," Jerry cried, gently picking up her hand. "Jenna, Cameron needs you," he added softly, caressing her fingers. "Has the doctor or any of the nurses been in to check on her?" Jerry asked, carefully placing Jenna's hand by her side."

"Yes. One of the nurses came in to check on her, but she didn't really make any comments. She simply smiled. Jerry, I'm so scared. I'm terrified. Now that my grandmother and grandfather have passed, especially with dad's death, I'm so afraid that mom might not want to stay. What am I going to do? Jerry, I can't lose her." Holding his face in his hands, Cameron sobbed bitterly. He was inconsolable.

"Cameron, please don't do this to yourself. You have to believe that she's going to be alright."

"Oh Jerry, if only I could believe that," Cameron cried.

"Cameron, I'm not leaving the hospital tonight. I'll be right next door in Kate's room. If you need me, just come over and get me or have one of the nurses call for me."

"Okay, thanks, Jerry. I hope Kate wakes up soon. I really do."

"I know, Cameron. Please try to get some sleep if you can. I'll have one of the nurses bring you in a blanket. Just hang in there. I love you."

As Jerry walked back into Kate's room, he got the surprise of his life. Kate was slowly beginning to move her hands.

"Jerry, Mom's waking up. Drew ran to get one of the nurses."

"Oh Babe, thank God," Jerry said, rushing to Kate's bed. "Babe, you're in the hospital, but don't worry. You're going to be fine."

Moving aside for the nurse to check Kate, Jerry felt relieved and grateful she had not sustained any life-threatening injuries.

"How is she?"

"I think she's beginning to gain consciousness. Her vital signs are all good. However, we can never predict for sure how long a patient might stay unconscious. If she continues to move her arms or legs or opens her eyes, please use the call button and let us know. In the meantime, maybe talking to her and trying to encourage her to wake up would help. It never hurts," Beth smiled, walking out of the room.

Nicole had an idea. It was brilliant. But first things first, she needed to talk with Drew.

"Jerry, can you stay here with Mom for a few minutes. I need a short break. Drew will you walk with me downstairs to get a snack. I'm feeling hungry."

"Sure, Babe, let's go. I could use something to drink. Jerry, would you like a cup of coffee?"

"Yes. Thank you. That would be awesome. Don't worry. I'll be right here. If anything changes, I'll have someone come down and get you."

"Oh, we won't be gone that long. Be right back," Nicole smiled.

"I'm kind of surprised that you would even want to leave your mom's room," Drew stated, reaching for the elevator button.

"Well, I needed to talk with you, and I didn't exactly want anyone to hear the news before I told you."

"What's news? What's going on?" Drew asked, looking utterly confused.

"Well, I guess if it has to be here in the elevator, so be it," Kate giggled. "We're having a baby. I'm pregnant," Nicole beamed.

Hearing the news, Drew scooped Nicole into his arms.

"Babe, really, we're going to have a baby," he screamed excitedly.

"Drew, we're in a hospital. For heaven's sake, be quiet," Nicole laughed. "Yes. I just found out today. I was going to tell you, but things spun out of control before I could give you the happy news. It is happy news, right?"

"Are you kidding? Babe, I'm thrilled. I'm going to be a father, and you're going to be a mom. Wow, wait till the boys hear this," Drew answered, kissing her all over as the elevator door opened to the surprised look of those waiting to enter.

"I'm going to be a father. We're pregnant," Drew exclaimed.

Receiving strange looks from one of the women waiting to enter the elevator, Nicole was sure after seeing Drew's Mohawk and facial piercings, she probably thought procreation wasn't exactly a good idea. However, the other woman offered her congratulations as she stepped inside.

"Thanks," Drew grinned.

"Babe, think you better tone it down a bit. Let's get some food. I'm starved," Nicole beamed, giving Drew one last kiss.

"You need a snack, and I need a drink," he laughed.

After grabbing sandwiches and milk, they got coffee for Jerry and headed back upstairs.

"Drew, I'm going to tell Mom. I think it might be just the encouragement she needs."

"Okay, Babe, whatever you think."

"Hey Jerry, how's Mom?" Nicole asked as she walked into the room, handing him his coffee.

"She's about the same. Thanks for the coffee."

"Oh, you're welcome."

Walking over to Kate's bed, Nicole paused. "Drew, come over here. I think we have something to tell Mom."

Putting his arms around Nicole, Drew had tears in his eyes.

"Mom, you're going to be a grandmother. Can you hear me? You've got to wake up. A grandmother, you're going to be a grandmother. Are you excited? We love you."

"What!" Jerry exclaimed.

"Yes. I suppose that's going to make you a grandpa," Drew laughed.

"Guys, I'm so happy. Wow, a grandpa. Now that's a word I've never thought about," Jerry smiled, giving them both a huge hug. "That should bring her around. So Grandpa is it," he laughed as he pondered the thought.

"Jerry, she has to wake up. She just has to," Nicole cried.

"Oh, honey, you've just given her every reason in the world to wake up," Jerry answered, wiping tears from his face. "Why don't you both go back to the hotel room tonight and get some rest. I'm not leaving her, so you don't have to worry."

"Yes, Babe, Jerry is right. However, it would be best if you rested, and there's nothing else we can do tonight," Drew pleaded.

"Oh, I don't know. I would feel better if I stayed."

"Sweetheart, you have to think about the baby now. You should go back to the hotel. Please. You need to get some rest," Jerry demanded.

"Okay, but you promise to call us if anything changes?"

"Yes. You have my promise." Then, looking over at Drew, Jerry smiled. "Please take our little mommy to be back to the hotel. I'll see you both in the morning," Jerry insisted, giving them one last hug.

After Nicole and Drew left the room, Jerry walked over to talk with Kate.

"Alright, babe, I know you heard your new title," Jerry laughed, taking

Kate's hand. "Can you even believe it? We're going to be grandparents. Yes, I know what you're thinking. We're too young, right? Well, that may be, but I've got to say that I'm over the moon, honestly. Can you even imagine having grandparents who manage a rock band? Wow, that does sound a bit crazy. Doesn't it? Oh, Babe, I need you desperately. Tonight was to have been our honeymoon, and here I stand at your bedside, begging you to wake up and come back to me. Babe, I can't live without you by my side. Sweetheart, you've been given another reason to wake up tonight. Please, give that new little one the chance to spend a lifetime loving you the way I do. Babe, I love you. It's still early. If you wake up, we still have time to be married before the day is over. I love you," Jerry begged.

He grabbed a blanket and tried to get comfortable, taking a seat in his chair. He had said everything he possibly could. Now, he could only wait. He must have somehow drifted off. He could faintly hear Kate's voice calling his name in his dreams. For some odd reason, the voice in his dream grew louder. Finally, loud enough that it woke him. Startled, he looked down at his watch. It was only 10:30 p.m. Wow, he had managed somehow to get a little sleep. Finally, once again, he heard a soft voice calling his name. It was Kate. Hurriedly leaving his chair, he ran over to Kate.

"Jerry, where am I? What happened?" Kate mumbled.

"Babe, you're awake," Jerry smiled. "How are you feeling?"

"Let me call the nurse. You're in the hospital. Sweetheart, you were in an auto accident, but you're going to be just fine."

"Jerry, how's Jenna?"

"Babe, she's in the next room, don't worry."

He would desperately try to avoid any further discussions regarding Jenna.

Calling the nurse and giving her the news, she came immediately.

"Welcome back. Let me recheck your vital signs," Beth smiled.

"Everything looks good. I guess your fiancé told you that you were in a terrible accident. You're one lucky woman. You've only sustained a mild concussion and a few broken bones. You're in intensive care tonight. However, now that you're awake, they'll be moving you downstairs in the morning. So there'll be no need to keep you on this floor. How are you feeling? Are you having any pain?" she asked.

"Just a slight headache. I'd like a drink of water."

Feeling an itch on her left leg, Kate felt the hard cast on her leg. She panicked.

"Jerry, there's a cast on my leg."

"Yes, you've broken your leg, but please don't worry. You're going to be just fine. Trust me," Jerry winked, trying to reassure her.

"Alright, just take a few slow sips," Beth instructed. "I'll check to see if the doctor left instructions for any pain meds."

As Beth walked out of the room, she knew that Kate was definitely one of those rare cases which a single word miracle can only define. No one ever walks away from an accident as tragic as she had been in and lived. Shaking her head, Beth couldn't believe it. But, unfortunately, she also knew that the other passenger in the next room probably wouldn't be as fortunate.

Walking back into the room, she gave Kate something to make her more comfortable.

"Okay, if you two should need anything, just use the buzzer. I'll come in later and check on you," Beth informed them, closing the door.

"So, Babe, what do you think?" Jerry asked rather amusingly, leaving her curious.

"Think about what?" Kate asked slowly.

"Getting married. It's only 11:00 p.m. The day isn't over yet."

"Jerry, you're crazy?" Kate whispered.

"No, Sweetheart, I think I'm saner than I've ever been," Jerry laughed. "Babe, I'm serious. I don't want to wait for a second longer. I want to marry you tonight, right here in this hospital room. I want you to wake up tomorrow as my wife, Mrs. Jerry Godwin." I never wanted a fancy wedding. I was doing that for you," Jerry said, wiping tears from his eyes. Do you think you can manage only two little words? *I do,*" he smiled.

He was being selfish. He knew it. Practically speaking, it made no sense to rush. What was he thinking? However, he knew. Life was fragile, and no one had a promise of tomorrow or any other day for that matter. He was not waiting. Having been in Jenna's room earlier made his decision easy. There was no better time than the present.

"Oh Jerry, I love you," Kate mumbled.

"Okay, let's do it," he smiled.

Ringing the buzzer for the nurse, Jerry was quite sure she had never received a request like this one before.

As Beth rushed into the room, thinking there might be a problem, she was perplexed to see that everything appeared fine.

"Yes. Can I help you?"

"Yes. You certainly can," Jerry smiled. "Our wedding was supposed to have taken place earlier today at Saint Michael's. But, unfortunately, it seems we've been held up by a tragic accident, and we want to get married right now, right here. Will you help us? Please," he begged.

"Oh, my," Beth replied in shock. I've never had a request like this before," she smiled. "But you know what, I understand your dilemma, and I don't remember any rules saying that you can't get married in the hospital. So let me make a call downstairs and see if we might just happen to have a clergy in the hospital. You never know, they're always in and out, and sometimes they keep late hours. So I'll be right back."

Walking out of the room, Beth almost felt giddy. She had now become part of something so out of the norm that it was virtually unheard of. Having worked for many years as an RN, Beth was elated to participate in such a scheme. Something which brought a huge smile to her face in a world of sickness and pain.

It was only a short time before Beth walked back into the room, followed by a priest. "Well, I think a higher power must certainly have approved. I happen to catch Father Joe as he was leaving the hospital," Beth smiled.

"Son, Beth filled me in on the way up in the elevator. It seems as if you two missed your wedding earlier today. This is most definitely one of the happier types of ministry I provide. It's been a while since I've performed a marriage ceremony in this hospital. But I must say, it's long overdue. I'm delighted to be asked up to your room. I assume you have your marriage license."

"Yes, Father, it's right here in my coat pocket."

"Okay, I think I have a marriage ceremony to perform," Father Joe smiled. "Let's get on with the ceremony."

Jerry walked over to the bed and took Kate's hand. It wasn't the Cysteine Chapel. It wasn't on the beach at an elegant resort or shores of a pristine lake or even in a beautiful meadow covered in green. It was perfect.

It took only a few short minutes as the vows were spoken, pronouncing them man and wife.

"You can now give your lovely bride a kiss," Father Joe suggested. "Congratulations."

"Yes, congratulations," Beth smiled. "Thank you for allowing me to witness such a special ceremony."

"Okay," Father Joe beamed. "If my services aren't needed any further, I'm going home to my bed for the night. May God richly bless your union and keep you in His loving care."

"Thank you, Father, you're kindness will never be forgotten," Jerry grinned.

After everyone left the room, Jerry quickly closed the door.

"Well, I guess we're officially on our honeymoon, Mrs. Godwin. I love you," he whispered, giving Kate a passionate kiss.

"Jerry, do you think they would let you lay beside me and hold me for tonight? I need to feel the warmth of your body next to mine."

"What do you mean, let me?" Jerry winked.

Slipping into bed next to his beautiful bride, it was only moments till they had fallen asleep. A few hours later, Beth observed Jerry asleep next to Kate. Knowing the details of the tragic accident and their wedding day, Beth quietly took vital signs and quickly exited.

Morning brought with it the normal loud noises and shift changes in personnel. It was early as the first nurse made her rounds.

"Oh, what have we here? Sir, you must remove yourself from this bed immediately," she demanded as she woke Jerry. You're in an intensive care room, and I'm afraid this chair will have to do," she reprimanded.

After giving Kate a quick kiss, Jerry hurriedly moved into the chair. No one was going to upset or bother him today. He now had a beautiful wife, and nothing else mattered.

"Good morning, Mrs. Godwin," Jerry grinned. "How are you feeling?"

"Well, I sort of remember having this crazy dream that we got married." Smiling, Kate glanced down at her hand. "Guess it wasn't a crazy dream after all," she teased.

"Babe, you've made me the happiest guy on earth. I promise you can still have that huge wedding you've always wanted. We'll redo our vows as soon as you're able if you want?"

"That won't be necessary. It was perfect. I love you."

"Sweetheart, I'll be right back," Jerry winked, giving her a quick kiss as he made a mad dash out of the room just as the nurse walked in. He was on a mission to find the nearest florist. Hopefully, he wouldn't have to go further than the downstairs lobby. Locating the florist shop, Jerry purchased a massive bouquet of red roses and arranged for her room to be filled with fresh flowers as soon as she was moved downstairs.

Seeing Jerry walk into the room, Kate smiled. She couldn't have been more in love, regardless of her condition. Then, however, she suddenly remembered Jenna being in the next room.

"Jerry, I want to see Jenna. I want to see her before they move me downstairs into another room."

"Babe, you'll need a wheelchair."

"Jerry, please. I have to see her."

"Okay. Let me get one of the nurses."

Jerry knew that Kate wasn't aware of Jenna's grave condition when walking out to the nurse's station. He hadn't had the heart to tell her. Last night was their night, so Jerry had chosen to wait. He knew morning would be soon enough for him to give her the dire facts. He wasn't prepared to see the love of his life in tears. Yet, he was resolved to be strong enough for both of them. After arranging for a wheelchair to be brought in, he now faced the dilemma of informing Kate. How would he ever be able to tell Kate? Why had such devastation entered their lives? How could things have changed so drastically in less than twenty-four hours?

"Sweetheart, the nurse is arranging for you to be able to visit Jenna," Jerry announced as he walked back into the room. "Babe," he hesitated for a moment walking over to take her hand. "I'm so sorry. I wanted to tell you last night, but I couldn't. I just couldn't. Please forgive me. You looked so fragile, and all I could think of was how very much I loved you. I wanted to tell you. But, Kate, I knew there was nothing you or, for that matter, anyone could do for Jenna. I just wanted to spare you the pain until morning. With tears in his eyes, he gently rubbed Kate's face. Babe, she's not going to make it. She's on a ventilator which is keeping her alive. Cameron is going to have to make a tough decision."

"Jerry, this can't be. You're lying. Why are you telling me this?" Kate screamed inconsolably.

"Babe, I'm so sorry. Trust me, you have no idea how hard this is for me. Let me buzz the nurse and see if they can bring you something."

"Jerry, I don't want anything. I want to see Jenna," Kate pleaded as tears streamed down her face.

Grabbing a tissue, Jerry gently wiped her moist face. The pain of seeing her so distraught was killing him. How was he ever going to get through this? He couldn't let the love of his life down, especially now and on their first day as man and wife. Yet, he was determined to keep his emotions in check.

"Okay. Let me get a nurse and find out about the wheelchair. I'll be right back."

Quickly hurrying back to her side, he found Kate still sobbing uncontrollably. "Babe, please, I'm going to need you to be strong. I know that you and Jenna finally became close and resolved your issues regarding Nicky. You have to find the strength to be strong for Cameron and Nicole. Those kids were the bond that allowed you and Jenna to put aside your differences. They're going to need you."

"Oh Jerry, Jenna was robbed of spending the rest of her life with

Nicky. She loved him so much. This past year has been so hard on her. She doesn't deserve this. Now Cameron will have to endure losing her. Life isn't fair. It just isn't fair," Kate cried, wiping her eyes.

"Babe, the way I see it, how do you really know this isn't what they both would have wanted, considering the circumstances. I know how much she loved Nicky. I was there when they first met."

It was only minutes later a nurse entered the room and wheeled Kate into the next room. Taking hold of her hand, Jerry was determined to be her rock.

Nothing could have ever prepared her. Jenna looked peaceful. Only the plastic tubes which connected her to the equipment and the sound of the ventilator indicated that she wasn't merely asleep.

"Oh Jerry, how could this have happened? We stopped by Nicole's room, and everyone was so happy. If it weren't for that damn road construction, none of this would have ever happened," Kate cried bitterly.

"Kate, you don't know that. But, unfortunately, that's something we'll never know," Jerry replied, handing Kate a tissue.

"Please, push me next to the bed. There are things I need to say."

"Sweetheart, please don't torture yourself. You know she isn't able to hear you."

"Babe, I know. But, it's more for me," Kate answered tearfully.

Taking Jenna's hand, Kate whispered.

"Jenna, I'm so sorry. My heart is broken." Pausing to wipe her eyes, Kate had to regain her thoughts. "I so regret that we didn't get more time together to share in the enjoyment of our children. But, please don't worry about Cameron. He's such a fine young man. You did a great job as a mom. Jerry and I will always be there for him. I'm so glad that we became friends. I love you. Jenna, I know that Nicky is waiting for you. You both have my heart," Kate sobbed, gently placing Jenna's hand on the bed.

"Oh Jerry, this is the hardest thing I've ever had to do. Please take me out of here now," Kate begged, wiping her eyes.

"Babe, I know. The nurse is waiting to take you down to a room on the next floor. I'm right beside you. I'm not leaving."

CHAPTER SEVENTEEN

The decision

It had been one week since Kate had left the hospital. However, Jerry would be returning one last time with Cameron. It would be one of the hardest things he would ever be asked to do. Once again, he would have to find the inner strength to support someone he loved.

Hearing the shower running in the bathroom, Kate opened the door. "Jerry, Cameron just called. The limo will be here in about fifteen minutes. Are you sure you don't want me to go with you?"

"Yes, Babe, I'm sure. Cameron felt it would be easier for him if it were just the two of us. Besides, you're still hobbling around in that cast."

"Is there anything I can do before you leave?"

"No. Just pray for Cameron. Today has got to be the hardest day of his life."

As the limo drove away carrying only the two of them inside, Jerry for once was at a loss for words.

"Hey, Jerry, would you like a shot of bourbon," Cameron asked, breaking the silence.

"Well, I guess it wouldn't hurt, just one. Cameron, I'm so sorry about Jenna. I just want you to know that Kate and I will always be there for you. We're all family. You're going to be an uncle soon."

"I know Jerry, and I do appreciate your kind words, but I can't even think about those things right now. I'm losing Mom today. You have no idea how hard this is going to be."

"You're right. I've never been asked to make a decision like this before, but I want you to know that you're doing the right thing. Jenna would never want to spend the rest of her life supported only by machines. So just know that you're making the right decision."

"Thanks, Jerry, I know, but it doesn't make it any less difficult."

The limo stopped under the entrance at the hospital. Stepping out of the car, Cameron stumbled. An overwhelming feeling of weakness suddenly came over him. Cameron began to wonder if his legs would even carry him inside to the elevator and up to the room where his mom still lay motionless, being artificially kept alive.

Seeing his dilemma, Jerry put his arms around him. He would become the strength that Cameron would so desperately need to get through the next few hours.

Things had remained unchanged as they walked into the room. It was only moments before hospital personnel walked in. After taking care of all the legalities required to remove someone from life support, the nurse explained what to expect as someone is brought off the ventilator. Jerry winced, thinking it was a bit too graphic for such a time as this. However, he was sure it was standard protocol. Staring at Cameron, Jerry was sure Cameron had probably not even heard a word.

"Why don't we give you a few minutes with your loved one? We'll come back in about fifteen minutes."

Jerry watched as Cameron bravely walked over to his mom's hospital bed and gently took her hand. He witnessed the bond of love between a son and his mother. He would never remember Cameron's exact words, but his heart ached for him. Afterward, with tears streaming down his face, Cameron turned around.

"Jerry, call me crazy, but I swear that I smell Dad's cologne. Do you believe in an afterlife?"

"Yes. Cameron," Jerry replied, putting his arms around him. Trying to remain strong, Jerry fought to keep back the tears and emotions consuming him.

Watching as Jenna took her last breaths, the machine which had been her only connection to life was slowly disconnected. Wiping tears from his eyes, Jerry watched as Cameron softly kissed his mom for the last time. He could only hold tight to his conviction of an afterlife as he felt the gentle touch of someone's hand on his shoulder. Turning around, there was no one—only an overwhelming scent of Nicky's favorite cologne.

Jenna was drawn into an immensely bright light and enveloped with an unknown peace. She smiled, hearing a familiar voice.

"Hey Doll, I'm here. It's time to go."

EPILOGUE

As the plane lifted into the air, Cameron again left Middleton. It seemed to be the epicenter from which everything constantly evolved. Jenna had now been laid to rest beside her loving husband. Taking one last look out his window, he took a deep breath. Middleton slowly began to fade into the distance, taking the grief that consumed him. Even though the band had also suffered the loss of Bruce, who was now living out his last years in an Alzheimer's facility, one thing had remained true. *The show must go on.*

Seven months later, while the band was on tour in Australia, a new life was added. It seemed Nicole had gone into labor earlier than expected, catching them off guard. As a result, there would be no time to travel back to Vancouver, where she had planned to give birth.

"Okay, just one more strong push," the doctor instructed. It was only moments before the doctor announced the arrival of Nicholas Drew Conner. Handing the tiny infant to the nurse to be cleaned and weighed seemed the perfect moment for the newborn to let out a loud boisterous wail. Nicole looked at Drew and beamed. It appeared their newborn carried more than his grandfather's name.

"Wow, this kid has a set of lungs," the nurse stated.

The room instantly filled with laughter hearing her statement. But, unbeknown to her was the baby's connection to the world of music.

"It's in the genes," Nicole smiled.